Strait of Hormuz

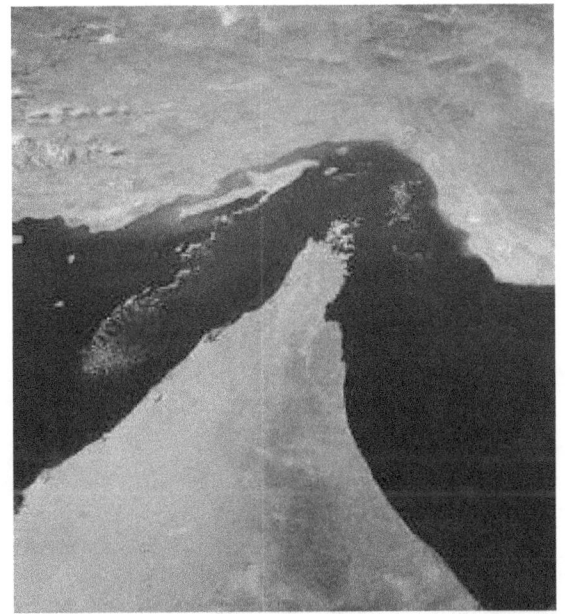

Choke point
34 miles wide
Oman to Iran
Sixteen million barrels of oil per day traverse
34 miles of treacherous water

Books by George Poncy
Published by Grey Knight Press

All-American Boy

Eternities of Darkness

Blackjack to Win: A Layman's Guide to Beating the Game

Strait of Hormuz

Grey Knight Press
Palm Beach, FL
mail@greyknightpress.com

Cover design by George Williams with Bryce Adkins

Strait of Hormuz

By George Poncy

Holy Qu'uran, Chapter 17, "The Children of Israel"

"If thou shouldst respite me to the day of resurrection, I will most certainly cause his progeny to perish except a few." – verse 62

1

Headlights, from behind and over the rise. At 2:08 a.m., it could only be a cop or a drunk.

Unless it was something really dangerous.

James Morrisey shaded his eyes as he turned. The lights were still far enough away, a corona silhouetting the roadway. Like a flock of blackbirds, the four man incursion team changed direction behind the ex-USMC Gunnery Sergeant and glided down the embankment from the shoulder of California SR-110. Despite their heavy weaponry, the men made no sound. In seconds, well before the vehicle appeared over the hill, they had melted into the brush, invisible from the two lane road. The light grew stronger, casting a faint illumination on their target, the twelve acre Jergens Research complex four hundred yards ahead. In moments, the car topped the rise. The men looked away to preserve their night vision. Morrisey sneaked a glance as the cruiser passed; he thought he made out the word Parkerville on the side.

The taillights receded, then disappeared over the next hill. As Morrisey led his men up the embankment, an ice pick of pain, souvenir of a patrol gone awry near Tikrit, jabbed into his left knee. He grimaced but refused to limp as they resumed their silent double time towards the installation. Morrisey took the pain because the money was too good to be true, even for a freelance job. Somebody wanted something very badly. He didn't know who or why, nor was he overly concerned with the answers. The job was sweet and the damaged ex-Marine, at age 34, too long in the tooth to be picky.

He fought the impulse to gulp cool September air as they approached the objective. It was third world dark. They had planned for no moon and were benefiting from a low overcast. Parkerville, glowing faintly over the hill, provided little illumination, but his PVS-14D Delta night vision goggles plainly showed the chain link fence yards ahead. He halted the team as they reached the barrier surrounding the research installation.

He checked his Dark Ops watch. 2:11 am. Right on time. The research facility was located in the middle of nowhere, just as the blond man had said; the only lights were dim low wattage spots mounted on the corners of the main buildings beyond the fence, and ornamental colored floods around the fountain in front of the main entrance. The silvery flicker from the gatehouse window, two hundred yards to his right, told him the guards were watching television.

Holman produced a pair of Ridgid bolt cutters and went to work. In fifty seconds, the opening had been created and Morrisey led his team through. Holman laid the red handled tool by the fence to mark the breach which, if all went well, they would clear in less than one hour.

Crouching low, they scuttled across the immaculate lawn towards the main building, largest of the three. Morrisey easily located the side door next to the large loading dock overhead door with the aid of his Delta goggles. The squad slipped inside; Morrisey led the team swiftly to the stairwell. As they took the steps two at a time, he imagined someone had shoved kebob skewers into both knees. He ground his teeth, willing the pain under control. The incursion team exited the stairwell on the fifth floor and transited a hallway to a heavy steel door marked:

LEVEL FOUR CONTAINMENT
STAGING AREA

Adjacent the door, a small LED mounted on the stainless steel keypad glowed green. Holman pulled off a Wiley X Tactical Assault glove and punched buttons. In moments, the team was inside the staging area, narrow and cluttered with equipment. Three large windows looked into the actual containment room, which was much larger. The men threaded their way through the maze of gear to the airlock.

Passage through the double doors took just over a minute. Davis and Holman stood guard while Morrisey and Switzer slipped inside the containment area, traversed the large outer room and approached a second door with built in combination lock. Morrisey removed a glove and worked the dial; in moments he and Switzer entered a small refrigerated room filled with glass doored compartments. Next to a door labeled **LASSA VIRUS**, Morrisey located one marked **G-11.** He opened the small cubicle and removed the stainless steel container, shaped like a mason jar, by its top handle. As he shut the compartment, he felt the exhilaration of having gained his objective.

The pair emerged from the refrigerated room as Holman wiped the combination dial clean of prints. The team threaded its way back through the staging area and closed the steel door behind. In sixty seconds, they had silently descended the staircase and were outside.

Crouching low, the four moved swiftly across the lawn and through the hole in the fence. Holman produced clear plastic electrical ties and quickly stitched the links together so that the breach was virtually invisible. In another five minutes, the squad had double timed down the side of the road far enough to be out of sight from the guardhouse, where they retrieved their gray Toyota panel van from a clearing behind a stand of oak trees.

Morrisey looked at his Dark Ops. 3:06 am. During the entire operation, which had taken less than an hour, not a human being had been sighted, not a word exchanged between the infiltrators, no flashlight snapped on, no weapon drawn. The mission had been white bread. In hours, Morrisey would rendezvous with the blond man and exchange the container, now packed in dry ice and safely resting in the cooler between the front seats, for the second cash payment.

What the ex-Gunnery Sergeant hadn't known was that there had been no need to bring weapons, especially since the man who made sure the side door by the loading dock had been left unlocked was Dr. Willard Jergens himself.

2

As dawn broke over the low hills some sixty miles east of Parkerville towards the Arizona border, James Morrisey took a moment to enjoy the beauty of the surrounding countryside from the front seat of his three year old F-150 pickup. The nighttime insects were silent now; birds chirped and leaves rustled in the slight breeze. It all looked California-bright and scrubbed. The temperature was perfect, the air invigorating – a great setting for one of those wine commercials, he thought. Maybe this wasn't wine country, what the hell did he know about that? Most of the little stunted trees he had seen the last several years were olive trees, anyway. Fortified with ibuprofen and a couple of bottles of Hard Hat beer, the soldier of fortune – he liked the term, especially now - felt fresh and alert and not as if he had been up all night as he waited for the blond man to pull up behind the deserted gas station. The van had been disposed of, and the container rested in the Igloo on the floor next to him.

Even his knee was quiet for the moment, Morrisey observed, no doubt owing to the anti-inflammatory and brew. His thoughts shifted as he waited. Maybe he'd get a new truck. He could afford one now, even with the alimony. The warranty on this one was just about over. Extended cab, maybe. Hell, he might just go for the Hummer, if he could still find a new one at a dealership somewhere. The thing wasn't too practical and got crummy mileage, but he had always wanted one anyway. Black, of course. If he—

The blond man's Suburban had just appeared over the rise and was approaching the gas station. Always careful, always professional, Morrisey cleared his thoughts. He felt the reassuring pressure of the Glock against the small of his back as he got out of the cab and stood next to the open door: instant cover if necessary. The Suburban slowed, then pulled into the dirt area ten yards from the ex-Marine. The engine died, leaving the birds chirping and the leaves rustling.

Both doors opened. A flush of adrenaline and Morrisey was suddenly on guard. What was this? A dark haired, attractive woman stepped down from the passenger seat as the blond man, in casual pants and golf shirt, got out the driver's side holding the briefcase containing, theoretically, the second half of the money.

Theoretically. Morrisey was damn sure going to count it.

"Hello," the woman said. She had a dazzling smile. It might have been the prettiest smile he had seen in a long time, he realized.

"Hello back." He smiled too, his best Special Ops smile. Everyone was smiling. Why not?

The blond man spoke up. "The container?"

Morrisey retrieved the Igloo from the passenger floor, keeping one eye on the pair as he turned, since after all he was a professional, although the woman's top was really low cut, and she had bent down for some reason, and so he was surprised to see that instead of holding the briefcase the blond man was grasping a SIG Sauer P226 handgun. He and the dark haired woman were still smiling, more broadly now, as she straightened.

How fair was this?

"What—"

Morrisey said this before something slammed into his chest with incredible force.

Strange, he thought as he fell, he hadn't heard a thing. He had always preferred the M9 Beretta to the SIG but maybe he had been wrong. He struggled to remove the Glock as he lay in the dirt but the blond man was standing over him now, still smiling, and there was another explosion in his chest, just for an instant.

The money really had been too good to be true.

3

The one who called himself Sharif sat at the grand Steinway in the Piano Suite of the Claridge Hotel playing the Brahms Piano Concerto No. 1 in D Minor.   He had completed the first two movements – the difficult *Maestoso*, the mysterious *Adagio* - and was well into the *Rondo*, eyes closed, seeing the sands drift into yellow swirls above the dunes, the hot wind coming from the north, carried by the fiery syncopations of the third movement when—

The telephone rang.   The landscape he had conjured turned orange with a flash of momentary anger, even though he was expecting the call. He knew Yousif would rush to pick it up before the intrusive noise repeated.

"As-salaam aliekom."   The aide hurried out of earshot.

His irritation faded as he re-entered the music.   Feeling the warmth on the side of his face diminish, he glanced outside.   The afternoon sun was sinking.   He saw the keys taking on a golden patina as he made the calmer transposition from D minor to D major. Perhaps Allah was accompanying him?   He smiled at the thought and closed his eyes again.   Engrossed in the intricacies of the *Rondo*, Sharif barely registered the chirp of a cell phone, one of a dozen laid out on the low table by the fireplace.

From nearby, a polite cough.   Another flare of annoyance; he opened his eyes and saw Yousif standing by the piano, holding out the phone. He finished the piece and took the instrument. Brahms and the concerto dissolved.

"Yes?" This in English. He thought it an irony that he preferred many of the English ways now. He felt more at home leveraging technological acquisitions than listening to the music of the *rababa* with his brothers, smoking the *shisha*.

"*As-salaam aliekom, Sharif.*"

"Yes?"

"I am downstairs. My words cannot be spoken on a cell phone, even with the precautions." The precautions, Sharif knew because he had devised them, included a special code designating which particular cell phone to use.

"Come." He allowed himself a current of anticipation.

Minutes later, a soft knock on the door to the suite. Yousif admitted a figure in traditional Arab dress, the white *thobe* with checkered *shumagh*. Sharif, perfectly tailored in a gray twelve ounce Anderson & Sheppard suit, sat opposite Fahd on the sofa next to the piano. It both pleased and irritated him that his western dress enhanced the gulf between them.

Although tea was brewing, he offered none. Sharif knew Fahd would get to the point quickly.

"Sharif, last night a twenty five gram container of the substance known as G-11 was removed from the Level Four containment area at Jergens Laboratories in California. Gafar was able to sequester a small quantity."

How serene. Allah has truly given his blessing, Sharif thought. "Where is the substance now?"

Why did he have to ask?

"On its way in a diplomatic pouch. It arrives this evening."

Sharif looked out the window, nodding slightly. With the movement, Fahd was dismissed, forgotten. Twilight approached, bringing a light fog. He watched the London streetlamps come to life, haloed fireflies stretching up Brook and Davies Streets. They were as the oil lamps, diffused through tent cloth, strewn through the camps.

In truth, he would have paid any price to obtain the bio-agent. His thoughts went to a distant relative, suffering in the mountains of Pakistan where only goats should live, wandering stone paths with a stick and being dialyzed in caves, a great bounty on his head from the Americans. He shook his head slightly. No one could fault his relative's sincerity, but his methods were crude, passé. No, with a little intelligence there was so much more damage to be done from the serenity and comfort of a location like the Piano Suite. Yes, how wonderfully ironic: the bee sucking the nectar before the sting.

Looking at the gleaming piano, he reflected again on the Brahms. The perfect metaphor for the sexual experience, with its rough, rhythmic brutality and spent dismissal. It was all as one: the concerto, the taking of a woman, the violent cycles of the desert. Few understood the true nature, the unforgiving hand of Allah.

A slight creak from the chair: Fahd re-materialized.

"What quantity is en route?" Sharif asked.

"Three and a half grams."

Sharif nodded, contented. It would be enough. Three and a half grams to unleash more devastation than all the wars, the battles, the *jihads* of the past.

Three and a half grams, Allah willing – and Sharif was certain he was – to fulfill the prophecy, to destroy Zion forever.

It was time for tea.

4

A breeze carrying the fragrant promise of cherry blossoms mixed with diesel fumes wafted down a road just off K Street in Washington, DC, drifting by an ordinary but upscale townhouse six thousand kilometers from the Piano Suite in London. Inside, past a paneled and wainscoted hallway painted a pleasant light peach and in a small, well-appointed study, two men sat in Baker chairs staring at a fire that threatened to extinguish itself and send threads of soot and smoke into the room. The wood shifted and complained. The older of the two, whose name was Richard Haycock, sighed. As was his custom, he wore a blazer and old school tie. This day, he had on a V necked sweater as well.

The older they got, the younger man realized, the more layers of clothing they wore, like tree rings. The chill of old age crept in slowly, it seemed. He thought briefly of his father, huddled against the cold on the wet concrete floor in a Hong Gai prison, soaked periodically with a hose. North Vietnam was sometimes cold in January. He had looked it up in the almanac when he was in eighth grade. His father had never spoken of it.

"Wet wood again," Haycock said. "It's ruining the furniture. Everything smells smoky."

The logs snapped and hissed, resisted the flames. An ancient dialogue between the two, almost painful to hear.

"Sir." The younger man, half his superior's age, sipped coffee and waited to learn the reason he had been summoned by the person who, over the years, he had come to regard as a second father. He put down his cup and tried not to wince. The old man's blend could melt metal.

Richard Haycock shifted his gaze to his guest. "Two days ago, a quantity of G-11 disappeared from the Jergens Research Laboratories near Parkerville. A twenty five gram container. You are of course familiar with the location and the substance." It wasn't a question.

"Yes sir."

"We have a general knowledge as to who is behind the theft. We have already discussed the possibility of a breach in containment and what measures must be taken to try and prevent an unthinkable inoculation. Yes?" Again, more punctuation than query.

"Certainly, sir." Both realized, the younger man knew, an inoculation was probably not preventable.

"More coffee? No? The situation is bad enough, but there is a complication." At that moment, there was a knock on the closed door of the study and William, in grey service jacket, hurried in. The elderly steward rushed to the fireplace.

"Sir, I smelled the smoke from the pantry. Let me just take care of this."

The younger man took a breath, sighed. Richard Haycock smiled, nodded, made a gesture.

As they watched, William poked and prodded with a tool. The wood groaned in protest, spit a cinder at him. Flames rose, feebly.

"I'm afraid we don't have much to work with here, sir," William said.

"Thank you, William." The guest thought: if it is the measure of a man how he treats his inferiors, Richard Haycock measured well.

The steward wobbled from the room and closed the door.

"Yes. As I say, there is a further complication. We believe a quantity of this stolen G-11, perhaps as much as five grams, is already offshore. This material may be utilized in an attempt to reverse engineer G-11. Is that possible, do you think?"

The younger man shifted in his chair, thought for a moment, waffled his hand. "Maybe. Depends who's doing it. Probably not from scratch." He had one eye on the fire.

"But you're not certain."

"No."

Haycock nodded. "Okay."

"Have we identified the infiltration team?" the younger man asked.

"Not entirely. A black ops type, former USMC Special Operations, was found shot to death yesterday morning sixty miles away at what appeared a rendezvous location. Tire tracks had been wiped away. The weapon was a military SIG Sauer. He or his team, if he had one, wouldn't have known what the substance really is or who they worked for."

"Yes."

Haycock inclined his head towards the younger man, raised an eyebrow. "I imagine that lead will be tracked down in any event." A gentle order, the younger man knew, that hadn't needed to be given.

"Yes." Finding the other squad members would take little time.

"I'm afraid I can't give you very much outside help on this one. We don't know how extensive this is."

"I understand."

"Play it close to the vest. Be careful who you trust."

"I will." Was this job any different? He was facing the only person he completely trusted.

"The major will brief you on details, although they're not much more than the sketchy outline I just gave you. Do you need instructions from me?"

"No, sir."

"Keep me informed, then."

The meeting was over. The younger man rose, looked into the fireplace. It wasn't working at all. Now there was more smoke than fire, and the crackling had turned to a constant hiss. Whenever asked to the townhouse, he thought of the fire. He always wanted it to work for the old man, and it never did. Why did it seem so important? Somehow he sensed the question was as meaningful as the answer.

The mean minimum temperature in Hanoi during the month of January was 56.7 degrees. He still remembered.

*   *   *   *

Richard Haycock remained in his chair for several minutes after his visitor had departed. He had served with the young man's father in Vietnam; they had known each other well before his friend had fallen from the sky in an NVA flak trap over Hanoi, flying the Route Package 66 strike zone. Later, after the war, the man that came home from North Vietnam was a shard of the robust fellow who had been Haycock's college knockabout.

And so Haycock had taken a special interest in the boy, mentoring him in college, seeing him become an effective weapon of war, perhaps with misgiving, a brilliant young man whose great strength was his ability to act alone, to move decisively and without hesitation when required.

And, most effective, his charm – the disarming grin, the engaging offhand mannerisms – that could be, and had been, deadly.

5

Parkerville, California:

The evening fog threaded its way through a stand of pine, then spread over the lake, rising to a curtain obscuring the sign at the water's edge. The words were not readable from the road forty yards away:

PARKERVILLE RESERVOIR
No Boating No Fishing No Swimming

Light from the quarter moon filtered through the gauze, silvering the surface. A daguerreotype in the stillness, broken by a suggestion of movement emerging from the trees.

A hooded figure dressed in black slipped a dark canoe into the water. Hidden by the pines, the man paddled almost delicately; soft ripples, eddying smoke marked his passage. An observer driving by – had there been one – would have seen nothing. Thirty yards out, the man shipped his paddle and the craft glided to a standstill.

The man withdrew a pair of latex exam gloves, donned them and flexed his fingers. He reached down between his feet and lifted a plastic gallon jug, placing it on the seat next to him. Carefully, he broke the safety seal, unscrewed and dropped the top into the water. He lifted the jug and, holding it close to the surface to minimize splashing, slowly poured the green viscous contents into the water. The soft burping noise from the jug was muffled by the fog. When the container was empty, he submerged it. The air bubbled out and it sank.

The man peeled off the exam gloves and dropped them into the reservoir. They floated until he picked up his paddle and pushed them under. He watched them sink before heading back to shore. As he did so, clouds covered the moon completely and darkened the scene.

6

Moon Valley, Arizona:

The migrant camp, an abstract of browns, lay untidily at the end of a rutted dirt road, a small capillary from the main artery miles away. Shacks, dust and flies, and then the road ran out, stopping at a field of produce that seemingly went on forever. An undernourished mongrel lay chained to a standpipe. Across the road, an open faucet, spigot broken, leaked water next to the dilapidated, unpainted general store, creating a muddy stain that ran to the adjacent barracks. Between the two buildings, an ancient black Ford, eviscerated, rested atop cinder blocks.

A heavy black woman in a once-colorful dress made her way around the standing water and waddled across the road, laundry basket atop her head. The dog licked a sore, watched her go. Beyond the largest building, barefoot children in shorts and ragged tee shirts hollered in Creole as they kicked a weather beaten soccer ball through the dust. From the shaded porch of the general store, two steps up from the street, old black men in overalls sat in rickety chairs as the time oozed like molasses.

The drone of a crop duster settled on the camp. The bright yellow Air Tractor AT-401, perhaps a mile distant, lined up along rows of lettuce. A few of the men on the porch watched idly as the plane swooped down and released a gray cloud. As it rose, the craft turned and circled. The pilot donned a gas mask and tightened the straps. Once finished, he turned the duster and headed for the town at an altitude of one hundred feet.

As the plane grew larger in the sky, and the engine noise grew louder, a Haitian child stopped playing soccer and yelled, pointing as the aircraft reached the end of the field and suddenly dove toward the camp. The other children stopped and followed his gaze. The old Haitian woman removed the basket from her head and looked upward as the plane, just yards above the ground, zeroed in.

In the cockpit, the pilot pulled a red knob.

A green cloud released from the wing jets and descended on the camp. As the plane reached the end of the settlement, the spray stopped and the craft climbed swiftly, loudly, gulping air and turning away. If anyone had noticed, the N numbers on the fuselage had been obscured by dirt and grease.

In the camp, the Haitians appeared befuddled as the cloud settled upon them. The old woman tugged at the faded kerchief atop her head, wheezed and spat in the dirt. One of the children coughed, echoed by two of the old men on the porch, no longer rocking. The mangy dog snapped at its open sore, rattling the chain.

The plane grew smaller, disappeared against the crystal sky.

*　　　　*　　　　*　　　　*　　　　*

On the same clear morning, forty miles away, jetliners traced a geometry of contrails high above the sheer cliff rising from the low desert floor to an altitude of eighteen hundred feet, ending abruptly in a plateau. The steepness of the rock, and its uncertain, crumbly composition made the climb a challenging one. Perhaps a third of the way up, two figures made their way toward the summit.

In the lead was Leslie Riordan, M.D., 32, in shorts and climbing boots. Attractive, athletic, her long blonde hair fell behind her as she negotiated her way up a difficult rock face. Ropes, camming devices, carabiners, and various climbing tools hung from her belt as she stopped and wedged a nut into a crevice that traversed the solid rock for a distance. A few yards below, Ben Moody, 23, unkempt dark hair framing his tanned, handsome face, looked upward.

"Ever take a break, Leslie?"

"There's a ledge about ten meters ahead," she replied. "What's the matter, can't keep up?"

The young grad student grinned. "Let's hear what you say a couple hours from now."

Leslie smiled back. "If you're close enough behind me to hear."

The obstetrician finished placing the wedge-shaped nut and yanked it twice. Satisfied, she clipped a rope. Smooth as a spider, Leslie scrambled upward.

Later, atop the plateau, the sun slightly lower in the sky, Leslie sat with Ben, contentedly looking out at the desert reaches. What an extravagant use of space, she mused. In the shadows of the buttes and crags, reds and browns muted to purple. They ate pbj sandwiches, polishing off their lunch with a package of Oreos. As she broke apart her cookie and licked the icing, Leslie studied the sediment layers on a nearby escarpment. They had broken and angled off, a mute display of some past calamity. It all led to thoughts of dinosaurs, giant ferns and theme park attractions. Why had they taken out the submarine ride? she wondered vaguely. It all looked so still and unchanging from the plateau, punctuated by the occasional smudge of a distant dust devil. Maybe God was some turbocharged version of Disney—

"Hey, you're eating all the Oreos!" Ben's exclamation jolted Leslie out of her reverie. Her thoughts seemed to get more random as she got older, she thought, before handing him the package with its last cookie. Was that bad? Maybe it was good.

Ben studied his climbing partner as well as the view: Leslie, the archetypical California blonde, bronzed and freckled with sunlight. One was as distant as the other, he thought wryly.

As they sipped from plastic water bottles, neither noticed the yellow Air Tractor speeding from its fierce errand as it crossed the horizon in the distance, three hundred feet below the plateau, and disappeared.

7

Two months after the crop duster inoculated the migrant camp population in Moon Valley, Arizona, twenty eight year old Husam al Din shuddered against the cold wind rushing down New Utrecht Avenue. He looked at the building numbers as he walked south on the Brooklyn street. The factory should be on the next block. Nothing could be written down and so he had memorized the address. The Syrian national tugged on his collar and thought of the warm breezes turning the wind turbines atop the hill on route 98 in Al Qunaytirah. Land of his ancestors. It comforted him to know that one day, not far off, Syria would again take the soil that was rightfully hers before Israel had wrenched it from his motherland. Even now, his countrymen were moving into the Golan Heights at the encouragement of Damascus. The entirety of the Heights would be Syrian if he were successful, he had been told, before embarking on the circuitous journey that was nearing its end with the factory on New Utrecht Avenue in New York City's Hasidic enclave. Whoever controlled the Golan Heights held a priceless military advantage; one that had shockingly slipped away toward the end of the Six Day War many years ago. The longstanding and illegal Israeli occupation was a festering splinter that had to be removed.

He passed Jew after Jew: black apparitions in doorways, picking over fruit, pulling bags of goods. Vile snatches of Yiddish, hurled away by the wind. Mothers drooling over babies. Old, old men, Israel in their eyes, sitting on stoops, dreaming in the daylight. Leather skin stretching, heads slowly swiveling as he passed, unclean gazes assailing him. His hatred was dispassionate, knowing what was in store. These were not like the Zionists in Israel with their Galil assault rifles and sunglasses and arrogant disregard for everyone. These were soft and fat and unfit to survive. Husam's name – Sword of the Faith – was a prophecy he was destined to fulfill, he knew.

There it was, across the street. Its appearance held no special significance: grimy and old, with filthy factory windows so dirty they reflected a rainbow sheen in the sunlight. Kashrut was one of seven Orthodox matzo factories in the borough, and primarily supplied shmura matzo to the Belz Hasidic sect. Not nearly as large as the Streit factory on the lower east side of Manhattan, whose product served a wide geographic area and many Orthodox variations, the Kashrut factory's output was small. The brand's distribution was concentrated in Brooklyn and thus easily tracked. It was perfect for their purposes.

Husam al Din crossed the street and picked up the Brooklyn Daily Eagle from a vendor's stand. He pretended to scan the front page as he studied the ancient building. The place was so old his superiors had had trouble determining the layout, as no plans were available for either the building or the machinery inside, much of which dated from the 1930's.

His concentration was interrupted by the vendor, an ancient Jew with a cloth apron, stained black with newsprint and grime. The man stood no more than five feet tall.

"You godda pay for dat."

Husam al Din looked at the creature, bug-eyed. The filthy—

"Twenny five zentz." The Jew was making gestures that said come on, pay up you deadbeat.

Husam al Din resisted the almost overwhelming reaction to smash the man's skull with the newspaper weight. It was vital that he stay unnoticed. He smiled, paid for the paper and strolled across the street with it under his arm. When he reached the curb, he glanced back but the vendor was busy with his papers.

He continued down the alley and stopped at the side entrance to the matzo factory, studying the lock that hung open during the workday. Satisfied, he turned and walked back to the street, mentally reviewing his information about the plant.

Much of the matzo inside was made by hand, and when Passover approached stringent rules for manufacture were observed. Nothing but flour and water, the requirements included baking for eighteen minutes and no longer. After each eighteen minute batch, the mixing bowls, mixing arms, and rollers were completely cleaned. Rabbis with stopwatches oversaw preparation: mixing, forming, rolling. Somehow the timing was very important to their God, he thought. Crazy Jews.

As specified, water in the Kashrut factory sat overnight. The three tanks were inspected by the rabbis and locked for the evening, to be unlocked by more rabbis in the morning. Similar guidelines prevailed for the flour; only after passing all the inspections could matzo be made. There could be no contamination of something man was making by something God had made. If by some circumstance such as mechanical breakdown the cycle was extended beyond the eighteen minute limit, the entire batch of matzo was thrown out and all machinery – mixers, matzo-cutting machines, chutes, rollers, etc – were thoroughly cleaned with towels, scrapers and compressed air.

Husam returned to the tiny apartment off Eastern Parkway where he and Aram Zada, his mission partner, had spent the previous night after arriving in Brooklyn by separate means. Husam did not know to whom the apartment belonged, only that the key had been left on the door sill, and the leather gym bag containing materials necessary for the operation was in the closet. He had been designated mission leader, and thus responsible for the precious container worth more, he knew, than their lives. They had been warned not to speak of personal things, and to reveal no unnecessary details to each other, but Aram in his excitement had volunteered his age. He was two years younger than Husam. They were supposed to rest and try to sleep until the evening, but Aram had discovered American television in the apartment and had been avidly watching since they arrived. Husam slept for four hours; when he awoke Aram was still staring at the set. The mission leader was making a mental list of his partner's violations. He would prove to Allah and his leaders he was a man to be trusted with future assignments.

At two thirty the next morning, under cover of a fierce rainstorm, Husam al Din and Aram Zada quickly unscrewed the hasp secured by an inexpensive model 1500 Master Lock padlock on the side door of the ancient matzo factory. Aram carried a plastic two liter container with two strips of masking tape on the side, marking the contents into thirds. Husam held the leather gym bag in his left hand. The two men slipped inside and snapped on their flashlights, taped to project a slit beam, although intelligence said the factory was unguarded. They moved cautiously and silently through the building, threading their way past machinery and conveyors, until they spied the water tanks to their left. As they turned past a large mixing machine, a soft light became visible. Husam, in the lead, stopped dead, tapped his partner's arm, and pointed.

Bending low, they crept forward. The light emanated from a window in an interior office on the plant floor. What was this? Husam wondered. He slowly unzipped his gym bag. To Aram, the noise sounded incredibly loud. Husam withdrew a SIG Sauer P220 Combat TB semi-automatic, improved with the Colt 1911-type magazine catch. Eyes on the window, he stuck the weapon, fully loaded with ten rounds of Parabellum 9mm ammunition, into his belt. He dipped into his bag again and came out with a 7.5 inch bladed Fairbairn-Sykes fighting knife, handing it to Aram. The pair crept forward until they could make out the shape of a black clothed, bearded man in an office chair, facing away, reading. The light came from a desk lamp. His coat was draped over a side chair. The man stroked his beard as he absorbed the words. A rabbi.

Rabbi Avram Hyman occasionally volunteered to spend the night at the Kashrut factory watching over the ingredients for the next day's matzo. He loved to read his Torah or, occasionally, a popular book. Tonight, it was *My Name is Asher Lev*. He had read it as a student, quickly, eagerly; now he savored the work.

Avram loved to think, as well, something many of his acquaintances spent their lives trying to avoid. He found the spartan little office a peaceful oasis from the clatterings and collisions of daily life in the borough. In truth, it was a respite from his *mame*, who had raised him, as well as his fiancé, Dvorah, who felt she must continue the task. Dvorah was of course lovely and devout and would soon make a suitable wife and, hopefully, mother but in the meantime she did love to talk. And talk.

Husam moved under the window and raised up slowly as Aram carefully set his container of liquid down next to a machine. Avram turned the page, engrossed in his reading, rocking slightly. Husam scanned the desk for a phone or buzzer. Nothing appeared within easy reach of the Jew. The Syrians looked at each other; their eyes met. Neither had killed before, and they were now faced with the reality of having to eliminate the unexpected man, a more personal *jihad* suddenly thrust upon them. Fortunately, he was not only a Jew, he was a rabbi, and their mission was vital to the cause, and blessed by Allah, as they had been told. So vital that Hamas and Hezbollah, two polar organizations, had apparently joined in an uneasy alliance for the operation. Or so Husam had inferred. Perhaps even Fatah, he had thought, but these were matters left to his superiors. He smiled slightly at the thought. Fatah was a reverse acronym of Hataf, or sudden death in Arabic. How fitting this night.

Husam, in the lead, crept around the office rectangle to the door, taking the pistol from his belt. He pointed to Aram and the knife, nodding. Aram nodded back. Husam thought he saw fear in the younger man's eyes, but it was dark. Aram positioned himself in front of the door, setting his feet as Husam reached for the knob. There was a moment of expectancy. Aram nodded in readiness. Husam took a breath and held it as he turned the knob and yanked, just as Avram Hyman coughed loudly.

Nothing. The door didn't open. Was it locked? The two Syrians looked at each other, wide-eyed. Aram, poised to leap into the office when the door was flung open, had nearly crashed into it. Both men stood stock-still for a moment. Inside, Avram turned towards the door. Had he heard something over his cough? What if a rodent had somehow gotten into the flour, or knocked over a scraper? This would be a calamity. It had happened before. He had best check. He put down his book and stood up.

Avram Hyman walked to the door and opened it, sticking his head through to look around, and came face to face with Aram Zada. Both men froze in shock.

"Aram!" Both men turned towards Husam, mouths open. Then Aram leaped forward and grabbed the rabbi's earlock, yanking his head around, bending the neck backward. The struggling pair lurched into the office. Avram's cry was cut short as the dagger penetrated the left side of his neck, almost to his ear, and Aram brought it around under the beard. The rabbi's legs caved and Aram let him go, stepping back to avoid the blood spurting, soaking the man's beard, his eyes darting between the two in incomprehension as he fell and lay face up on the floor. The amount of blood was shocking. Because the Fairbairn-Sykes was a killing weapon, designed to cut cleanly through the arteries rather than tear them, the vessels did not contract and stanch the blood flow.

Avram's brain struggled through the shock and intense pain to try and make sense out of what was happening. He could not. Where was he? His dwindling thoughts were not of Dvorah at all, but of the playground and games of his youth, and the wind ruffling the water on Jamaica Bay, and the Hasidic rituals of growing up, and his father on his park bench, backlit in the sunlight.

Husam realized this mess would compromise their mission. He quickly hopped over the fallen rabbi, yanked his coat from the side chair, bent over and wrapped it around Avram's head. He saw the light in the man's eyes was fading now, eyes glazing, mouth working like a guppy out of water. And still the blood oozed into the beard, slower, darker. Then the coat was over his face.

Avram was cold, now. The sunlight behind his father dimmed, went dark.

"We have to get him out of here!" Husam said.

"Wait!" Aram held up his hand. "We can't let him drip."

They hurried out of the office, scanning the factory floor with their flashlight beams. Behind, the rabbi's legs jerked spasmodically, became still.

"There!" Husam pointed. In a corner, a blue plastic tarpaulin covered an ancient piece of machinery. They ran to the machine and yanked the tarpaulin off, returning to the office.

"Take his wallet!" Husam hissed. "Search his pockets!"

Aram nodded. As he pulled the wallet from Avram's pocket, the rabbi jerked again. Aram, startled, cried out. Husam yanked the wallet from Aram and smacked him on the arm.

"Shut up!"

Carefully, they slid the tarp under the body and rolled it, wrapping the rabbi twice. Avram twitched once more, became still. The body was soaked with blood, but, surprisingly, it appeared little had worked through to the floor. Aram retrieved the cords that had held the tarp over the machine and they wrapped their ghastly package, dragging it out the office door. Husam and Aram stepped back inside and looked around more closely. There was blood on the floor, drying, but it was limited to a small area. There were no bloody footprints. They scanned each other, playing their lights over their clothing. Both men were spotted with dark red, but nothing had dripped.

There was no shortage of towels, scrapers and other cleaning supplies, thanks to the religious requirements of the factory. They rounded these up and went to work on the floor. Aram had to use the scraper where the blood had dried, but twenty minutes later the office had been cleaned up. Husam retrieved the rabbi's book and put it in his pocket next to the wallet. He stood back and looked the room over. Had he left evidence of the crime? He didn't think so, but it would have to do. Satisfied, he turned out the light and closed the door. The two men picked up the body, handling it carefully, keeping the ends higher so as not to drip, and carried it to the side door. They placed the rabbi down and retraced their steps. Aram retrieved the jug. They moved to the water tanks, taking the steps two at a time until they were at the lids.

Husam al Din's intelligence had not extended to the locks securing the water tanks. As a result, he carried a Peterson Professional lock picking set and an assortment of replacement locks in his valise. The two men quickly observed the arrangements were more ceremonial than preventive and in short order Husam had picked the lock, lifted the lid on the first tank and nodded to his partner. Aram donned exam gloves, unsealed the jug and opened it. He poured a third of the contents into the tank, down to the first line of tape, and screwed the top back on as Husam relocked the lid.

It took less than fifteen minutes to inoculate all three tanks, lock them, seal the empty jug and another ten to exit the building. The rain was still falling. They quickly spotted a pair of dumpsters at the end of the alley. Aram ran over and checked; one was nearly empty.

Retrieving the rabbi's body, they carried their package to the dumpster, where they struggled to heft it over the rim. Aram lost his grip on the wet, slippery plastic. He shifted his hands; suddenly his end lowered. A river of blood poured out, soaking his shirt. Cursing, the men struggled and finally heaved Rabbi Avram Hyman over the side, where he fell with a hollow clang to the floor of the dumpster. Aram had no option except to tear off his sodden shirt, wad it up and throw it in after the body. He stood in the rain, wearing his sleeveless tee shirt, cursing. Husam looked at his partner, inclined his head towards the other dumpster. The pair raised the lid and grabbed bags of garbage, covering the body and the shirt until both dumpsters were approximately half full. Husam undid a garbage bag in the second dumpster, took the rabbi's book from his pocket and dropped it in. He extracted the wallet. Twenty three lousy American dollars. He pocketed the money and stuffed the wallet in with the book, retying the bag. They closed the dumpster lids and walked quickly back to the factory, retrieving the gym bag. The cold rain was a welcome blessing, washing both men after the grisly night's work. Husam retrieved the screws from his pocket and reattached the hasp to the door, leaving it locked.

Each man left in a different direction. At 4:44 am Husam al Din made one call from his cell phone before dropping it into Jamaica Bay, along with the gym bag. He kept the SIG Sauer but not the knife. By the time the sun had risen fully above the horizon, the water from the tanks was being mixed with flour and baked in the eighteen minute window under rabbinical blessing, Rabbi Avram Hyman had been picked up by the Department of Sanitation and was on his way to the Brooklyn landfill on Memphis Avenue, and Husam al Din and Aram Zada were on a freighter steaming out of New York harbor, praising Allah not only for their success but their good fortune in the slaughtering of the rabbin. It was still raining. Neither man remembered they had left the empty container just inside the side entrance to the Kashrut factory, where the rollers were being scraped for a new batch of matzo, depositing infinitesimal particles of Avram Hyman on the equipment.

8

Sharif had chosen to play Mozart's Allegro in Bb Major, a contemplative piece, as he mulled over the situation in the Piano Suite. The Americans were as children, lurching on a steady decline into impotence and insolvency. While their population was mesmerized by amateur singing contests, grotesque racial chants that passed for music and professional football, the feeble intelligentsia had been neutered by a series of Presidents that could only have been a blessing from Allah. The country was suicidal. They had never realized it had been better to have a criminal for a President than a series of drooling dreamers, unfit and ungrounded in the real world, dismantling their own intelligence operations and giving away invaluable assets from the Panama Canal to the most sophisticated weapons technology. And what they didn't give away, they published and spread all over the web. No, the Americans were not to be feared. Let them pursue their dwindling self-importance, alienating allies and fueling hostility; let them start their ridiculous irrelevant wars and create ever more enemies, sliding towards bankruptcy and able to see no context but their own. As a result, his distant relative was now safe, having benefited from the West's short attention span. Yes, let them misread the signs but let their eager news media report those signs.

And yet they still had the scientific ingenuity, the resourcefulness and intelligence to develop the material he had stolen, the material now paying priceless dividends. Analysis of the G-11 had accelerated their own program, allowed them to gain perhaps two full years, and now they were underway in just under eight weeks. Allah had truly blessed this holy mission.

It was late afternoon again, and although he was waiting for a telephone call he gave no indication. He carried inside him the patience of a people who had waited for rain where there would be no rain for years, a people who outlasted the furious sandstorms for days on end, and who would continue to survive because of that patience, surviving even the liquid wealth that Allah had vomited up from black lakes below the sands.

He thought again of his brothers. He had left them behind, irretrievably, irrevocably; they were lost to him as they jockeyed for the crown like children for the party favor, the cheap whimsy of the moment, without the knowledge that they would never attain it. His brothers, papier-mâché princes cruising the pleasure halls of Bahrain and Dubai, lurking in the dark corners of Tehran, floating on liquid MDMA, the empty dream of forever-oil and disrespecting *Sharia*, the ancient code of Islam, turning the sacred Kingdom into the sandbox of a profane playground.

Theirs was not the destiny of the firstborn, the chosen. Sharif knew his manifest was to rely only upon himself and the firm belief in *Wahhabe*, the most violent of Islamic sects, and *jahiliyya*, the vilification of all societies – even Islamic societies – allowing impurity.

His gaze went to the window. Outside, it had begun to rain. He watched the glistening taxicabs crawl up Brooks Street, swarm around Grosvenor Square, black beetles against the charcoal of Mayfair in the twilight drizzle.

And then the phone did ring. The aide went through the same ritual as before, and in minutes there was the knock on the door, and the brief conversation with the messenger on the sofa. Again, Fahd's presence was forgotten as soon as he had finished delivering the message.

Allah had blessed the adventure in Brooklyn. The bearers of *jihad* had been successful. After Fahd had left, Sharif nodded to the aide, who activated a satellite telephone. It was time to probe the belly of the beast.

9

Twenty three kilometers miles west of Damascus, outside the town of Qatana, a phone rang just before lunch in a drab single story building, nondescript except for the camouflage netting above the roof concealing a forest of antennae and satellite dishes of varying sizes. The call was a relay from London, carrying a message from Brooklyn, New York that the baby had been baptized. The Syrian Special Forces captain receiving the call hurried into an adjacent office and repeated the message to his superior, Colonel Hassan al-Hassad, the officer in charge of the GSD installation. Although in theory a civilian organization, the General Security Directorate overlapped with Special Forces on certain intelligence matters.

Shortly thereafter, Mohammad Kanan and Farouk al-Hassad hiked to a hill within sight of the U.N. building in Kunetra, near the Golan Heights demarcation. They walked at a leisurely pace. The two men, born on the same day twenty years earlier, had grown up together in southern Syria, in Salkhad, a small town 30 km south of the city of Suweida. They had spent their youths climbing the ancient Ayyubid fortress, built in the volcanic crater towering 1500 meters above the town, and playing with their toy wooden rifles among the tombs and ruins, ancient remnants of Damascus' southern defense ring. When they reached their teens, the wooden rifles had been replaced with AK-47s. This day, they had been told, they carried a weapon more powerful than they could have dreamed. What could be more potent than the AK-47, more devastating than the Russian-made RPG-27 they had been promised? Farouk wondered. Both were anxious to perform their first mission for Hezbollah. Or so they had been told.

It was a balmy afternoon. Trees shrugged in the light breeze. Mohammad and Farouk opened their backpacks, spread a cloth and sat, eating falafel and drinking Pepsi Cola. They left their mission cargo, the heavy four liter jug sealed with security tape, in Farouk's backpack. They finished with a small sack of dates, idly chucking the pits at nearby palms as they spoke of their girlfriends in Salkhad, laughing, growing excited with the thought of the upcoming adventure. After waiting for nightfall, the pair skirted checkpoints and security fencing and entered the Golan. They wended their way around the many minefields to a dirt road, carrying only the jug and exam gloves in their remaining backpack. At nine fifteen, as predetermined, Farouk and Mohammad saw a flash of headlights and stood out in the road. A battered Toyota four by four stopped, motor running, and the Syrians clambered in.

The driver, twenty three year old Khaled Faris, was also keyed up. His briefing had stressed the vital nature of the mission. He was to transport his cargo to the springs at Salukiya, as close to the objective as possible without being seen, then wait on the side of the road with the hood up and lights off. When the two men returned to the Toyota, the orders were to drive them back to the pickup point.

Khaled knew enough not to introduce himself. The ride was not far. He glanced at the pair as he drove.

"You look so young," he said.

"You're not exactly a grandfather," Farouk said.

Mohammad and Farouk looked at each other. "Guess who's older," Mohammad asked playfully.

"You?"

"Ha! Guess again!"

"Well, that's not much of a trick, then. You." He nodded his head towards Farouk.

The passengers laughed loudly. "Wrong again!"

"How could that be?" Khaled asked.

"We were both born on the exact same day!" Farouk exclaimed.

"So you grew up together, or what?"

"Yes. And we both liked the same girls. Big rivals." More nervous laughter.

Farouk jerked his thumb towards his companion. "His sweetheart's the prettiest girl in Salkhad!"

The Toyota bumped along; as they approached Salukiya lights became visible perhaps a quarter mile away. The daytime breeze had stilled. The road began to parallel the stream of spring water. Khaled slowed and crept forward until the vehicle was just outside the minimally lighted area. He watched as Farouk hefted the four liter jug and climbed out with his companion. Crouching low, they moved down the embankment towards the water and were lost from sight.

Moving along the bank, the young Syrians stayed in the shadows of the trees until they were yards from the building that loomed ahead. Peering into the rushing spring, they were able to ascertain the correct location for the insertion, recognizing the layout from the rough schematics they had memorized days ago.

Donning the exam gloves, Farouk moved to the water's edge and unsealed the jug. He emptied the contents into the spring directly above the intake pipes. In the darkness, they could barely make out the outline of the Mey Eden mineral water bottling plant yards away.

Retreating quickly, they moved along the embankment to where the Toyota sat at the side of the road. Farouk submerged the jug until it filled and sank. He tossed the exam gloves in the bushes.

36

Then the pair clambered up the bank and hopped in the Toyota. Their heavy breathing was more from excitement than exertion. Both experienced the euphoria of having successfully completed the mission. Allah was doubtless pleased.

The ride back to the drop off point was uneventful. Unlike their Brooklyn counterparts, there were no unexpected occurrences. They were back in Syria before dawn, unaware their brief banter with the driver had sealed their fates.

10

Gaspari Vanucci stuck his hand under the plastic raingear, reached into his pea jacket and extracted a hip flask. Through long experience, he knew just how much Jack Daniels would last him through the first shift on his job at the Brooklyn landfill. No one in his right mind could be a sorter for very long, at least without the help of a flask or controlled substance. Everything was gray in the early morning rain. Memphis Avenue was gray, the buildings were gray, the conveyor was gray, except—

Something was very red. A shirt, he saw, as it approached on the conveyor. A bloody shirt. Gaspari saw a lot of things in the Brooklyn trash, including bloodstained clothing, but this was different. The shirt was not spotted with drops, but had been saturated with a sheet of blood. Curious, he signaled for the conveyor to be stopped. Of course, he had to signal twice as that lazy Armenian on the controls wasn't paying attention. He moved past a rolled blue tarp to inspect the garment. Except the blue tarp wasn't shapeless exactly, and the ends were also soaked in red.

*　　　　　*　　　　　*　　　　　*

Detective-Second Grade Harris Mulvaney knew it would be very difficult to trace the body back to a particular dumpster. With luck and hard work he might be able to pin down a particular route, and thus a string of receptacles, which could then be inspected one by one. In his stint with Brooklyn homicide, he had never heard of a rabbin murder, if indeed the unidentified corpse was what it seemed. If so, this would likely be a high profile case, with all the attendant headaches and opportunities. He mulled over the developing facts as he sipped his coffee, sitting in a tiled anteroom at the Brooklyn morgue on Clarkson Avenue. The shirt, on its way to the lab, belonged to someone other than the corpse, which had been fully dressed. The logical assumption was that it came from the perpetrator. The tarp looked like a common nylon-impregnated vinyl affair, stiff and weathered from age. Tracing its origin would be impossible. He was going to need some manpower to try and track down the dumpster, and from there, hopefully, the murder site.

All that changed with the phone call from Dvorah Ashkenazy. It did not take very long to match the parcel found in the Brooklyn landfill with the report that her fiancé was missing. By early afternoon, a hysterical Dvorah had been brought to the morgue and identified Avram Hyman. Someone gave her an injection. It was thirty minutes before she could be questioned. She sat in a chair, head in her hands.

Mulvaney sat across, leaned forward and touched her shoulder. "I'm sorry," he said. She looked up.

"When did you see him last?"

"Yesterday evening, maybe at seven o'clock? He would read, watch over the matzo until morning." She clutched a small handkerchief. The embroidered initials were frayed, Mulvaney saw, the dress faded, shapeless.

"Watch over the matzo?"

"At the Kashrut factory. On New Utrecht Avenue."

Mulvaney, an Irish Catholic, nodded. He had learned a considerable amount of Hasidic ritual in the two years he had been assigned to Brooklyn.

"How often did he do that?"

"I don't know, sometimes. Maybe once or twice a week."

"Did he have a schedule at all?"

"No. If he felt like it, he'd phone Rabbi Goldman and tell him he was coming. He would take a book. But I phoned the rabbi this morning. Avram wasn't there. Who would do this?"

"I don't know."

No book had been found with the body. If Rabbi Hyman had brought one, it was missing, along with the wallet and identification.

At 3:30, Mulvaney was at the Kashrut factory. He parked in back, next to the loading dock, where workers were loading the morning production into the distributor's truck. Inside, he found Rabbi Aaron Goldman standing over a mixing machine.

"Let's go to the office," Goldman said. "It's quieter there." He led the detective toward the small room in the center of the factory.

"His custom was to read in the office. This was maybe once a week. He said he was going to come over last night."

"Did you see him last night?"

"No, I was gone by six."

The pair threaded their way through the machinery towards the rectangle.

"When did you arrive this morning?"

"A little after eight."

"Did you expect to see him when you got here?"

"No. He would have been gone hours ago. When Dvorah called, I looked in the window here. No Avram. For all I know, he never came over. You haven't found him?"

"We found him."

The rabbi raised an inquisitive eyebrow as he reached for the doorknob, but Mulvaney put up his hand. He had peered through the glass. The detective's trained eye had noticed – what - a chair out of place, maybe?

Mulvaney opened the door with a handkerchief and looked at the floor. Traces of dark stains here and there; silent marks of the evening's mayhem.

"Has anyone been in this room today?" he asked.

"I don't think so. Some days, no one goes in there."

After studying the room for a few minutes, Mulvaney was sure Avram Hyman was assaulted and probably slain in the factory office. He called for CSI. The lab would find fingerprints that did not match those people with access to the office, as well as scratch marks on the screws that attached the hasp on the side door lock. The prints belonged to Aram Zada and Husam al Din. Naturally, they were not on file anywhere in the country.

The Kashrut factory, unthinkably violated, was immediately closed. The New York City press and television news gave considerable ink to the homicide of a rabbi. Speculation was that Avram Hyman, while at the Kashrut office, surprised two nighttime burglars and was slain in an ensuing confrontation. His missing wallet supported that conclusion.

Detective Mulvaney did not share this theory. What thieves, he reasoned, would take the time and trouble to wrap the body, dump it in the trash, screw the hasp back on the door frame, and stroll off in the rain?

When the police had finished gathering evidence and removed the yellow tape, the office and factory were cleaned and purified under rabbinical supervision. Everything in the plant was thoroughly cleaned, scrubbed and inspected. Kashrut Matzo reopened two days later and production resumed. Product made the morning Detective-Second Grade Mulvaney pinned down the murder site had been distributed throughout its market area. It was sold and consumed over the next few weeks. No one had thought to recall it.

11

Mohammad Kanan and Farouk Al-Hassad had spent close to S£2000 – two thousand Syrian pounds, or about $40 – for dinner with Farouk's young cousin Usaid and his friend Nasif, both twelve, at the Café Latakia in Suweida. An exorbitant sum, which surely impressed the youngsters, who laughed and joked throughout the meal of *kibbe, burak* and *toshka* after appetizers of *hommas*, white cheese and *falafel*.

The four had been greeted by Hassan, the café's owner, who was a family friend of the Kanans and perhaps a distant relation.

"Please express my warmest regards to your parents," Hassan said to Mohammad, after hugs and kisses to the cheeks. He showed them to, as he pointed out, the best table in the house. It was by a window overlooking the road.

"I will order for us," Mohammad said, taking charge. He ordered from the waiter – also a distant cousin – with authority, impressing everyone. It was a time for celebration. The young men could not tell their younger companions of their heroic adventure in the Golan, of course, but somehow the secret made the night even more delicious. Rather than take the bus, Farouk had prevailed upon his uncle Ziad to lend them his battered Fiat, an ancient vehicle of uncertain color and reliability, but they had made the 30 km journey successfully and would soon ride back to Salkhad under a starry Syrian sky, bringing the twelve year olds back for a festive weekend visit with the Kanans. Mohammad had not seen his younger cousin, who lived in Suweida, for a year.

After the feast, Farouk, in a moment of frivolity, suggested smoking from the *erghilly*, which, rather than show their manliness and worldly ways, brought about a fit of coughing and tears, making the boys giggle.

Hassan made an appearance at the table. "Was everything satisfactory?"

"Oh, yes, wonderful," they chorused.

"I have a treat for you," Hassan said, smiling, and led them to the back room of the café, where they sat around a small wooden table. He brought out a bottle of *Arak*, a can of Pepsi Cola, five tiny glasses, a pitcher of water and a quantity of ice. He took off his apron, a small gesture to show he was a part of the festivity, but not so close in family that he didn't charge an additional S£200 for the bottle. He showed them how to pour the *Arak* and then add the water, and, lastly, the ice. The four watched the clear liquid turn cloudy, and then white, as if by magic, the young boys laughing all the while. Hassan examined the glasses closely and announced it was time to drink, and naturally he poured Pepsi Cola for Usaid and Nasif, and they all drank together, including Hassan, celebrating no one knew what, exactly, except of course Mohammad and Farouk who knew Allah would not mind their imbibing after such an important accomplishment. Usaid and Nasif broke up with laughter as Mohammad and Farouk began to cough, and their eyes watered with the powerful beverage, similar to Turkish Razi or Greek Ouzo, which took their breath away.

Finally, at 9:30, they climbed into the Fiat and headed back towards Salkhad, after jovial and exaggerated goodbyes from Hassan. Mohammad was thinking they would be home by 10:15. He glanced out the window; there were many stars on this soft night. Two of them were for himself and Farouk, he thought, rising stars in the Hezbollah firmament. After leaving Suweida, traffic thinned until there were no cars on the road. They were approximately halfway home. Laughter spilled from the open windows as they drove under the canopy of Paradise, the only visible lights except for the glow of Suweida behind them and—

Headlights rapidly approaching from behind. Farouk would have a mind to race the approaching vehicle, but the tired Fiat could only manage 70 kmh anyway. The lights came very close now, and flashed at Farouk. What? There was plenty of room to pass. Should he ease over? He did so as he strained to see in his rear view mirror. The vehicle pulled out and came alongside. Men with uniforms in a military vehicle. Farouk couldn't quite place the uniforms. Police? Soldiers? PSD, the Political Security Directorate? GSD?

He turned to Mohammad. "Who are these guys? Should I pull over?" Maybe they just wanted to pass. But no, they were waving Farouk to stop. They were holding automatic weapons. Mohammad exchanged a look with Farouk that said I'm scared too, but we're heroes in the *jihad* against Zion and once they find out who we are we'll be all right. In the back seat, Usaid and Nasif gaped at the armed intruders.

*   *   *   *

It was the next morning before a truck driver delivering a load of grain to Salkhad found the Fiat twenty meters off the road. Lying alongside, not visible from the highway, were the bodies of two twelve year old boys. They had been shot in the head at close range with 5.56mm rounds, standard ammunition for the Israeli Galil assault rifle, Russian AK-47, and American military/NATO M-16 weapons. There was no sign of Mohammad or Farouk.

The police were as puzzled as anyone.

12

Detective-Second Grade Mulvaney was smart. He knew he was smart. As a history major graduating with a 3.2 average from CCNY, he had won the Paul Aron Award for the best undergraduate research paper on, as he had argued, the folly of the War of 1812. He badly wanted to make Detective-First Grade as quickly as possible. There was another baby on the way. The Avram Hyman case could do it for him, and it was bothering him.

The case was wrong. Something was missing. The fact that the body had been moved told him something. The hasp being screwed back on the door frame and the factory relocked told him something. People who would kill a rabbi, apparently without compunction, and leave indiscriminate prints when they had plenty of time to clean up, prints that matched nothing on the local or national database, told him something. He was convinced this was no burglary. What did they want to steal, matzo? What could have been in the office that was so valuable? There was no cash on premises. The rabbi was a quiet, unassuming man with no known enemies. Was there a strategic reason to ambush and kill him? Was that the original intent? Maybe the encounter wasn't chance after all. Maybe these two guys, whoever they were, picked a perfect spot for an assassination. Maybe, but Mulvaney wasn't inclined to think so.

The two intruders didn't want it known they were in the factory. Perhaps they were buying time, but only a little time. The connection between the corpse and the Kashrut matzo factory was too obvious. He swiveled in his chair and looked out the window of the 77th precinct at the traffic on Union Avenue. In all his time at the Crown Heights station, he had never heard of a rabbin murder. Avram Hyman got in the way, all right, but it wasn't a robbery. It was a surprise encounter, because his fiancé and the other rabbis told him Hyman's schedule was erratic.

There was nothing to do but go back out there again, walk the premises, look at the facility with fresh eyes. What might someone want to get out of there? He got up and put on his jacket. He stopped with the flash of insight.

What might someone want to put *in* there?

*　　　　*　　　　*　　　　*

Mulvaney had not always found the Hasidic community entirely cooperative, although after two years the Irish Catholic was beginning to find a grudging acceptance. This case was different. This was not something to be kept in the enclave and dealt with by elders. Unknown monsters had taken a holy man's life, slit him like a lamb and let him bleed out, and when the life had run out of him wrapped the body in a plastic shroud and tossed it in a dumpster, to be hauled to a landfill. This was an unspeakable crime, one that must have been committed by outsiders. This scared people. They were glad to see the detective at the Kashrut factory, willing to answer all his questions. The fact that he had returned showed his determination to solve the homicide.

Mulvaney wandered the plant with no real agenda. It was an odd tableau: gleaming, spotless machinery in an ancient Industrial Age setting, the light filtered through windows that had become yellowed with age and decades of grime leached from the Brooklyn air. The place, in operation, was noisy, but the sounds insulated his thinking. He went into the office where Avram Hyman was slain.

There was no safe, no real hiding place. He tried to picture the rabbi's surprise. Did he perhaps surprise the intruders as well? Yes, if it was a chance encounter. No, if it was an ambush. As Mulvaney thought about it, he began to lend some credence to the latter theory. But why? And why leave so many indiscriminate prints, so many careless smears of blood?

He walked past the water tanks, then turned and headed back to the entry point, stopping just inside the side door. He looked around. He opened the door and stood in the doorway, looking back into the factory, out at the alley, down to the dumpsters. Mulvaney looked for something to prop the door open with while he let his mind play over the possibilities.

There was a plastic container on the floor, almost hidden in the shadow of a disused umbrella stand. He nudged it with his foot. It was empty, too light to hold the door open. Something about the jug caught his eye. He bent down and looked, careful not to touch it. The container was marked with masking tape in two places, apparently dividing the container into thirds. The screw top had another piece of masking tape around the threads, but it was loose, dangling. Now that he looked closely, it wasn't masking tape. It was smoother, like the stuff plumbers used to ensure a waterproof seal around pipe threads. It was as though the container had been unsealed and a hasty attempt made to reseal it.

Mulvaney stuck his pen through the jug handle and lifted it. There was writing indented into the bottom of the jug. It was Hebrew, and –

Mulvaney was not a linguistics expert, but he knew he was looking at Arabic. Arabic? What the hell was an Arabic container doing in a Hasidic matzo plant?

The question would remain unanswered for the next two months as the Avram Hyman homicide grew stale, fading from the front pages of the New York papers.

13

The single story, neat adobe professional building, framed tidily with mannered landscaping, stood back fifty feet from the street. The adjacent parking lot was nearly full. The sign on the lawn proclaimed:

2499
MOON VALLEY PROFESSIONAL BUILDING

and underneath, along with other physicians and lawyers:

LESLIE RIORDAN, M.D.
FRED JAMISON, M.D.
OBSTETRICS AND GYNECOLOGY

Leslie, in her exam coat, pulled a stethoscope with bright red tubing from her ears as she straightened from examining Lydia McConnell, 34, who was nearing term on her second baby.

Lydia sat up, covered her distended belly and buttoned her dress as Leslie wrote on her chart.

"Right on schedule, Mrs. McConnell," she said.

"Still the fifth?"

"Still the same. I want to see you in three weeks now."

Her appointments continued in a steady stream until well after 4 p.m. After the last expectant mother, she went to her office and reviewed the day's patient charts, making notes as she drank a diet cola. Leslie's office seemed almost an afterthought: small, cluttered, with inexpensive paneling and furnishings. She had become reconciled to the fact that between Medicare and the migrant camp, obstetrics in rural Arizona was not a particularly financially rewarding profession.

The migrant camp. Something about the place had been bothering her, and she wasn't quite sure what it was. Normally, Leslie visited her patients at the settlement once a week, except for emergencies. Yet—

She had to check her records. They weren't organized that way, she realized. She'd have to go through the files one by one. Still, it shouldn't take more than a half hour. No need to bother Mary Jo on the front desk; she was too new to help and would be leaving in fifteen minutes anyway.

The sun was edging towards the distant hills when Fred Jamison, Leslie's partner, opened the door to her office and sauntered in. Fred, at six foot three and 190 pounds, was as fit as his partner. Racquetball was his game; he played it Saturday and Sunday at the country club.

Leslie looked up from her desk, pen in hand. She noticed Fred was wearing his glasses, a sign he had been to the hospital. She knew he didn't wear his contacts in the O.R. or Delivery Room.

"Oh, hey, Fred. Didn't see you much today. Everything go okay at the hospital?"

Both were still in their white exam coats, names embroidered in pastel cursive.

"Yeah, busy one. Betsy Keller's delivery ran overtime, but everything was normal. A girl." He took off his glasses and rubbed his nose.

"Glad to hear it. She finally got her daughter after three boys."

"Yeah. They were afraid to find out ahead of time, you know? Didn't want to see the sonogram."

Leslie nodded. When she had begun her practice she thought most of her patients would want to know the sex of the fetus, and had been surprised when some actually didn't.

Fred sat in the ancient leather visitor's chair Leslie had resurrected from Moon Valley's secondhand shop. He absently peeled a fragment of cracked leather from the arm, then looked at his watch.

"You going to be able to get out of here in time for dinner?" he asked.

"I think so," Leslie said.

"Better get to bed early," Fred continued. "Gotta be sharp for that big climb tomorrow, hey?"

"Yes, daddy. I'll tuck in at ten. Can I get a bedtime story?"

"We tried that once, remember?" Fred said. It had been some time ago, and Leslie had realized quickly it was a mistake, too soon after Donald had died, when she still could recall his face by glancing at young Derek when he smiled, or turned just so, without having to look at the pictures scattered around her house, pictures forming a kaleidoscope of emotion she hadn't wanted to dim in the fading light of time. She had cut it off, fearing the partnership would suffer in one way or another, she told herself, before they would have become intimate. Fred, for his part, recalled the time with the wistfulness of a determined romantic. It was a cherished memory, for its sadness as well as its uplifting moments: points of light through, he had not realized, cotton candy. Leslie was his only personal catastrophe. He had wanted military service, to be flung to some distant exotic theater, but failed the physical with a separated shoulder. He had insisted her name be listed first when they became partners. Then, it had been chivalrous, perhaps romantic; now it was a small scar, part of the smaller tragedy.

Leslie put down her pen.

"Listen, Fred," she said, interrupting his reverie. "There's something kind of – I don't know – odd, I think."

"Odd?"

"Have you noticed anything in the last couple months?"

Fred tried to remember if Leslie had cut her hair. Maybe the color was different, but he didn't think so.

"Like what? You feeling okay?"

"Of course I'm feeling okay. I mean with our practice."

Fred made an I-don't-know gesture. He hoped she wasn't talking about the books. He didn't really review the accounting.

"Well, here's the thing," she said, fiddling with the stethoscope that sat on her desk. This one had lime green tubing. "I've just been checking here. Now Moon Valley's got a large ethnic population, right? Maybe thirty per cent? I mean, look at the migrant camp."

Fred knitted his brow in thought. "I dunno, I guess so. Something like that."

"Okay, what started me thinking is that I haven't had a new pregnancy at the camp in four months."

"Yeah? Is the camp still pretty full?" The settlement was not Fred's bailiwick, but he knew the migrant population ebbed and flowed during the year, depending on the season.

"Pretty full."

"That does sound a little odd, I suppose."

"It gets odder. I checked all the new patient files. Not just the camp. I haven't had a single pregnancy in four months that isn't white, and I don't think you have either."

"What?" Fred asked. "What do you mean?"

"Caucasian, you know," Leslie said. "No Mexican, no black, no Guatemalan. And I see all ends of the spectrum, normally. Haven't you noticed?"

51

"Can't say I have." Fred ventured a thought. "Maybe somebody's opened up we don't know about? A clinic maybe?"

Leslie shook her head. "No, I asked. We'd have heard anyway. Stop that."

Fred quit picking pieces of dried leather off the chair arm. The stuff was so old its mottled appearance resembled a skin disease. "Oh, sorry. Well, I don't know. I'll double check my new patients. I'm sure it's just coincidence."

Leslie was dubious. "Maybe. Let me know, though, all right?"

"Sure," Fred said, as he picked more bits of dried leather from the arm.

Leslie barely noticed the short drive home, lost in thoughts of standard deviations and probability, wishing she had paid more attention to her statistics classes in college. She was startled to find herself turning into the driveway.

*   *   *   *

The door from the garage opened and Leslie entered the house, shuffling through the mail, reading the envelopes. Entering the kitchen, she dumped the magazines and bills on the center island and was greeted by Naomi, busy at the stove. Naomi kept the single story ranch house reasonably clean, besides minding Derek and preparing dinner.

"Hello, Ms. Riordan," she said cheerfully. Despite Leslie's entreaties, the black housekeeper refused to address her employer informally. On the other hand, she found the term Doctor too distant, and so had settled on Ms.

"Hi, Naomi. How're you? Derek?"

She looked around for her five year old.

"Oh, we're just fine. He's–"

A blond rocket in overalls streaked into the room and leaped into his mother's arms, a huge smile on his face.

"Mommy!" he cried.

"–around here somewhere!" Naomi smiled.

Mother and son hugged warmly.

"Dinner's on the stove, Ms. Riordan," Naomi said, as she removed her apron and hung it behind the pantry door. "Gotta get along now, Mr. Williams be wanting his supper on time, too." She headed for the door.

"Thank you, Naomi," Leslie said. "See you in the morning." As soon as she put Derek down, the youngster shot away and down the hall towards the television, faintly audible from the kitchen. She thought she heard Sponge Bob.

Naomi turned. "Oh, ma'am? The dryer man said the hose was kinked, that's all. Can you imagine? Sixty bucks to come out here just to straighten a hose? He left the bill on the counter."

Leslie shook her head. "Yeah, well, that figures. I get fifty five for an exam out at the migrant camp."

The maid opened the front door. She was stepping out when Leslie called.

"Say, Naomi? You've got lots of relatives, I remember. Right?"

"Just about every black person in Moon Valley, and then prob'ly somes I don't even know," she said.

Leslie asked the question that had been troubling her. "Anybody pregnant?"

Naomi hesitated, hand still on the doorknob. "Well, now that you mention it, I can't think of one. First time I recall. 'Sides, you'd be seein' 'em anyways."

"Thanks, Naomi," said Leslie.

The maid chuckled. "Maybe it's somethin' in the water."

Naomi walked out and closed the door behind her as Leslie cocked her head, thinking. She was interrupted by Derek, who launched himself upward into her arms for the second time. Leslie smiled.

"Mommy, I colored today. I'll show you after supper, 'kay?"

She nodded as she carried her young charge to the stove. The pot of beanie wienie steamed invitingly.

"Come on, you, let's eat."

Maybe it's somethin' in the water.

14

By the time Sharif had reached his 23rd birthday, he had grown his $500,000 birth stipend, given to each of the five thousand plus members of the Royal Family, into an eight million dollar fund. He had done this by investing in western stocks and UAE real estate, primarily in Dubai. Although he could draw on additional monies, a birthright, he did not avail himself of the communal wealth.

As a youth, he had done well at the Princes' School in Riyadh. He excelled both in music and mathematics, which he found to be in complex relationship. At the London Business School, he was a thoughtful student, realizing the tools he was learning would translate into power and control. At home with algorithms and probability, he had anticipated the worldwide recession and divested his holdings before the real estate meltdown, selling off the last of his Dubai properties just before the country cratered.

Sharif, then known by his given name, had a small circle of important friends from both cultures. Like many members of his generation, he embraced Western methods of business, and certain classical aspects of culture, while still maintaining, without question, the principles of *Sharia*, the feudal code governing many aspects of Arab life, from religion to politics to criminal law. In other parts of the Middle East, however, *Sharia* was coming under increasing attack from the generation maturing to adulthood.

There were a number of Arab women among the fourteen hundred students at the London Business School in Regent's Park.

In his compartmentalized mind, Sharif's reaction to seeing Princess Haifa in Western dress was as if she were naked. Distantly related, of course, they had seen each other at gatherings and religious occasions for years. At home, deferential and inoffensive in her *jallabia*, she was little more than furniture. Yet Sharif, in the currency of his feelings, had spent perhaps a small coin on Haifa: she had beautiful, dark eyes; the pupils glowed almost violet. He had been bemused by the very concept of that feeling. Now, to see her in Western dress, long black hair cascading down her shoulders, offended him. It was almost as if she were a person. He, a prince who glided effortlessly through the cultures of East and West, at home in any social milieu, and well-liked: that was one thing. This woman's effrontery was quite another. Unlike Sharif's rank, the title Princess was an obligation, not a right. Did she not know?

As a true Royal, rather than a prince of the Cadet branch, Sharif was theoretically eligible for the Kingdom throne, although this was not likely and not a consideration in his thoughts. Nonetheless, he was a favorite among those for whom the possibility was more realistic.

In 2007, with little fanfare, the Kingdom revoked the King's right to choose his successor, bestowing that power instead upon a council who would name a crown prince from a short list of nominees. This immediately opened possibilities. The old men who passed power to other old men would no longer be able to keep the Kingdom firmly in the past. Suddenly now royal princes, younger, better educated and vigorous, became viable candidates for the throne. Sharif began to consider the strategy of placing himself in a more visible position with the council.

The sudden possibility of attaining the Crown had had a divisive effect amongst many princes of the Royal branch. Alignments had formed and were forming. As a result, Sharif had acquired a small but important group of enemies, of which he knew nothing.

15

The annual Moon Walk ball brought out most of the professionals in the town, even the few who were not members of the Moon Valley Country Club. The dining room was festooned with streamers and silvered balloons, cleverly altered to look like space helmets and celestial objects. In the center of it all hung a fake ball of green cheese, sequined to reflect the light as it revolved. Leslie felt the thing was an apt commentary on the affair, but every year she went anyway, usually with Fred as her escort. It was one of the few times she got to consort with her fellow physicians in the area. Besides, she thought, her dress-ups were getting permanent hangar marks in the closet.

A three piece combo played a salsa tune while a few of the well-dressed couples wafted across the dance floor. Leslie, in a smashingly simple black dress, watched the operation as she sipped her glass of Bourgogne Aligote. Not a wine connoisseur, she had been introduced to the unusual chardonnay by Fred, whose modest cellar fueled his painting hobby. He had prevailed upon the club to buy a case.

The ersatz Mariachi trio had launched recklessly into *Joy to the World*. Leslie thought she'd scream. Instead, she sighed and looked around the lunar disco.

"Ever think there's more to life than this place? After work, I mean."

Fred chewed on his roast beef. He gestured around with his fork. "The club? What's wrong with it? They just redid the dining room here."

Leslie liked the old dining room. Now it looked like something in a strip mall, minus the cafeteria line.

"No, I mean the whole place. Moon Valley," she said.

Fred swallowed. "Well, there's the new movie."

"Wow."

Joy to the fishes in the deep blue sea, the band said.

"They've got maybe sixteen screens. Something like that," Fred said. In a way, Leslie envied her partner, she reflected. Simple pleasures, simple rewards.

"Yeah, we're a regular Hollywood. Be right back."

Leslie took her black matching purse – big enough to hold a tissue and stick of gum – and walked across the edge of the wooden dance floor. She spied Ted Winslow, M.D., seated at the bar as she passed. He waved.

Leslie walked over. "Hello, Ted."

Ted put down his vodka martini and took her hand with both of his, a big grin on his face. Like all the men in Moon Valley, he had a crush on his colleague.

"Leslie! How are you? Beautiful as ever. Is that what they call that little black dress?" Leslie was glad Ted hadn't recognized the outfit from last year's gala, when it was new.

She smiled. "I hope so. Where's Betsy?"

Ted's wife was also his receptionist.

"Who?" he said with a grin.

Leslie gave him a look. He gestured with a jerk of his head.

"She's in the can. Doesn't give us that much time," he said with a mock grimace.

Leslie gave him a scornful look. "Nice," she said.

Una poca de gracia, the band said. Now they'd crossed the line, Leslie thought. The band was trampling on hallowed ground, crucifying Richie Valens and Los Lobos.

"Listen, Ted, I know your practice is pretty upscale, but do you ever get ethnic pregnancies?"

Ted sipped his drink. "Ethnic pregnancies?"

"Well, anything other than, say, WASP women. Caucasian, you know."

"Sure, maybe . . . fifteen percent or so? I mean, I guess."

Leslie pressed. "How about right now?"

Ted sipped again, raised an eyebrow. "Well, offhand, can't think of any right now," he said.

"Thanks, Ted. See you at the board meeting next Tuesday," Leslie said, as she started for the ladies room. Both were members of the hospital's advisory board.

"How 'bout lunch Monday?" Ted offered.

Leslie turned and smiled. "Sure, can Betsy come along?"

Ted winced, "Ouch." He watched her all the way to the ladies room, where the music was only a muffled thumping. Leslie lingered inside, exchanging pleasantries with Betsy.

*　　　　*　　　　　　*　　　　　　*

Lunchtime on Monday found Leslie on the phone from her office.

"That's right, Doctor," she said. "Four months. I ran a statistical analysis using our population base and ethnic make-up over that time period. It's not my field, but I don't think I made an error."

She hoped she hadn't, anyway. She had been lucky to get a C in Statistics.

"That's right, ninety five per cent confidence limits . . . thanks. All right, I'll wait to hear from you . . . Oh, and doctor? Can you give me your direct line? I must have talked to every CDC employee in Atlanta before I got you."

In fact, she had spoken with three CDC employees, one of whom was precisely the wrong person.

16

Menachem Yitzchak took his *shtreimel* from the closet shelf and placed it in his lap. Being *Shabbat*, the Hasidic Jew would wear the fur hat instead of the weekday fedora. He sat patiently in his favorite chair, where he read the Brooklyn Daily Eagle as well as his medical periodicals, and looked out the front window. The Gitelmans, with their four children, all of whom he had delivered - and Sadie had not been the easiest of births - were walking by, on their way to services. Sadie and Brina were skipping in circles around their parents. He could faintly hear their laughter through the window pane, mixed with sounds of the familiar last minute ruckus drifting downstairs as his own family got ready for temple. He pulled out his pocket watch. They were going to be late for services. Again. His friend, Rabbi Ben Zvi, would notice. He sighed. Being an obstetrician in Borough Park, Brooklyn meant he routinely worked ten to twelve hours a day, including night and odd hours. Hasidic families multiplied geometrically; as many as ten children per household were not uncommon. As a result, many of the older houses in the neighborhood sported additions and backyards had been usurped for additional living space.

Shabbat was no day of rest, really, he thought. He needed another day. In fact, today was complicated by one of the thirty-nine areas of restricted behavior on Saturday. He needed to transport a number of texts to his sister's husband, who was more than four cubits away in Crown Heights, and the complicated laws of *eruv* needed to be observed. He didn't know how he was going to solve the problem. Perhaps he would ask Rabbi Zvi. It was God's restriction; maybe God had the answer. Life was a series of small problems interrupted by big problems, he reflected.

Although lately the pace at his office had eased up, dramatically so, in fact. He wondered if his young friend Mordecai Rubin was stealing his patients. (Young? How old was he when thirty seven seemed young?) Maybe Mordecai wasn't his friend. There were mouths to be fed. He would see him soon if his own family ever finished getting ready for temple. Maybe he should ask? What if it were true? What if it wasn't?

His thoughts were interrupted as Sadie, ten, bounded down the stairs and jumped in his lap, crushing the *shtreimel* into the shape of a dead animal.

17

The Jew was named Morris Fine and he was a first year American student at the London Business School. He was short, with frizzy hair, and he came from Miami Beach, Florida. He registered on Sharif's consciousness as would a stain on the wallpaper. Sharif was in his second and final year pursuing his MBA. The school had opened a Dubai branch, but he had preferred the advantages of London. The self-awareness of that preference annoyed him. There were Jews, of course, both students and faculty; Sharif dismissed them in his mind as if waving away insects. It was a beautiful spring day in Regent's Park when Sharif wandered through the quadrangle and down a path to the lake, contemplating strategic modeling and algorithms of oil pricing when—

He stopped in surprise. Hidden from view by shrubbery, on the grass by the lake, two people embraced on a blanket. Princess Haifa faced him, eyes closed. When her eyes opened and fixed upon him, they widened in shock. Her partner, sensing something, turned and looked.

It was Morris Fine. Sharif did not know his name, but his ancestry was unmistakable.

A Jew was kissing Princess Haifa! It was so unthinkable, his mind almost rejected it. The vermin was drinking from the Muslim cup, profaning the vessel. For long moments, the three remained frozen, staring at each other. The shadow of a small, puffy cloud passed across the grass, the Princess and Morris Fine: a visible sign of the blasphemy to all of Islam. An almost palpable wave of hatred flowed from the prince. His eyes narrowed and a tight smile crossed his face. The nod was almost imperceptible, its meaning unmistakable. As the sunlight returned, he turned and walked away.

On the blanket, Princess Haifa shuddered.

Sharif returned to his room, placed a phone call. He reached Yousif immediately. His instructions were explicit.

Six days later, most of Morris Fine was found inside the disused entrance to the demolished East Brixton rail station off Barrington Road, six km south of Charing Cross. The body lay half-naked in a lake of blood. A common hand plane, sticky with dried blood and clogged with tissue, protruded from the mouth. A carrot peeler, in similar condition, was jammed in an ear. The most veteran Metropolitan Police investigators winced at the sight: some type of clamp was fastened around what was left of the man's penis. The organ had been shaved away, leaving a bloody thread. As there was no wallet, twenty four hours elapsed before Morris Fine was identified, and that was only because Princess Haifa had phoned the MPS to report her friend and fellow student missing. Interviews with classmates quickly uncovered the romance between Fine and the Princess, but nothing else out of the ordinary. Fine had been a serious academic, if somewhat brash. As far as could be determined, he had never been anywhere near the largely Caribbean neighborhood before. Everything about the horrific crime seemed bereft of any discernible rationale.

18

Five hundred feet above and a half mile east of Moon Valley Municipal Airport, the 1979 Piper Arrow banked for final approach. The single engine aircraft gleamed with its new color scheme. A birthday present from David Livingston to himself on his thirty second birthday six weeks prior, the blue and white polyurethane paint job had set him back several thousand dollars. He turned the aircraft and applied the third notch of flaps as runway 23 appeared in the windscreen.

"Moon Valley Unicom, Piper four three one three Uniform turning final for runway two three, Moon Valley."

Thermals toyed with the Arrow, tilting the wings, bouncing it along its path, but David kept the runway in the windscreen with a minimum of control input. He knew, as skilled pilots do, that when it's bumpy it's usually best to let the airplane sort things out by itself.

Two months after Leslie Riordan's initial phone call to the Centers for Disease Control, David Livingston touched down uneventfully and taxied to the visitor's parking area. He shut the plane down, gathered his overnight bag, exited the plane and tied it down. After asking the line boy to fuel his craft, David walked to the small building that served as the office. Once inside, he passed the vending machines and approached the counter. Jeff, the airport operator, flight instructor and car rental clerk, came out from his office munching a fossilized Clark bar and soon had the scientist on his way in a dusty Pontiac, along with directions for the Moon Valley Professional Building.

Twenty minutes later, as Leslie studied the papers in front of her, a knock on the office door broke her concentration. She looked up as David Livingston stuck his head in. There was a friendly grin on his face.

"Come in," she waved. "I won't say it," she said, returning the smile.

"Go ahead, it won't bother me," David replied. His first thought was that Leslie Riordan was bottled sunlight.

"Okay, I will say it. Doctor Livingston, I presume?"

David gave a slight mock bow. "At your service."

"Please, sit down." Leslie gestured toward the decrepit leather visitor's chair. "Any trouble finding us?"

"Not at all," came the reply as David folded into the chair. "Took me only three hours."

"What? It's only a twenty minute drive from the airport."

David laughed. "I meant the flight this morning. I flew myself."

Leslie looked puzzled for a second, then brightened. David thought that if she beamed any brighter, he'd need sunglasses.

"Oh, I didn't know. How exciting. You seem – younger that I thought you'd be."

"That makes us even," David replied with a wink. "Listen, I didn't have lunch yet. You hungry?"

It was Leslie's turn to grin. "You read my mind."

The Moon Valley Diner looked like something carefully constructed to look like a 1950's diner. It was, in fact, a 1950's diner, and in the desert climate had held together for over fifty years. Many of the juke boxes on the booth walls worked some of the time, and a patron took his chance for only a nickel. David looked around at the working class crowd as he attacked his hamburger stacked with jalapenos, mustard, pickles and grilled onions. Many of the diners had waved or said hello to Leslie, as did Sally, the waitress, who told David his lunch partner had delivered her little Samantha a year ago.

"You're a popular customer," David said. She really was very easy on the eyes, he thought.

"Well, most of these guys' wives are my patients," Leslie responded.

"This is some place," he said.

"Sure it's all right?" Leslie asked.

"Listen, this is a real milkshake." David poured a second glass from the mixing tin into his glass, held by an old-fashioned metal holder. "It's great. Not so easy to get in Atlanta. Plus they'd never give you the tin. Reminds me of when I was a kid in a small town like this. Hope you don't mind the grilled onions on my hamburger."

"Where's your small town?"

"Two Spot, Alabama. Makes Moon Valley seem like a big city."

David had lost much of the Deep South from his voice; what remained was pleasant and understandable. He picked up the last of his chocolate shake, upended his glass and tapped the bottom to dislodge a glob of ice cream.

"Okay, here's the deal. I'm primarily a CDC researcher, but I also do work for EIS. That's the Epidemic Intelligence Service branch of the Centers. You finally got an EIS officer, who funneled your inquiry to me. Actually, that's kind of amazing."

Leslie interrupted, alarmed. "Epidemic? You think this could be the start of an epidemic?"

"I don't necessarily think anything yet. I did my doctorate on selective genetic defects. Like why do certain illnesses, certain defects, only affect particular ethnic groups? Sickle cell anemia, for example."

The waitress brought Leslie a cup of coffee. As she stirred in real cream from a pitcher and sipped, David dropped a nickel in the jukebox, punched buttons. Leslie grinned at the opening guitar riff from the Alabama state anthem.

"Homesick already?" she asked, smiling. David grinned back.

Turn it up, said Lynyrd Skynyrd. Few people, even Alabamans, knew the line was not meant to be in the song, but Ronnie Van Zant had wanted more volume in his earphones.

"I understand that anemia can affect some other racial groups besides African Americans," Leslie said.

"That's right," David nodded. "With sickle cell, the black population is the largest, but it's present in Arabs, Greeks, Latin Americans and Dots."

Leslie was puzzled. "Dots?"

David smiled, pointed to his forehead.

"India type Indians. It's possible to have the trait as a Caucasian, but very unlikely. You can't catch it, only inherit it and carry it or develop the disease."

Does your conscience bother you? asked Ronnie Van Zant.

"What we're finding is that most of the time there's a specific gene issue, a molecular affinity for a specific ethnic problem. They're just different in each case. The principle's the same."

"And that's what you look for?" Leslie asked, sipping her coffee. The diner was quieter now, as most of the lunch crowd, on the clock, had left.

"Yeah. It's just detective work, that's all. There are also diseases caused by cultural mores, of course. Certain spirochetes infect the Chinese because they work barefoot in the fields. They cure it with herbs, like they do syphilis. Although that's certainly caused by a universal behavior. I don't get into that kind of stuff. I've been studying alcoholism among Native Americans for three years now."

Leslie's eyebrows went up. "It's really true, then?" she inquired. "And not just cultural?"

"Haven't proven anything yet, but I'm on the right track," David replied. "Look at this: for alcohol related offenses, native Americans are arrested at eight times the rate of blacks and over twenty times that of Caucasians. These are hard numbers. The rate seems unaffected by tribe, location, social conditions, values, or anything else we can think of. It leads to a genetic hypothesis."

Leslie put down her cup. "What are you doing?"

"Looking at gene-related potential causative factors. Technically, bonding of alcohol compounds with unique cellular structures. I'm probably a year away from proving it."

"That has tremendous implications for society," Leslie replied. The diner had completely emptied out now; they had the place to themselves. Sally dropped off the check.

Leslie was finding the subject fascinating. In medical school, she had intuitively suspected genetic causation of things like alcoholism amongst the Indians.

"Sure it does, but look. This kind of research is potentially volatile. Unpopular."

"What do you mean?" Leslie asked.

"Just saying a scientific fact, like Indians tend to be drunks, gets everyone upset no matter how you phrase it. It doesn't matter that I'm trying to prove it's not a moral issue. You know what I mean. Funding's difficult, especially since we're federal, as you can imagine. Should I have another shake, do you think?"

Leslie laughed. "I've just been envying your eating habits. If I drank that, I'd put on three pounds. Try genetically altering that, Doctor Livingston."

Sweet Home Alabama

Lord I'm coming home to you.

Leslie reached for the check, but David was quicker. He decided the vivacious obstetrician was bright and observant as well as attractive. It was good, he thought, that much of his cover story was actually true.

19

David, in the passenger seat of Leslie's white Jeep, pulled his Atlanta Braves baseball cap low over his forehead in the dazzling sunlight. The migrant camp was a few miles distant. He eyed the saguaro, joshua trees and flowering palo verde as they passed: spines and lineaments of a harsh world. Leslie saw his look of curiosity.

"I love the desert, you know. It's beautiful – so peaceful. Takes awhile to realize it when you're not from the southwest, though."

"Did you grow up here?" he asked.

"Phoenix. Before it got to be all pavement and traffic and humidity."

"Humidity? From people? Can they do that?"

"They come here from green climates. They look at the desert landscape and don't appreciate the natural beauty. They think it's a vacant lot, so they plant grass in their yards. Then they irrigate. Doesn't take long. Phoenix's humidity's way out of control. When I was a kid, it was maybe less than twenty percent. Now it's more like fifty. It was always hot, but it was a dry heat."

"So's an oven," David said, chuckling. He pointed to a giant saguaro. "I had no idea those – saguaro? – were so tall. They're huge," David said.

"Know something? They don't start to grow those arms until they're maybe 75 years old. They don't even mature until they're 125 or more. You can make jam, syrup, all kinds of things from the fruit."

David smiled as he listened, enjoying her passion for the land. "What's that big tree with all the yellow flowers?"

"That's a palo verde."

"Doesn't verde mean green?"

"The flowers are yellow but the bark's green. They shelter young saguaro sometimes. Then the saguaro takes over. It's all pretty neat, isn't it?"

It certainly was, David thought. Not exactly Spanish moss, live oak and cypress stands.

The two lane blacktop petered out. They bumped and clattered along the dirt road, raising a trail of dust as she approached the migrant camp.

Leslie gave her passenger some background as the settlement came into view. "These camps exist all over the country, of course. Here in Arizona, most are filled with illegals from Mexico, up for the season. This particular site is Caribbean, though, mostly Haitian. They used to be here for just a few months, then move on to another crop," Leslie said, stretching.

"What do you mean, used to be?"

"Well, now they grow crops pretty much all year round. Lettuce, cantaloupe, onions, in the fall, different stuff in the spring. The settlement's just about permanent now." She slowed as they entered the camp and pulled up in front of the general store.

As they climbed out of the two year old vehicle, David looked around. "This looks like something out of 'Grapes of Wrath,'" he remarked, grabbing his field pack from the back seat.

"This is actually one of the nicer camps," Leslie said. "In some places, they live in tents alongside the crops."

Both doctors wore jeans; David had on a Dave Matthews tee shirt and desert boots. Leslie thought he looked like an Abercrombie ad. David, in turn, thought she reminded him of Naomi Watts in *King Kong*. Or maybe it was *Eastern Promises*.

"I'll start over there," he said. David walked over to the dripping standpipe, squatted down and collected a water sample in a vial. He labeled the container with a permanent marker. Moving to the muddy pool, he repeated the process. As he worked and Leslie watched, several black passersby nodded and exchanged greetings with the obstetrician. From the porch, the old men in their chairs eyed the goings-on incuriously.

David stood. "Okay, all set here." He put the samples in his pack. "Where's our blood sample volunteers?" he asked.

"Should be here in a couple of minutes," Leslie replied. "I told them ten bucks a head, right?"

David nodded. "Cash on the barrel head."

Leslie wasn't familiar with CDC procedures, but she felt sure their protocol would normally require a study review board before authorizing payments for blood samples. Either David Livingston had more clout than she realized, or the Centers were taking this very seriously. Or both.

They mounted the steps and entered the general store. The old men paid no mind as they passed. The place looked like a rundown Cracker Barrel, without the tourists. There actually was a checker board sitting on a barrel. The wooden, unpainted walls were festooned with provisions, many of which were unknown to David. Strange Caribbean fruits and vegetables sat in loose bins. A variety of spices and nuts with exotic names were displayed in jars or small mesh bags. Crude figurines with feathers and what appeared to be dried chicken feet stood here and there. David guessed they had religious significance; he thought he recognized a small doll that might be Baron Samedi, guardian of the crossroads, with miniature top hat. A blue tobacco haze drifted over everything, eddying around the slow-moving ceiling fan like ethereal taffy, flowing in and out of the sunlight that streamed in through the filthy windows. Galaxies of dust hung in the redolent air.

To David, it all smelled like – he closed his eyes and placed it - Cuba. If time flowed like a slow river outside, he thought, in here it had meandered back a half century.

Behind the counter a black man in overalls, perhaps seventy years old, nodded to Leslie.

"Hello, Doc Riordan," he said.

"Hi, Merion. How's business?"

"Oh, you know, can't complain. Chaw tobaccy, cigs and beer keep the place runnin'."

David looked around. "Is this like the social center?"

"Yes," Leslie replied.

While they waited for their volunteer subjects, David perused the vegetable bins. He recognized guava, breadfruit, and plantains, but hadn't seen items like star fruit, sapodilla, sugar apple and tamarind. He examined them with interest. As he picked up a bag of lychee nuts, two black women in their twenties, in old faded dresses, entered the store. David noted that one was strikingly beautiful, with delicate features and a willowy figure. He wondered idly if she were of mixed blood, which might affect their findings.

"Here comes our first group," Leslie observed.

20

Princess Haifa had no illusions about what had happened to Morris Fine. She told no one. The investigation had been taken over by the Metropolitan Police Service Specialist Operations, the branch that dealt with counter-terrorism as well as matters of royalty and other high profile inquiries. Before interviewing the Princess, Detective Sergeant Peter Wilhite visited his friend, Forensic Medical Examiner Colin Blake, who had reviewed the autopsy. They were seated in Dr. Blake's office in Clive House, Petty France, which smelled vaguely like chemicals, old books and vintage tobacco: a not unpleasant combination, Wilhite had decided years ago.

"What do you make of it?" the detective asked.

"Never quite seen anything like it," said Dr. Blake, as he lit his pipe. The portly physician was nearing retirement and was a wealth of information with over thirty years of service. He enjoyed his role as a medical sleuth and had a theory about this bizarre case.

"You don't know where the poor bugger was tortured, I take it," he continued, "except that it clearly was somewhere else. He was alive when they dumped him in Brixton, though."

A cloud of smoke rose slowly over Blake's head in the still air.

"All the blood."

"Yes. He bled out in that godforsaken filthy place."

"What was that device around what was left of his penis?"

"It's called a Mogen Clamp. It's used by some for Jewish circumcisions. The thing's outdated in the West. I think you may find this was done by Islamics."

"Why do you say that, Colin?"

"The symbolism of the whole thing. It's a bizarre – what? – mockery of the Jewish rite of circumcision. That plus the savage nature of the crime."

"Hmm. That's interesting. A bit dramatic, eh?" Wilhite didn't smoke, but thought the tobacco in Blake's pipe was nicely aromatic. He must have changed the blend: it killed the lab smell.

"It's a dramatic crime. And that's not all. Guess what we found in his system."

"Can't imagine."

"Viagra. An overdose of Viagra. Know what that means?"

Wilhite winced at the thought.

"That's right, Peter. They wanted to make sure he had an erection so they could—" He left the thought unfinished.

Wilhite found his mind going where he didn't want it to go. "Do you think it worked?"

"Who knows?" Blake said, with a wicked grin. "Be a hell of a testimonial for the stuff, though, wouldn't it?"

"Jesus, Colin."

"Yeah. If your erection persists more than four hours, see your doctor straightaway."

He laughed at his own joke as the detective shook his head. The FME's bizarre sense of humor was well known throughout the department. It had gotten stranger as he edged closer to retirement.

"Anyway, this was deliberately done to send a message. That's what I think. I understand he was seeing an Arab student. Princess, wasn't she?"

"That's why we've got the case. She called in the missing person report."

"Well, then?"

"Yes, of course. We're putting together a list of her Islamic classmates."

The FME puffed away. "They're all princesses, aren't they?"

"Only when they're here."

Blake smiled and looked at his watch. "Touché. Lunch? I reserved a table at Quilon. You'll love the lobster with ginger. All this talk makes me hungry," he grinned.

*   *   *   *   *

At three o'clock, Wilhite sat with Haifa in an alcove of the study lounge on the London Business School campus. A long walkway, lined with wood and glass doors, stretched before them. It was a sunny and pleasant spot.

"I met Mister Fine three months ago, shortly after term started. I suppose it seems illogical, but we became friends." Her English, while accented, was excellent. Wilhite, who was very good at his job, observed her effort to remain composed. He already knew she had been seen wearing a head scarf the last two days, although all term she had been without. After venturing from the path of Islam, he thought, she evidently had beaten a hasty retreat.

"What do you mean, illogical?" he asked, knowing perfectly well what she meant.

"Morris is – was - a Jew, I believe you know that. He was perhaps the first Jew I ever met, certainly the first I talked with. We were as different as two people could be. I imagine that was part of the . . . interest."

"Do you think this might have upset anyone? You and Mister Fine being involved?"

"Involved?"

"Please, Your Highness. Do you think your relationship might have upset anyone?"

"I don't know who that could be," she said, shifting. Her body language told the Detective Sergeant it was an evasion.

"Any of the other Arab students at the school, perhaps."

"I don't believe so. Besides, we were very private. People didn't know."

Either the princess was covering up or believed she lived in a vacuum, Wilhite thought. Everyone knew about the two of them, their improbable romance, he had learned right away. An American pursuing his doctorate had already told the detective he thought the princess must like to live dangerously; there were plenty of Arab students at the school.

"What led you to phone the police straightaway?"

"We were supposed to meet for breakfast that morning. He did not come."

"Sometimes people miss a meeting but the police aren't called."

"Morris was very reliable, very punctual. His roommate said he did not return the evening before. He had never done that."

"The roommate didn't think it serious enough to raise an alarm," Wilhite said.

"I cannot speak for his roommate," was all she would say.

True or not, the Princess was hiding something, he was certain.

Detective Sergeant Wilhite learned little else from the interview. With over 1400 students from 131 countries on campus, the London cop was not able to speak with all the Arabs. He concentrated on her first year classmates, which did not include Sharif.

Local interviews near the rail station proved fruitless. No one had seen anything. The crime scene itself yielded nothing useful. Morris Fine's parents came over from Miami Beach and took the body home. Wilhite met with them briefly; they were from another generation of Jews, a generation whose parents had seen unspeakable things in the bowels of Europe, experienced true horror in the dark barbed wire archipelagos of the Continent and had left the scars on their young. The Fines seemed almost accepting, unlike their son.

The file would remain open.

21

Just after 3 p.m. on a Thursday afternoon, Yousif exited the underground station at Baker Street and headed towards Regents' Park, crossing the busy A41 and walking through the pleasant, upscale neighborhood. A slight wind ruffled the trees; the sky overhead was unusually blue and clear. He failed to give the elegant mansions on Hanover Terrace a second look as he strode purposefully towards his destination. The address on Hanover Terrace Mews was approximately a half mile from the London Business School. Yousif walked past the building and crossed the street to avoid a young woman pushing a pram. He stopped a short distance away at the corner. Across the Outer Circle, the greenery of Regents' Park stretched to the lake, shrugging in the breeze, but again he paid the landscape no mind. In a few moments, the woman had turned the corner and the Mews was deserted.

Yousif walked back to the building and entered. He climbed the stairs soundlessly to the second floor, donning a pair of Marigold featherweight disposable lab gloves as he did so. It was 4:10 p.m.; he knew the flat would be empty. He withdrew a SouthOrd lock picking set and extracted a tool as he studied the apartment door. Careful to avoid scratch marks around the keyhole, he slipped inside a half minute later.

His quarry would return after five, Yousif knew, when her Thursday classes were over. It would still be light, but that made little difference. He looked around the flat and in five minutes had located what he wanted. He pulled a pocket edition of the Koran from his jacket and settled down to wait.

At 5:14 he heard the key in the lock. In a moment, Princess Haifa entered and shut the door behind. As she turned, she gasped at the sight of the stranger in front of her.

"*As-salaam aliekom, Princess,*" he said, smiling.

*   *   *   *

Five days later, a tenant in a downstairs apartment phoned the St. John Wood Police Station to report a foul odor emanating from the flat upstairs. An investigating officer found the door locked. When the police broke in, they found a young woman hanging from a ceiling fan, strung up with what appeared to be a robe.

Within a half hour, Detective Sergeant Peter Wilhite received a telephone call from the MPS station on Harrows Road. The deceased had been identified as Princess Haifa. She had been strangled with a black *jallabia*, subsequently identified as her own, the sleeve knotted around her neck.

22

Next to the country club, O'Shea's was Moon Valley's upscale dining experience. Specializing in steaks and chops, the décor was cowboy sophisticated: dark wood-grained plastic, red leatherette and faux Tiffany lampshades. It was six thirty. David and Leslie were seated at a corner table after returning from the migrant camp. Their window overlooked a fountain surrounded by colorful plantings. In the distance, the low mountains framed the picture, softened by the fading light.

Both sipped Bloody Marys garnished with celery and olives. David looked over at the visible kitchen, where busy chefs worked over flaming grilles as rising blue smoke was sucked into stainless steel overhead vents. He nodded towards the mayhem.

"Looks like a scene from hell," he said.

Leslie laughed. "The steaks taste from heaven."

"I hope so. I'm starving," David said, as he popped his olive into his mouth. He looked around the restaurant. "People eat early around here."

"You're too used to Atlanta."

"Maybe so. In Alabama, we ate early, too."

"Are your folks retired?" Leslie asked.

"My dad died when I was still in grad school," David said.

"Oh, I'm sorry."

"No, it's all right. It was a while ago." There was a silence that seemed weighted. David sipped from his drink. "He was a

POW in North Vietnam. He made it home, but never really recovered from what they did to him."

"I am sorry, David."

"My mom lives with her sister. She's a war widow, too. First Iraqi war. I see them when I can. What about you?"

"We moved around a lot when I was a kid. My dad's dead, also. Liver disease."

"It's my turn to be sorry."

Leslie stared at her drink, then looked off. "We're a product of our past, I guess."

David sensed something behind the remark. The quiet moment was broken by the waiter.

"Your steaks will be here in just a minute," he said, replacing their table knives with steak knives.

Leslie refocused. "When will you be able to analyze the samples?"

"A couple of days after I get back to Atlanta. Then we'll see what we'll see. I'll probably head out to Parkerville for more samples. They've got nine more Caucasian pregnancies – that's it. No minorities. The timetable's about the same. Six months out there."

"Did you get anything promising from the interviews?"

"Maybe. Looking for location-specific clues, habits, stuff like that."

"So why would the same thing happen hundreds of miles apart?"

"No idea. That's another thing to look for – some commonality. I'll compare the answers to what I get in Parkerville. The two towns seem like night and day. Maybe somebody went from here to there carrying something. Some fertilizer, whatever. Could be a million things, could be nothing. It's more detective work. Do you come to this place often?"

David changed subjects with disconcerting ease, Leslie had noticed.

"I'm usually eating at home with Derek," Leslie said.

"Is he in school yet?"

"Half days. I drop him off and Naomi picks him up at lunchtime. She stays with him in the afternoons. She's a good cook."

Leslie was taken aback by David's next remark. "I'd like to meet him sometime."

"Why, I'm sure he'd enjoy meeting you, David." Leslie's natural inclination to keep a personal distance meant she didn't often use first names. She wondered if he noticed, feeling a bit awkward. She was glad the waiter came at that moment with the steaks. It had grown dark. Outside the window, the fountain was now lit with changing colors. Leslie had never noticed it before.

Later, as she tucked in to bed after patting the sleeping Derek on the bottom, she decided it had been a most interesting day.

*   *   *   *   *

In his motel room a few miles away, David Livingston also thought it had been a most interesting day, with perhaps a more ominous slant. As he had feared, the migrant camp was a perfect site for the first wave of attack. He was anxious to see what Parkerville would bring, and perhaps what conclusions he might be able to reach. Everything would be a clue.

David thought about Leslie Riordan for a second time. Good-looking, intelligent, personable, she was the type of woman almost any man would feel an attraction for. He could afford no distractions, though, and he had to keep her out of harm's way. The stakes were too high, and he harbored no illusions about the ruthlessness of the perpetrators. He probably shouldn't have said anything about meeting her young son. In normal times, he might follow through with his interest. But, he reflected wryly, there weren't many normal times for David Livingston.

23

"Green what?" Detective Sergeant Wilhite asked his friend Colin Blake, as they sat at a balcony table in The Cinnamon Club on Great Smith Street. The restaurant in St. James' was the site of the old Westminster Library; books still lined the walls behind their table. The place was full at lunchtime. Aside from the view to the busy main floor below, their table offered a measure of privacy and quiet. Blake was attacking a dish of tandoori king prawns.

"Green moong kedgeree," the doctor replied. "You're an embarrassment, Peter. The recipe's over a thousand years old. I should have taken you for a Wimpy Burger, I suppose, and saved a few quid."

"Squid." Wilhite chuckled at his own joke. "Besides, one day it's going to be euros, I think."

"Don't remind me of the great empire's sellout. Just eat the Indian food. They're still a colony, aren't they?"

Wilhite chewed his Portobello mushroom. Along with the layered bread, the lunch was wonderful.

"I'm not too up on Indian fare. What's this stuff?" He poked at his plate.

"Morels and girlles."

"Boys and girls?"

Blake put down his fork. "I know why you're doing this."

His friend tried to look innocent.

"All right, Peter. Want to know what I think?"

"Sure. That's why I'm eating this—food."

"It's the penalty for picking my brain. Anyway, the forensics and the evidence at the scene support the suicide theory – chair tipped over, door locked, no forced entry, all that. Cause of death was strangulation. No bruises or other marks on the body. No sign of a struggle. No witnesses to anyone coming or going, right? Neighbors heard nothing, right?"

"Yes." Wilhite wished for more bread. It really was amazingly good, but he needed to lose a little weight.

"And the room itself showed no evidence of a recent visitor. But I'm not buying it," the FME continued. "In my opinion, she was hanged by the same person who offed her boyfriend, the Jew, what's his name, Feingold?"

"Fine. Morris Fine."

"Right. Anyway, one reason I conclude this is the jallabia. These crimes are very symbolic. The princess violated the laws of *Sharia*, and paid the price. Using the jallabia to hang her is just like what happened to Fine. Hoisted on her own religious petard, so to speak, quite literally."

"Hmmm." Wilhite's mouth was full of layered bread.

"Besides being very careful, the killer is inventive and quite clever, you'll find. If indeed you do find him. If he's still in the country."

"Interesting."

"Which he is most certainly probably not."

"Certainly probably?"

"Plus you said the princess was partially packed. She was scared. She was getting ready to bolt."

"We don't know that."

"You may not, Peter, but I do. Did she tell the school anything?"

Wilhite shook his head. "Nor anyone else, as far as we can determine. We checked to see if she might have been moving to another apartment. She hadn't given notice."

"Another Islamic hit, I'm telling you. What about her cell phone?" Blake said, as he ate the last king prawn.

"She wasn't much of a talker. We looked at every phone call after the Fine killing. A few friends and a couple of calls home."

"Middle East home?"

"Yes. We found two calls to a cell phone we believe was owned by her brother. She had an older brother Hayyan. He was in Jeddah at the time. The last call was the day before she died. He hasn't responded to our query, at least yet."

"He may not."

"That's right, he may not. She disgraced her family."

"These people are insane."

"Some of them."

They ate in silence for a few minutes, broken by a crash as somewhere downstairs a waiter dropped a dish.

"I could use a few more prawns," Blake said, laying down his fork. "Peter, it's an obscure vendetta by Arabs against Arabs. Just like the Russians. She crossed the line with the Jewish boyfriend. The truth is, no one here really cares and she had, as you say, disgraced herself. This case will die. Look at it this way - at least they didn't stone her in Piccadilly Circus. Would you like more bread?"

In fact, Hayyan never responded to MPS Specialist Operations, but not because he felt his sister disgraced the family. The day before she was slain, Princess Haifa had called to tell her brother she feared for her life, and that she was sure Sharif had murdered her 'friend'. Hayyan said nothing to MPS because he knew vengeance belonged to him, and not England.

24

Monday morning found David Livingston peering through a microscope in a well-equipped Bio Safety Level 2 laboratory. He had spent the weekend flying back across the country. From the cockpit, the world below was a clean, beautiful place, free of strife and danger. Perspective brought serenity. He loved to see the rolling view of the United States from less than ten thousand feet, winging almost due east: the harsh, bare browns changing to soft green, crags and peaks to rolling hills and prairie. David never failed to marvel at how empty the country seemed from the flight deck, once he cleared the coasts.

The long hours in the air built up his flight log and afforded him time to ponder the situation further. Being posted to the CDC had paid off. Leslie Riordan's phone call had revealed the beginnings and location of what Richard Haycock and David had feared and what they knew was inevitable. He almost felt a sense of relief that it had started, and he could move into action.

Just as at Jergens Laboratories, the CDC labs in the special bio-containment section were organized into four Bio-Safety Levels. Pathogens such as rabies were confined on Level 2, where David was working, and Level 3.

He straightened, picked up his phone and dialed three digits.

"ETEC, Eberling."

"Hey, Mark, how's it going? This is David Livingston upstairs."

"Oh, hey, David," came the reply from the microscopy specialist.

"Listen, I need a little time on the ETEC. What've you got this afternoon?"

The ETEC Autoscan scanning electronic microscope produced dramatic three dimensional ultrastructural images and was particularly useful for observing the attachment of microorganisms to cell surfaces. Prep for ETEC was extensive, though, and involved things like sputter coatings, special drying apparatus, and carbon and metal shadowing evaporators – items not found in the average commercial lab.

"No can do, buddy," came the reply. "Got West Nile stuff all afternoon and SARS tomorrow, pretty much."

David pressed. "Come on, Mark. I only need maybe forty-five minutes. They've been putting the West Nile virus through so many times it's like a summer rerun."

"Hey, I don't book the movies, I just run the projector."

"How about the Philips?"

The Philips 201 was a high resolution, versatile instrument with 2 nm ultimate resolution. Another powerful tool.

"The 201? You can have that tomorrow morning, but I can't help you with prep." Samples for the Philips also required careful preparation. "Can't spare anybody. Whatcha got?"

"They're already on a coated grid and air dried. I need maybe a hundred and fifty thousand magnification. The 201 handle that?" David asked.

"Yeah. Okay . . . say nine thirty. I'll give you an hour. You have to give it a name and description, though. I gotta book it. And don't say ham and swiss sandwich analysis or crap like that. Some dipshit did that last month and I caught hell for it."

"Call it Parkerville slash Moon Valley Environmental Analysis."

Mark switched gears. "Don't forget softball tonight, hey."

"Yeah, yeah."

"We need your golden glove."

Mark hung up and bent over his microscope again.

*   *   *   *

At 2 pm, David Livingston was seated in a large office with a view of the parking lot. The neat, uncluttered office belonged to Dr. Nicholas Day, the fifty-five year old head of ETEC and the overseer of LRN. The Laboratory Response Network, a 1999 CDC creation, was an affiliation of public and private lab facilities across the country that could be coordinated to respond to biological and chemical terrorism, as well as other public health emergencies. Day was David's boss. His expensive suit and impeccable haircut contrasted with David's rumpled appearance. He sipped coffee from a china cup.

"I checked her math, Doctor Day," David was saying. "She's right, statistically. It's virtually impossible for this to be random. It's been over six months now in Moon Valley, about the same in Parkerville."

"She seem pretty sharp to you?" Day inquired.

"Well, she picked up on this at four months," replied David.

"She did?" Dr. Day said with surprise. "Nobody told me."

"Just found out myself," David said. "Slipped through the cracks, I guess. Anyway, she's sharp, all right. Doesn't miss a trick."

The section chief nodded, swiveled and looked out at the parking lot.

"What are you going to do about samples from Parkerville?" he asked.

"Well, I figure I'll go out there later in the week. Might have results from the electron microscope by then."

"And you're on in the morning?"

"Yes," David replied. "I sent the samples down to Mark. Everything's all prepped and ready."

Doctor Day nodded. "Good. Are you flying commercial to Parkerville?"

David was surprised at the question. His boss had never asked how he got from here to there.

"No. I'm flying myself. Parkerville's out of the way. Don't worry, the money's about the same."

Doctor Day nodded as David checked his watch. "Oh, lemme run," he said. "I've got a conference call in five minutes."

Dr. Day watched David pop up and leave the office. He steepled his fingers thoughtfully, then picked up his phone and dialed.

"We've got a problem," he said.

25

Facility 1391 did not exist. It did not exist between Hadera and Afula in northern Israel, just off the main highway, beyond a double high fence, watchtowers, vicious attack dogs, thick concrete walls and iron gates. There was no large single story building shimmering in the heat; it was surely a mirage. The compound, known as – or rather, not known as – Facility 1391 was not listed as one of Israel's eleven prisons, nor was it found on any map. The most secret maximum security prison in a land dotted with maximum security facilities, admittance to International Red Cross workers, lawyers, Amnesty International or other organizations was consistently denied. Admittance was consistently denied because, simply, Facility 1391 wasn't there. The official reason given by the government of Israel was that the prison, if it had existed, lay on a secret military base and was thus inaccessible. Being nonexistent, Facility 1391 did not fall under the jurisdiction of any of the three major Israeli intelligence agencies: the Shabak – or Shin Bet - Israel's General Security Service, The Mossad, Israel's intelligence agency involved in counter-terrorism and covert operations, or Aman, the military's intelligence arm.

Facility 1391 specialized in torture – physical and psychological. Prisoners of extraordinary value or high national risk were held there, in solitary, often with black, vile smelling hoods over their heads for protracted periods of time. A specialty of the house was the "Shabak technique", wherein a subject was forced to sit on a short kindergarten stool, angled forward so resting became impossible, arms and legs tied, hooded, with loud noises or music constantly reverberating at high volume in the cell.

Mohammad Kanan and Farouk Al-Hassad were imprisoned for two days, held in separate cells. Aside from being subjected to the Shabak technique, they were violently shaken a number of times while hooded. After two such episodes, Farouk had difficulty breathing; there was an excruciating pain in his neck whenever he moved it.

On the third day, Mohammad was brought for interrogation. When the hood was yanked from his head, he blinked and looked around a small, rough room. His hands were tied behind him. He saw a man in mismatching suit jacket and pants, with a white dress shirt, sitting at a wooden table. He wore no tie. Behind the man stood a sturdy guard in an unidentifiable uniform, leashed attack dog at his side. Where the young Syrian stood, there appeared to be dried blood and fecal matter. Mohammad swayed before catching his balance and blurted out the words every prisoner did when summoned for interrogation. "Where am I?"

"You are in Hell," came the reply. The man's Arabic was without accent. "You will ask nothing further. You will answer my questions. If you do not answer my questions quickly and truthfully, you will see something so horrific you will never get the image from your mind, and then I will ask you again. After that, if you have not answered quickly and truthfully . . ."

He turned to the guard, who bent low and whispered something to the dog. Immediately, the animal sprang forward with a terrible bark, mouth open, directly at Mohammad Kanan. Saliva flew. The chain cut his leap short as Mohammad gasped and immediately urinated in his filthy pants.

". . . you will never be able to answer anything again."

26

David's apartment, on a pleasant, tree-lined northeast Atlanta street, cost him more per month than he had wanted to spend, but his need to be near an airport and still within commuting distance to the CDC limited his geography. Since the new paint job on his beloved Arrow, the researcher had opted to pay for more expensive hangared space at DeKalb-Peachtree Airport, rather than tie his craft outdoors on the tarmac where the southern sun would exact its toll on the Piper's appearance.

Wearing his softball uniform and carrying his glove, David opened the door and automatically reached for the light switch, stopping when he realized it was already on.

He tossed his glove on the couch as he looked around. The room was in disarray. His desk drawer was open, papers scattered on the floor. All the drawers were open, he saw. The place had been ransacked.

"Uh-oh," he said.

As he walked toward the kitchen, the pantry door burst open. David caught a glimpse of an exam gloved fist flying towards his jaw. He ducked, but caught the blow on his forehead, staggering him backward. The thug, short and heavyset, leaped forward but David had quickly assumed a karate stance and managed a kick that just missed the groin, catching the assailant's thigh. Both men grappled and fell over the couch as the table lamp thunked to the floor. David rolled on top of his assailant and landed a hard blow to the midsection before his opponent grabbed the lamp and shattered it over his head. David, stunned, lay on the floor as the man sprang up and darted out the door.

In a few moments, David got to his feet unsteadily, holding his head. He wobbled to the open door and looked out.

Nothing. It had started to drizzle, haloing the streetlamps, glistening the roadway. He felt his head gingerly, a knot already forming.

Twenty minutes later, ice bag to his head, David was cleaning up the broken lamp when the doorbell rang. He opened the door to two Metro uniformed policemen.

"Can I help you?" David asked.

The cops looked at David's ice bag, then at the room beyond.

"Sir, we had a report of a disturbance here."

David looked at the cops. "Must've been the TV," he said, finally.

*   *   *   *   *

The next morning, at ten minutes to nine, David entered the microscopy lab that was Mark Eberling's domain. A true lab rat, Mark was at the CDC twelve or thirteen hours per day, and David knew he'd be working when he arrived. Although he was David's age, Mark looked five years older, perhaps because he weighed 260 pounds. Eberling pitched for the ETECs, probably because he held ultimate power over who got time on the various microscopes. Other than Thursday night softball, he had no life at all, being addicted to video games and online porn.

David looked around and spotted Mark sitting on a stool, hunched over as he prepared a slide, surrounded by instruments of varying sizes, slides, reagents, tubing and a variety of apparatus.

Mark looked up and took in David's scraped forehead and swollen, discolored eye.

"Morning, Da – whoa. What the hell happened to you?"

"Tripped over the ironing board."

Mark looked at David's clothing. "You own an ironing board?"

David ignored the jibe. "Where's my slides?"

Mark gestured towards a counter top across the room. "They're right where you left 'em." He bent back over his slide.

David walked over and looked around the area. "Don't see them," he said.

Mark looked up. "Come on, they're right –"

He got off his stool and went over to the counter. He scanned the area, then frowned.

"What? What the hell?" he said.

"Mark, you're kidding me, right?"

Mark bent down and opened the cabinet doors below the counter. He looked inside, then straightened. His frown had deepened.

"Listen, David. I saw your stuff there last night and I'm the only one who comes in here."

Both men looked around, examining each surface and opening every cabinet. The slides were gone.

"There's nowhere else to look," David said. "What happened to my slides?"

"Hey, it's a mystery to me," Mark answered.

That evening, David phoned Leslie. He had finished tidying up; the apartment looked like it had before the attack, minus the table lamp. He told her about the missing samples.

"Probably someone didn't know what they were and tossed them all," he told her. In truth, David knew the only other person with access to the lab was Doctor Day.

"That doesn't sound very likely," Leslie said. Curled up on the couch with chips and salsa, she had been watching Derek as he built a Lego structure on the carpet. He hadn't wanted any help, just company.

"Listen, all I can do is start over. When I told my boss, he kind of discouraged me. Said it all could wait. He wants me up in New England for the flu breakout."

"I read about that," Leslie observed.

"That's not my field," David said. "And we've got half the staff up there now anyway. If the weather's good, I'll try and fly out Thursday. Think you can line up some more women for blood samples?"

"Sure," came the reply. "I'll do it tomorrow."

"Don't be alarmed when you see me. I had a break-in last night."

Leslie sat up sharply. She winced as a glob of salsa flew off the chip she was holding and splattered on the cocktail table. "What?! What do you mean? Did they take anything?"

"We got into it a little bit. I think I look worse than he does."

"David!"

"I'm okay." There was a pause. "Leslie?"

"Yes, David?"

"Be careful."

"What do you mean?"

"I don't know. Maybe I'm overly suspicious." He normally would not have mentioned the burglary, but would rather err on the side of caution.

"I can't believe there's any connection between the man in your apartment and the missing samples. I mean – it's crazy," she said, wiping up salsa with a napkin, receiver to her ear.

Two hours later, she fell asleep, mulling over David's last remark.

At 2:10 a.m., a noise woke Leslie. She sat up, feeling her heart pound. The doorknob was plainly turning. Her eyes grew wide.

The door opened and Derek came in, rubbing his eyes. She sighed as he approached the bed sleepily.

"Mommy?"

She patted her son's shoulder. "Yes, Derek?"

"I heard something by the window."

She lifted Derek into bed. "Stay here, honey. Mommy'll make sure everything's okay."

Leslie opened her night table drawer and took out a black rubberized flashlight. In pajamas, she moved noiselessly to the hallway and snapped on the light.

Nothing.

Except the noise of a car starting and driving off. She ran to the front door and opened it, stepped to the end of the porch in time to see a dark Suburban turn the corner and vanish. Leslie stood, remembering David's remark. Although it was a balmy evening, she shivered before returning inside.

27

"Why were you in Israel? Did you know the man who drove you? Why were you dropped off by the springs at Salukiya? What did you do there? Who sent you?"

Mohammad had closed his eyes. How could they have known? He reacted to the first question without thinking. "Golan is not Israel. It is Syria." He opened his eyes, in disbelief at what he had said.

All was frozen for a moment. The man in the chair cocked his head slowly and raised an eyebrow, as if appraising the mettle of his prisoner.

"Very well," he said, a small smile forming on his face. He got up leisurely and walked over to Mohammad, standing very close. He looked into the young man's eyes, nodding slightly. Then he turned and left the room.

Mohammad's legs began to tremble as fear radiated outward from the pit of his stomach. He tried not to think. He became aware of the sound of dripping water, somewhere close. For some reason, the noise terrified him.

He tried to pray, but could not concentrate. Time passed: fifteen minutes, an hour?

A lifetime?

The door opened and two guards came in. One carried a length of rope. He tossed one end up and over a pipe above Mohammad's head, a pipe he had not noticed. Perhaps it was a water pipe, the source of the dripping sound? The guard moved behind Mohammad and grabbed his wrists where they were bound together. The dangling rope was attached and pulled taut before being tied. The movement thrust him forward and his arms upward behind him, parallel to the floor. Mohammad knew if he lost his balance, his shoulders would separate.

The second guard grabbed him at the waist and yanked his pants down around his ankles. His underwear followed. He saw the hood in the guard's hand, and then it was dark. He gagged on the stench inside the foul, thick cloth.

Terror and nausea flooded together, heightened by a growing pain in his shoulders. He could hear the guards' footsteps as they left without a word. It grew completely silent.

Again, he tried to pray but feared that Allah could not hear him through the coarse fabric. The sensation in his shoulders had grown to agony, his legs trembled with the strain of staying upright. Pain shot through in his calves.

Sounds from outside the room. Relief began to flood over him; they were coming to let him down. But it was the sound of the dog again. The fierce barking grew closer. He became acutely aware he was naked from the waist down. The door opened and suddenly the animal was very near.

28

For the second time that month, David approached the Moon Valley Airport, entering downwind at one thousand feet AGL. He spoke into his headset.

"Moon Valley Unicom, Piper four three one three uniform downwind for runway two three, Moon Valley."

It was another cloudless day over the desert. With the winds light and variable, and Moon Valley's long, wide runway, the landing wouldn't be much of a strain. As David continued the approach, he pulled the gear wheel on the panel out and down.

The three lights failed to glow green. There was no slight pitch change or loss of airspeed that normally accompanied gear deployment.

"Oh, shit," he muttered. He tapped the lights, then checked the panel light rheostat wheel. If the panel lights were on, the aircraft would think it was night and automatically dim the three greens, rendering them invisible in daylight. More than one red-faced pilot had been fooled by the Piper system.

The rheostat was off.

He leaned over and looked at the circuit breakers in front of the co-pilot seat. He tripped several off, then back on.

Nothing.

David reached between the seats and pulled the emergency gear down lever.

No pitch change, no slight loss of airspeed.

The lights stayed dark. Holding the gear lever up, he mashed the right rudder pedal, then the left, fishtailing the Piper, trying to dislodge the gear and let it fall.

It didn't fall.

David pushed the talk button. "Uh, Moon Valley Unicom, Piper four three one three uniform breaking off the approach. I've got a problem."

In the airport office, Jeff had been restocking stale candy in the vending machine. He picked up the mic from the counter.

"One three uniform, Moon Valley. What's the prob?"

"Ah, got a gear malfunction. No green lights. Gonna do a flyby, you can tell me if it's the lights or the gear's really stuck."

Jeff's eyebrows went up. "Roger, one three uniform." He put down the microphone and hustled out the door towards the active. He looked up and spotted the Arrow approaching runway 23 at one hundred feet. In a few moments, David flew over. He had deployed two notches of flaps to allow the craft to fly slowly enough for a good look. The airplane was clean – the wheels were up. Jeff hustled back inside and picked up the mic.

"One three uniform, Moon Valley. Your gear is definitely up. Repeat, no gear."

"Roger, no gear. I'm gonna burn off fuel for awhile, shake the tail again, hope to get a free fall."

Fifteen minutes later, Leslie's Jeep pulled up to the small facility. She spotted the sheriff's car, fire truck and ambulance outside the terminal, lights flashing. She jumped out and hurried inside.

Sheriff Winfield, two ambulance attendants, and several firefighters stood around the counter. The lawman, having driven more than one tardy soon-to-be-mother to the hospital where Leslie awaited, greeted her.

"Hey, doc. What're you doing here? Hear it on the radio?"

"No, I don't –"

She was interrupted by David's voice over the loudspeaker.

"Okay, I'm pretty low on fuel now. Coming on in."

Leslie's eyes grew wide. What was happening?

The sheriff looked at Leslie again. "Somebody having a baby, Doc?"

"What's the matter? I'm supposed to meet Doctor Livingston. Is he in trouble?" She felt her heart pound.

"You could say that." He turned to the crews. "We better get out there now."

Leslie's hand flew to her cheek. She felt helpless, an unusual feeling for the physician. In a few moments, the firefighters and ambulance attendance were in their vehicles and had driven to the end of the runway where they stopped, lights flashing. Leslie stood outside the office, perhaps a hundred feet off the side of the runway, watching in horror as the little craft descended towards the tarmac. Even to her untrained eye, things looked unnatural with no gear down.

In the cockpit, David yanked the flaps handle, applying the third notch at forty degrees. Thinking furiously, too busy to be scared, he talked to himself.

"Flaps forty. Airspeed eighty five. Boost pump off." As he crossed the runway threshold, David turned the fuel selector to off and killed the mixture, hoping the prop would stop in the horizontal position. The Arrow continued in eerie silence, floating in ground effect, unnaturally low with no wheels. The plane inched toward the runway surface as the airspeed bled off.

There was a tremendous screeching noise and a shower of sparks. The Piper skidded a surprisingly short way down the centerline, turned slightly and stopped. It had taken but a few moments. The rescue vehicles, too far down the runway, sped back toward David's plane, lights flashing and sirens wailing.

The door to four three one three uniform opened and David emerged, stepping onto the wing before hopping to the tarmac, which, without gear, wasn't far below. He looked first at the prop. Fortunately, it had stopped horizontally, and was undamaged. He bent down and peered at the belly of his precious Arrow as the caravan roared up and squealed to a halt several feet away. The firemen tumbled out, unreeled a hose and ran towards the airplane. The men waved to David to back off.

"Get away!" one yelled.

David appeared unruffled, but backed away. There was an electrical smell, but no apparent fire. He turned in time to see Leslie run up and almost crash into him.

"Hi, Leslie," he said.

"David!" she exclaimed. You're all right?"

"Sure," came the reply. "Look at my plane." He peered at the undercarriage. "Actually, it doesn't look too bad. Except for the six thousand dollar paint job," he remarked ruefully.

The firemen stood poised with the hose. David thought they looked disappointed when the little Arrow didn't explode.

"You could have been killed!" Leslie said, unconsciously squeezing his arm.

"Yeah," he replied. "You hungry?"

Sheriff Winfield walked up. "You better have a candy bar now, Doctor. You're gonna be awhile. FAA's on the way."

Being a typical FAA inspector, Raymond Towne right off made clear that he was a pilot too, and sympathetic, while all the time certain David had merely forgotten to lower the gear and looking for evidence to prove it. Towne was forced to rule out pilot error, though, in light of the radio transmissions and attempts to shake the gear free. Two hours later, after a lot of paperwork, photographs and official questions, the FAA inspector cleared the wounded aircraft for removal. David watched anxiously as Jerry's Crane Service attached a sling underneath the wings and lifted the plane. He and Towne inspected the undercarriage before it was loaded onto a flatbed truck and driven to a hangar across the runway. The damage was surprisingly minimal.

Eventually, David sat with Leslie in a booth at the Moon Valley diner. The place was empty again, being well past lunchtime. David was grateful the food came quickly. He inhaled his burger. Leslie wasn't far behind him.

"God, I was starving." He munched on a dill pickle slice.

"Adrenaline will do that. It's amazing it turned out so well," Leslie said. "The landing, I mean. I've seen a couple on TV that didn't."

A half hour later, with Leslie at the wheel of the Jeep, David turned in the passenger seat, eyes narrowing as he looked through the rear window. A vehicle was maintaining a constant distance. Leslie sensed something new was amiss.

"What's the matter?"

"Nothing. I don't know. When do you turn?" David asked.

"About two miles up the road."

David shifted around, turned towards Leslie. "Listen, do me a favor. Turn before then. Someplace where you can get back on the main road without having to turn around or back up."

"What's the matter?" Leslie repeated, looking in her rear view mirror. She was becoming alarmed.

"Maybe nothing," David said. "Let's see."

Leslie continued to a side street that entered a rabbit warren of new homes. She turned in and pulled over straightaway. In a moment, a dark Suburban with tinted windows drove past. They watched it go.

Leslie expelled a breath she hadn't realized she'd been holding. "You had me spooked," she said. "I told you about the car the other night."

"That was a Suburban too, you said. Did you see what color it was?"

David hadn't taken his eyes off the Chevrolet. He watched it turn at a bend down the road and disappear before looking over at Leslie. She was staring at him.

29

A penthouse suite at the Burj al Arab had arguably the best views in the Emirate of Dubai. Shaped like the sail of a giant *dhow*, the $650 million dollar hotel soared skyward from an artificial island connected to the mainland by private bridge. The Burj featured, among other things, the largest atrium in the world. When viewed from offshore, the entire affair looked like a giant Christian cross, surely an accidental act on the part of the British architects. Just to the west and jutting into the blue green Arabian Gulf was the Palm Jumeirah, an incredible man-made island in the shape of a palm tree, whose fronds offered 4,000 waterfront villas and apartments. To the south, just across the eight lane Sheikh Zayed Road, past the Mall of the Emirates and the Gold and Diamond Park, lay the Dubai Camel Racecourse and the beginnings of desert sands. A sleepy fishing village as late as 1990, Dubai had all sprouted like a giant concrete and steel beanstalk on the edge of the Gulf, fertilized by seemingly endless wealth. Now most of the villas and apartments stood empty, victims of the cratered economy.

The occupant of the suite, however, was concerned not with the view nor shopping but rather the news from Syria that the two men sent into the Golan had been captured after their successful mission. Sharif pondered the implications of their disappearance as he played Brahms' Piano Concerto No. 2, a favorite since having been inspired by the brilliant Czech Ivan Moravec's 1988 recording.

The short list could only consist of Mossad, CIA or MI6. MI6 was unlikely, since two young boys, presumably unarmed, had been shot at close quarters during the operation. There was also the possibility, however slight, that the coalition of Arab organizations involved, the discordant groups he had cobbled together, was already falling apart. They always did eventually, Sharif knew, because it was their nature, and in their blood, something usually lost to the bunglers at Langley and Vauxhall Cross. That was the joke: the best way to defeat any Arab coalition was to let it alone. Old tribal rivalries and religious differences ran deeper and were much older than any conflict with the West. Sharif glanced out the window as he played, at the waters whose name couldn't even be agreed on - the Iranians insisted on Persian Gulf, to almost everyone else it was the Arabian Gulf. No wonder jihad was still a dream, and he the would-be dreamweaver.

Keeping Hamas and Fatah from each other's throats was an impossibility for very long; only the monumental objective and the pending reality of its attainment had allowed him to hold things together so far. This was too important and too soon and besides, he would know if his axis had fallen apart. The most reasonable assessment was a CIA - Mossad collaboration. The Brooklyn experiment might have been compromised in some way, providing a lead.

A complication, and potentially serious, but not overwhelming. Of course, the two missing men knew nothing. But the fact they had been abducted meant someone knew something, if only that they had ventured into the Golan. He would begin to ferret out the answers. Contacting the American would be distasteful, and the likelihood was he had no information anyway. He would save that option.

He gazed northward to the horizon, where beyond lay the Strait of Hormuz and Iran. Nothing must disturb the work across the water.

30

Fear radiated outward from the pit of Mohammad's stomach and shot fire down his quavering legs. The dog's breathing was very near. He involuntarily drew up his testicles as the seconds passed. The guard moved behind Mohammad and grabbed his wrists where they were bound together. He led him towards the door, forcing Mohammad to walk backwards quickly. He knew that if he stumbled and fell, the man would not let go and his shoulders would separate.

The suffocating hood was yanked off. The hallway was very dark and completely silent. The guard led him to the end and opened a door. Then he whipped Mohammad around and pushed him into a sandy courtyard, where he was blinded by the sunlight he had not seen for three days. As his vision returned, he recognized Farouk. He felt a rush of relief at seeing his friend. What was he doing?

Farouk, shovel in hand, was digging in the bare earth. Another guard stood a few feet to the side. Mohammad recognized the man's Galil SAR assault rifle as standard Israeli army issue, triggering a realization: Farouk was digging their graves.

The light was dazzling. The sand from Farouk's shovel seemed to dance in the shimmering air. With all hope suddenly gone, a calm descended on Mohammad. Soon he would see Allah, who would be pleased. Like his friends and compatriots, the many whom had fallen before, the young Arab would not flinch at the barrel of a gun.

Farouk looked over at Mohammad and attempted a smile. The guard hefted his weapon; Farouk returned to his digging. Mohammad noticed a scarred wooden table to the side. Something metal was attached to it; something vaguely familiar but he couldn't place. After a time the man in the mismatched suit came through the door.

"Stop!" he said. The grave was not finished. The man walked to the table. "Bring them here," he said, gesturing towards Farouk. Both Arabs were led to the table, stained dark where the attachment was mounted. Suddenly Mohammad recognized the implement bolted to it, the device with the open chute and crank handle. He recognized it from his mother's kitchen. It was a sausage grinder. Nausea rushed up from his stomach.

There was a noise behind him. From somewhere, two guards had appeared leading a pig on a leash. Mohammad's mind froze as they approached and tied the leash to a table leg. The other guard grabbed Farouk's right hand and held it over the grinder. His partner pulled a Sheffield Commando knife, bent down and quickly slit the pig's belly, then with another quick movement came out with a dripping section of entrails. He dropped it into the grinder.

"Farouk al-Hassad," the man in civilian clothes said, "Why were you in Israel? Who was the man who drove you? What did you do by the springs of Salukiya? Who sent you?"

Farouk's mouth worked, but no sound came out. His eyes were white all around. The man nodded to the guards. One jammed Farouk's hand into the grinder as the other turned the crank with two hands, jerkily, straining with the effort. Farouk screamed then. There was another noise, a wet grinding noise, punctuated by sharp cracking of bone. The air began to go dark around the edges of Mohammad's vision. He retched; the bile reached the back of his throat, burning. He swayed, but the sudden pain of his shoulders being wrenched kept him conscious. He did not fall. Below, on the ground, Farouk lay, unconscious. The fingers on his right hand were gone, all the way to the knuckles. Blood oozed into the dust, mingling with that of the pig, which was lying on its side now, screeching and jerking its legs as the blood continued to seep from its belly in slow sheets. A guard reached down and stuck Farouk's hand into the belly of the pig. The other guard reached inside the animal and wrenched organs free, stood and smiled at Mohammad. He slapped and smeared the gore on Mohammad's face, his shirt, his pants. He tied a section of entrails around his neck. The stench was overwhelming. The guard with the Galil stood over Farouk and cocked his weapon. The noise was lost in the squeals of the wounded pig, its life ebbing into the dry sand. The guard shot Farouk in the groin; the young Arab jerked and groaned, drew up his legs.

Soon the squeals stopped. The wind shrugged; dust rose briefly.

The guards dragged Farouk to the grave and dumped him in. They returned and hauled the gutted pig over and dumped it on top of Mohammad's friend. Farouk grunted as the weight of the pig fell on him, the animal's legs faintly moving in response to some belated instinct. Glistening innards of the pig slid out over Farouk. One guard picked up the shovel and began to fill the hole. As the dirt hit Farouk's face, his eyes opened. The guard noticed, and lifted the shovel high over his head. He brought it down as hard as he could on Farouk's face. Blood and teeth flew. The sound sickened Mohammad further.

A door in the courtyard opened and yet another uniformed guard entered, leading a pig on a leash. He brought it over and tied the leash to the table leg.

The man with the mismatched suit, a student of history and admirer of General Black Jack Pershing, leisurely lit a cigarette. He took a deep drag and regarded Mohammad. Then he stepped very close. He saw the Arab's pupils were contracted in shock. He spoke gently.

"Mohammad Kanan, do you think Allah will welcome you or your friend into Paradise when you and the pig are one? What did you do at Salukiya?"

31

David sat on Leslie's sofa sipping a glass of Bourgogne Aligote.

"What is this stuff?" he asked, holding up his glass. "Chardonnay?"

"Not exactly. Fred, my partner, found it. It's a young white wine from Burgundy. Do you like it?" Leslie asked.

"Sure. It's different. Is Fred a connoisseur?"

"No, he's an obstetrician," she laughed. "I think he just wanted to get me drunk."

There was a momentary silence, an unasked question.

"Derek's dad died two years ago," said Leslie, anticipating the researcher.

"Oh, I'm sorry."

"Stomach cancer," Leslie went on. "We met in medical school. We were married after graduation, then went into practice together for four years. Know what he told me? When he was in the hospital?"

"What was that?" David asked.

"He said all that education, planning, always looking forward. The future. He said it's quite a shock to realize there is no future. He said he started looking back, and realized he already was a rich man."

David pondered the remark. "He must have been quite a guy."

Leslie stared into her wine glass as she slowly swished the dark liquid. The air in the room had thickened. Outside, it had grown dark. David sat up.

"Okay, anyway. You asked me if I was worried. I'm worried as hell, actually," he said. He put down his drink and leaned forward. He ticked off items on his fingers.

"Look. My missing samples, my boss trying to get me to New England, that thing with you and the car outside the other night, the guy in my house, the airplane—"

"Your airplane!?" Leslie exclaimed. "You think—"

"I think it's not safe for us anymore. I'm curious to see what the shop turns up when they finish with my plane."

"Why, David, that would be--!?"

David drained the rest of his drink. He stood and walked to the window, looking out.

Leslie put her drink on the cocktail table. "I don't think it's safe for you in that hotel. Besides, they've probably canceled your reservation. It's after nine. I've got a guest bedroom, you know."

      *   *   *   *   *

Leslie awoke with a clear head. She looked up at the time. The soft red digits projected onto the ceiling glowed 4:11. 4:11? She'd never even *seen* 4:11 on the thing. The always accurate atomic clock had been one of Donald's fascinations, along with vintage electric guitars, amplifiers and old British sports cars. There was still a cabinet in the garage with metric tools and spare Lucas tinker toy electric parts for the long gone MG TD, the defunct Austin-Healey 3000, the mortally wounded tiny yellow TR3A. Faded oil stains on the garage floor and in the driveway marked the resting places of the wounded – what Donald had called his MASH unit: Mobile Automobile Surgical Hospital.

Why was her mind wandering through the Donald-past with David sleeping in her house? She was never up in the night. Now she felt wide awake, as if sunlight would make the blinds glow any minute. Why had she invited him to stay, really? Was she frightened for him? For her? Was it something else?

Did it make sense?

From the kitchen, Leslie heard the familiar sound of the ice machine dumping another load into the receptacle. It seemed to crank out an amazing quantity of ice for the little use she gave it. The thing ran all day and all night. The sound reminded her of a bowling alley. When they had moved in, the ice machine had been a distraction; now it was a familiar comfort, the little ice people bowling in the kitchen.

She eased from the bed and slipped out of the bedroom. Not really knowing why, she entered the room she seldom visited, the room containing Donald's desk and personal effects. She turned the desk lamp to the low setting and sat on the couch, looking at the guitars hung on the walls. Donald's enthusiasm for the instruments had been infectious, although as a player he hadn't gotten much beyond the garage band stage. Here was a 1961 Telecaster, one that had belonged to the tragic genius Roy Buchanan. There was a 1992 Mark Sampson hand-wired Matchless SC-30 amplifier, complete with hot box tube floor pedal. He had revered this stuff and she would have felt it a betrayal to sell any of it. Donald had gotten an appraisal for the homeowners' insurance policy, and she had learned the rare gear was worth a small fortune. Actually, not so small. The Trainwreck Express amp in the corner was valued at over twenty thousand dollars. Because he had loved it, she loved it too. Maybe some day.

Rumble, kerplunk. Another load of cubes. She vaguely remembered a Laurel and Hardy movie featuring an ice truck and an endless set of steps. Laurel and Hardy were very funny, much funnier than the characters Derek watched. Amos and Andy, Ernie Kovacs, The Honeymooners: they all were much funnier than the characters Derek watched. A legacy from her father, who used to roar in front of the television enjoying the vintage comedy network. Leslie had often been by his side, he with his beer, she with her soda, sharing popcorn or nonpareils or Jujubes that threatened to pull out her fillings or some other wonderful snack and laughing at the black and white hilarity.

She thought of the words she would have used to describe her life: words like order, purpose, planning. Even after Donald died, and she had reached out and tested her capabilities, it was always after careful thought and having measured potential risk. She never winged it, really, although it might seem so to others. Leslie knew she was not quite as adventurous as she appeared. Her boldness was something in spite of; her mountaineering an overcoming, her travels not carefree but rather done with a planned determination.

Leslie had known she was going to be a physician when she was ten years old. She thought again about her father. An alcoholic who bounced from job to job as a male nurse, he had always managed to put bread on the table, albeit sometimes a single slice or two. She saw the toll it took on her mother. Leslie had loved her dad dearly, but the fear of the unknown he had engendered and the insecurity of moving from place to place with little notice had shaped her. Education meant safety, she knew, a barrier against the fear, and so she had studied with the voracity of great purpose.

And Donald had fit right in. Not quite as serious as she, not afraid to enjoy life without setting enjoyment as a task to be accomplished. She thought herself sometimes as an egg, smooth, without features, difficult for others to gain a purchase. Strong from end to end, but perhaps fragile in the middle. The protective shell protected – what?

She was sleepy now; her brain felt thick with dust. She got up and headed towards the bed. Everything would sort out eventually.

*   *   *   *   *

In the guest bedroom, David was sound asleep. Under his pillow was a .40 caliber Glock 23 handgun. He wouldn't normally keep a loaded weapon there, but a child was in the house. He had an ulterior motive for accepting Leslie's invitation, but it wasn't to hook up, attractive as she was. He knew the dark Suburban was probably trouble, and things might be becoming dangerous for the inquisitive obstetrician.

32

At nine thirty on the morning following David's unconventional landing, Leslie drove the Jeep along the two lane blacktop, headed for the migrant camp. The green lettuce fields had come into view, eventually giving way to onions stretching all the way to the distant hills. It was still a couple of miles until the road turned to dirt. There was no traffic.

"Are you sure you can do this today?"

"It's my off day, anyway. I was going climbing," she said.

"Maybe you can teach me," David said. "We only need to be here long enough to get another batch of samples. Maybe a half hour."

"What I really want to do is have you teach me to fly," she responded.

"Even after yesterday?" he asked. He smiled at her spunk.

"Well, if you're right, that was no accident, so—"

"There's a deal," David said.

They continued on in the clear desert morning. The temperature was very comfortable, but would soon climb another ten to fifteen degrees before the sun reached its peak. David looked out at the distant lettuce fields, then noticed something in the side view mirror. He sat up.

"What is it?" Leslie asked.

"Behind us. Suburban. Looks like the same one from last night." He had been checking the mirror since they'd started the drive.

Leslie turned to look.

"Oh, no," she said, gripping the wheel with both hands.

She sped up just as the blacktop disappeared and the road turned to dirt. They bounced along at teeth-rattling speed, but the Suburban gradually closed the distance until it was tailgating. David reached into the back seat, grabbed his field pack and brought it to the front. He rummaged through the bag.

"What are you doing?" Leslie asked, sneaking a glance over to the CDC researcher as David pulled out the Glock 23 handgun.

"What?! Where did you get that?" Leslie was fast becoming unglued.

"From my bag."

"No, I mean—"

Bam! The Suburban had rammed the Jeep's bumper. Leslie let out a screech and fought for control as the Jeep fishtailed and drifted to the left. Behind, the Suburban dropped back a few yards, then sped up to ram the Jeep again. David leaned out and fired three shots at the pursuing Chevrolet. Bullet holes appeared in the truck's windscreen; it swerved sharply.

Leslie fought for control as the Jeep continued to slide, sending up billowing clouds of dust. The Suburban gunned its engine and sped past. She felt helpless as they drifted off the road and slid towards a large palo verde tree. She knew they were going to hit it.

The Jeep slammed into the trunk at slow speed. She was vaguely aware of David hopping out and aiming at the Suburban, but it disappeared over a rise. He ran around and opened the driver's door.

"Leslie!"

Leslie sat, stunned. A rivulet of blood ran down from her hair and down her cheek. It felt warm. She put her hand to her face and looked disbelievingly at the blood on her fingers.

"I'm – I'm all right, I think," she stammered.

"Well, don't move," David said. "Let me get my cell phone."

"Mine's right here," Leslie said, picking it up from the console. Some detached part of her mind watched as if from above as she carefully dialed 911. She wondered with dismay if the blood from her fingers would screw up her phone. They weren't supposed to get wet, she knew.

*　　　　*　　　　*　　　　*

Sheriff Winfield leaned against his patrol car, watching Jerry's tow truck winch up Leslie's Jeep. There was a sizeable dent in the driver's door and a smashed front headlight.

"Pretty lucky, you folks," he observed.

"I guess," Leslie said. She was having trouble believing what had just happened. She sat in the patrol car passenger seat with the door open, feet on the ground. The law officer looked over at David.

"What the hell kinda doctor are you, Livingston? Doctor Doom?"

David suppressed a smile. "Not hardly," he replied. "I'm just a CDC research guy."

"Well, you two are sure tearing up this town," Winfield remarked. "Suppose it's time you let me know what the hell's going on?"

"Wish we knew," David said, not entirely untruthfully.

Leslie looked up. "Sheriff, can you give us a lift to the migrant camp?"

Winfield regarded the pair as if seeing a new species. "I suppose that's as good a way as any to find out what you two are up to," he said, finally.

Later, at the camp, David loaded the fresh samples into his field pack. As he had estimated, it took about a half hour to gather new samples from the water and camp volunteers. The word had spread since the first trip; at ten bucks a head David had no shortage of volunteers. Sheriff Winfield looked on.

"I dunno, I don't get it. What're you looking for?" he asked.

David replied, "We don't know what we're looking for."

"Sounds like the government," the sheriff remarked.

"I've got to get to Parkerville," David said to Leslie.

"I'm going with you," Leslie replied. David was surprised.

"What? How—"

"Don't argue," she said with a resolve he hadn't seen before. David looked at her for a moment, then seemed to accept her statement. She might be safer with him than alone, he thought. At least he could keep an eye on her.

And besides, someone already knew who she was.

"Anyway," David said, "all I need to do is get back to town and pack this stuff with dry ice."

"Taking it back to the CDC?" asked the lawman.

"No, not there," David replied. "It's a lab in California. I've got a few calls to make first."

The sheriff looked at the pair. "All right, doctors. If you two are leaving town, maybe something won't get bent for a day or two. Even if it is all your own stuff."

33

While the desert sun dominated a cloudless Arizona sky, it was raining steadily in Washington, D.C. Although just after 2 pm, it seemed like twilight under the leaden clouds rolling slowly over the capitol. A low pressure system blanketed the eastern seaboard from Virginia to New England, and it wasn't supposed to clear for two days. Steady rivulets of water ran down the windows at NSA headquarters, streaking the dirt on the panes. Inside, the paneled double doors of a fourth floor wing read:

EXECUTIVE OFFICES
NATIONAL OPERATIONS SECURITY PROGRAM

Beyond, the area was jammed with interior cubicles surrounded by windowed offices, filled with serious people in white shirts and ties, suits and heels. Florescence mixed with the glow from computer screens created an uneasy atmosphere that somehow hinted of ill health.

The paneled door to a corner office bore the legend JACK MOSS, DIRECTOR. That door was closed. Inside his two windowed and carpeted office, Moss, the forty three year old head of OPSEC, paid no attention to the miserable weather as he studied a file. He wore his hair close-cropped and favored muted ties against his white shirts. Moss' resume, otherwise unremarkable, was interesting because of the gaps between NSA appointments.

He picked up a phone and punched a button marked SECURITY. An amber light sprang to life as he punched digits. The phone connected; Moss began to speak as soon as the ringing was interrupted.

"Sir, it's Moss," he said.

"Yes?" came the reply.

"The horses are still out of the barn, sir."

The voice continued. "That doesn't sound promising, does it? And . . .?"

"Well, do we have a green light, sir?" Moss asked, as lightly as possible.

"That's nothing you'll get from this end, Mister Moss. Am I clear?"

"Yes, sir," Moss replied.

"You're on your own authority," the voice continued. "Consequences stop with your office. Clear?"

"Crystal, sir." Moss hung up. He steepled his fingers, swiveled and looked out at the Washington landmarks. He noticed it was raining before picking up the phone again and pressing the Security button.

*   *   *   *   *

As Jack Moss hung up the phone from his second call, Leslie and David sat in her living room. Naomi walked in from the hall.

"Ma'am?"

"Yes, Naomi?"

"Derek's up from his nap. I can see you two got things to do, so if you like I can take him to the park."

"Oh, that would be great, Naomi. Thank you."

They exchanged smiles before Naomi retreated down the hall.

"She's a bargain at any price," David remarked.

"You said it."

"I've got to call a friend of mine in California, tell him the samples are coming. It's another facility with electron microscopy."

"You really don't trust the CDC?" Leslie asked. "Your own office?"

"After what happened, I'm not going to take a chance," David replied. "In the morning I'll go to Parkerville."

"I'd like to go with you, if that's all right." She hadn't changed her mind. "I want to see this through."

David looked at her as if weighing the idea. "What about Derek? Your practice?"

"I was going climbing for four days, anyway, so my schedule's all covered, and Derek's supposed to go to my sister's," she said.

David looked off for a moment. "Okay," he said quietly. Leslie studied his expression for a moment. Her eyes widened.

"You don't think—?"

"I'm just trying to be careful. I do know I'm not going to phone California from here or use my cell phone. I'll call from a pay phone."

He stood and looked out the window, thinking about –

From behind, very near:

"David?" Leslie said in a soft voice. "You'll stay here tonight, won't you?"

It might have been an awkward afternoon, growing more so as she played out a charade about the guest room, and it would have weighed on her mind for the rest of the day and into the evening. Dinner could have been especially clumsy. But suddenly she moved forward and kissed him, and they were in each other's arms, and Leslie's bottled emotions were uncorked with more intensity than she could have imagined.

Naomi, who was a wily judge of people anyway, had left the two of them alone and didn't bring her little charge back for another two hours.

*   *   *   *

Later, in the darkness, after meat loaf and mashed potatoes and playing with Derek and making love again, they found they spoke surprisingly little. Neither felt the need to fill the night with words. Leslie had smiled when she turned the lock on her bedroom door for the first time; she had often wondered if and when it would happen.

And still later, when she heard the sound of David's breathing, even and regular, she felt an unexpected warmth as the Donald-past assumed its rightful place in her memory, fertilized with this new relationship, no longer needing to be held so tightly, no longer required to feed her needs by itself. It was what it was, and all her emotional coinage no longer needed to be spent there.

34

David was up at 5:30 a.m. Not wanting to wake Leslie, he lay beside her for several minutes, mulling over this new development. He didn't spend time on the emotional aspect of their relationship, nor could he afford to let it affect his mission. Her attractiveness and his natural feelings were beside the point. He really hadn't wanted them to become intimate under the circumstances. It was an unnecessary complication and brought a new set of concerns. But it had happened.

It was becoming clearer that the forces they faced were organized and determined, and likely had governmental ties, especially as far as the CDC was concerned. Those ties could include law enforcement, when he considered the Atlanta break-in. As Richard Haycock had cautioned, it might be dangerous to call for help. They simply didn't know who was involved. His best lead now could be a damaged dark late model Suburban with bullet holes in the windscreen. He should be able to locate it if repairs were made, but he doubted the vehicle would be taken to the nearest Chevy dealer.

He was still on his own, and the lethal game that had begun behind an Arizona gas station was escalating.

The drive to Parkerville was going to take a good three and a half hours. David and Leslie had planned to leave by 7:30 a.m., but it was an extra thirty minutes before they situated her son at his aunt's after stopping at a drive-through, bringing doughnuts and coffee. Little Derek was delighted to see his cousin Terry. Seated at the breakfast table, they exchanged secret smiles while their cheeks filled like chipmunks, stuffed with glazed doughnut. If he had looked, Derek might have seen that smile mirrored on his mother as she looked at David, who thought Catherine was Leslie's twin. The women were actually eighteen months apart. The younger sister, pursuing her doctorate in English literature, would drive Derek to school in a little while and pick him up at noon. It was obvious Catherine felt an undercurrent of agitation in Leslie mixed with the glow of after-love.

"Is everything okay?" she asked. Leslie assured her it was, but remained vague about the purpose of her California trip. She could tell from her sister's look she had not allayed her concerns. Finally underway, David steered the Jeep along the desert highway towards California as Leslie took in the scenery.

Leslie found his hand and squeezed it, but they avoided talking about the prior day's intimacy. It seemed better for each of them to compartmentalize, at least for the time being.

"Derek seemed excited go to your sister's," David said. The stop had been along their way.

"She spoils him rotten," Leslie said. "And he loves little Terry. She's one year younger than he is."

"There's a family resemblance. And that's a compliment."

"Thank you. I could tell she's concerned. I guess I didn't seem my usual bubbly self. Wait, I mean—I don't mean about last—"

David laughed. "I know what you mean. Anyway, I don't know if I told you – I used to work just outside of Parkerville."

"No, you didn't," Leslie said, glad David had changed the subject. "I thought you went with the CDC right from school." The craggy, low desert terrain spread out in every direction, punctuated by tall saguaro and dry arroyos. Washed by the distance, she thought she saw the Superstition Mountains well to the east, but it might have been cloud.

"I did," David replied, "but I interned at Jergens Labs. They've got very sophisticated electron microscope capability. The guy I called last night's a friend of mine I worked with, Ken Holliday. He's still there. He'll run the samples for us."

"Oh," Leslie said, snapping her fingers, "I checked and there are only two obstetricians in Parkerville. I was able to reach a Doctor Garrison. He already knew about the pattern, of course, and he says he may have information for us."

David suddenly stiffened. "You called from the house?"

"No, I used my cell—"

Her hand flew to her mouth. She looked at David in horror.

"Maybe that wasn't so smart," she said. David was expressionless.

In Washington, Jack Moss was at his desk, impatiently waiting for the phone to ring on the scrambler line. He'd been there since six thirty that morning. When a call came in, he looked at the I.D. screen, then pressed the security button and picked up when he saw the amber glow.

"Moss."

"This is Blue Sky One," came the response.

"Go."

"Subject two made a call from a pay phone at 2100 hours local time from a convenience store outside Moon Valley. Call completed to one Ken Holliday, Columbia Valley, California."

"Who is he?" Moss asked.

"Get this. Columbia Valley's six miles from Parkerville. Holliday works at Jergens Labs. Genetic research."

Moss became agitated. "What the hell is that? What could that be?"

"Coincidence, maybe. Probably not. One other call. Subject one. Cell phone call to Richard Garrison, M.D."

"And he is . . . ?" Moss asked.

"One of the two practicing obstetricians in Parkerville. They've got a meeting set up for this afternoon."

Moss' jaw clenched. "This is getting out of hand. Shut it down *now*."

Without waiting for a reply, Moss disconnected. He sat for a moment, thinking. After pressing the security button again, he dialed another number.

"Jergens Laboratories," came the greeting.

"Doctor Jergens, please. Thomas Keller calling."

   *   *   *   *

Richard Garrison, 64, looked exactly what he was: a kindly small town obstetrician. Grey-haired, handsome, he stood almost as tall as he had twenty years earlier, although he could no longer jump as high. He had given up recreational basketball a couple of years ago after the left knee followed the right one into arthroscopy. When the occasional storm chugged in from the Pacific, one or the other joint seemed to know in advance.

The doctor had finished a late breakfast, rinsed his dish and loaded it into the dishwasher, which was getting full. For some reason, he couldn't bring himself to run the machine half empty. It might have had something to do with his recent widowhood, but he didn't care to analyze it. He had watched his wife slowly rot from cancer. The reality of her illness – his knowledge as a physician - had been a cruel curse.

Last year, for the first time in his life, he had picked up an iron that wasn't a golf club. He figured out which was the washer and which the dryer, although he had no idea what many of the settings were for. He found he didn't mind ironing in front of the television. He watched more TV now than he cared to admit.

Garrison had been easing off from his practice, especially since he no longer was the only OB/GYN in town, and enjoyed his two rounds of golf per week. His score had settled into the comfortable mid-eighties range, with a 79 or two scattered in now and then to give him palpitations. He deluded himself that he was still quick as a bunny on the tennis court, but suspected he was more a tapir. He had scoffed at doubles in his salad days: now, that's all he and his tennis buddies played.

As he got into his Volvo SUV, he reflected on none of this, instead thinking about the upcoming cruise to Mexico he'd be taking in two weeks from Los Angeles. He was going to enjoy himself. He still had time to drop that annoying five extra pounds and brush up on his dance skills.

The drive from his home to the office normally took fewer than ten minutes, and much of the time he saw not a single vehicle until he was inside the town limits. The Garrison home was isolated at the end of a road that served a half dozen houses over a five mile stretch. As he rounded a bend at a comfortable thirty five miles per hour, he came upon a dark Suburban with a damaged front bumper and tape on the windscreen, flashers blinking. The vehicle appeared to have hit a tree. A young blond man stood in the middle of the road and waved his arms.

Garrison stopped his Volvo in the middle of the road and put the window down. The blond man leaned in.

"Help us, please! My wife's having a baby! I don't have a cell phone!"

"I'm a doctor," Garrison said. "Just a sec." Garrison looked over at the Suburban, but couldn't see anything through the dark windows. He pulled to the shoulder opposite, reached into the back seat for his black bag, and got out of the car.

"Over here!" the blond man said, waving Garrison to his Suburban. He opened the door and the doctor saw a woman in her thirties, with brown hair, in the back seat. She was breathing hard.

"How often are your contractions?" he asked.

Concentrating on the woman, he failed to notice as the blond man took a hypodermic syringe from his pocket, removed the cap, and came up behind. Swiftly, he yanked Doctor Garrison's neck in a chokehold.

"Aargh!" he cried, before his breath was cut off. The pain was intense.

The blond man plunged the needle into the physician's neck and pressed the plunger. Garrison felt a slow fire begin to spread, and then he felt nothing at all.

35

Harry Deutsch (D-NY), ranking member of the U.S. Senate Permanent Subcommittee on Investigations, wasn't hearing any of the testimony droning on from the staff witnesses. Terrorist financing was the agenda for the week. Again. He already knew all about the use of checks under ten thousand dollars each for phony automobile purchases, sent to car dealerships in the States through the Cayman Islands, manipulated to appear as if the funds were drawn on domestic banks. After all, Harry had made his money on Mercedes-Benz and BMW car dealerships in New York City. His uncle's car dealerships, technically. Well, actually, his uncle had made the money, but Harry's father had been his only heir.

Harry was familiar with the relationship between terrorist groups and certain charitable organizations, and how the charities always performed semi-legitimate functions to obfuscate their real purpose. This guy eating the microphone was describing the cross border complexities and legal difficulties in seizing laundered funds from U.S. correspondent banks in multi-jurisdictional settings.

For Christ's sake, they had gone over this stuff three years ago anyway.

Harry was an expert, he thought, and normally attentive, but today he was physically distressed, almost nauseated. The Senator had a tendency to sweat even without stress or physical exercise, an idiosyncrasy he hated but not enough to lose the fifteen extra pounds he lugged around. Well, thirty pounds. He suspected his wife hated it too, not that Harry was overly concerned with her emotional well-being. Right now his shirt was soaked, sticking to his skin. He had the helpless feeling that things were unraveling and there was nothing he could do about it.

When, in 2007, the United States minority population first exceeded one hundred million, Harry had known it was the death knell for the greatest country in the world, a toll that called him into action. After all, it was his Teutonic heritage. Foot washing stations at Phoenix Sky Harbor Airport, for Christ's sake. Illegal aliens crossing the Mexican border every day to go to U.S. public schools. Salsa outselling ketchup nationwide. The federal government permitting – no, *enforcing* - head scarves in Muskogee schools. Muskogee! A mongrel arrow straight into America's heartland. And on and on. Those minorities bred like fruit flies, with about the same intelligence, and decent white America, like his Baby Boomer generation, was going to disappear. Disappear, just like in Europe, rotted from within. France was the saddest example. Well, not on Harry's watch.

Someone was investigating the situations in Parkerville and Moon Valley. It was one thing to formulate a grand plan with other powerful men, pursue a vision of a better tomorrow, one without tacos and head scarves, but quite another when his compatriots turned out to be ruthless and prepared to act with swift finality. Harry thought himself street tough, having come up through the wards, but this was on another level. The risk meter had just pegged.

His messages to the Arab had not been answered. He needed to talk to him. The raghead had his own agenda, Harry knew, but they were all in this together.

Weren't they?

36

David and Leslie had crossed into California after stopping at a fast food restaurant for a late breakfast. Leslie wouldn't use the drive-through, having found too many of Derek's fossilized meals on the floor and under the seats. David continued to drive. Leslie noticed the countryside greening as the desert loosened its hold on the terrain.

"Do you think the break-in at your apartment has any connection with this?" she asked.

"I know it does," came the reply.

"Why?"

David adjusted the cruise control to 74 as the speed limit dropped to 65. "The cops showed up. I never called them. Said they got a call about a disturbance."

"Well, maybe that's true."

"Yeah, but about a half hour later this Detective Ryan came by. Said he was following up. Thing is, break-ins are about a dime a dozen in Atlanta."

"Maybe it was a slow night," Leslie said.

"He asked some interesting questions. It was like he was trying to find out what I knew. What I thought. If I'd look for anything specific to be missing. Anyway, I didn't tell him much. For instance, Thursday night's softball night, so normally I wouldn't have been home for another two hours. More, if we went for a couple of beers, which we usually do. But here's the thing. We only played one inning. Irrigation pipe broke and flooded the field."

Leslie frowned. "I don't know, David. Seems like a stretch."

"Well, see how elastic this is," David replied. "I asked him for his card – he said he didn't have one with him. I called Metro after he left. Detective Ryan just had his appendix out."

Leslie gasped. "Oh, shit," she said. A lifetime of relative normalcy made her struggle to get her mind around the increasingly sinister events. She kept wanting to push them away.

They rode in silence for a few minutes, passing into an area of low green hills. The Jeep passed a highway sign: Parkerville 4 miles. They rounded a bend. Leslie sat up sharply.

"Hey, what's this?" she exclaimed. A white Volvo SUV was off the side of the road, engine running. Someone was slumped over the wheel. A blond man was climbing into a Suburban, which was facing the same direction David and Leslie were traveling.

David slowed and pulled alongside. He noted the taped windscreen and bashed front bumper.

"That's our Suburban," he replied, jerking completely upright. A dark-haired woman was climbing over from the back seat. The blond man behind the wheel looked shocked when he saw David. He gunned the engine in reverse, spun around and sped off the other way.

"That man's hurt!" Leslie said as she looked at the Volvo. "Stop!"

David looked hard in the rear view mirror as he pulled the Jeep over. The truck had an Arizona plate, but he couldn't read the tag.

Leslie grabbed her medical bag and jumped from the Jeep as David called 911. Garrison was sweating heavily, unconscious and gasping. His thready pulse weakened as Leslie worked frantically to save her fellow obstetrician. David administered CPR. As he failed, his color turned blue, then gray.

Later, as Leslie oversaw two ambulance attendants loading the covered body into a flashing ambulance, David talked with two uniformed Parkerville police officers.

"Damn shame," said the cop whose ID read Officer Freitag. Both men were in their early twenties. He looked at his partner, Officer Jeffcoat.

"He must've – he was the only baby doc in town back then, wasn't he?" Jeffcoat asked.

"Yeah," said Freitag. The officer turned to David. "Great guy, he was. Delivered both of us, I guess. He'd help anybody who needed it."

"Coached my Little League team," Jeffcoat said. "I remember he had to leave in the middle of a playoff game to deliver a baby. We won that game."

David asked the cops, "Think they'll do an autopsy?"

The officers looked at each other. "I dunno," Freitag said. "I guess not." He waved his arm towards Leslie. "I mean, your doctor friend said it was a heart attack, right?"

As the attendants closed the ambulance doors, Leslie spoke to one of the EMTs. "The symptoms were consistent but I don't know if it was a heart attack. I'm an obstetrician. Another physician will have to examine him at the hospital to issue the death certificate."

The cops took down David and Leslie's contact information and brief statements. In a few minutes, everyone had gone and David drove the Jeep towards town. He looked over at his companion; her eyes were narrowed in thought.

"Not much further," he said.

"The medics thought it was a heart attack," Leslie said. She gazed out the window.

"I know."

"There were bruise marks on his neck. I looked for a puncture wound. Didn't see anything I could tell for sure," Leslie said. "Why didn't we want to tell the police what we knew?" she asked.

"Not yet," David replied. "We just needed to get the hell out of there. I think time may be working against us now. We'll call the coroner later, tell them what we suspect. We'll stay anonymous for time being."

"How did you know he was Doctor Garrison before we checked his wallet?"

"The medical plate on his car and the Suburban pretty much told me," David said.

Leslie shook her head slowly. "I've entered another world."

They drove on.

"David?"

"What?"

"I killed him with my phone call, didn't I? With my cell phone?"

David looked over at the obstetrician. "No, you didn't," he said.

Leslie stared out the window. "Yes, I did," she said softly.

The game had become deadly. It had only been a matter of time, David thought.

They topped a rise and the Jergens Laboratories complex came into view. To the right side, the parking lot was fairly full. They pulled up to the gatehouse, manned by a uniformed guard. David put the window down and noted the holstered weapon and the name of the private security firm on the man's jacket.

"Can I help you?" the guard asked. He appeared around fifty years old and in decent shape.

"Doctor Livingston for Doctor Ken Holliday," he said.

The guard consulted a list on his clipboard. "Okay, here we are. Can I get your name, ma'am?" he inquired.

"Doctor Riordan," Leslie said.

The guard handed them a parking pass and pointed to the lot. "Anywhere in the visitors' section," he said. He raised the gate and watched as David drove the Jeep slowly through and towards the parking lot. He returned to his booth and picked up a phone.

David turned to say something to Leslie, but she was staring out the window.

37

Sharif was becoming annoyed. The moans from the bedroom had persisted for several minutes now. He had already shut the door, kicking aside the *jallabia* that lay in the doorway, flecked with blood. White carpet had been a poor choice.

The American was panicking. His frantic message indicated elements of domestic intelligence were tracking a civilian inquiry into the G-11 disappearance. Sharif looked out over the calm waters of the Gulf and smiled to himself. So what? Did the cretin think the theft would have gone unnoticed? Did he not know even fools could be clever? Perhaps a quarter mile offshore, a *dhow* was sailing west to east, while beyond, a supertanker trekked across the horizon in the opposite direction. A perfect metaphor, he thought. It was of little import what, if anything, a few scientists flailing around chasing ghosts could uncover. The American would have to handle it. And if the trail began to lead overseas, he would deal with it himself: swiftly, decisively. The affair in the United States could succeed or fail, it wasn't really critical. For the American to expect anything from him showed the shallowness of the man. From that standpoint, at least, he had been a perfect choice.

He looked at his watch. Soon the aide would arrive to tidy things. She had been – he already thought of her in the past tense - tall and lithe, with long dark hair. She must have long dark hair; that was a condition. The aide knew exactly what he required. Above all, she must wear the *jallabia*. Yousif was expected to clean up any mess afterward, should things become - unclear. This had only happened once. It was the aide's business to discard the husk once the kernel had been removed. It could, on occasion, be complicated business. In London, she would be a Jewess, but that was of course impossible in Dubai, although this one, a Lebanese, had looked the part. For the Jewess to also wear the garment was a requisite. Some were surprised; most shrugged and a few, he could tell, enjoyed the concept. One had objected briefly until he enlightened her. It did not matter in the end, but their reactions added seasoning, shading, nuance.

He would play now, the Allegretto from Beethoven's Seventh. As a sensitive person, he sometimes wept as he progressed through the struggle and eventual triumph of the piece. In that manner he would not hear the moans, if they persisted. If he heard more sounds, he would have to enlighten her. He was not a sadist, of course, so he would complete the eight minute work if Yousif did not arrive before then. If he finished, well, then, it would be Allah's will.

38

The modern, expansive reception area of Jergens Laboratories hinted at federal grant money and the company's history of successful patents. The size of a tennis court, the ceiling rose two stories. Expensive art hung on the gray walls, a new addition since David's last visit. Outside in the circle, manicured rose bushes bloomed around the sparkling fountain. It was all so elegant, and it all belied the work done upstairs, David thought.

He and Leslie were seated in soft leather chairs to the side of the double glass doors. Roses of many colors, obviously cut daily, rested in a vase on the low glass table between them, filling the air with fragrance. In the center, behind a curved desk, a pretty blond receptionist in her twenties was busy typing on her keyboard. In a few moments, the door from a sweeping, curved staircase one floor above opened and Ken Holliday burst through. The big, exuberant scientist with flaming red hair bounded down the stairs and strode up with a big grin as David and Leslie stood.

"David! Hey, buddy! How the hell are you?!" He grabbed David in a bear hug and pounded him on the back before letting go.

David returned the grin. "Hi Ken! Backhand any better?"

"Worse!" came the reply. Ken turned to Leslie.

"He never was that good, just smart. He just kept hitting to my backhand!"

Leslie smiled politely, still stunned by the death she had witnessed. Ken was roly-poly soft, she noted as David introduced them. He probably didn't play much tennis or any other sport.

"Come on up," Ken said, waving them forward. He led them up the staircase and through the door.

Ken Holliday's laboratory was on the second floor, not far down the hallway. He sat behind a metal desk facing David and Leslie, who perched on stools. Journals, notebooks, beakers, printouts, a computer and various apparatus were everywhere. Shelving, jammed with the odds and ends of a working laboratory, stood in front of the windows, blocking the view. They all had coffee in Styrofoam cups. Ken listened to David's narrative, leaned back and expelled a breath.

"That's one hell of a story," he observed.

"That's just the summary, Ken," David said.

Ken shifted in his chair. "Well, it's a hell of a story for another reason, anyway."

David sipped his coffee. "What do you mean?"

"About two years ago, we were funded for a project that got assigned to me. If you'd have been here, I'm sure we'd have worked on it together. More coffee?"

David and Leslie shook their heads. The lab coffee hadn't improved since David left.

"Creepy habit, anyway. Project *Oeuvre*," Ken said.

"Project Egg?" David inquired.

"No, no, that's *oeuf*," Leslie remarked. "Egg is *oeuf*. *Oeuvre* means works."

"It does?" Ken asked. "I thought it means open."

"That's *ouvrir*," Leslie said.

David looked puzzled. "Works?"

"Like the works of an artist," Leslie replied.

Ken shrugged, then addressed his buddy. "Well, anyway, I don't know what it means. Remember the stuff we worked on? Race specific pathogens?"

"Yeah, sure," David said. "It's the same stuff I do at CDC."

Ken looked surprised. "Oh, really? I didn't know. Then you're probably aware of the German studies published two years ago."

David replied, "The alcohol study, sure. I reference it in my Indian study."

"What's the alcohol study?" asked Leslie.

Ken turned to Leslie. "Well, about five or six years ago they were able to turn white guinea pigs into alcoholics, brown ones alcohol-intolerant. Stuff like that. But the newer study is much more sophisticated."

"How?" Leslie asked.

"For one thing," Ken continued, "they used more complex animals. Different species of cats, for example. And a variety of addictive substances. Also, they advanced from addiction to reproduction. That's the stuff we've been working on."

Leslie and David looked at each other.

"You've been working on reproduction?" David asked slowly.

"Yeah. I mean, some other stuff too, but mainly reproduction. I thought that's why you called," Ken said.

David shook his head. "No, I didn't know that. Is this a sponsored study?"

"Yeah."

"Who?" David asked.

"Who else?"

"Uncle Sam," Leslie said.

Ken turned to the obstetrician. "Of course. In fact, it requires a pretty high security clearance. Which I kind of forgot about in our conversation here."

David hefted his cooler up and plopped it down on Ken's desk.

"Here are the samples," he said.

Ken nodded. Leslie had never thought her job delivering babies was mundane, but now it seemed like another life. Now she was – what? – down the rabbit hole, spinning through events that were happening faster than her ability to comprehend their meaning. Curiouser and curiouser, she thought. Still rocked by the murder of Doctor Garrison, the thought of her own personal danger hadn't really registered with her. Not yet.

39

Emily Painter loved her job; children were a joy. Derek Riordan was one of her favorite students at the Little Tots Preschool. Maybe a little too energetic, she thought; he had his mother's curiosity and ready smile. The soft spot for Derek was in part due to the fact that Emily knew the boy's father had died. Leslie Riordan had delivered Jeffrey Painter four months before giving birth to Derek, and the two were in Emily's class. The boys played well together. An additional benefit of teaching at Little Tots was free tuition for her son. She had just learned she was pregnant again and Leslie would be taking a sonogram soon. Did she want to know the sex? Emily wasn't sure.

The class was at recess; eighteen of her charges were romping through the fenced playground. Two of the girls were out sick. Emily hoped it wasn't something that would spread throughout the school. Derek, Jeffrey and two other children were in the tree house, taking turns on the slide. Today, recess was at the end of the morning and dismissal was in thirty minutes. One car was already parked across the street, where the mothers usually lined up ten to fifteen minutes before school let out. It was not a vehicle she recognized. In fact, the dented SUV was peculiar. For one thing, the windscreen was taped. For another, the windows were tinted way too dark. It was illegal under Arizona law to have opaque windows – allowing less than a third of the light through – a cause Emily had campaigned for along with law enforcement, other teachers and parents. Something didn't feel right.

She unclipped the pager from her belt. Mrs. Whitney, Head of School, should be apprised.

Minutes later, Emily saw Mrs. Whitney exit the front door and walk across the street to the SUV. The driver's window went down and she glimpsed a blond man behind the wheel and a dark haired woman in the passenger seat. They spoke for perhaps a minute. Evidently things were on the up and up, because Mrs. Whitney nodded, turned and went back across the street and into the school.

40

The trio went to lunch in the Jergens cafeteria, located on the ground floor behind the reception area.   Leslie and Ken unloaded their trays while David paid the cashier.

"How long have you known my friend?" Ken asked.

Leslie lifted her fish plate to the table and sat down. "Seems like years, but really it's only - a few weeks?" How weird, she thought. Her life before meeting the scientist/sleuth seemed a distant past. How much of it was the mayhem she had experienced, she couldn't say. Was she getting hooked on adrenaline? Or just David Livingston?

David arrived, unloaded his tray and sat down.

"Still the cheapest food in town, I see," David said.

Ken turned to Leslie. "And the lousiest."

"So what do you think?" Leslie asked Ken as she cut her fish.

Ken ruminated over a bite of his meatball submarine. "Well, I don't know what to think. I can't believe this is our stuff, but then again, it's government, so who knows what the hell they're doing with it?"

"When can we get on the electron microscope?" David asked. "We'd like to stick around if you can do it today."

Ken smiled. "Hey, we got funding up the wazoo. We'll do it right after lunch."

It took a good hour of delicate and tedious work to prepare the specimens. Finally, the samples were ready.   Ken sat at a console fiddling with dials, keypad and video screen. David and Leslie stood behind watching the scientist work.

"Leslie, know much about these devices?" Ken asked over his shoulder.

"Only from med school," she replied, "and that's a while ago."

"They've progressed light years in the past few years. I have to learn new techniques couple times a year. This is a state of the art S E M. The images are three dimensional."

"Why do they take so long to prep?" Leslie asked.

"They've got to be dried in a special way so they don't shrivel up. Since the photograph is really made with electrons, they've got to conduct electricity. It's called sputter coating."

An image appeared on the screen. David and Ken craned forward.

"This is a blood sample from an African-American woman at the migrant camp in Moon Valley," Ken said.

"Okay," David acknowledged.

"Jesus Christ," Ken said.

"I see it."

"What?" asked Leslie. She couldn't make heads or tails out of the image.

The lab door opened. Two burly security guards in uniform and side arms appeared in the doorway. One spoke.

"Doctors, will you come with us please?"

The trio looked at each other. The second guard hooked his thumb on his belt, fingers resting on the holster cover.

"*Now*, please."

*　　　*　　　*　　　*　　　*

The décor in Dr. Jergens' corner office was another eloquent testament to the string of lucrative medical patents owned by his firm. Original oils graced the walls, more traditional than the works in the lobby. A large, ornate Philippine mahogany desk rested on deep, light blue burber carpet. Behind the desk, custom silk drapes framed the large window overlooking the manicured grounds.

Stainless steel and glass objects, artistic renditions of ordinary lab apparatus, rested on the cocktail table grouped with a leather couch and matching chairs. The two guards ushered David, Ken and Leslie inside and closed the door as they withdrew.

Behind the desk, Willard Jergens, the sixty two year old CEO, stood and buttoned his jacket. He cut an impressive figure, with his grey hair and expensive suit. He could appear in ads for his company, Leslie thought. Seated in one of the leather chairs was another man, perhaps forty, in an off the rack suit. Neither Ken nor David would know the difference in the clothing, she knew. To Leslie, the man had a slightly oily appearance. He remained seated.

"Well, we meet at last," Doctor Jergens said, looking at David and Leslie.

"Sir, we met at the company picnic last year," Ken volunteered.

"Of course," said the CEO, "I mean Doctor Riordan. I remember you, Doctor Livingston, very well. One of our brighter bulbs. Please, sit down. I'm Willard Jergens."

David hesitated, weighing whether to make a move with no guards present or wait and learn what he could.

Jergens gestured toward the seating area. "Please. I'm sorry if your escort seemed a bit . . . heavy handed."

After a moment, they all sat. Doctor Jergens folded his hands on top of his desk. "I've been following your travels with a great deal of interest," he said.

"You have?" David asked.

"Oh, yes," Jergens replied. "From day one, actually. When you first got the call from Doctor Riordan."

David, momentarily surprised, realized he shouldn't have been. "How did you know about that?"

"Aah, well, it's not a concern. Tell me, what have you deduced?"

The three glanced at each other. No one said anything for a few moments.

"Oh, come now," urged Jergens. "Surely we're past game playing, aren't we?"

"All right," David said, "who's this?" He indicated the man in the chair, who spoke for the first time.

"The name's Smith," Smith said.

"Do go on, Doctor Livingston," said Jergens.

David leaned back in his chair. It was very comfortable. "Parkerville and Moon Valley. No ethnic pregnancies for over four months. Is that a good start?"

It was Jergens' turn to smile. "Very good start. Coffee?"

Heads shook no.

David continued. "Project *Oeuvre*. Your turn."

Smith piped up. "It's a federal project, Doctor. Highly sensitive. You can appreciate why."

"You're selectively breeding. How'd you do it, reservoir? Aerosol?" David asked.

Smith crossed his legs as he regarded the trio with some amusement. "Both, actually," he said. "Parkerville, we used the water. We sprayed the migrant camp at Moon Valley. It's vital to know the best method of delivery."

David nodded. "Of course." Something caught his eye and he glanced outside. The crimson helicopter sparkled in the California sunlight. The grass looked like a fairway. It was all so pretty.

Ken was incredulous. "Wait a minute, I'm slow. You've been using my research to *stop* pregnancies along ethnic lines?"

It was Jergens' turn to answer. "Not just your research, doctor. But yes."

A moment passed.

"Why?" David asked.

"Isn't it obvious?" replied Jergens.

Smith shifted impatiently in his seat. "Let's cut to the chase. We'd like you to help us, Doctor Livingston. We'd like to move along at a faster pace."

Leslie found her voice. "This is monstrous," she said.

"Know something, doctor," Smith said. "The end product is not for manipulating our own population or that of our friends. It's a weapon, like any other, for our arsenal. And the beauty of it is, it doesn't kill anyone."

"I want to say you're not serious, but I know you are," Leslie said with intensity.

Dr. Jergens spoke soothingly. "Look, the effects are reversible, anyway."

"Reversible?" Leslie echoed.

"Let's take India, for example," Jergens continued. "China. Wouldn't they and the rest of the world benefit if they took a rest, if I can put it that way, for a few years? Or look at our strategic enemies. The North Koreans, for example. They'd just . . . fade away. Isn't this a more humane weapon than a nuclear warhead?"

Leslie was more than taken aback. "I can't imagine—"

David interrupted. "I didn't think of it in that light. Maybe because the whole thing seemed so – surreptitious, I guess. But of course everything needed to be secret." He paused, shifted in his chair. "We need to think about this, Doctor Jergens, Mister Smith. If this could be an alternative to weapons of mass destruction, then maybe—I dunno—"

Leslie whirled. "David!"

"All I'm saying is we need to weigh all the ramifications. Ken?"

The portly scientist was slack-jawed. "I'm still in shock, I guess. I don't know."

"Listen," said Mr. Smith, "Why don't you talk this over amongst yourselves? We'll take you to a private area."

The door opened and the two security guards entered. There must have been a buzzer somewhere, Leslie thought.

Smith looked at his watch. "We'll discuss this again at, say four o'clock? You'll have lots of questions. By the way, we're very well funded on this. We really can use your help."

Leslie looked up at the burly guards. They didn't look friendly. "We can find our own way," she said.

"Oh, no, they'll escort you," said Smith. "Things are already set up."

There didn't seem to be much choice. Leslie, Ken and David stood up and filed out. The guards followed, closing the door behind them.

Jergens leaned back. "They didn't buy it, I think."

"Of course they didn't," said Smith. "You know what to do."

Jergens was visibly taken aback. "What? What do you mean?"

Smith eyed the scientist coldly. "You know exactly what I mean," he said evenly.

"We can't just – they've got friends – how would we explain—"

"Simple," came the response. "They were in the containment lab and there was an accident."

Jergens was horrified. "Is that where they're going?"

It was Smith's turn to lean back. He cocked his head. "You surprise me, Doctor Jergens. We've already been down this road."

41

Detective-Second Grade Harris Mulvaney looked at the drawing sitting on the desk in front of him. Actually, the drawing was on top of a mess of papers that had been growing ever taller. Mulvaney hadn't seen the surface of his desk in months; he was afraid to look at what might be buried in the pile of department memos, circulars, pay stubs, safety bulletins and God knew what else. He was no artist and so his partner, Detective-Second Grade Milt Levin, had duplicated the writing on the bottom of the jug. He hadn't even needed to trace it. Mulvaney couldn't believe there wasn't a single Arab cop in the 77th precinct, but apparently law enforcement wasn't high on the Islamic agenda. He had done the simplest thing and faxed Levin's paper to the Research & Reference desk of the Brooklyn Public Library, with a cover note saying a translation was urgent police business. Of course, they hadn't gotten back to him. He'd have to haul the damn thing over there, most likely. He could probably just flag down any taxi and show it to the driver, for that matter. If there was a cab to be found on Union Avenue.

And now his stomach was bothering him. Once again Levin had talked him into the sausage, onion and peppers sub from the vendor on Union Avenue. Once again, he was glad he wasn't out in the field after eating the damn thing. Come to think of it, the vendor looked like an Arab. Maybe he should take the drawing outside and let the guy look at it. He looked over at Levin, happily checking the

NBA scores from last night, having bet on the Knicks. Nothing bothered Levin's stomach.

"Hey, Milt," he said. His partner looked up. "That vendor guy. What do you think he is?"

"Ha! Knicks beat the Sixers 104-89. I told you to give the spread. Whadja say?"

Mulvaney repeated the question.

Levin frowned. "What do you mean? He's a vendor, for Chrissake. He's the sausage guy."

"No, I mean, what is he? Think he's an Arab? He looks like an Arab."

"He's probably a Jew," Levin said. "We all look alike."

"Jews look like Arabs sometimes."

"See if he shortchanged you. That'll tell you," Levin said.

"I'm gonna see," Mulvaney said. He picked up the drawing and headed for the door.

"Lunch says he's a Jew," Levin said. "A raghead wouldn't have kosher hot dogs on the truck."

"A Jew wouldn't have lamb kabobs."

"A Jew would have anything he could sell," Levin said.

"Besides, we already ate lunch, if that's what it was."

"Tomorrow's lunch."

"No bet."

"Five bucks says he can't read that writing," Levin said. "He probably can't read anything. He's probably illiterate anyway."

"Then I'll know he's Irish," Mulvaney said as he walked out. First, he was going to have to stop in the head, he realized.

Ten minutes later, Mulvaney wished he had taken both bets.

42

David took in his surroundings: gauging, thinking, looking for the exits. The group of five was up on the fifth floor. As they approached the steel staging area door, Leslie's eyes grew wide. Ken looked confused. Only David seemed composed as he quickly constructed an action sequence. The guards' weapons were holstered. Mentally, he whirled and slammed the nearest—

Two more uniformed security personnel appeared, weapons drawn but at their sides. They took up positions several feet away. There were no viable options, David realized. One of the guards pressed buttons on the keypad and they heard the click of tumblers unlocking. Leslie had started to protest when she followed David's gaze to the drawn pistols. She paled at the sight.

They moved single file through the staging area. As David had expected, the guards opened the airlock to the containment area and gestured them through. Ken seemed befuddled, perhaps in shock. Leslie's eyes darted everywhere as they entered. The large room, twenty four feet square, held a lab table, equipment of various kinds, benches and, along the far wall, a series of empty stainless steel cages. Most of the cages were four feet square; a few were smaller. The ceiling looked to be perhaps twelve feet high with a large ventilator grille at its center.

Ken whirled when the airlock door closed behind them.

"We're locked in!" he cried.

"Of course," David replied matter-of-factly as he explored the room.

"You weren't really serious about entertaining their proposal, right? You were just buying us time, weren't you?" Leslie asked.

David nodded. "They weren't selling."

Ken's mouth was open as he slowly gazed around. He wandered here and there, idly picking up lab equipment, putting it down.

"There's going to be an accident, isn't there, David?" Leslie said.

"An accident?" Ken repeated.

"Yes," David replied.

Ken's jaw dropped.

"How else can they solve their problem?" David said. "Afterward, there's going to be suspicion, and an investigation, but it'll all stand up."

Leslie examined everything quickly. She seemed to have shifted into a higher gear. She approached a reinforced door at the far end of the room.

"But they said!" Ken exclaimed. "It's just a weapons project. They wanted us to help them!"

David gave Ken a look as Leslie tried the door unsuccessfully and twirled the built-in combination lock.

"No," said David, as he felt the door's surface; it was cold. A refrigerated room containing pathogens, he was sure.

"What?" Ken's eyes were huge; he was sweating.

"No, it's not what they said. Think about it. Experimenting on our own population? How many deaths so far? Doesn't add up."

There was a heavy silence. Finally, Ken spoke.

"You're right," he said.

David had picked up a pair of crucible tongs from the floor and was trying to jam them into the fitting around one of the large glass panes to the staging area, without success. "We don't have much time."

Leslie was looking up at the ceiling.

"Okay," she said, nodding, in a determined voice. "I've got an idea."

"Do I know where this is going?" David asked.

"Up." She pointed to the large louvered vent cover in the ceiling. "Ventilator shafts," she said. "They've got to be fairly large for a containment area, don't they?"

"Well, yeah, sure, I guess," said Ken.

Leslie moved to the lab table and swept everything off in a single motion. Glass shattered on the floor, startling Ken.

"Come on," she said, "let's move the table."

The trio grabbed the table and tried to lift it. Nothing. David looked underneath.

"Bolted down. Maybe we can—"

"The cages! Quick!" Leslie exclaimed. They hustled to the row of cages and pushed two of them to the center of the room. It was a difficult job.

"We've got to stack them!" Leslie exclaimed. "Right under the vent!"

Ken and David shoved one of the cages directly under the vent, then tried to pick up the other. They grunted as they lifted the second cage; it wobbled unsteadily.

"Christ, these are heavy," Ken said.

"Stainless steel," David said. "Heave!"

They managed to catch a corner on top of the first cage, and then slid the top cage into position, centered over the one under it.

"David! How much time do you think we've got?" Ken asked.

"Well, it's not a normal procedure, is it? They'll have to get the pathogen, aerosol it – unless they already prepared for this, maybe ten, fifteen minutes."

As he spoke, Leslie climbed up the cages with ease and stood on top.

"How the hell'd you do that?" Ken asked.

"That's what she does on weekends," David said.

Leslie reached up and yanked the louver under the ventilation shaft. The retaining clip broke; the louver came loose and clattered to the top of the cage, then fell to the floor. Leslie looked up the shaft.

"There's other stuff in the way here," she said, craning to identify the obstruction.

"Probably baffles and micron screens for containment," David said.

Leslie stood on tiptoe. "Wait a sec. I think I can get it," she said, reaching up and yanking something from inside the shaft. A baffle fell out, clattered through the cage bars and landed inside. A micron screen followed.

"That's it," she said. "Now I can see. Goes up maybe two feet, then branches off. To the main shaft, I guess. Seems wide enough."

"You gotta be kidding," Ken said.

Leslie looked down at the pudgy researcher, thought for a moment. "We need another cage. There's a smaller one in the corner there." She pointed to a three by three cage. "We can reach the main shaft then." Leslie slithered down to help.

Inside David's head, a clock was ticking. Moving quickly, they dragged the smaller cage to the center of the room and hoisted it atop the other two.

Leslie clambered up like a monkey and centered the smaller cage, lining it up with the shaft. She jumped on top.

The ceiling was now lower than her full height. She ducked under and straightened inside the vent shaft, which was perhaps three feet square. Her legs disappeared, following her torso as she clambered up.

"Okay, I'm in the shaft. Come on up," her voice echoed.

Suddenly the distant sound of an air compressor starting up and running penetrated the room.

43

Three floors below, Willard Jergens, Ph.D., felt as though all the air had left his office. His armpits were clammy. He was going to ruin a custom shirt. Smith had left fifteen minutes ago, presumably to arrange the containment lab "accident". How could things have gotten so far out of control? Who on his payroll would do such a thing? He realized he wasn't really a hands-on manager. He wasn't even sure who really controlled his own security force. Their personnel had multiplied with the G-11 contract, but he didn't remember okaying the increase. The uniforms were everywhere, it seemed. Like those armed guards that had brought the three doctors to his office – he had never seen them before. And when had they been issued weapons anyway?

These doctors were not criminals or terrorists. Two of them had worked at Jergens and the third delivered babies, for Christ's sake. Plus she was a hell of a lot better looking than his own secretary, even. Maybe, with more time, he could convince them the G-11 program was for everyone's betterment. Everything but this seemed to be going well; the plan was working. He was sure they would see the light, without Smith or armed security about. That was certainly off-putting. He had persuaded Appropriations Committees and government agencies; surely he could talk to these scientists. They seemed reasonable enough.

Did that slippery Senator know about this deal? Maybe he'd better call Deutsch. Sure, each had scratched the other's back.

Deutsch had steered a deal or two his way, and had influenced the G-11 contract, but he'd gotten paid, and damned well.

He'd best get him on the phone right now. He had the guy's cell number. There wasn't much time. Smith was, now that he thought about it, the next thing to a psychopath. Why hadn't he seen it before?

It never occurred to Willard Jergens that anyone could have tapped his phone line, and that his call to Senator Deutsch was monitored in the main security office of Jergens Laboratories.

44

In the containment lab, David and Ken looked at each other as they stood next to the stack of cages.

"We'd better hurry," David said.

"You first," Ken urged.

David grabbed the cage and tried to climb, but his hands kept slipping down the smooth bars. The stack wobbled.

"Shove the second cage sideways to make a ledge!" Leslie yelled. "Offset it a little!"

It seemed to make sense. Ken and David tried to follow Leslie's suggestion, but the middle cage would barely move with the extra weight of the top cage. They had to pull, straining and heaving to creating a foot wide skirt. Now David was able to get his foot on top of the first cage and, by grabbing the bars, stand on it. The structure wobbled further as he did so. Despite the instability, it wasn't too difficult to make it to the top of the second cage, which had a much wider ledge.

"Good, David, good!" Leslie exclaimed. "Now the rest of the way!"

David moved the smaller cage directly under the shaft again and hoisted himself on top as it threatened to upend. He ducked under the shaft opening and stood straight. Only his legs were visible from the floor.

"Okay, Ken!" he yelled.

Ken's eyes were large with fright. He started to climb, but had a great deal more difficulty. He fell with a heavy thump before he could make it atop the bottom cage.

Leslie's voice came down from the shaft. "You all right?"

"Yeah," Ken replied. Desperately, he pulled himself up and finally made it to the top of the first cage. Sweat poured off his brow. He stood on the ledge, petrified as the unsteady structure wobbled with his efforts. He grabbed the bars atop the second cage and tried to hoist himself up.

Suddenly, the pile toppled with a tremendous crash. Ken hit the floor hard again as David's legs, now unsupported, dangled in the air, sticking out of the shaft.

"I gotcha!" Leslie exclaimed. "Come on, climb!"

David's legs flailed as he grabbed for purchase, then suddenly disappeared as he hoisted himself onto his elbows on the floor of the intersecting horizontal shaft. Below, Ken slowly got to his feet and watched David crawl to safety. David's voice echoed down into the room.

"Ken!" he yelled.

"Yeah, buddy," came the response.

"I'll come back down!"

"No, you won't," Ken said. "I can't lift these cages by myself and you'd just break a leg jumping down." It was probably true. There was no way for David to fall twelve feet without risking serious injury.

"Besides, there's no time," Ken said. His voice was flat.

"We're not gonna just leave you!" David exclaimed.

"Listen, my chances are better if you get your ass moving and try to open this door from the other side."

"He's right," Leslie said to David.

"We'll hurry!" David yelled. "Good luck, Ken!"

"It's you gonna need the luck. Go!" Ken urged.

The horizontal shaft, like its vertical component, was perhaps three feet wide. Leslie began to crawl, David behind. There was little light. The shaft was either well-reinforced or rested on a solid structure, as the aluminum barely sagged as they moved along.

A hissing noise from behind.

"Oh, shit." Ken's voice was muffled. "David?"

"Move!" David said. Leslie sped up.

From behind, coughing.

Leslie hesitated. "David, was that-?"

"No. He's all right."

The shaft seemed to be angling down. She reached another opening. "There's no screen. Hard to tell through the louvers, but it looks like maybe a utility closet."

"That's what we need," from behind.

Leslie wedged herself in the vertical shaft and eased downward. She kicked hard; the louvered vent clattered to the floor below.

"David!" she whispered loudly.

"What?"

David crawled to the edge and looked down at Leslie, wedged in the shaft.

"It's less of a drop!" she exclaimed. "We must have been angling down a little. Just have to miss that mop bucket."

She disappeared. David heard a thump.

He cupped his hands over his mouth. "You all right?" he whispered.

"Well, you don't have to whisper after that," Leslie said. "Come on down. I'll move this crap out of the way."

David reached across the shaft and balanced himself with his hands as he lowered his legs into the shaft. He tried to wedge himself as Leslie had done, but suddenly slipped and fell directly to the floor. Fortunately, he landed on his feet, tumbling sideways onto a pile of rags.

"Ow!" He grabbed his ankle.

"Are you okay?" Leslie asked.

David flexed his foot and nodded. He stood up and looked around the small closet. A little light filtered through the vented door; he found a light switch and clicked it on. There were shelves stacked with janitorial equipment and supplies and a wheeled cart to one side.

"Let's see what we've got," he said, rummaging around. He reached for a container of bleach.

Leslie clutched at his arm.

"We've got to hurry. Ken—" She left the thought unfinished.

David turned; their eyes met. Her hand went slowly to her open mouth.

"Oh. Oh, no. Oh my God."

"I'm sorry, too," David said. "He was my friend."

45

At the Little Tots Preschool, things were definitely not on the up and up, Mrs. Whitney concluded after speaking with the couple in the SUV.

"Excuse me," she had said, "can I help you? I'm Mrs. Whitney, Head of School."

"We're here to pick up a student," the man replied.

"Who would that be?"

The dark haired woman leaned across. "Doctor Riordan is my cousin. She asked me to take her son home today. She's out of town. Are we early?"

"Yes. They're not due out for awhile."

Mrs. Whitney had not wanted to pin down the dismissal time. As she walked back across the street, she knew something was wrong. Every parent knew the school would not release a child to an unknown person without written consent. Doctor Riordan had expressly instructed at the beginning of the year that only she, Naomi or her sister Caroline could pick up Derek. She entered the building and went straight to her office and picked up the phone.

*　　　　*　　　　*　　　　*　　　　*

Moon Valley Deputy Sheriff Daryl Phillips had been on the job eight months. He loved his work and took his responsibilities very seriously. Sheriff Winfield had let the young lawman arrange his schedule to allow night classes at the junior college. Winfield put him in a cruiser two months ago, and told him he could take the vehicle home at night after a year's employment. Daryl looked forward to the day the cop car would sit in his driveway, even though he still lived at home. His younger brother had pestered him for rides and, despite feigning annoyance, Daryl had been proud to let Jamie ride along on two occasions. It was technically illegal but he had bent the rules. He could always let his brother off if something serious arose. Daryl had handled a few routine calls during those shifts and felt his brother's admiring gaze.

Less than two minutes after Mrs. Whitney had phoned the sheriff's office, Daryl had gotten the call from dispatch and driven over to the Little Tots' Preschool on Linden Lane. As he pulled up behind the Suburban he noted two violations: the damaged windscreen and dark tinted windows. He started to enter the license plate into his computer when his radio crackled. An eighteen wheeler had swerved to avoid another vehicle over on Grove and taken out a utility pole. Live wires were down.

Deputy Phillips lit up the cruiser, wheeled around and sped off towards Grove. He arrived within minutes and began to police the scene. The wires sparked and crackled as the pole, not fully down, wavered unsteadily. The driver of the semi had managed to jump out and dart across the street unharmed. The car causing the accident had failed to stop, but was located minutes later outside the beauty shop on Somerset Road. Its driver, Mrs. June Laney, was inside getting her hair done and claimed to know nothing about what had happened. After interviewing two witnesses, she was cited for careless driving and leaving the scene. It was a full two hours before the accident was cleared and repair crews replaced the utility pole and restored power to a twelve block area.

A thorough officer, Phillips checked back with Little Tots Preschool regarding the damaged vehicle waiting outside. Mrs. Whitney repeated the conversation with its occupants and told

Deputy Phillips her concerns. She said that Mrs. Painter had seen the SUV drive off as soon as Daryl's cruiser had left Little Tots. No, she hadn't gotten a license number, but with that dent and broken windscreen it shouldn't be too hard to find, should it?

Deputy Phillips wrote up the incident and mentioned it to Sheriff Winfield. The lawman nodded thoughtfully and told Daryl it was important enough to put on the screens of all the deputies. The SUV was not seen again.

46

Leslie leaned heavily against the wall while David poked through the utility closet.

"We're on borrowed time, Leslie. As soon as they check the containment room they'll see the vent. Take a peek outside."

Leslie took a breath and composed herself. She turned the knob and opened the door a crack. She saw an empty hallway.

"All clear," she said. "What are you doing?"

David replied, "Lots of times there's household chemicals, cleaning products, stuff like that. You can make things."

"Make things? What things?"

"Say, like an impact grenade."

"You're a chemist, too?" Leslie asked.

"Well, high school. That's where you learn that stuff. Anyway, there's no time. Come on. "

Leslie thought back. She had never learned anything like that in high school. Who *was* this guy? Before she could contemplate the question further, he took her hand and they slipped out the door.

David led her quickly down the hallway past rows of doors. Some were marked, some not. A few were locked. Several had small windows in the doors; they were various small laboratories. David peeked inside the unlocked and unmarked doors as they went.

"What are you looking for?" Leslie asked.

"It's somewhere around here, I remember . . ."

He had opened a door and saw what he was looking for. He guided Leslie inside and followed. They had entered a combination locker and shower room. David moved quickly and starting opening lockers. In a few moments he had extracted two lab coats, both with Jergens employee picture I.D.s attached.

"Put this on," he told Leslie.

"Who would leave their I.D. badges on?" she asked as she donned the white coat.

"Just read their names and you'll know," David replied, buttoning his.

Leslie looked at the badge on her coat. Margaret Carella was pretty enough, if careless, but looked nothing like Leslie.

"This'll never work," she said, staring at the image of the dark-haired woman in her fifties. "Besides, your coat's too small."

"Sure it will, you'll see. Come on, we've got one stop to make."

They came to a bank of elevators. David pushed the down button. A moment later, two young male technicians in similar dress came around the hallway from the other direction.

Leslie' breath quickened as her heart picked up speed again. She turned slightly away to hide her identification badge. David smiled and nodded at the pair; they smiled back. All four waited for the elevator in silence. They looked away, as strangers do.

Except the younger technician. He was openly eyeing Leslie.

"Hi, haven't seen you around. I'm Mike Lampart." He stuck out his hand.

"Hi," Leslie said, smiling a dazzling smile. She almost said she was Margaret Carella, but maybe this guy knew Margaret. As she shook hands, she put her left hand to her throat, hiding her badge. Lampart was obviously trying to read her name.

David stepped in front of Leslie and stuck out his hand. "Hey, Mike. Working hard?"

Lampart couldn't hide his annoyance. He grunted in reply, never looking at David. About three years went by, it seemed. No elevator showed up, although they could hear the motor whining and the car clacking below.

"Going to the picnic this weekend?" Lampart pressed. His partner impatiently hit the down button, although already lit.

"Maybe," Leslie said. "Not if it's like the last one."

"I know what you mean," Lampart said, smiling – no, he was beaming. "I must have had too much beer, because I don't remember you." He tried to edge around David.

"You did have too much beer," Leslie said.

Finally the doors opened and they entered the car. Leslie was relieved they all faced the front so no one could read her badge. David pressed the button for the second floor. Why are we going to two, Leslie wondered? She just wanted to get the hell out of there. The doors opened and they left the technicians.

Lampart's voice floated out the doors as they closed. "See you Saturday."

David looked around. "Aah," he said, "it's this way."

She only recognized Ken's lab when David opened the door and they stepped inside. He moved quickly to Ken's desk and opened drawers. One had a steel cover and what appeared to be a substantial lock. Leslie watched as Ken rifled through Ken's top drawer and withdrew something she thought might have been a paper clip. He went to work on the lock. In a moment the top was open; David reached in, took out and held up two bound notebooks. Leslie looked at them.

"What are those?" she asked.

"Ken's research notes," David replied.

"Did you learn to open locks in high school, too?" Leslie asked.

"Aah, you know," he said, brushing off the question. Leslie looked at him.

"I took some lessons from a magician," David amplified. He shrugged, "Anybody could have gotten in there."

No they couldn't, Leslie was certain.

She peered at David's badge as he stuffed the notebooks in his waistband, in back, like a waiter.

"This is a black guy. On your badge. It's a black guy!"

"Equal opportunity employer."

"This'll never work," she said.

"Nobody ever looks," David said as he ushered Leslie out the door and towards the bank of elevators.

In a few moments, the doors opened and they stepped onto an empty elevator. David pushed the button marked L1.

"The basement?" Leslie asked, as they descended.

The elevator doors opened; David and Leslie stepped out into an underground parking garage. David took her arm and steered her left along the rear wall.

"I'm pretty sure they keep the utility trucks down here," he said. They hurried along the perimeter. As they turned the corner, a row of windowless white vans with the Jergens logo came into view. Leslie trotted to the first van and tried the door. It was locked. She moved to the next van in line.

"Forget it, they'll all be locked," David said. He took a large red fire extinguisher from the wall.

"Can you open this?" After seeing David pick the lock on Ken's drawer, she half thought he could. She turned to see him approach, carrying the heavy canister.

David hefted the cylinder. "I think so. Back up a step," he said, and as she did so he crashed the extinguisher into the passenger window. The noise was loud, echoing throughout the garage. The glass shattered, but held together. David pushed hard and the webbed glass fell inside. He reached in and opened the door as Leslie looked around, but saw no one.

"Come on, let's go," he said. Leslie jumped in. David moved swiftly around to the driver's door while she reached over and unlocked it. He got in, still holding the extinguisher.

"What are you going to do with that?" she asked.

David climbed in the truck, put the extinguisher between the front seats and rummaged around in the back.

"Spray the guard at the gate if I have to," he replied. Leslie heard him say "Aah," as he found a battered toolbox. In a moment, he hopped back in the driver's seat carrying a large screwdriver and a small hammer. Leslie watched as he quickly jammed open the steering column, smashed the key mechanism to reveal the rotation switch, and manually started the truck. The engine came to life.

Leslie looked at David. Little surprised her anymore, it seemed. She glanced back toward the elevator. The doors remained closed.

"No one's following us yet," she said.

"It won't take them long. We've got to get through the gate first." David didn't mention the uniformed guard's sidearm.

He drove out of the garage and proceeded at thirty miles per hour toward the guardhouse. As he slowed for the barrier, Leslie found herself holding her breath until the gate went up automatically. David waved at the guard, who waved back. He glanced in the rear view mirror; the guard had picked up his phone. Was he dialing? Answering?

But they were through.

Once out of sight, David stepped on the gas until he was clipping along at sixty five. Leslie picked up glass from the shattered passenger window and tossed the pieces in back. She looked at the mangled steering column as they sped along the two lane road.

"You're a car thief, too?" she said.

David shrugged. "This is a truck."

Silence. She did not acknowledge his quip. In truth, David felt about as grim as Leslie must, he guessed, but he knew she would have had no frame of reference in her entire life for what had just happened. She had performed remarkably, saving their lives, but as the adrenaline wore off she could crash. He kept an eye on her as he drove.

David Livingston had that frame of reference, but he wasn't as confident or as nonchalant as he hoped he appeared. They had come within a whisker of getting killed, and his friend *had* been killed, gassed to death in the containment room. But he was an experienced operative, having acquired the soldier's skill at keeping his emotions in check when there was a task at hand.

The glass fragments on the floor sparkled as Leslie picked them up. It was a gorgeous sunny afternoon. It seemed so incongruous, she thought. The whole world was having an everyday normal afternoon, just another ordinary workday, and she was – not.

"It's a beautiful day. You'd almost think this was—normal," she said, tossing the last pieces in back.

"Good thing it's not raining, because there's no glass in your window," David said, in another weak attempt to lighten the situation. He looked over; she was staring out the window, biting her lip. He glanced in the side view mirror. The road was still clear.

Leslie gazed out the opening, unseeing. After a time, she muttered to herself. "Well, I guess we're not in Kansas anymore."

David knew he needed to get her mind working in a productive way. "Listen, it won't be long before they figure this out," he said. "We've got to ditch this van."

"I wonder if I'll get my Jeep back," she said. Suddenly, she let out an involuntary sob. David reached over and patted her shoulder. Leslie tilted her head back against the headrest and closed her eyes.

"Oh, my God. Everybody I meet in the last week winds up dead and I'm worrying about my car," she said.

David comforted her. "It's a natural reaction. I know this seems all insane."

Leslie opened her eyes and inclined her head towards David.

"Doesn't this seem insane to you?"

"Yeah, sure," he said, but not very convincingly, she thought.

"But you're so calm."

"Am I? It's a good front, I guess." Whether it was the truth or not didn't matter. He had a job to do, and he couldn't fail: end of story. He smiled and patted her with, he hoped, some reassurance.

"Seems like days since I talked to Derek, but it was this morning," Leslie said. "So much has happened."

"Yeah," David agreed.

Another sob.

"I'm sorry. I can't help it," she said softly.

"No, don't be sorry," David said forcefully. "It's okay. Listen, I've got to get back to Washington with these notebooks."

Leslie registered surprise. "Washington?"

"I mean Atlanta," David said. Leslie's eyes narrowed.

"You said Washington."

"Yeah, I know. I've got to go to Washington first. I know some people there that can maybe help us. Then back to CDC in Atlanta. I can rent you a car."

David was still checking the van's side view mirror as he put distance between themselves and Jergens Laboratories. Nothing.

Leslie lifted her head from the headrest. "Could you do that?" she asked. "Would they know if you used one of our credit cards?"

"They might. I've got a different credit card," David said.

Another surprise. No, that was the wrong word, Leslie thought. She really was moving beyond surprise.

"I suppose I could have known that."

"I'll explain later," David said, glancing again at the side view mirror.

There was a pause. Leslie had a clear vision of a time, months ago, on a ledge a thousand feet above the desert floor. She had to reach way out to grasp the outcropping above, and she had hesitated for long moments. The longer she had waited, the more hesitant she had become, and finally had reached out only when the realization struck that fear was capable of paralyzing her. She knew she needed to take charge of her emotions right now.

"Listen, David, I don't know where you're going but one thing's for sure." David recognized her tone of voice as complete determination. It was the third time he'd heard it.

"What's that?" He thought he knew.

"I'm going with you."

David was glad Leslie thought it was her decision. What the obstetrician hadn't yet realized, and David had not wanted to tell her, was that she really had no choice. She couldn't go home. She was a marked woman, and in this world of shadows the enemy wore no uniforms.

47

Jack Moss' eyes were bugging out his head. "What do you mean, gone? How the hell could that be?"

Although it was still afternoon, the little light that filtered through the clouds and drizzle over Washington seemed dirty. The distant cars were driving with their headlights on. Moss didn't notice. On the other end of the scrambler, Blue Sky One's voice was as calm as ever.

"They appear quite clever. They got out through the air vents, would you believe that? It was just about impossible, Jergens said. He's panicking – he phoned the Senator. They stole a company van and took off. In light of their actions, capabilities, we backed off until we could inform you and regroup. We found the van this morning in a hotel parking lot in Palm Springs, near the airport. Also, the Parkerville obstetrician's been neutralized. There was some trouble there, by the way."

"Do I want to know?"

"Not now, but containment may become a problem. The immediate situation is the inference they took a flight. We matched credit card payments at the hotel – there were fourteen overnight bookings – with airline payments. We came up with an untraceable credit card. This guy's priority is scary."

"Never mind that."

"Tickets for two to Washington, D.C. Another set, different airline, to New York."

"Naturally. Forget New York. It's probably a feint."

"Right. It was a direct flight and they would have already landed anyway."

"If they've gone anywhere, it'd be Washington. How do we know they're really on the plane?"

"We don't. Like I said, they're very resourceful."

"What time do they land?"

"Four fifty nine, Delta through Atlanta. They could've gotten off in Atlanta, maybe, that's his home base. But we missed it anyway. What do you want to do?"

Moss looked at his watch. It was 3:55 pm. "What the hell do you think I want to do? Have it met in Washington. Is there time?"

"No prob. Will do."

"One other thing."

"Yes?"

"Make sure Jergens calms down. We can't have a loose cannon."

"Already taken care of."

Moss sat back in his chair. He realized the two doctors had accumulated valuable information. It would be useful to find out what they knew, what they suspected before removing them. There were other possibilities, but Moss was willing to bet they had either deplaned in Atlanta or would be landing at Reagan. Of course, as he had been told, they were very resourceful. They could have done anything, even remained in California.

Smith was already en route to Washington. Day was in the city to testify about LRN preparedness in front of Harry Deutsch's subcommittee. Moss would set things up.

He pushed the scrambler and dialed another number.

48

David and Leslie walked up the jet way towards Terminal B with the other deplaning Delta Airlines passengers. It was 5:15 pm. They had gone to ground in Palm Springs, spending the night at the Courtyard Marriott two miles from the airport. Leslie, at least, had needed the rest of the afternoon and evening to recover any sense of balance. Finding a pay phone had been surprisingly difficult, but she finally located one at a nearby shopping mall where they purchased necessities. She called Catherine: Derek was fine, he was already asleep, and sure, she'd be glad to take him to school again tomorrow and call Naomi, and was everything ok? Leslie assured Catherine it was, uncertain how convincing she sounded.

David and Leslie ate at a Chinese restaurant in the mall. The obstetrician never got past her wonton soup. They returned and went to bed before ten pm. David, knowing Leslie was not used to people dying around her, held her until she fell asleep. Even after, she twitched in his arms and let out a few distressed sounds before he too faded out.

Leslie was awake at four, staring at the ceiling. In the darkness, the day's bravery was replaced by a hollow, almost paralyzing fear. She propped herself on one elbow and looked over at David. David, the man who had collided with her life just weeks ago, and taken it over. And she, used to being in charge of her own destiny, depending only on herself, was along for the ride. She'd read about women like herself, women who were in charge, who had accomplished much, but who completely flipped the other way and become totally dependent on some man. There was that headmaster and the diet doctor, for example. Of course, she had wound up shooting the guy. Well, David was a doctor. Or the Clintons, maybe. There was a whack ball relationship.

What was there to think about? Everything and nothing. Not at four a.m. anyway. She lay back down and managed to drift back into an uneasy sleep until the five o'clock wake-up call.

At 5:45 they took the courtesy shuttle to the airport and caught the 7:14 am Delta flight connecting through Atlanta, arriving in Washington National at 4:59 pm. Leslie had plenty of time to mull over the tangle of events as they winged their way eastward. David was a black and white thinker, it seemed, even more so than Donald had been. Whys and wherefores were not his paramount concern – at least while action and problem-solving were required. She still needed to sort things out emotionally as well as logically. How did it all fit together, if indeed it did? She wanted to push the puzzle pieces around, but dozed off whenever she tried.

David's cheap carry-on bag, purchased the day before, held the few store bought items, another underwear change, one shirt and Ken Holliday's two notebooks. He carried it up the jet way as he walked next to Leslie. He leaned in.

"So far, so good."

David's remark jolted Leslie's fledgling sense of well-being. "What do you mean?"

"I mean we haven't been stopped," David replied.

"Why should we—"

Suddenly David looked straight down at the ground as they approached the gate area. He spoke with a low intensity.

"Let somebody get between us and go left. Go left out the gate and meet me at the Travelers Aid counter in fifteen minutes."

"What?" She had heard him, but was uncomprehending.

"Five thirty. Do it!" There was no mistaking the urgency in David's voice.

Leslie slowed and let a business traveler pulling his luggage pass between them. She watched as David, holding the carry-on, walked through the gate area and turned right towards Terminal A. The gate was crowded with passengers for the next flight; there was a line at the counter. She noticed two men in suits waiting just across the hallway. One was leaning against a pillar as they scrutinized the deplaning passengers. They looked like serious characters with their close-cropped hair and intense looks. Pillar man nudged his partner as he spotted David; they began to follow as Leslie passed through the gate area and turned left. After a few steps, she snuck a glance behind to see the two closing in on David, moving fast. She gasped and continued walking away.

David, walking rapidly past numbered gates, veered into a men's room. The men in suits hesitated.

"Wait or go in?" the younger man asked. He was shorter and more muscular than his partner.

"He's buying time for the woman, that's all," came the reply. "That's not our priority. We go in."

The men walked through the open entrance and around the privacy wall, passing the utility closet on the way. Apart from a teenager at the washbasin, the men's room appeared empty. The older man signaled his partner to stay by the entrance, then cautiously approached the stalls as the youth finished drying his hands and left. The younger man stood next to the utility closet as his partner bent down and looked under all six stall doors. Inside the closet, David could see the man's legs through the louvers near the bottom of the door.

The older man moved to the last door and kicked it open. As he did so, the closet door burst open and slammed into the second man, who staggered back with a grunt. Before he could regain his balance, David had delivered a vicious chop to the throat. The man fell, choking. As he did so, David reached inside his jacket and yanked a Beretta 92F pistol from the man's shoulder holster.

The older man was reaching inside his jacket when David leveled the 9mm at his head. The man froze, then slowly moved his hands away, palms upward.

"Take off your pants," David ordered. "Now."

The man started to undo his belt. He seemed in no hurry.

"Why don't we talk this over?" he said.

In reply, David delivered another kick to his fallen partner's midsection and the man sped up. In a few seconds he stood in socks, shirt and jacket, glaring at David with a what-now? look.

"Leave your weapon holstered. Take it off and slide it over. Then chuck your pants in the toilet."

In a few seconds, the taller man's pants were very wet and the holstered weapon lay at David's feet. Another 9mm Beretta. He slid the weapon into his waistband and dropped the man's shoes into the nearest toilet. Without another word, David stepped over the man on the floor and walked out of the men's room, passing two business travelers on their way in. They would get quite a surprise, he thought.

Leslie had found a seat in the lounge area; she had the Traveler's Aid booth in view. She had picked up a newspaper and used it to cover her face. She looked at her watch. David was due any minute. She glanced upward at the television and gasped; the picture was an exterior shot of the Jergens Laboratories. She strained to hear the announcer.

"Just hours ago, a laboratory accident claimed the life of well-known industrialist Willard Jergens and an employee, Doctor Ken Holliday."

Hours ago? Leslie was uncomprehending. The shot switched to a file photo of Willard Jergens.

"Doctor Jergens, scientist 'til the end, was conducting an experiment in a containment area when something went horribly wrong. We have no further information at this time, but we'll be bringing you details as they become available."

Where was David?

49

At that moment, David, after leaving a Federal Express box, had taken a left turn off the main corridor and was walking down a side hallway. He stopped before a door marked NO ADMITTANCE. It was locked. David looked both ways, then slid a credit card into the jamb. He shut the door quietly behind him.

The terminal was crowded; people hustled to and fro in front of Leslie as she sat by the Traveler's Aid booth. She looked at the newspaper without seeing it. The curious migrant camp anomaly she had discovered a short few weeks ago had become an unending nightmare. She prayed David was all right. If he didn't show by 5:40, she'd go look for him. For the first time in her life, she wished she had a gun.

Leslie's thoughts were as tangled clothes tumbling in a dryer. As a result, she failed to notice the man in coat and tie, carrying a briefcase, who sat two seats to her left. Nor did she see a second man, similarly dressed but without briefcase, position himself to her right.

"Doctor Riordan?"

This from the man on the left. Leslie gasped, jerked visibly.

"Doctor Riordan, please don't be alarmed. My name is Lindell, FBI."

He extended his identification wallet. Leslie's eyes, big as saucers, automatically went to it.

A second voice from the right. "I'm Special Agent Ent." A second wallet came into view from the opposite side.

"Time to come in from the cold, Doctor Riordan," Lindell said.

Leslie tensed. Lindell continued, "Please. We know how harrowing this must be. You don't need to run. You're free to go if you wish."

Leslie appeared in shock. She pointed to the television.

"They just killed Doctor Jergens," she blurted.

"We know," Lindell replied.

"Who are you?" she asked. Both men felt the tinge of hysteria in her voice.

"It's like we said," Lindell replied soothingly. "We're with the Federal Bureau of Investigation. The FBI. We'd like you to come with us. You're in danger, Miss Riordan. You already know that. We're the good guys."

Leslie regained her focus. "How do I know I can trust you? Where's Doctor Livingston?"

"We're not sure at the moment. But believe me, ma'am, he can take care of himself." Lindell formed a wry smile.

"What do you mean?"

"Why don't you come with us?" he asked.

Ent saw Leslie's knuckles turn white as she gripped the armrest. She was ready to bolt. He spoke up.

"Look, Doctor. Agent Lindell and I are going to get up and walk over to the Traveler's Aid counter. I hope this makes you feel more comfortable. If and when you decide to come with us, just come over. We've got a car waiting and you'll be safe."

There was a pause, then the two men stood up.

"I'm supposed to meet David right here in—" She looked at her watch. "Oh, no. Five minutes ago."

*　　　　*　　　　*　　　　*

Two minutes later, agents Ent and Lindell flanked Leslie as they emerged from the terminal. Lindell looked left and raised his arm towards a white van parked fifty yards away in a red zone. When Lindell signaled, the van's lights snapped on and it eased from the curb. As the trio watched the vehicle approach, Leslie read the lettering on the side: POTOMAC PLUMBING. Behind them, a man in pilot uniform walked through the terminal doors, head down, cap obscuring his face. He carried a folded Washington Post.

The van stopped; Ent slid open the rear door and held his arm out for Leslie. As she stepped in, the pilot reached the group and raised his head. Visible behind the newspaper was the 9mm handgun.

"David!" Leslie exclaimed.

Neither FBI agent moved as David slid into the van. He stepped over Leslie and sat behind the driver.

"Stay inside, Leslie. You, driver, hands on the wheel." The driver complied as David looked towards Ent and Lindell. "You two, lean in and with two fingers remove your weapons and place them on the floor."

Passersby on the busy sidewalk were unaware of the drama unfolding in front of them.

Ent spoke up. "You're making a mistake, Doctor Livingston. We're on your side."

"Yeah? Maybe. We'll see. Now do it. You first." He nodded towards Lindell.

Agent Lindell leaned in and did as David had directed. When he backed off, Agent Ent did the same. Now two Glock 23 .40 caliber steel and polymer handguns rested on the front passenger floor.

David addressed his companion. "Leslie, I want you to move up to the front seat, reach in and pull out the driver's weapon."

Leslie moved easily to the front without having to get out of the van. She felt for the driver's pistol. It wasn't there.

"If it's not in a shoulder holster, it's on his hip," David said. Leslie reached around the driver's waist.

"Here it is," she said, pulling out another Glock 23 and holding it with both hands.

David addressed the driver. "Get out. We're leaving."

Ent spoke up. "I told you, this is wrong."

"Call me on the radio and convince me you're the white hats," David said. The driver got out of the van, stepped around to join his companions.

"We could have taken you out right here," Ent said. He was still trying.

"Well, then maybe you are the good guys. Leslie, please drive."

Leslie scooted over behind the wheel just as a uniformed Washington police officer leaned in the driver's window.

"Gotta move it, ma'am."

A startled Leslie reacted, "Oh, yes sir."

As she pulled away, Lindell reached for his cell phone as the three FBI agents watched them go.

50

Things seemed really to be falling apart now, Harry Deutsch was thinking. He could read the signs. He sat in his office in the Hart Senate Office Building on Constitution Avenue, feet up on the desk, balancing a vodka tonic on his stomach and looking out the window at the same dismal weather Leslie was driving through. Besides the curt message from Moss, no one had told him anything, except Willard Jergens, and the man had been on the edge of panic, Harry could tell. He had tried to calm the scientist down, and Harry wasn't very calm himself. Now Jergens was dead, a national news story. Harry was sure it wasn't an accident. What the hell was going on? Did they want to kill everybody?

It was too late to disassociate himself from those nut cases, he knew. He was in up to his neck. But he wasn't going to panic. Harry Deutsch always landed on his feet, always the survivor. He had even survived his re-election campaign, despite the newspapers having uncovered the situation with the I-287 Stage III Reconstruction Project. What the hell, who could be expected to do an important executive job for a lousy hundred and sixty five grand a year anyway? But they could never prove a damn thing. And here he was again.

He swiveled in his chair and looked at the large framed picture of himself on the credenza, positioned directly in the line of vision from the visitor chairs. Taken three years ago, Harry was shaking hands with the President in front of the I-287 construction site. The moron had no idea why Harry was smiling.

He needed to talk to the Arab, needed to find out what was happening on that front, but the son of a bitch wasn't communicating. Neither was Jack Moss, except his message warning him to stay away from the *Tradewinds*. He didn't care to ask why. Not that he was going near the yacht anyway, especially in weather like this. He needed another drink, that's what. Edna, his new secretary, would be coming in the office with some important papers to review. Never mind the papers were tucked in her panties, and smelled of *Obsession*.

He went to the side cabinet and poured himself another stiff one. Not only did he have to deal with this new situation, but he had to go home for a late dinner as well. It was either his wife's birthday or their anniversary or some damn thing. At least he'd have Edna for an appetizer.

He hoped she'd wrapped something appropriate.

51

In a few minutes, Leslie was crossing the 14th Street Bridge as David, now in the front passenger seat, checked the agents' weapons. He was accumulating quite an arsenal. Outside, it was completely dark and had started to mist. Leslie turned on the wipers. Rather than clear the rain, the worn blades just smeared water and dirt running down from the roof.

Leslie glanced around the dashboard, up at the overhead.

"I guess you weren't too serious about them calling us on the radio."

"What?" David was looking at the S&W jacketed cartridges.

"You told that FBI guy to call us on the radio if he really was an FBI agent."

"Did I?"

"There is no radio in here."

"Mmm." David said. He finished with the handguns.

"It seems all we do anymore is drive around in vans with people chasing us. Were they fakes?" she asked, looking for the defroster and craning forward to see the road. She found the knob and cranked it on high.

"I doubt it," David replied. "For one thing, these are standard FBI issue weapons."

Leslie was puzzled. "Then why'd we run?"

David turned to her. "Remember that guy in Jergens' office?"

Leslie jerked. "Oh! Did you hear what happened to Doctor Jergens?"

"Saw it on the monitor at the airport," David replied.

"What about that guy? Smith, he said his name was."

"Yeah. He's either FBI or NSA, probably."

"NSA?" Leslie inquired.

"National Security Agency," David said.

"What? How do you know that?"

The van neared the end of the bridge. David made a gesture. "I don't for sure. Turn left at the light."

Leslie turned on the blinker. "What do they do exactly?" she asked.

"NSA primarily monitors overseas transmissions, looks for threats to security, things like that. But lately they've been kind of an offline clearinghouse for all kinds of stuff."

Leslie turned left. The drizzle continued. At least the dirt had stopped smearing across her view. She turned to David. "What do you mean?"

"Keep going straight for awhile," David said. "Activity that various agencies might not want attributed directly to them. All this stuff kind of tightened up with the Homeland Security deal, and this was a new way to operate and bypass normal channels."

A pause. "How do you know this?" Leslie asked.

David shrugged. "Think I read about it in Time or someplace."

She glanced sideways at David. Something didn't sound right to Leslie, but she had a new thought before she could mull it over. "Wait a minute. If Smith, or whatever his name really is, was FBI, and those agents were real, then they probably weren't going to kill us!"

David shrugged. "It's a possibility."

"Can they do that?" Leslie asked. "I mean, we're Americans!"

David suppressed a laugh. Leslie drew back. "I'm sorry," he said, but the smile remained.

"Am I that naïve? I guess I am. But wait. That means our own people – the whole thing – like that guy Doctor Mengele the Nazi guy—"

Just as David noticed a Suburban heading towards them in the opposite lane, a second Suburban swung out from behind it, blocking the street.

"I see it!" Leslie exclaimed. Reacting swiftly, she squealed the van into a hard left turn down an alley to the left just as David said, "No! Don't—".

"Too late now." She accelerated down the narrow passage.

Suddenly a truck roared across the alley from between two buildings, blocking their path. As Leslie stood on the brakes, she read the truck's sign:

CAPITOL PROVISIONS
Fresh Meats

The van slid on the wet pavement, screeching slightly sideways as it slowed and bumped the truck, caving in the van's fender. The windscreen cracked.

"Damn it, this is getting old," Leslie said.

David grabbed one of the seventeen shot FBI Glocks as the Suburbans turned into the alley from behind, pinning them in. It had been neatly done.

"Give me one of those," Leslie said, gesturing. David looked surprised, then handed her a weapon.

"It doesn't have a safety lever. You have to—"

But Leslie had already flung open her door and jumped to the street. As he followed, a small part of David's mind marveled at how quickly Leslie was adapting to a high risk environment. He aimed at the Suburban from behind the hood of the van, Leslie alongside, her Glock pointed at the windscreen. Pumped with adrenaline, she barely noticed the cold rain.

All was still for several moments. Finally, the Suburban's passenger door opened.

"Doctor Livingston!" Hands appeared, palms up. Mr. Smith stepped slowly out into the street, arms outstretched.

David trained the Glock on Smith as he approached slowly. How did he get here so fast? David wondered. He knew they'd had a fair head start. Another indication of the scope of this operation, David thought.

"Surely you can see I'm not armed," Smith said conversationally. "We could have shot you right here." David inclined his head towards Leslie, keeping his eyes and weapon on Smith.

"It's bullshit," he said in a low voice. "We're on a public street." He had said it for Leslie's benefit. In reality, the alley was completely deserted.

He straightened as Smith continued to approach. "Stop right there. What do you want?"

Smith stopped. "We'd like you both to come with us."

"Another containment room?"

"Please," came the response. "You've got it all wrong." Smith looked around. "We don't want a scene, do we?"

"Oh, I think we do," David disagreed. A puff of wind carried the drizzle sideways up the alley.

"How about if we just shoot Doctor Riordan?" Smith said, in the same conversational tone of voice. He nodded, and an AR-15 rifle appeared from the truck cab window. The red dot danced ominously across Leslie's chest. From that short distance, it was an easy shot.

With incredible swiftness, Leslie dove back into the van.

David flashed through and discarded all the available scenarios. It was too risky. He lowered his weapon.

"David!" Leslie hissed from below the dashboard. "We can get out of this!"

David compressed his lips and shook his head. He would have tried it alone, but not with Leslie. He knew they would shoot her. He called out to Smith. "Where are we going?"

52

The rain had stopped; the thinning clouds revealed a full moon. David recognized the Washington Navy Yard as they rode with their captors down M Street, turning onto Delaware Avenue, past Fort McNair to a marina at the confluence of the Anacostia and Potomac rivers. They pulled into an empty parking lot. As they stepped out of the Suburban, Leslie saw a low building marked Dockmaster, and beyond a series of wooden docks. The vessels moored in the slips ranged in size from small skiffs to large yachts. At the end of a T dock was the largest vessel in the marina: the *Tradewinds*. The sleek Benetti motor yacht appeared to be streaking through the water while tied up at the pier. Leslie estimated the vessel exceeded one hundred feet in length. It reeked of money, and something else, at first unidentifiable to Leslie, as it gleamed immaculately, rainwater sparkling on the stainless steel fittings. There was a light chop on the waters outside the marina. Fireflies of reflected moonlight danced on the hull as Leslie and David, escorted by agents Ent and Lindell, approached the gangway. Smith brought up the rear. David noticed the smaller letters B V I painted on the hull underneath the vessel name. They had seen no one on the walk from the parking area to the T-dock; the marina was deserted.

They mounted the gangway as the B V I red ensign flapped from the masthead overhead. Leslie recognized the trappings of power, existence above accountability; that was what she had felt, and an icy finger of fear brushed her. They came aboard and went directly into the salon. Leslie took in the off-white Italian leather couch and matching chairs, expensive wall coverings, wet bar and built-in electronic comforts, including a high definition screen that seemed almost life-sized. She was certain the interior to the salon cost more than she made in a single year, but she was only half right.

David was not registering the yacht's creature comforts; rather he was focusing on the man sitting on the couch, cocktail in hand. Doctor Day, in a light grey suit, smiled. After a moment, David smiled too.

"I might have guessed," he said.

Doctor Day motioned the pair to sit.

"Oh, how so? Please. Drinks?" he inquired. Leslie shook her head as she sat down on an opposite chair. It was very comfortable. The dry, processed air smelled clean, like leather and fiberglass. The salon had the aroma of money, she thought.

The four – David, Leslie, Smith and Doctor Day – sat in an expectant silence. Agent Ent stood aside, watchful.

Doctor Day repeated his question. "Drinks? No? You'd appreciate the bartender. Knows his stuff."

David could think of a number of drinks he wouldn't mind having at the moment, but he knew he was going to need all his faculties.

Day continued, "Anyway, you were saying?"

"I wasn't," David replied. He looked over at to Smith. "How did you get here so quickly?"

Smith just smiled. Doctor Day turned toward Leslie. "Where are your manners, David? Doctor Riordan, I'm Nicholas Day, David's boss. Very pleased to meet you. I have some business with your friend here. I wonder if you'd be good enough to allow us some privacy? We've got very nice accommodations below; I'm sure you'd like to freshen up."

Ent looked at Leslie and pointed to a spiral staircase. She got up and headed towards it, squeezing David's hand as she passed. Ent followed her down. David watched them go.

"Don't worry, she'll be fine," said Doctor Day. "You know, you're so clever, David. I wondered if you'd figure out I buried Doctor Riordan's first request. And that New England deal, that was too clumsy, wasn't it? I'm afraid I didn't improvise very well there."

David's director sipped his drink, looked at Mr. Smith and nodded. Smith took up the reins.

"We made a mistake, Doctor Livingston. I know you saw right through our story at Jergens. I'm afraid you panicked in the containment room, though. We had no intention of harming you or Doctor Riordan."

David shifted his gaze. "And Ken Holliday?"

Smith shrugged. "A pawn in the game."

"Willard Jergens was no pawn."

"A complex situation."

"I'll bet."

The engines came to life. Inside the well-insulated salon, there was just the slightest rumble, more felt than heard.

"We going somewhere?" David asked.

Doctor Day smiled. "A little moonlight cruise." David knew he and Leslie weren't traveling on a round trip ticket.

Smith stood and paced as he continued. "It's a taboo subject, isn't it, Doctor Livingston? You know what I'm talking about. The real purpose for Project *Oeuvre.*"

David took a breath. "*Oeuvre d'lentraide aux enfants de la grand-route.* The Swiss program from 1934 to 1975 for the systematic elimination of Yenish gypsies. For starters."

Smith was visibly taken aback.

"I told you he was smart," Doctor Day said.

"They weren't alone, Doctor Livingston," Smith said. "Much of Europe set up similar programs. It's been universal. Far away as Australia and Aboriginals. But we're not trying to emulate them or Adolf Hitler. We're not harming anyone."

David could think of a string of people they'd harmed, starting with Ken Holliday.

53

One level below decks from the salon, Ent gestured Leslie down a narrow passageway. There were doors on the starboard side.

"Right here, Doctor Riordan," he said. Ent opened a stateroom door and motioned Leslie inside. The room was well-appointed, although too glitzy for Leslie's taste. A queen sized bed took up virtually the entire width of the cabin, leaving narrow aisles that could only be navigated sideways. A television was built into the opposite corner. Ent checked the closet, which was empty. Leslie caught the fragrance of cedar. Without another word, he walked back through the door and shut it. She heard the click from outside.

She waited a few moments for Ent to leave the hallway, then pulled the lever down. The door was locked. Leslie tried to turn the little locking knob, but it wouldn't budge. How could a stateroom lock from outside? They always did in the movies, but in real life? They must have done something, she thought, before looking carefully around the room and in all the drawers. She pulled open the small drape to find a port light. The view was across the river to the Anacostia Naval Station.

Just then, the vessel's engines turned over. The throaty sound was slightly more audible than in the salon. Leslie felt a lump in her throat. She flopped down on the bed and tried to think.

*   *   *   *

Upstairs, Doctor Day was appealing to David with scientific logic.

"David, we don't have to bore you with statistics you already know. Your Indian project and alcoholism. Of the eight million annual arrests nationwide, a third are blacks. They comprise half the prison inmates, but only thirteen percent of the general population. Over twenty one percent of black males will be incarcerated by age thirty versus one point four percent of white males. There are more Negroes in prison than in college." He drained his drink. It seemed to fuel him up. "They're six times more likely to be imprisoned over their lifetime than whites. On any given day, a third of all black males in their twenties are somewhere in the criminal justice system."

David was wondering why Doctor Day was boring him with statistics he already knew. More importantly, where they had stashed Leslie? He was pretty sure she was all right, at least until they were well offshore, but then again he had never thought Ken Holliday or Willard Jergens would be sacrificed either. And Jergens had, evidently, been one of their own.

He heard voices outside as lines were being cast off. Looking past his captors, the view began to change. He saw a Boeing 767 climb out from the glow of Reagan National across the water. They were underway, slowly at first.

Day continued passionately.

"Look at Iowa, for example. For every hundred thousand people, 309 whites are incarcerated compared to 4,200 blacks."

Did he know the state by state statistics? David wondered as Day waved his empty glass around and continued, even louder than before.

"But can we talk about it? Oh, no. Twenty seven of twenty eight defensive backfields in the NFL are black, we can talk about that." The fact that there were thirty two teams didn't seem to bother

Day. "When's the last time you saw a colored airline pilot? You want to fly with one? There ain't no affirmative action in the sky, when it really matters." David recalled the film he had seen on the Tuskegee Airmen. He supposed they didn't count, somehow, being military.

Smith piped in. "The browning of America," he said. "Look at MTV. Their fantasy mix of a mixed racial society is in danger of coming true."

"Can I have something to drink?" David asked.

Smith pushed a button. In a few moments, a steward in white service jacket appeared.

"Just some ice water, please," David said. Doctor Day would be happy, he thought. The steward was fairly dark-skinned. All these guys needed were a couple of bed sheets and a burning cross.

The steward moved to the bar and was busy with tongs and ice. He poured from a bottle that looked French. Doctor Day was recharging as the steward brought David's water in what appeared to be a wine glass. Is that right? David wondered. Must be, this guy would know. Day picked up speed again.

"We'll be heroes, David. It's something everybody wants, but won't admit. You know I'm telling the truth. Look down the road thirty, forty years. We'll be spoken of like Washington, Lincoln," he enthused, gesturing grandly.

Smith formed a wry smile. "Well, maybe not Lincoln."

*   *   *   *

In the stateroom below, Leslie had pulled the curtain back and was working on the porthole retaining screw. It wasn't moving. Evidently housekeeping hadn't extended to the brass fitting; verdigris marred the surface and the screw was stuck fast. As she pondered the problem, she saw the yacht was moving faster now.

They were passing a large airport. It must be Reagan National, she thought, where she had arrived not long ago, when the future seemed a little brighter, at least. Wherever they were going, she reasoned, it wouldn't be someplace good. She needed to hurry. After almost breaking a nail on the wing nut, she decided to search the cabin.

There was little in the stateroom, and what there was had been fastened down, except for the television remote. Leslie wished she could change the channel on the whole evening. She opened the door to the connecting head. She tried that outer door without much hope, and was rewarded: it was locked. Leslie went through the drawers. Nothing but a soap dispenser by the sink, washcloth and matching towel hanging on a rod.

Soap. Washcloth. Rod.

Leslie backed up and kicked the rod as hard as she could. She succeeded in jamming the brass pole into its retaining fixture. One more solid kick and the rod came loose; she pulled the other end free. She wet the washcloth and soaped it. Returning to the stateroom, she soaped the area around the screw. She looked at the mutilated rod end. It might work.

Leslie shoved the rod end onto the wings of the retaining screw. It didn't quite fit. She put the washcloth over the other end as a cushion and smacked it with the heel of her hand. The soft brass started to deform over the retaining screw wings, but not enough to jam itself on. Holding the rod with one hand, she lifted her foot and stomped on the rod, not easy in the horizontal position.

Leslie had succeeded. The rod was now jammed over the retaining screw, and she had a lever. She thought for a second. Righty, tightie, lefty, loosie. Okay. She carefully applied leftward pressure against the rod. She felt the screw start to turn, but the rod was riding up and threatening to pop off. She kept up the pressure. Something gave.

The retaining screw had loosened. The rod end had come off, but it had done its job.

54

Sharif squeezed the phone, more in anger than frustration. Why was it so difficult keeping things cobbled together for just a little while longer? Once again, Hamas and Fatah were at each other's throats in Gaza, this time another incomprehensible dispute involving the disruption of a Hamas funeral, allegedly by Fatah militia. The funeral was for a young girl killed by a mortar round while on her way to school. Although as it turned out the girl was perhaps not so young, and likely not on her way to school, but maybe ferrying ammunition between buildings. Of course, nothing could be proved.

His conversation with the deputy to former Palestinian P.M. Ismail Haniyeh was on the level of a four-year-old, he judged. He looked out at the Gulf as he listened. He thought he saw a tanker, but the glare was dazzling, even through the polarized and treated glass.

"The young girl was on her way to school," the deputy was saying. "The mortar shell blew off her legs and she bled to death in the street. Eleven years old. These people are animals."

Sharif ignored the posturing. Patience and diplomacy were called for.

"I have spoken with the deputy to Mahmoud Abbas." Sharif knew to keep things on an even plane; in fact, he had spoken to the leader of Fatah himself. "He is equally distressed and assures me the jackals disrupting the funeral were Israelis."

"Naturally he did!"

"There is footage on CNN," Sharif responded. Of course, it was a lie. "The vermin of Israel will do anything to drive a wedge and advance their tanks."

Sharif could sense the man retreating. When the deputy spoke, he was more subdued.

"In any event, these are unimportant details. Disrupting a funeral. These are the actions of jackals."

"Yes indeed they are," Sharif responded. "But they are Israeli jackals."

"And what is all of this to you, Sharif? Your interests are over a thousand kilometers away."

Sharif knew he had to be careful. The deputy was probing.

"We are all brothers against Zion," he said. "We stand with you from over a thousand kilometers away. Israel has once again fomented violence and made Gaza a parking lot for their military vehicles. They fire fragmentation shells and thousands of cluster bombs and phosphorus shells against your people, people of Allah, all in defiance of the Geneva Convention."

Sharif knew his words were the truth. So did the deputy. There was silence for a time. Sharif prodded.

"If they are not stopped in Gaza, a thousand kilometers is not so great a distance."

"This is true," came the voice.

It was working, Sharif thought. Just a little while longer. He looked outside; a scattered layer of light cumulus had formed near the horizon. A breeze had sprung up offshore. He could see it move towards him, ruffling the water, rocking the solitary dhow as it trudged slowly across on its unknown journey. He had one more phone call to make.

55

Leslie quickly finished unscrewing the port light and pushed it, but it remained fast. She pulled; the window opened inward and up. The sound of engines and rushing sea water roared into the stateroom, carried by the cold, wet air. Leslie fastened the retaining clip, noting the porthole was recessed several inches inside the hull. She stuck her head through and peered in all directions, eyes watering when she faced into the wind. Perhaps four feet above her was a slight step, it appeared, an architectural line perhaps. Then again, it might be a shadow. She looked fore and aft, but in the darkness couldn't tell for certain. She thought hard, mentally reboarding the vessel some twenty minutes ago. Yes, there had been a step, a slight ledge running all the way fore and aft, breaking the solid line of the hull and aiding the illusion of speed. Eyes closed, she visualized further, and pictured the hull above. Above the step, a considerable distance, would be the railed deck. Satisfied, she retreated into the room and sat on the bed. She visualized the climb. The porthole was recessed. The hull step would be wide enough for a handhold, if nothing else. She had battled higher winds at altitude. It would be dangerous, but not impossible.

Probably.

If she fell, at least she would drop into the cold Potomac rather than four hundred feet to the desert floor. She wasn't a great swimmer, but they weren't in the open ocean yet, either. Would the propellers suck her in? Likely not. Maybe not. If she felt herself slip, she'd try to dive away from the hull. The lights gliding by onshore didn't seem that far away. Okay. She stood on the bed. With her hands on the overhead, she leaned –

What?

There was a bulge in the overhead liner. Leslie looked up and saw a Velcro retainer, almost invisible with its upholstered covering. What was this concealing? She pulled the Velcro and a hinged panel swung down, revealing an aluminum ladder and a hatch.

A fire escape? Yes, it must be. Leslie breathed a sigh of relief. This would be much easier. She loved a climbing challenge, but not when their lives were at stake. She unhinged the ladder and lowered it to the bed. Reaching up and slowly pushing on the hatch, Leslie hoped she wouldn't emerge in the middle of the galley or a crew card game. She knew she was too far forward to pop up in the middle of David's tête-à-tête in the salon.

The hatch didn't open. Now what? she wondered. It couldn't have a lock; it was an escape hatch. Could it? No, there was no lock, she knew, only nightclubs and textile workshops had locked fire exits. There was, however, unknown to Leslie, a chair leg directly on the hatch one deck above. In the chair the ship's chef dozed as he watched a DVD of The Sopranos last season. It had been a long day, and everyone had ordered a different entrée.

*   *   *   *

In the salon, David was sipping from a sparkling glass. The steward left. Doctor Day continued right where he left off.

"We'll have saved America," he concluded.

Maybe he's waiting for applause, David thought, or for him to stand and salute something. Instead, he asked, "Who's in on this?"

There was a pause. They were at cruise, David noticed, making maybe fifteen knots. To starboard, the city lights of Alexandria were moving by at a slightly faster clip. To port, he could make out headlights moving on the Anacostia Freeway. Doctor Day and Smith looked at each other.

"Go on, tell him," Smith said. "He pretty much knows, anyway."

Why not tell me? David thought. I'm not supposed to be coming back anyway. David could visualize Day mentally rubbing his hands together.

"The top people, David," he chirped. "Our top people with vision and guts. In the NSA, FBI, law enforcement at all levels. Especially law enforcement, wouldn't you know? We're it, David. The future. With your talents and knowledge, there's a big place in it for you."

Smith chimed in. "And the future belongs to those who prepare for it."

*   *   *   *

Leslie knew time was her enemy, increasingly so; the ship was steaming towards some place that would likely be the end of her and David, and she had lost considerable minutes without solving the problem. The aluminum ladder, not meant for heavy duty and designed to save weight, proved flimsy enough. She kicked one of the rails off as well as all the rungs but one at an end, leaving an L shaped affair six feet in length. Leslie poked the L out the porthole ahead of her, and then, leaning forward, pushed both arms through the opening and stretched. Now she was halfway out. Having planned her course of action, she swiveled her body so she was facing upward. All the while, the aluminum wavered in the rush of air. The piece threatened to fly out of her hand and spin into the Potomac.

Leslie's hair streamed behind; her clothing flapped in the wind. They were steaming at close to twenty knots, but to Leslie felt more like forty as the dark water rushed by below, seeming to come alive around the yacht with a malevolent hiss and eerie phosphorescent glow. Outside the cabin, the roar of wind and the sound of water streaming by were louder than the engines. Carefully, Leslie stretched upward as far as she could with her empty hand. Not far enough. Her left foot was still touching the bed; now she had to inch outward a bit more and rely on her sense of balance without assistance. Still not enough. She strained every muscle and tightened her buttocks. The tip of her middle finger felt the smooth fiberglass of the hull step, but she wasn't quite high enough to grip it.

Leslie knew there would be a moment when she would be beyond recovery, shifting her weight outward to gain another two inches or so in height. In her other hand, the remnants of the aluminum ladder vibrating in the wind didn't help. It was the moments she'd faced on the rock face months before: the fulcrum of no return. But she'd overcome her hesitation then, when a slip would have been fatal. Now, if she missed, she was going to get very wet, but not fall hundreds of feet to the rocks below. She kicked out and strained upward. She felt her fingers close on the step above, and she pressed against it as hard as she could. Would they slip off the wet, smooth surface? She kept maximum pressure with her fingers while she shifted her buttocks out the porthole. The aluminum L was hard to control; it wanted to oscillate. Her wrist was already aching, but she secured her grip on the step above as she pulled one leg onto the porthole recess and heaved upward. In seconds she was upright, standing on her porthole, balancing against the hull while squeezing the step, lashed by wind and spray.

She barely noticed, deep in concentration. Slowly, she brought the L upward with her free hand, turning it so the rung would face inward when she reached the overhead position. The aluminum clanged on a stanchion. Leslie now had three points of purchase. She focused and took a breath. Bending slightly, she sprang upward with one deceptively simple movement, trying to minimize her pull on the L, and grasped the stainless steel railing. In a moment, she had vaulted the rail and was standing on the deck. She looked at her improvised climbing tool; the rung had bent and the aluminum had ripped. She shuddered and let it fall into the black water.

Leslie looked both ways. There was no one in sight. She was amidships. Which way? Six and one half dozen of the other. Hugging the bulkhead, she moved rapidly aft. There was no need for silence; noise was lost to the wind, sea and engines. She came to a hatch and debated whether to open it. The decision was made for her as she caught a glimpse of a crew member in white start forward on the deck from aft. She darted inside and closed the door.

Leslie found herself in a utility locker. She opened a large toolbox. In a few moments, she was back on deck, a large wrench in her hand and a hammer in her waistband.

Leslie saw the large windows of the salon perhaps twenty feet aft. She crept under the window, raised her head cautiously and peered inside. David, Doctor Day and Smith were still inside. Doctor Day seemed to be talking. He made expansive gestures as he moved about.

Suddenly, from the rear of the salon, light slanted across the deck. A man appeared, smoking a cigarette. Leslie saw his shoulder holster before the hatch closed, cutting off the light. Her heart pounded; they were yards apart. She took the hammer from her waistband. He was looking aft when she wound up and threw it at his head. It wasn't even close. The hammer continued past, clanged on the rail and went over. Leslie gasped.

Casually, the man moved to the rail and leaned overboard, evidently looking for the source of the sound. Leslie quickly ran forward, lifted the heavy wrench with both hands and with all her might brought it down on the man's head as he straightened. To her horror, his knees buckled but he didn't go down. He grabbed his head with both hands; blood streamed down his wrists.

"Ow, ow, goddamn it!" he yelled. He turned. As their eyes met, she swung again and cracked him in the face. Instantly, blood spurted everywhere as the man's nose shattered. He went down, completely out. Quickly, Leslie bent down and withdrew his weapon, a Glock 18. She had no idea she held a fully automatic machine pistol, capable of spewing out thirty three 9mm rounds with a single pull of the trigger.

56

Sharif felt drained from his efforts at diplomacy. Fortunately, he thought, once again the United States had misread the dynamics of the Middle East and stepped up covert operations against Hezbollah in Lebanon, part of the CIA's desperate and misguided soft war against their most natural ally, Iran. They were so consistently inept; only the geography of a vast ocean had saved them – up until now - from disaster. As a result, Hezbollah was firmly supporting Sharif and the bio-agent operation, and now threads from the cloth of war were already inside American borders. The phone call he would make to an influential Emir should be instrumental in quelling the violence in Gaza. Or so he hoped. There was little more to be done.

And now Syed was calling him from London with another problem. Again. Something involving a girl and a night club owner. Little brother Syed, who still went by the title of *Samu Maliki*. His Royal Highness. It was a mockery. He was a royal pain in the ass is what he was. Sharif could make a phone call and that would be that; the problem in London would disappear. Or he could make another phone call and the wrath of his family would descend upon little Syed, who wasn't so little anymore, except his brain had turned to *hummus* with all the controlled substances he ingested. Or he could whisper a word to Yousif and the problem would be solved permanently. It was a temptation. He found he didn't care much one way or another.

It was no wonder Sharif's faith was firmly in *Wahhabe*. Western culture was a systemic chancre spreading its poisons, even throughout the Kingdom. It could not be stopped except by extraordinary means, and it would be stopped in due course. There were other priorities though. Sharif was content to glide on the waves of western society, sailing with little effort on the pleasant societal breezes rather than becoming immersed in its foul humors. He moved to the piano. Perhaps Liszt's Sonata in B Minor would be appropriate, given his thoughts. The problematic piece required more than dexterity and interpretation; the work had been criticized for a century and a half by those lacking the ability to weave the motivic elements into a coherent structure of four seamless movements.

Sharif knew he did not lack that architectural knowledge, and that the only imperfection in his performance was the instrument itself. The Steinway Music Room Grand was a full 47 cm shorter than the Concert Grand, a regrettable compromise in the Burj suite. Perhaps only he and Allah could hear the difference, he mused as he played, one part of his mind mulling over the annoyance that was Syed. Sharif finished flawlessly, preferring the long-discarded triumphant ending for the quieter one Liszt had penned in sometime in 1853.

He stood and moved to the glass, three hundred meters above the Gulf, gazing north across the water: a billion diamonds set in blue, shifting, gleaming, a kaleidoscope leading his eye towards Persia, invisible over the horizon. Yes, to Iran, where, Allah willing, the holy work would soon bear ultimate fruit. He walked across the room and sat gazing into the dark fireplace. When Yousif returned, he would speak to him about his brother. He looked at his Vacheron Constantin Minute Repeater; it was just past 2:30, time to speak with the Emir. He picked up one of a row of cell phones and began to punch buttons when—

Sharif was startled by a noise behind him. He whirled to see the Libyan, a green-eyed dark haired beauty the aide had brought to the penthouse an hour ago. She – Fatima, wasn't it? - had emerged from the bedroom and padded across the floor to the piano, unseen and unheard as he sat absorbed in his thoughts. What was this? When the meal was eaten, the dishes were cleared. They weren't supposed to reappear.

She wore the *jallabia* carelessly now, more as a drape than clothing. Sharif was surprised at the powerful response evoked by the swell of her breast, the caress of the fabric, so soon after having spent himself in her. He couldn't believe this woman had the temerity to walk out of the bedroom, without asking permission, perhaps listen to his phone call and sit at the piano. *The piano.*

Her hands went to the keys. Sharif had a sharp intake of breath. He looked around and eyed the poker from the nearby fireplace; if she touched the keyboard he would – he could - he didn't know what - smash her fingers. Her bare feet went to the pedals. Anger flashed. He started to stand up, charged with adrenaline. What profanity was this—?

She began to play Rachmaninoff's Fourth Piano Concerto.

The Fourth Concerto! Sharif was stupefied. No one played the tragic Fourth! Her fingers were alive! Rachmaninoff's desolate longing for Mother Russia, the infinite sadness of that infinite white expanse, beyond melancholy: it swelled from the instrument, filled the room, and out, stretched before his eye across the steppes to the horizon and beyond. He stood, and she became backlit by the Gulf, haloed in the glare, a spectral dark figure at the piano, and now the *jallabia* was death's shroud, the keys the mighty armies laid to waste on the way to Stalingrad. Beyond, the sparkling blue water became white, frozen, the endless steppes beyond Moscow, snow crystals blowing west to east across the limitless waste. Notes glistened as they danced between silent flakes, rendered *pianissimo* by the falling snow.

White wolves trotted across the carpet! Beyond, *dhows* became farmhouses. Solitary figures bundled in fur chopped wood for pitiful little houses, chimneys breathing, smudging the icy blue sky. Horses' breath frozen in their nostrils. Cannon stuck fast in congealed mud.

Overcome, Sharif began to weep. Fatima – yes, it was Fatima – looked over at him, expressionless, and still she played, passage after passage, snowfall after snowfall, skipping across the ice crystals settled on the tundra of the keyboard, and Sharif knew rapture.

57

Inside the *Tradewinds* salon, all three men heard the guard cry out. Doctor Day froze, wide-eyed; Smith leaped to his feet and reached inside his jacket. David sprang across the room as the salon door burst open and Leslie jumped in, holding the Glock with both hands. Smith fired before Leslie could train the weapon on him, but David had managed to reach him and tip his arm. The bullet splintered the doorframe inches from her head. Instinctively, she scrunched her eyes and ducked as David wrestled with Smith. Doctor Day, wide-eyed, retreated to the far wall. Leslie aimed at Smith and pulled the trigger. Nothing.

"Leslie! The safety!" David had recognized the Glock 18 with its triple internal safety system but had no time to explain. Leslie stared at the weapon uncomprehendingly, looking for safety levers and finding none save the toggle that set the weapon on automatic fire. David delivered a vicious chop to Smith's arm. As the pistol fell to the carpet, Smith shoved David onto the couch, darted through the salon doorway and out on deck.

David took the Glock from Leslie. "Let's go," he said. They rushed on deck as Doctor Day looked on, mouth an O. The yacht was just passing through the Woodrow Wilson Bridge. The open draw spans loomed overhead.

David looked around, saw no one. "Okay, get on the foredeck. Undo the straps on the life raft container. It's a big fiberglass box. Stay there."

"What's the foredeck?"

David looked at her with amazement. "It's up front there. Just go up ahead of the cabin and there'll be an open area. The box is up there."

"What are you going to do?" she asked.

"Just be ready with the raft. Now go!"

Leslie ran forward to the foredeck as David ducked in a hatchway. Above the din of the cruising vessel, he heard yelling and rapid footsteps. Spotting a red metal box mounted next to the door, he opened it rapidly, extracted a flare and jammed it into his pocket. He opened the passage door and hurried inside.

David clambered down steps, Glock at the ready, but all the action was above and he met no one. He descended past the deck where Leslie had been held captive, and followed his ears down the passageway to the heavy engine room door. He yanked it open and ducked inside.

The engine room was painted a gleaming white enamel, with two bright rows of florescent fixtures on the ceiling. The din in the closed compartment was deafening. The yacht was making 24 knots, maximum cruise, and David winced at the roar of the Man 2842 V12 diesels, each thrumming along at 1800 rpm, churning out 800 horses. As quickly as he could, he located a large standing tool chest, rummaged through drawers and took out tools.

He darted to the rear of the engine room, where twin hoses came through the bulkhead. The openings were banded in red; above each hose the sign read HAZARDOUS – FUEL. David unscrewed the heavy clamp from one of the hoses, loosening it until a steady stream of diesel fuel shot out and began to accumulate in the bilge between stringers. He eyed the leak for a moment. Too fast. He adjusted the rate of flow with the screwdriver on the clamp.

Satisfied, he took the flare from his pocket and pulled the end. It ignited immediately. Thick smoke billowed out; David looked away from the intense light. He tossed the flare in the adjacent bilge area, turned and hastened back to the engine room door. He looked back. The diesel fuel was slowly rising toward the top of the stringer separating the compartments. Then he opened the door and ran out.

On deck, Leslie crouched behind the life raft container. The yacht had slowed and the ambient noise level decreased. She could see little, but heard commotion as the crew and Smith looked for them. She thought David must still be free, or the noise would have stopped.

Suddenly David reappeared alongside, startling her.

"David!" she said.

"Let's go now!" David shoved the Glock in his waistband, stood and unclasped the raft container. He pushed it to the edge of the deck. The action made a considerable racket. As a clattering of footsteps closed in, David kicked the container overboard and motioned for Leslie to jump. There was no time to think; together they leaped over the side. The water was cold, but not debilitating.

"There they are!" someone cried as the yacht slid past. A hail of small-arms fire pocked the water, so close David felt a splash. The raft had deployed from its container, and a beacon had begun to flash, making an easy target. The yacht turned steeply. On deck, Smith yelled "Wait 'til we're right on them!"

A searchlight burst to life; the intense beam quickly found the pair next to the floating raft. As Leslie squinted under the blinding glare, David fired three rounds and shattered the light. The vessel completed its turn and headed back towards them. There was no chance to make shore; the river had widened considerably since the bridge. Maryland and Virginia were too far away.

The *Tradewinds* slowed further as it closed the distance. Leslie could make out men with weapons on deck, taking aim from behind cover. David got off several rounds and pointed down; they both took deep breaths and—

A tremendous BOOM! and a fireball mushroomed skyward where the yacht had been. Leslie and David, together in the water, felt the stunning concussion and then the roasting heat from the blast. Leslie saw with horror the fireball was rolling towards them, and then David was shoving her underwater and the river lit up orange and green from the hell storm above.

       *   *   *   *

It seemed like hours before Leslie surfaced. She feared her lungs had been burnt, but when she took a great draught of air realized it was just lack of oxygen. David's hand was under her arm. The raft seemed to be undamaged; the fireball had flashed over in an instant. David moved to help her climb aboard, but of course she was already inside reaching back to help him.

They looked in awe at the sight spread out over the Potomac. There seemed to be a hundred fires from flaming debris. Acrid black smoke from melting fiberglass billowed upward; Leslie recalled pictures of burning Kuwait oil fires. There was nothing recognizable from the yacht; no sign of life, just pieces. One by one the floating remnants extinguished themselves. There was little current. Presently, they heard the distant wail of a U.S. Coast Guard cutter, growing louder. As the vessel approached, lights flashing, it slowed before easing up alongside their blinking raft.

58

The dark green SUV stenciled United States Coast Guard pulled to the curb in front of the upscale but otherwise ordinary townhouse just off K Street in Foggy Bottom. David and Leslie, dressed in borrowed Coast Guard denims and white sneakers, emerged. Leslie's shirt was several sizes too large. They thanked the two midshipmen for the ride and the dry clothes and got an informal salute from the driver in return.

They mounted the steps to the entrance. "Who lives here?" she asked.

"No one exactly," came the reply. David rang the bell; two longs, one short, one long.

"Some kind of code?" Leslie asked.

She noticed movement from the corner of her eye. She looked up and saw a small, unobtrusive camera, not visible from the street, swivel over them. After a few moments, the door opened. Leslie was surprised – or, she thought, maybe she wasn't – when a U.S. Army sergeant with sidearm opened the door.

"This way, please," he intoned. David motioned Leslie in. The sergeant led them down the paneled hallway to the study. In one corner sat an expensive walnut desk and leather swivel chair. Mounted on the wall, opposite bookshelves filled with an eclectic collection of volumes, were banks of television monitors.

David and Leslie sat on the couch. William entered with a steaming tray of de Havilland service. The smell of rich coffee filled the room. The orderly nodded to David, unloaded and left. Within

moments, the tall, lean, distinguished man in his sixties entered wearing a blazer and old school tie. Leslie thought he looked familiar somehow, with his kindly eyes and patrician demeanor.
He might have been an Ivy League professor, she thought, but probably wasn't. He closed the door and turned.

"Hello, David. Doctor Riordan," the man said. David stood; Leslie followed suit. They shook hands. Leslie suddenly thought of her hair; she had washed it hastily but hadn't been able to blow dry.

"Sir," David said.

The man motioned David and Leslie to sit. The pair returned to the couch while their host took one of the facing Baker chairs and poured coffee.

"Why doesn't it surprise me anymore when everybody knows who I am?" Leslie asked.

The man formed a warm smile. Leslie decided she liked him. "I know this has been quite a series of events for you, Doctor."

"I heard that same line from some else recently. David got us away from them at gunpoint."

"Yes. He's got a lot to tell me. But first, let me bring you into the picture more fully. David says you're brilliant, so I know this won't take long. Sugar?"

"No, thank you," Leslie replied. "He's seen me on my good days." She sipped her coffee; it was quite good and incredibly strong. The warmth spread throughout her chest.

A knock. In a moment, the door opened and the sergeant reappeared.

"Doctor Livingston? A phone call."

David looked at Leslie. "Excuse me." He put down his coffee and left. The older man glanced at the door.

"He probably would have preferred hot chocolate," he said with a chuckle, shifting to face Leslie. "I don't think he likes my *illy* espresso. Okay, from the beginning," the man said. "David works for me, Doctor Riordan. My name is Richard Haycock."

Leslie felt a slight shock. "Special Assistant to the President? *That* Richard Haycock?"

"Well, David's right. You're sharp as a tack."

"I *knew* he wasn't just a CDC scientist," Leslie said.

"Hardly. Although he is a doctor, all right. Everything I tell you now is highly classified and normally you would not be hearing any of what I am about to say. But of course these haven't been normal circumstances, and we are still going to need your help monitoring the Arizona situation. No doubt David has told you some of this. And you have earned your country's gratitude, although no one is going to know it."

"Thank you. Can I guess you've done a background check on me?"

"You can guess," Haycock said with a small smile. "Doctor Riordan, the area of selective genetic targeting is a pretty hot one right now." He put his coffee down. "It's complex, but not so complex that certain nations, ours included, haven't made significant progress towards developing these selective agents. We've been monitoring three or four locations around the globe. Our own efforts are confined to a classified military lab and the contractual program at Jergens."

Leslie leaned forward. "You said selective genetic targeting. Is that a synonym for genetic warfare?"

Haycock replied. "Not necessarily, but that's one of the more obvious applications of SGT. The whole program's been under intense controversy since it began."

Another knock. William had returned with an assortment of pastries. As he put down the tray, Leslie suddenly realized she was famished. She eyed the layout. There was some sort of seal embossed on the tray, underneath the food.

Haycock smiled. "Please. I don't know when you've eaten last."

"I can't remember myself," Leslie said, taking a small cinnamon bun. It was warm and delicious. She picked up the thread of their conversation.

"I can imagine the controversy. Who knows about it?"

"These do smell good, don't they?" Haycock selected a butter cookie and bit into it. "Not many – the President, U.S. Army, NSA, and of course the actual scientists at the Army lab and at Jergens. One or two Senators on key committees. There were elaborate security measures in place from the start. Nonetheless, nine months ago, a team of commandos infiltrated Jergens Labs and made off with a small quantity of a material known as G-11. No one could trace its disappearance. Partially because there have been such intense feelings about the program, the President directed me to find out what happened to the stuff. That's when Doctor Livingston – David – was assigned to the CDC."

Where was David, Leslie wondered?

"Why?" she asked.

"Because of the nature of G-11."

A moment passed as Leslie thought. She bit her lip, narrowed her eyes, and finally nodded.

"Let me guess," she said. "I think I can start to put the pieces together. G-11 inhibits procreation in all but Caucasian hosts. You were afraid – or maybe you knew – the stolen material would be used domestically. So . . . the way to find out was to hope some local O.B. saw a pattern somewhere and called the CDC. Am I close?"

Haycock smiled. "And someone did. Maybe we should put you on the payroll."

"But why didn't something happen when I first phoned Atlanta?" Leslie asked. "Why did it take a second call two months later?"

Haycock was on his second cookie. "That's a very good question. Doctor Day buried the request. I have to stop eating these."

The Special Assistant was just like David, Leslie thought. Where *was* he?

"Anyway, let me jump ahead," Haycock continued. "Thanks to you and another alert physician—"

"Doctor Garrison."

"Yes, Doctor Garrison. Unfortunately, he was just an innocent victim that got in the way of— well, you know that tragic story. We deduced that SGT had been applied to two population segments – Parkerville, through the water system, and the migrant camp outside Moon Valley, in aerosol form. They appear to be tests."

"How, in Moon Valley?" Leslie recalled their detective work. There was no central water supply at the camp.

"Crop duster," Haycock replied. Of course, Leslie thought. How easy. How perfect. Who would know?

"So now you know where, but not who?" she asked.

"Yes, but it's even more complicated. G-11 alters the female; its molecular changes are traceable in the blood. It was vital for us to test the affected population."

"Why?" Leslie was not following.

"We had to make sure it was G-11. Parallel research programs, one particularly in the Middle East, target the male. We didn't think they were that far along, but we had to be sure."

"Wouldn't that be a long shot?" Leslie asked. "I mean, your own material was already missing."

"Maybe, except that NSA – they monitor foreign transmissions, you know – had been intercepting communications concerning selective bio-agents. And, eight months ago, they picked up a couple of Middle East communiqués that raised the probability of foreign bio-activity on our soil. Such an attack would show a signature of male targeting, unless they had the G-11, and we hadn't ruled that out."

"And . . . ?"

"Your migrant women were affected by G-11," Haycock said. "It was our own material."

Leslie felt a sense of outrage at the insult to her patients in the camp. "I see," she said.

"We don't. Not completely. Lots of loose ends. Some of this may become clearer when we analyze Doctor Holliday's notebooks."

"Oh!" Leslie exclaimed. "Last I saw David had them, but I don't know what happened to them." Maybe they were lost in the explosion? She couldn't recall seeing them after the flight from California.

"When things got dicey at the airport, David dropped them in a Fed Ex box. They'll be here tomorrow."

"Who was that Smith person? Was Jergens a traitor? Why was he killed? Why did David get us away from the FBI? Were those two guys really the FBI?"

Haycock held up his hand, chuckling. "Whoa. One at a time. Smith was likely NSA, from David's description. Not his real name, of course. We'll know just who he was when somebody doesn't show up for work after a few days. Same with the two agents – if that's who they really were."

Hard to punch in when you're dead, Leslie thought, eyeing another cinnamon bun. Best eat it while it was still warm. "There was at least one other guy, the driver."

Haycock nodded, continued. "You see, we became aware that a loose confederation of powerful men – and at least one woman - were interested in subverting the research into a population manipulation program at home. They came from agencies already involved, from NSA to Jergens Labs to, we think now, FBI. And one U.S. Senator."

"How could you know who to trust?" Leslie asked.

"We didn't," came the reply.

"So you – you brought in David. To find out."

"He was the ideal choice. He had the scientific background and prior connections to Jergens Labs. Plus his other – talents."

Leslie nodded. "I've seen some of those talents. Can you tell me just what he does?"

"No," Haycock said, with a slight smile. "Besides, I'm not even sure I know."

"And now what?" she asked.

Haycock reached for another cookie as he took a breath. "Jergens, Day and Smith are dead along with the two FBI agents, if that's who they were. We know who the Senator is. They know we know. The domestic crisis is over, and I have no doubt we'll root out the rest of the participants."

"And the town of Parkerville? The migrants in Moon Valley?"

"In rats, the effects lasted six months. In hamsters, four months. Humans, we don't know. It may be transient, it may be permanent. We'll just have to wait and see. You'll no doubt be the first to know, Doctor Riordan."

A red phone began a steady ring from the desk. Haycock put down the cookie, jumped up. He took very small bites, Leslie had noticed.

"Excuse me, please." He picked up the receiver. "Haycock."

He listened for several moments, writing on a pad.

"I see. Certainly, sir."

He hung up. The Special Assistant to the President wore a pensive look.

"Where's David?" Leslie asked.

"Oh – I'm sorry. David's changing into something more appropriate," Haycock said. There was a trace of a smile.

"What? For what?"

"My boss wants to see him. He asked for a personal briefing."

It was several seconds before it dawned on Leslie that David was only going a few blocks.

59

Leslie had been back for two weeks. Richard Haycock had offered her a protection detail, at least until they were sure all the perpetrators of the domestic scheme had been identified. Over Haycock and David's objections, she had declined, wanting her life to resume a semblance of normalcy. Fred had asked if she enjoyed her vacation, assuming she had gone climbing as planned. It seemed to Leslie like she had been gone two years. She had replied vaguely and Fred nodded absently. A few days later, he asked in passing, "Say, think there was ever anything to that thing with the Caucasian babies?"

Leslie shrugged. "Probably not," she had replied. And that was that. Thoughts of David crept in at the oddest times: she could control her emotions – after all, she told herself, she was a grown woman and a responsible mother and physician – but she would be listening to a stethoscope and hear his laughter.

David had been busy in Washington and Atlanta, helping tie up the loose ends Richard Haycock had alluded to. The dominos were falling rapidly. Smith was identified as NSA, as David had surmised, and agents Lindell and Ent were indeed found to have been with the FBI. The van driver was located and interrogated. In all, five additional law enforcement figures were identified and detained. Bit by bit, the domestic eugenics scheme was dismantled. The blond man and his female accomplice who had driven the Suburban, rammed Leslie's jeep and slain Doctor Garrison had not yet been identified.

The death of Richard Garrison left Walter McReady, M.D., as the only obstetrician in Parkerville. McReady, whose practice was normally limited to the town's affluent, would be taking over the area's entire patient load, if temporarily. When David called to request an appointment, the ob/gyn nurse had been inquisitive and standoffish, stressing her employer's busy schedule. She attempted to put the meeting off for two weeks. David was forced to ratchet up the stakes a bit.

"The CDC is very concerned about a potential situation with some of Doctor McReady's patients. We would hate to launch a field investigation before discussing the matter with the doctor." The appointment was set for two days hence. When David arrived on time, he waited thirty minutes before being ushered into the obstetrician's office, easily twice the size of Leslie's and expensively furnished. Luckily, he had found an issue of Your Baby that was less than two years old.

"How can I help the CDC?" McReady asked, looking at David's card. He was thirty four years old, trim and well-groomed in his starched, immaculate exam coat, with an air of competence and, underneath, faint disdain. David noted the lack of clutter; there were no files stacked here or there. The polished desk was clean.

"Doctor Garrison was helping us with a study of minority pregnancies," David was saying, "and now of course, with his unfortunate passing, we need to see what we can do to continue."

"I didn't know that. What sort of study?" Doctor McReady asked.

"Fetal growth as correlated to certain socio-economic and geographic factors," David replied, knowing it was just the thing the government would spend taxpayer money on. "Locations around the country had been chosen based on various statistical criteria, and Parkerville is one of our test sites. We'd like to continue and hope you can help us out. We're defining minority as any non-Caucasian pregnancies."

McReady shifted in his chair. "Of course I'll do what I can," he said, "but you should know my practice has been fairly limited to the more – umm, I don't take Medicare, for example. I don't believe I have any minority patients at the moment."

"I understand," David replied. "For the time being, anyway, I'm assuming you probably will get all the pregnancies in Parkerville?" McReady shrugged in grudging assent. "At least until someone else takes up the slack? If you could help us out until then."

"Of course." The physician picked up a pen and tapped on a prescription pad, as if he had other things to do.

"Good. The primary thing is to notify me as soon as you see a qualifying patient so we can interview the subject for background data."

McReady apparently bought David's story and agreed to cooperate. In truth, he had been annoyed beforehand, but the whole thing had taken less than fifteen minutes and he could still get in nine holes before dark.

The Parkerville Reservoir also served a section of nearby Palo Vista, a third of whose population was of Mexican descent. In addition, there was a pocket of native California Indians. It was among these groups that Doctor Garrison had first noted the cessation of pregnancies. Before leaving the area, David paid a visit to the Bureau of Indian Affairs field office as well as the nearby Head Start Clinic, which was just closing. Both agreed to notify him when they learned of new pregnancies. Satisfied with his efforts, David headed to the airport and caught a flight to Dallas. After changing planes again, he arrived at Thurgood Marshall Airport, very late, rented a car and checked into a nearby hotel. He made one phone call and went to bed. He slept for eight hours, tired from the long day.

Next morning, after a leisurely breakfast of eggs, corned beef hash and toast, David drove to Piney Orchard Ice Arena where he sat in the mezzanine watching the Washington Capitals practice on a cold morning in Odenton, Maryland.

60

David had been watching the action for perhaps five minutes when a familiar figure came through the entrance and looked around the arena. David waved to Owen Hamilton and caught his eye, being rewarded by a big grin as his old teammate bounded up the steps and grabbed David in a bear hug.

"You look like you haven't gained an ounce," David said with a grin. "You can still take 'em two at a time."

"I hated those drills, man. All the way up to the press box? I can't believe we used to do that every day."

They spent several minutes dusting off old football memories as the Capitals whizzed around the ice.

"Those were fun times, all right," David said.

Owen nodded. "Hey, at least you got your uniform dirty. I figure I averaged twenty minutes a year playing time."

Both had warmed the Lehigh bench for three years, gaining only sporadic playing time as utility players, and had become fast friends. David had finally been rewarded as a starting senior receiver for the Engineers. He had enjoyed his undergraduate years in Bethlehem, Pennsylvania although the first semester had been an adjustment, having experienced culture and climate shock moving up from rural Alabama.

Owen gazed down at the Capitals. "Look at those guys," Owen said. "They can't even spell their name right. Haven't had a winning season since 2002. Sold everybody off."

The Caps were running through shooting drills from the blue line. David was taken aback at the velocity of the puck. Shots that missed the net caromed off the boards. With no crowd, the booms were like cannon fire.

"So what's up, old buddy?"

"I need some information about a yacht. Who owned it. What their circles of interest are, who their friends are. Stuff like that."

"It's a little out of my line."

"Only a little," David said.

"The fact that you're asking me tells me the inquiry's pretty sensitive. I take it this is not a domestic vessel."

"You take it correctly,"

"What's the name of the boat?"

"*Tradewinds*. It carried British Virgin Islands registry."

Owen paused. "That's the yacht blew up last week out of D.C.," he said quietly, looking at his friend. "It was in all the papers. Half a dozen casualties. One or two very interesting people."

"Is that right? I was on the west coast."

Owen looked askance at his friend. "West coast of what? The Potomac? Truth is, we were interested anyway," he said. There was a pause. Both looked down at the rink. The Capitals were skating sprints from blue line to goal line and back.

"You know, your name never crosses my desk," Owen said with a slight smile.

There was nothing for David to say. Owen looked at his watch.

"I gotta get back. Got a meeting at noon." The drive back to NSA headquarters in Fort Meade would take but a few minutes where, David was sure, they weren't flying their flag at half mast for the yacht victims. "How's tomorrow afternoon?" Owen asked. "That fast enough for you?"

61

In the townhouse just off K Street, Richard Haycock nibbled from an English biscuit tin as he sat in the study watching the fireplace smolder. Again. The flames had withered and gone out, replaced by rising soot. A strand floated out of the fireplace and gently landed on an armchair. He sighed. It really wasn't worth the effort.

The Special Assistant was reading David's update. The notification system regarding any new pregnancies in the affected areas seemed in place. They could turn their attention to urgent matters. He heard the code on the front door buzzer, and asked William to bring the hot drinks. When David came in, his hair was matted down. It was raining in Washington again, a cold rain in the cold weather.

"Don't you carry an umbrella?" Haycock asked. As soon as he had, he realized what a silly question it was. Another generation.

"Uh, no, sir," came the reply.

"The spy who comes in from the cold," Haycock chuckled. "Hot chocolate's coming." David thought the old man seemed delighted to have ordered the stuff. In truth, he would just as well have had a shot of Jack Daniels. Within moments, William arrived with the de Havilland service.

"William, would you get our guest a towel for his head?" Haycock asked.

David had a stray thought about where he might be going and a towel for his head. Was it precognition?

"Certainly, sir," came the reply. Moments later, David was drying his soaking wet hair. He felt like a schoolboy as Haycock waited for him to finish.

"Senator Deutsch," the old man said, when David had handed the towel to William with a nod of thanks.

"Yes, sir," David replied, one eye on the smoldering fireplace.

"We will need to speak with him. We should discuss the best strategy. Is he worried about being exposed? One would think he'd be quaking in his boots, but on the other hand when the yacht blew up so did the key players that could place him smack in the middle. I'm sure he was insulated anyway. He may be feeling fairly safe." Haycock paused to sip his coffee. "Where are you on the yacht business?" he continued.

"Sir, I've initiated a search into the ownership of the *Tradewinds*," David said. "The vessel had British Virgin Islands registry and was flying the British red ensign. We tracked ownership to a Channel Islands corporation, Red Crescent Limited."

"Hmm. Middle Eastern?"

"Not on paper, at least. The listed owners are probably straw men. We're still running that down. If we penetrated the corporate veil using normal channels we might have aroused someone's curiosity, probably MI6. I didn't want to do that without your input, so I went another way."

Haycock nodded. "How's that? Do I want to know?"

"No. Yes. Contact at NSA. College buddy. Quid pro quo normally would be to supply some feedback, since they were already curious about the explosion and the passengers. We'll have to be a bit inventive there."

"Yes." Haycock wondered briefly what David might have been like as a college friend. Probably exactly the same, especially as regarded his palate. He had been Class President, the Special Assistant knew.

David paused to sip his chocolate. It was hot and rich, and probably better than Jack Daniels, he decided. "Maintenance and crew expenses for the *Tradewinds* were paid through Red Crescent," he continued. "Income was the occasional charter. Those seem legitimate, but we've only had time for a cursory examination. We went back to the vessel survey, while the *Tradewinds* was being acquired, figuring maybe the company hadn't been formed yet. It hadn't. The survey bill was paid by a Delaware LLC. That entity is owned by two people – one is Herbert Harris. The other is Lawrence Massimo."

Haycock's eyebrows went up.

"Isn't that cozy?" David said.

62

Cozy was not a word Sharif would have used as he too mulled over ramifications of the *Tradewinds* incident, sitting at a small table in the penthouse of the Burj al Arab in Dubai, United Arab Emirates, clothed in traditional *thob* and *ghutra*. It bemused him to understand that his manner of dress influenced his thinking, especially with regard to his food. He broke off a piece of *arikah*. He shaped the bread – brought to him fresh from the Asir region – and dipped it in honey. As he chewed, he reread the newspaper coverage of the accident in the Washington Post and the New York Times, ironed and spread before him. There was little information beyond the obvious. Now he would be contacted by the American, a distasteful thought.

From almost 300 meters above sea level, the prince looked out over the Gulf. A few ships were visible on the horizon, carrying their liquid loads of energy. With two thirds of the world's proven oil reserves – somewhere between a billion and a billion and a third barrels – lying in the Middle East, those ships should continue to plod around the globe for the balance of his lifetime. He knew, though, that the real measure of oil included recoverable reserves, and by that standard the Middle East was dwarfed by Venezuela. With four trillion recoverable barrels in the Orinoco heavy oil belt, that country had the means to change the balance of power for generations. And yet the Americans treated their neighbor with disdain while kowtowing to Zion.

Sharif had studied oil and the politics of energy, both at the London Business School and throughout his steady progress towards the center of power. He had considered all the energy studies and weighed various prognostications: the Hubbert Theory on global oil production, the numbers put forth by the Association for the Study of Peak Oil and Gas, and others. As far back as 1974, Hubbert had predicted world production would peak in 1995, a phenomenon that did not actually occur for another ten years. In the United States, production had reached its height in 1971. No one believed the hopelessly optimistic U.S. Geological Survey, which had claimed there was enough oil in the ground to last for another fifty to one hundred years. Even the Jack 2 field, the deep water find in the Gulf of Mexico, would only sustain two years of U.S. consumption at then-present levels. Compounding the problem, BP's Deepwater Horizon disaster had interrupted drilling in the region. All the easy fields of gas and oil had been found and largely exploited. World consumption, at 88 million barrels per day, was already outpacing the 85 million barrel daily production rate. The U.S. Energy Information Administration predicted usage rates of 97 million barrels by 2015, and 118 million by 2030. Perhaps the most ominous statistic was the rate of discovery of new reserves, which had dwindled below eight billion barrels per year. With emergency reserves measured in months, the world's consumers were happily unaware they were forever standing on a slope made slippery with oil.

But what was the difference of a few years, more or less, especially to his people who measured time so much more slowly?

As the Americans would say, the handwriting was on the wall. Sharif knew better than to indulge the luxury that those Americans, those morally bankrupt children, should be treated as the enemy. Despise them, yes. Enemy? Hardly. No, their all-consuming engine sucked the black blood from the ground in the Middle East, and they paid heavily for their thirst. The Americans could not be a target, not for years: the country that financed everything must continue to do so. Never mind that they consumed everything, polluted everything, a foul kudzu that smothered the world with horrendous music and corrupted with dissolute morality, obliterating tradition and culture everywhere. These were transient bagatelles. Let others rant and rave in the streets and in the halls of foolish governments, as long as they kept the petrodollars coming. Only when the oil was done could they be dealt with.

The real enemy was always, would always be Israel. Israel, the festering sore, the chancre, the nest of vermin blaspheming the holy lands by its presence. Torn from the heart of the Middle East in its infernal creation, it must be destroyed forever. As an instrument of Allah, and with, through his grace, the means at his disposal, it was a holy obligation.

As if punctuating his thoughts, a large LNG tanker plodded into view. He mused on its contents, which would perhaps light barbecues in the American west, fire hot water in the north of England, heat baths in Copenhagen. He watched the vessel's progress as he chewed. Perhaps he would finish with a dish of locusts and camel milk.

63

Leslie bit her lip as she watched the needle and ball. Things were definitely out of synch. The ancient flight instrument had never really been improved upon, and she was still green at interpreting its information as she developed her cockpit scan. At this stage of proficiency, it was slow and erratic.

Seeing David's airplane had crystallized a new challenge, despite his scary belly-up landing. Her days were slower now, with the reduced patient load, lack of camp visits, and no one trying to kill her. Soon the last crop would be picked in any event, and the camp would clear out for a few months. She had signed up for flying lessons as unhesitatingly as she had taken up climbing.

"Your nose is dropping," Jeff said. "Watch your altitude." Leslie's eyes darted to the altimeter. Damn! She had indeed lost 150 feet without realizing it. There were so many forces to control - she knew her turn was awkward and unbalanced. If she could accomplish a standard rate turn - thirty degrees of bank - while keeping the little Cherokee in balance and maintaining altitude, she would gain in confidence. Right now everything was awkward and unnatural.

"Don't worry, it's natural to feel awkward and unnatural," Jeff said. "Let's level out and try it again. Bring her back to fifteen hundred feet."

In the weeks that had passed since David left for – who knew where? - , Jeff had proven a friendly and knowledgeable instructor. He offered constant encouragement, but Leslie was used to rapid results from her efforts. She was frustrated and discouraged that things hadn't yet jelled in the air for her.

"Don't forget, increase back pressure during the turn. You've got to counter the nose drop due to decreased lift. Step on the ball to keep it centered. Use small movements, you'll find it works better. Let the aircraft react to your control inputs."

And so it went. Leslie felt like every lesson – she had had a half dozen – was a step backward before going forward. She was anxious to solo, but nervous about the concept.

"How many lessons before the average person solos?" she had asked when they first began. Jeff wouldn't quantify an answer for Leslie, knowing the competitive physician was measuring herself against an artificial standard.

"Everybody's different," is all he said. "It's not a contest." Of course it was, she thought.

Leslie was back in her office by two o'clock. The phone call came at 2:30. Merion was on the line.

"Doc? I think we got some business for you," he said. Leslie hung up, tingling with excitement. If Merion was right, then it would seem the effects of the G-11 were indeed temporary on humans. Within the hour, Leslie was at the camp, talking with the proprietor in his store.

"Lizzie's not married, you know," he said. "She don't want this around too much." Leslie nodded. This wouldn't be the first time. Merion left to fetch the nineteen year old. Leslie passed the few minutes cutting up a star fruit for a late afternoon snack. Soon she was in the back room with Lizzie.

"Miss Leslie," Lizzie said, "I missed my friend two times now."

Leslie nodded. "Who's the father?" While G-11 altered the female, it was important to know if the father had been subject to the aerosol as well. Lizzie looked around.

"Well, Miss Leslie," she said, avoiding eye contact, "I believe the daddy is Emmanuel, my cousin, but it ain't necessarily so."

"Oh? Who else?"

"It could be Bobby Ray. I'd appreciate the fact that you didn't – uh…"

"It's okay, Lizzie, I'm not going to say anything. I just need to know for medical reasons. Are both Emmanuel and Bobby Ray here at the camp?"

"Why sure they are."

In the next half hour, Leslie took a history and administered a field pregnancy test. Lizzie was indeed with child. This was all big news, and as soon as she had the specifics she would need to get the word to David. Although she couldn't reach him directly, he had provided an emergency phone number. Back in her office, she left a message as instructed. David called within the hour. After warmly greeting each other, Leslie brought him up to date.

"I'll let you know as soon as I hear of any others, of course. Will you tell me if and when there's any news out of Parkerville?" she asked.

"Of course," David replied. "Leslie? I'd like you to monitor this pregnancy as closely as possible. We've found a statistically higher incidence of abnormalities in the offspring of the affected rats. The hamsters, too."

"I can do a sonogram and blood test at ten weeks," she replied.

"I thought you could do that earlier, no? Maybe eight weeks?"

David's remark surprised Leslie. He was correct; it was a matter of conservative procedure. She told him so. "If anything, I'd rather err on the side of caution," she said.

"Okay, sure. How many conditions can you monitor for?" David asked.

"It's growing all the time. The last journal I read, they were up to over seven hundred. I don't know how many the local lab can process, though."

"Can you do the sonogram at your office?"

"Sure."

"How old's your equipment?"

"It's not even two years," she said.

"Is it 3D/4D?" he asked. Leslie was taken aback again.

"Well, it's not *that* sophisticated," she said. Medicare and migrant camps.

"Okay, Monday morning you'll have digital recorders so you can send the data where I tell you. Run whatever blood tests you can there, but take duplicate samples. I'll arrange courier service to Jergens or CDC for the more sophisticated analyses."

"There's a complication," Leslie added.

"What?"

"The father may be the mother's first cousin. There may be a greater propensity for an abnormality, and I can't take his family history."

"Yeah, I get you. We'll just have to see."

"David? I don't suppose you can tell me where you are."

"Just as far away as the nearest phone," he said.

The possibility of Lizzie's child suffering a birth defect was sobering. She thought about the ramifications if G-11 tended to increase their incidence. No one in his right mind would want a substance like that loose on any population, she was certain. She remembered reading about the tragedies in the U.K. and most of Europe with thalidomide in the late 1950s. She had seen films like *Erin Brokovich* and *A Civil Action*. The effects in Moon Valley and Parkerville could be horrific. And that was just two towns.

64

Prince Hayyan was a realist. The brother of Princess Haifa was as distant a royal relation to Sharif and his brothers as genealogically possible. A member of the Cadet branch, and thus ineligible for the throne, he knew there was little chance to avenge his sister's murder without higher assistance. Hayyan seethed quietly and awaited his opportunity. After *Umrah*, the Lesser Pilgrimage, he arranged to cross paths with Prince Syed in Tehran.

They had met once only, but Hayyan was aware of Syed's reputation. Sharif's youngest brother was a profligate, constantly skirting trouble in both the Islamic and Western worlds as he drifted aimlessly between them. Small, almost waif-like in appearance, Syed's unblinking, rheumy eyes had a disquieting effect. He looked unwell. Syed had used the *Umrah* as an excuse to travel to Jeddah, and thence to Mecca, completing the short pilgrimage in two days. He continued on to Bahrain, hopping from one hotel bar to another, passing out in Trader Vic's at Le Meridien, getting into a dispute at BJ's night club. Hayyan followed Syed's itinerary. The next day, the diminutive prince flew to Tehran. Hayyan arranged a chance encounter that evening at a private party in the *darband* section of the city.

The gathering was upstairs, above a commercial establishment. It was a balmy night, with many stars and a crescent moon. The streets were crowded. Hayyan entered through the unmarked doorway and looked around. It wasn't quite a night club, but more a series of rooms. Music played in the largest of these;

there was space to dance. Hayyan wondered if the premises were rented out expressly for parties like these.

He wandered through the crowded rooms before he spotted Syed on a leather sofa, accompanied by two lithe, dark-haired women definitely not wearing *jallabias*. There was a lull in the loud music. Hayyan approached.

"*Samu Maliki*." Your Royal Highness.

Syed looked up, then furrowed his brow; the face was familiar but he could not place the tall, thin handsome fellow.

"I know you."

"Yes. We have met. I am Prince Hayyan. You knew my sister as well, Haifa."

A smile crossed Syed's face. "Ah, yes. The lovely Haifa. We were sorry for your family, Hayyan. What brings you to Tehran? Join us." He indicated the lounge chair opposite. From Syed's cordial invitation, Hayyan judged that Syed probably was without knowledge that his sister had been murdered.

The small table between them was sprinkled with white powder.

"What brings you to Tehran?" Syed asked again, as Hayyan sat.

"I have some business tomorrow. Tonight is for relaxation."

Syed was drinking 18 year old Sazerac whiskey. The women, who might have been sisters, were sharing a bottle of Domaine Carneros. Syed made an indication towards the rye; Hayyan nodded. Syed poured him two fingers. Hayyan, not inured to alcohol, refrained from coughing only with effort. He hoped Syed did not notice the water in his eyes. Syed indicated his companions and said something that sounded like Aisha, but the music had started to blare again and Hayyan didn't catch it. The women smiled and nodded.

Over the next half hour the potted plant behind Hayyan became exactly that, as Haifa's brother surreptitiously fertilized the soil with the most expensive rye whiskey in the world. Syed was clumsy with the two women, who made little effort to hide their disdain for his groping. Yet they did not leave right away. The one who might have been Aisha gave Hayyan liquid glances; she was not unattractive. There was small talk, made difficult by the noise and Syed's wandering concentration. The music, a mixture of Arab and Western songs, continued uninterrupted. After another fifteen minutes, one of the women nodded to the other and they left, perhaps for the bathroom or more fertile pastures. Hayyan had not returned the woman's silent advances although, he thought, another time he might have.

Syed's smile was without focus. He poured himself another drink.

"I hear your brother's in London," Hayyan said.

"What?"

Just then the music stopped. Hayyan repeated the question.

"Which one?"

"The one who now calls himself Sharif."

Syed snorted derisively. The white powder below his nose blew off.

"The Black Prince? He is too good for the rest of us."

Hayyan, surprised, had not heard that before. He did not have to wonder why his brother called him such a name. He let it alone.

"He seems very dedicated, that's true," he observed.

Silence for a time. Syed seemed to drift. Hayyan prodded again. "Do you think he believes he can attain the throne?"

"Who knows what he believes. I'm not concerned about it. Where are the girls?" He looked around.

"If Sharif were not a consideration, you are not so far down the line, are you?"

Syed looked at Hayyan as though for the first time. "What are you saying?"

"I am saying that if for whatever reason your older brother was not a consideration for the throne, the natural choice down the line could be you."

Syed narrowed his eyes. Cunning substituted for intelligence, Hayyan realized. From somewhere beyond, laughter.

"Why are you saying this?"

"Is it not so? I am just making conversation."

"I don't think so."

"It's only conversation."

"Is it?"

"Yes."

"There are other princes. Many others."

"Just so."

The evening played on. The women returned – a mild surprise - and started another bottle of Domaine. The music resumed, grew louder; the action became more frenetic. The whiskey bottle was nearly empty. Don Henley was singing *All She Wants to Do is Dance*. The girls got up. Syed tried to stand, but swayed and sat back down. The women danced with each other: close, closer but not touching. Syed and Hayyan watched the women flow across the floor.

They're pickin' up prisoners, and puttin' them in the pen,
And all she wants to do is dance, dance.

Their undulations were like the soft motions of a tide pool.

Syed spoke as he continued to watch. "And what is your interest in the line of succession? Do you know people on the council?"

Although Syed was drunk, and high on the white powder, Hayyan knew he had to be careful.

"I know people, yes."

"You are not a true Royal," Syed said.

"Nonetheless, I know people on the council."

"And are you saying you can influence their vote?" Syed had stopped drifting.

"No. I would not say such a thing. I am only making conjecture."

Googoosh, the legendary Iranian icon, was singing the tear-jerker *Hamzad*. Hayyan looked around. No one seemed to realize who she was. Another generation, he thought, as the girls returned.

There was a crash, followed by laughter. Someone had knocked over a lamp. The place was getting unruly. In a few minutes, Hayyan bade his goodbyes and got up to leave. Syed grabbed his sleeve.

"Come back tomorrow night. We will talk."

Hayyan gestured around. "Will there be another party here tomorrow night?"

Syed smiled. "No. It will be the same party."

65

Hayyan, as arranged, returned the next night. The streets were more crowded, noisier than before. He entered and looked around but Syed had not yet arrived. Hayyan wandered through the rooms while he drank orange soda and chatted with several of the fifty or so people milling around. Half the attendees were Saudis, it seemed; he knew one or two. There were no Westerners, although he had seen a few the previous evening. The Saudis seemed drunker than the rest of the crowd.

After a half hour, Syed came in. He was accompanied this time by a taller, older man, perhaps thirty, with piercing eyes and a serious look. The stranger was introduced as Prince Abdul-Haq. The trio found a sofa and chair in a corner where the music was less intrusive. Syed drank beer, while Abdul-Haq sipped fruit juice. A few women drifted by and eyed the group, but were ignored. There was a minimum of small talk before the tall stranger steered the conversation to the prior night's topic.

"Syed mentioned you were discussing succession last night."

"I believe the subject came up briefly," Hayyan said.

"Syed said you brought it up."

"I may have."

There was a lull in the music. Abdul-Haq leaned forward. "Prince Hayyan, you were the brother of Princess Haifa, were you not?"

"Yes."

Abdul-Haq nodded slowly. Hayyan was shocked. How could this fellow know? He realized he could be on dangerous ground. He needed to be careful. Who was this Royal, anyway? He seemed to be waiting for Hayyan to continue.

"Sharif is a . . . strong personality."

Abdul-Haq looked at him with his smoldering eyes. The look said Hayyan's answer was incomplete.

From somewhere, a burst of laughter, a tinkle of glasses.

"Strong personalities invite strong opinions. Do you have such an opinion, Prince Hayyan?"

"Perhaps."

Abdul-Haq leaned back, nodded slightly. "Very well," he said. It appeared they had an understanding; a danger had passed.

Hayyan ventured a query. "And you, Abdul-Haq? Have you a strong opinion?"

"What will follow requires courage, Hayyan. Courage and determination as well as utmost discretion. Do you believe you have cause for these qualities?"

"I have cause. What is your cause?"

"It is of no consequence to you. What matters is that we are aligned. The next steps will be mine. Enjoy the rest of the evening."

66

An invitation to lunch at the White House was impossible to turn down, even for a United States Senator. Harry Deutsch was not about to be the exception. He had met Richard Haycock a few times, once when the Permanent Senate Subcommittee on Investigations asked Haycock to testify. The President had put in a word, and the Special Assistant never did go under oath. He had met informally with the ranking members, including Senator Deutsch. This was the legislator's second term.

Haycock had discussed their approach with David before issuing the invitation.

"I'll let you get into the specifics. We're only going to show as many cards as we have to," he said.

"I researched the guy a little bit," David said. "It's amazing. He got elected mostly with the urban vote. He carried New York City, Albany, most all of the cities."

"Why is that amazing? He's a Democrat."

"So why would he want to kill off the people that elected him?"

Haycock shrugged. "Some species of female spider eat the males after they've mated."

"Maybe he's like some of those Nazi SS troopers. The most fanatic ones that hid the fact they were part Jewish. I did hear some rumors about his family's wartime activities in Germany."

"I'd like this to be more of a subtle warning," Haycock said.

"Why?" David asked.

"We don't have irrefutable proof, at least yet."

"We're getting closer."

"At this juncture we just want to make sure the activity has stopped. We don't know if they used all the G-11. Above all, we have to make certain that any remaining stock is destroyed."

It had not occurred to the Senator that his involvement with G-11 was the reason for the invitation. The destruction of the yacht and its passengers had seemed to insulate him from any consequences. The message indicated he would be participating in an informal briefing regarding ongoing investigations in general. When he arrived at the White House, Deutsch was shown into the Green Room, where a small dining table had been set up. The room encouraged informality, with its large fireplace and intimate atmosphere.

"Seems appropriate," Haycock had told David. "Jefferson signed the Declaration of War in here." He saw David's puzzled look. "War of 1812."

Lunch for the trio was rigatoni with green and black olive puttanesca, accompanied by greens with a very light Italian dressing, walnuts and feta cheese. David found the meal delicious. He said little during the lunch conversation, which revolved around the Subcommittee's current activity. Over coffee – Richard Haycock's cast iron blend - , the Special Assistant fired the first volley after the dishes were cleared and an assortment of pastries set out.

"Senator, we've been looking into some population anomalies out west. Specifically, Arizona and California. Read anything about it?" Haycock knew there had been no press coverage.

The Senator pretended to knit his brow, thinking. After a time he said, "Can't say as I have, actually. What sort of anomalies?"

"Anomalies that might be connected with the yacht that exploded in the Potomac a few weeks ago."

Deutsch looked from one to the other. He seemed to be getting a little flushed. "Yeah, I read about that. Terrible accident."

Haycock turned to David.

"Senator," David began, "there were a couple of very interesting people aboard that yacht, as you may know. One was a Doctor Nicholas Day, head of LRN at CDC."

"Of course I know. Day was supposed to testify before our subcommittee the day after he was killed."

"Another was a Mr. Smith, a member of our intelligence community."

"Don't believe I knew the man," Deutsch said. "How can our committee help?"

"That yacht was owned by an offshore company headquartered in the Channel Islands, Red Crescent LLC. Cash flowed into that entity through a Delaware corporation owned by Lawrence Massimo and Herbert Harris."

There was no reaction from the Senator.

"Harris was the largest contributor to your last re-election campaign and Massimo your campaign manager," David continued. "As you may recall."

"Of course I recall." Deutsch sounded annoyed. "Seems like a coincidence."

"Yes, an amazing coincidence," Haycock said. "Have you ever heard of G-11?"

"Isn't that a new Air Force fighter program?" Deutsch wasn't going to be easy.

"David will bring you up to date on what we're doing," Haycock said, nibbling on a wafer.

David leaned forward. "We have begun a very intensive investigation, Senator, and wanted to keep you in the loop. We're going to be interviewing Messrs. Massimo and Harris, among others. It seems a transparent organization, a conspiracy of shadows if you will, may have existed, may still exist, which embraces eugenics at its center. Testing on our own population appears to have occurred.

Of course, because of your committee position and closeness to those two gentlemen, we'll keep you informed."

Deutsch was expressionless. "Yes. Please do so. Who could commit such an unthinkable crime? You know, that coffee is delicious once you get used to it. I do believe I'll have another cup," he said.

*   *   *   *

After Senator Deutsch had left, Haycock turned to David. "You know, I love this room." He looked around.

"Yes, sir, it's very nice." David waited for his boss to say what was on his mind.

"He's a tough cookie, that one. Ward heeler from the streets. He hardly flinched."

"But he did blink, sir. He knows we know."

"Well, I think it went pretty much as we thought. I'd have liked to see the Senator hung out to dry as much as you, but this was the best way."

It had all been a tap dance, David thought, with the Senator admitting to nothing. Everyone would go on. The only people who would suffer any consequences were either dead or pregnant.

67

Leslie studied the printout in front of her. There seemed little doubt: Lizzie's baby had a serious problem. One of the tests performed at the ten week interval -chorionic villis sampling, or CVS – had revealed a fragile X mutation. Fragile X, a genetic condition, was the generic name given to abnormal changes within the FMR1 gene, and, occasionally, the FMR4 gene. The most likely occurrence was that the gene had somehow become corrupted, much like computer code, and shut down. Consequences of FMR1/FMR4 mutation included mental impairment, ranging from learning disabilities to full-blown autism or autistic-like behaviors. Symptoms also expressed themselves physically, and were often accompanied by delays in language development, gross motor development, sensory integration, and other problems. It was serious stuff, and there was no cure.

Leslie would confirm the presence of fragile X at sixteen to twenty weeks through amniocentesis, but there it was. Complicating matters was the fact that fragile X was an inherited disease, but the parents might never exhibit any symptoms on their own. Since Lizzie was unsure of the father, the situation was muddy indeed. Leslie needed to talk to David. Just as she was about to call, however, Merion telephoned. There was a second pregnancy at the camp. Leslie decided to interview the subject before calling David, in case there was anything to be learned from the visit.

When she reached the migrant settlement, Merion rounded up twenty two year old Lonnie Belle Carter. Leslie took her history in the back of Merion's store, as she had with Lizzie.

"Daryl gonna be right pleased," Lonnie Belle said. She and Daryl had been married for six months and wanted children badly. This would be a more clear-cut case, Leslie thought, as she took down the history and administered a field pregnancy test, which detected 14.5 mIU of hCG – an early pregnancy hormone. There was no doubt – Lonnie Belle was pregnant. In fact, she had conceived at roughly the same time as Lizzie, but hadn't realized it. Leslie took blood samples and scheduled the woman for a sonogram. Before she left the camp, she tracked down Lizzie, who was taking a batch of clothes off her wash line.

"I ain't due for another exam, am I?" she asked.

"No, I just dropped by to see how you're doing. Anything I should know about?"

"Well, it ain't slowed me down none."

"That's good. Listen, Lizzie, have you spoken with Emmanuel and Bobby Ray?"

Lizzie avoided eye contact. "I did have a word with Bobby Ray. He wasn't too pleased, I can tell you. He said it for sure weren't him, and said if it was I woulda had the baby by now."

"Is Billy Ray right?"

"I don't rightly know, Miss Riordan," Lizzie said, eyes on the ground.

"What about Emmanuel?"

"You don't know Emmanuel. That's not a thing to be tellin' him."

Leslie saved her next question. It would be useless to try and trace a genetic disorder from the male side. She moved on, and hoped the last query would sound innocuous. "Say, Lizzie, have you ever had any history in your family of babies that – weren't quite the same as everybody's? I mean, they weren't completely normal?"

Lizzie looked up sharply. "No, ma'am, not that I knows of. Why are you askin' me that?"

*   *   *   *

Back in her office, Leslie left a phone message for David and went about her practice. At four p.m., he returned her call. While she was dying to tell him about her fledgling pilot career, and that she had soloed, she had decided to wait until she was licensed and surprise him.

"Has something happened?"

"We have a problem with the pregnancy at the camp," she began. She reviewed Lizzie's test results with David and explained the ambiguity regarding the hereditary trace. Leslie confirmed she had sent hard copy to the CDC address he had given her. She went on to say that a second pregnancy had been discovered, and that testing was underway. David said that he received a message from Doctor McReady in Parkerville and he had gotten one pregnant Mexican housewife, Rosalie Ramirez.

"Listen, I was going to call you anyway," David said.

"What for?"

"I'd like you to check over Mrs. Ramirez in Palo Vista. I'll get her over to your office. You should have results of your second pregnancy by then, maybe, and we can go over that. Plus I haven't had a decent hamburger and shake in awhile now."

"Oh! When? When are you coming?"

"Tomorrow. Is that okay?"

68

The next day passed quickly. For a change, Leslie had a full load of patients. At three thirty, David arrived in a rental car and they met in her office. Her perfume transported him: someplace wonderful, but he didn't know where.

"The kitchen," Leslie said. "It's vanilla."

Fifteen minutes later, an unmarked, dark green humvee drove up and parked on the side of the building. The Marine driver and his companion, requisitioned out of MCAGCC 29 Palms, remained in the vehicle. They would wait until the examination was finished and transport their passenger back to Palo Vista. Leslie retrieved a sturdy Mrs. Ramirez from the waiting room, who turned out to have a wonderful sense of humor and a keen eye. She "made" David and Leslie right away.

"*Su novio, si?*" she asked, with a sly smile, wagging her finger between the two of them. Fortunately, she didn't wait for an answer, but nodded, answering her own question. "I want to know if it's *muchachito*, a little boy," she said. "Carlos said to find out; he said you could see the little *pene* with your magic *maquina*. He read about it, you know."

Leslie drew enough blood for the duplicate samples and whisked Mrs. Ramirez in for her sonogram. The state of the art equipment David had provided enabled an unprecedented level of detail. After Mrs. Ramirez left, Leslie showed the recording to David. He was awed by the miracle of life as the baby, quite active, clearly sucked its thumb for a few moments, withdrew it and waved its arm.

Its only arm.

*   *   *   *

David phoned Doctor McReady, who came on the line after several minutes. He briefly introduced Leslie, who explained the findings to the Parkerville obstetrician.

"I haven't informed Mrs. Ramirez," she said, "but she has a copy of the recording for you. Since she's your patient, I thought you'd want me to leave that to you."

McReady sighed. "Well, thank you, Doctor, I suppose. I'll take care of it. Put Doctor Livingston back on the line, please."

Leslie handed David the phone. "Doctor McReady?"

"Will you be continuing the program? Do you still want to know about minority pregnancies?"

"Yes, Doctor, it's probably more important now than before."

"Well, we have two more," McReady said.

There was a pause. "We'll see them right away," David said.

'I don't know that I realized you were doing sonograms and blood testing. Will you want to be doing invasive procedures? I'd need to have input on that."

David answered indirectly. "Certainly we would confer with you before amniocentesis, Doctor McReady."

There was another pause. "I've got a full load today, but sometime soon I'd like you to tell me just what socio-economic and environmental factors you're concerned with," he said.

The problem of containment was just beginning, David realized.

After the phone call, Leslie's nurse buzzed through. "Merion's on the line," she said. Leslie looked at David before picking up. There was another pregnancy at the migrant camp.

69

Hayyan did not hear from Syed or Abdul-Haq for three weeks. When he did, it was an invitation to a dinner at the Millennium Hotel in Doha, on the Arabian Peninsula. It seemed an out of the way location. Hayyan reserved a suite for the evening and flew to the capital of Qatar on the indicated date. He gazed out of the airport limousine as it drove up Jawaan Street. The hotel, in the commercial district, probably had been chosen so as not to attract attention.

A half hour after he checked in, the phone rang. He muted the television and answered. It was Syed.

"We will have dinner in two hours and you will meet some important people. I will come to your room and pick you up."

A private dining room in the hotel had been arranged. As they rode in the elevator, Syed turned to Hayyan.

"Tomorrow we will go to the Jassim Bin Hamad Stadium for a match; Al Zaeeis is at home. Is that all right with you?"

Hayyan, an Arsenal fan, knew that Syed owned a team that had done well a few years ago in the Asian Cup competition.

"I would be delighted to go."

The dining room was intimate, with windows overlooking the mall and nearby park. Aside from Syed and Abdul-Haq, the other two other attendees were introduced as Princes Hashim and Mamdouh. Both were true Royals: powerful, influential, people the council would consider when succession became an issue. Hayyan realized he was with the men who could well determine his nation's destiny. Following the meal of chopped herb salad and *kabsa* with meat, desserts of *tirmania* and *terfizia* sprinkled with powdered sugar were served along with coconut dates and Saudi coffee with rose water, crushed cardamom and saffron threads. Hayyan sipped; he tasted ginger or cinnamon, he couldn't be sure.

He glanced out the window. Over the park, stars shimmered against the dark blue vault of the desert night. Abdul-Haq addressed Hashim and Mamdouh.

"My esteemed guests, Prince Hayyan is an acquaintance of Syed and we are honored by his presence. Nonetheless, you may wonder if that presence is appropriate here. I believe you will find that it is. He may choose to explain his reasons."

Everyone looked at Hayyan. Abdul-Haq had made it impossible to keep his own counsel.

He hesitated, than spoke in formal tones. "Less than three years ago, my sister Haifa was put to death in London. The stories that circulated at home concerned a liaison with a non-Muslim, disgrace, and suicide. The Black Prince took it upon himself to punish my sister for what was an unproved and vicious rumor."

The princes looked at each other.

"I know this to be true," Abdul-Haq said. Under *Sharia* there was only blame and punishment for the victim, often more than for her partner. Only the year before, a rape victim had received ninety lashes. Another had been stoned to death for adultery, although the assailant had forced himself upon the victim.

Hayyan had no idea how Prince Abdul-Haq knew his sister had been slain. In the end, though, did it really matter?

"And may I ask why you are all here?"

There was a silence. After a time, Abdul-Haq spoke. "We are here for political reasons. We believe The Black Prince is a dangerous person; his unwavering belief in Wahhabe would be disastrous should be become King. Your experience is further proof."

Prince Hashim leaned forward. "An extraordinarily dangerous person."

Hayyan interpreted this to mean they wanted the throne desperately. The four would have formed an alliance, regardless of which was chosen, casting their lot as a group. After all, they were all true Royals. Men of will and substance, except for Syed, but Hayyan guessed the diminutive prince would have been included because of the likelihood he would follow Sharif in line. Or he may have been the catalyst to bring this group together.

The dinner ended soon afterward. Hayyan was told he would be contacted through Syed only, and that they would all not meet again alone. Sharif was known to have many friends, many eyes and ears, and there might be risk. Hayyan was told he would be the hand, the instrument, as required; all would be arranged. The others would set things up, provide as much help as possible.

*   *   *   *

Within two hours of the dinner meeting at the Millennium, CCTV tapes from the hotel lobby within a four hour window of Syed's check-in were being reduced to stills and transferred over the internet into a computer in Sharif's suite at the Burj al Arab. Yousif, skilled in technology, supervised the activity. One by one, pictures of the meeting's attendees - everyone except Hayyan - flashed on the screen. Sharif knew them all, of course. He smiled. He expected nothing else from his wastrel brother. He would have to thank him for identifying his enemies.

70

David hurried along K Street and turned the corner towards the townhouse. He looked at his watch. He didn't like to be late anyway, but late to meet Richard Haycock was unthinkable. When David had been pursuing his doctorate, Haycock had been his advisor as well as university Dean. Even then, the old man was a special liaison to the former President and had turned down an important ambassadorship. Busy as he was, he always had time for David and had never cancelled a meeting. When David's eleven year old Peugeot had blown a cylinder four blocks from Haycock's office, he had grabbed his books and sprinted the whole way, arriving out of breath, sweaty and thirty seconds early. That was the first time William had gotten him a towel.

It had been two months since the first defective pregnancies had been detected in Moon Valley and Parkerville. The rate of conception had returned to its pre-inoculation levels. Subsequent fetal anomalies were running at a tragic seventy percent. The western newspapers picked it up first and the CDC was inundated with calls. So far the reporters were sniffing around the Central Arizona Project and other improbable sources.

Haycock was waiting in the study.

"Morning, sir," David said.

"Hello, David." Haycock gestured him to a seat. In moments, William came in with coffee. David thought he caught William glance at his head with the slight trace of a smile on the elderly steward. Well, it wasn't raining and the Peugeot was long gone.

"When I got your last message, I thought it best you drop by."

"Yes, sir."

"Have you been reading the newspapers?"

"Yes, sir, I have."

"Review this for me, if you will. Bring me up to date."

"Certainly. Ten days ago, I received a phone call, routed through the CDC, from an obstetrician in Brooklyn, New York, a Doctor Yitzchak. He's in a neighborhood called Borough Park. That's right in the middle of the Hasidic enclave."

"Orthodox Jews."

"Yes, Orthodox Jews. To give you some frame of reference, they breed kind of like the Amish, with lots of kids per family. Most don't have televisions, you know how they dress, very insular society. Anyway, the guy noticed right away when pregnancies dropped to zero. He said he went from working ten, twelve hour days to half that, almost overnight."

"Did you check the surrounding area?"

"Yes. No anomalies outside the Jewish neighborhoods."

"How could they have done that? What kind of selective agent? Couldn't be the water supply, could it?"

"No. Brooklyn's water, in fact the whole city, comes mostly from the Catskill and Delaware reservoirs. We checked the water mains and routing. There is no way to tamper with the water supply and just cover the Jewish neighborhoods."

"Neighborhoods plural?" Haycock asked.

"Yes. It didn't take long to check with the surrounding obstetricians. The phenomenon affected all the Hasidic areas, and saturated them completely. We suspect a selective genetic bonding, harmless to non-Jews, but there is reason to believe if it's not G-11, if it's an agent developed overseas, it wouldn't be as sophisticated. We're only theorizing there, so we're also looking for a way to deliver a generalized agent to a selective population. We don't have a valid theory yet."

David pretended to sip his coffee.

"Publicity?"

"The first New York story broke in the Brooklyn Eagle two days ago, when I called you. The paper treated it as a curiosity, fortunately."

"That's just a temporary reprieve, I suppose," Haycock mused.

"Yes, but we have some time here, because I got a call from Doctor Yitzchak that afternoon. The pregnancies have resumed. We immediately had blood samples taken from the affected women to determine if G-11 is involved, if there is any G-11 remaining outside the secured areas. Because of the ethnic choice, there is reason to suspect we will find nothing. We are taking blood samples from the men."

"So we're waiting for the other shoe to drop?"

"Yes sir. The shoe, pants, belt, the whole thing."

71

David entered the new VIP section of Terminal One at Ben-Gurion International Airport, fifteen kilometers from Tel Aviv. The flight from Washington had been pleasant enough; the IAI G150, built in Tel Aviv, was equipped with a bed and David spent most of the air time asleep after a detailed cockpit tour. Ever the pilot, David had been keen on learning about the state-of-the-art Israeli jet, cruising at 41,000 feet at Mach .75. His economical hosts had arranged a free ride as the brand new aircraft was returning from its fitting out in Dallas. He was met by two Israeli Defense Force field grade officers in civilian clothes who ushered him to a waiting Mercedes Benz S550 sedan. During the fifteen minute ride from the airport, the three chatted amiably, but the Israelis never introduced themselves. David didn't know their exact destination, but they seemed to be heading in the general direction of Lod. The vehicle turned onto a pleasant, wide tree-lined avenue and then through a gated entrance into a compound. The house beyond was not extravagant; flowers, shrubs and competent looking men in uniform carrying Galil assault weapons populated the small yard.

The interior was also modest. David theorized, correctly, that since all three Israeli security services would likely be involved, the meeting was being held at a neutral site.

He entered an ordinary living room where seven men sat, three of whom were in uniform. They all nodded and looked the visitor over. To David, the whole tableau was an eerie reminder of the scene from the film *Munich*.

No time was wasted. A tall, thin soldier with penetrating eyes introduced himself.

"Doctor Livingston, I am General Ephraim Ben-Reuven. Thank you for coming."

"Thank you for the ride. The flight was very pleasant."

The general introduced the other participants. The military men were also of general officer rank. He did not specify affiliations, but it appeared two were Mossad, two Aman, and a fifth, David reasoned, was Shin Bet. The lone scientist was a Doctor Meir.

Ben-Reuven indicated a tray of half sandwiches. David suddenly realized he was hungry; he picked up one he hoped was salami. It was. He grabbed a bottled soda and sat where the general indicated. They got down to business.

"Doctor Livingston, not long ago two young Syrian nationals, under the direction of Hezbollah, entered the Golan Heights at night carrying a four liter container of liquid. These low level operatives were told by their handlers the contents were a great weapon in the final *jihad* against Israel, that their mission was of vital importance and their lives were nothing as compared to the critical nature of their goal. They made their way past a number of minefields to a prearranged location along a dirt road, where they were met by an off-road vehicle. They were driven to a spring upstream from a mineral water bottling plant that serves a wide geographic area, including all of Israel.'

'The four liters were dumped into the stream, directly over the intake pipes. The Syrians were driven back to their checkpoint and made their way back to Syria before dawn."

He noticed David was looking askance at his drink. Ben-Reuven formed a wry smile. "Not to worry, Doctor Livingston. I am drinking a soda also. These were bottled in a completely different region."

The general turned to a man in civilian clothes, who had been introduced as Major Ya'ari. The major shifted in his seat to face David.

"As you know, Doctor Livingston, the Shabak relies on HUMINT to extract and gather information."

Human intelligence, David thought. Always the best way. Something vitally lacking in the United States intelligence gathering services for a long time; now they were playing catch-up ball after a series of Presidential blunders.

Ya'ari continued. "Suffice to say the driver, a Syrian settler in the Golan, mentioned the strange mission to his friend the next day. That was a mistake. We picked up the driver and extracted whatever information we could. While he could not identify his passengers, he said they had chatted nervously about returning to their girlfriends in Salkhad. They mentioned in passing that they were both born on the same day. He estimated their ages at twenty or twenty-one. That was, of course, all we needed."

No doubt, David thought. It certainly would be. Especially in their hands, despite recent Israeli misjudgments regarding Arab troop strengths that had gotten so much publicity.

"The two Syrian lads were kind enough to help us. They did not know who gave the orders, naturally, but we were able to ascertain how and from where they were instructed. We traced the immediate source to a location in southern Syria, not far from Damascus. That entity, more or less a relay point, has a number and variety of secure communication facilities. We were able to monitor transmissions and frequencies emanating from the location and, while we have not yet deciphered the communiqués, determined they were linked to some very major entities in the Arab world, crossing several borders. I will defer now to Doctor Meir."

Doctor Meir offered a tight-lipped smile. "Doctor. Well, the first thing we did was shut down the mineral water plant.

Unfortunately, it had taken us two days to deduce what these men were doing. This was confirmed several days later by the two Syrians, as General Ben-Reuven has told you. A search of the topography around the plant revealed a pair of exam gloves in shrubbery near the intake pipes. An empty plastic four liter jug was recovered from the spring bottom.'

'Several shipments of product had been distributed as far west as Safad. Nothing had been sent south. We immediately set out to retrieve the water. We recovered eight pallets intact, two partial pallets, and various cartons that had been stacked in stores. Working backwards, we realized that a total of thirteen and a half pallets were beyond recovery."

Doctor Meir stopped to drain a glass of Coca-Cola. He grinned. "All this talk of liquid makes me thirsty." He put down the empty glass. "Okay. So there are several questions. First, what about the contaminant that was not sucked into the bottling plant, but continued downstream, if any? We assume it has become too diluted to be of concern, but that may not be true. There's nothing we can do, in any event. So, how potent is the substance? How far were the four liters designed to stretch? A couple of pallets? A whole day's output? We simply did not know. We put the recovered mineral water under intense chemical scrutiny. We would like you, Doctor Livingston, to help us evaluate our findings. We are of course aware of the difficulty you have had in the States – even if we hadn't been filled in by Richard Haycock, we read the papers – and we are assuming for the time being that we are working with something other than G-11. It is logical to think so. And the larger question – what is in store for us?"

He paused and looked expectantly at David.

"Yes. I need to tell you about Brooklyn."

72

David had found Menachem Yitzchak delightfully droll. As Yitzchak cheerfully admitted while they sat in his front room, he was not in the forefront of obstetrical progress. He was a simple baby doctor who delivered offspring in Brooklyn, just about all of whom had been healthy, and when he needed help he wasn't too proud to ask his younger friend and very brilliant colleague, Mordecai Rubin, who after all had graduated third in his class from a top five medical school, East Carolina (Brody), as ranked by U.S. News & World Report, for assistance. Yitzchak said, though, that he wasn't so dim that the sudden cessation of pregnancies had gone unnoticed, nor their just as inexplicable resumption.

David took it all in, including the heavy furniture in the Yitzchaks front room (as Menachem had called it) that looked as though it had come by way of Ellis Island perhaps a hundred and fifty years ago, brooding in the weak sunlight that managed to struggle through the layers of window coverings, the innermost layer being lace yellowed at the edges.

By the way, Yitzchak continued, he had the issue showing the East Carolina (Brody) ranking, and would his guest like to see it? It was right in the next room. David smiled and declined, steering Yitzchak back to the subject at hand.

The simple baby doctor insisted David have dinner with his family, a raucous affair indeed. There had been no way to refuse. There were innumerable children, all moderately well-behaved in a strange sort of way, and, although they peppered him with questions about, what David came to realize partway through the dinner, was 'the outside world', the experience was just as strangely enjoyable. It was difficult to conceive that in many ways he was on foreign soil, with less in common than he had with the average European. Weirder than the clothing, stranger than the earlocks, odder than the innumerable small culture shocks, including the tablecloth that appeared to be made of the same lace as the curtains, the absence of a television – HD LCD display or not – was irreconcilable. Nomadic Mongols and Bedouins had flat panels in their tents, David knew.

Apparently the intent of much Hasidic cooking was to kill a chicken as dead as possible, boiling it for geologic time until nothing remained but a whitish substance that fell apart when touched with a utensil. David learned about horseradish the hard way. He bit into what he thought he recognized as a matzo ball, but wasn't, rather a thing called gefilte fish. The fish had evidently been massaged into a kind of meatball shape, because it certainly didn't come that way in the field, for whatever reason David could not guess. He did not drink from his seltzer glass and hoped no one noticed.

Mrs. Yitzchak - a durable woman, clearly – shooed the children away as she served coffee. The doorbell rang moments later, and she ushered Mordecai Rubin into the dining room. David had thought favorably of Yitzchak's suggestion to include the younger physician.

Mordecai Rubin, who, as pointed out again by Menachem Yitzchak, had graduated number three in his medical school class at the top five school, and the U.S. News & World Report issue was in the next room if David cared to see it, proved indeed intelligent and capable. When the pregnancies resumed, he had immediately taken blood samples of both mother and father and performed as much prenatal testing as practical. As a result, his findings preceded David's, which were identical. The conclusions were inescapable.

There were still vital answers needed, but now they knew what they were up against. The implications were staggering.

David left his coffee untouched.

73

Everyone in the room on the outskirts of Lod was peering at David intently. He took a breath, looked around at his audience and began:

"In California and Arizona, we knew from analyzing the female blood that the agent used was the G-11 stolen from one of the domestic labs under contract to the United States government. The mothers were affected. Where we could identify the paternal partner, they presented no anomalies. G-11 has the ability to bond with virtually all females except Caucasians, with whom it passes through harmlessly. Therefore the method of delivery need not be very selective. We subsequently learned the two locations were utilized to test method of delivery as much as effectiveness among differing minorities. One, like the springs at Salukiya, compromised the water supply. The second was delivered by aerosol in the form of a crop duster over a camp of migrant agricultural workers. Haitians and Dominicans, mostly, and a few Guatemalans populate the place. While the Arizona location was minority-specific, if you will, the Parkerville inoculation – that's the California site – was more democratic, covering Caucasian, Mexican and Indian populations."

David paused. "I should point out that in the affected areas there is no Jewish population. We don't really know if G-11 would have any effect, but we suspect not, for reasons which will become clear. Okay.'

'We have not been able to pinpoint the exact dates G-11 was introduced in either location. We have made informed judgments. As a result, we can only speculate as to the incubation period, if any, and draw parallels with our animal testing. There is no incubation period with either rats or hamsters. All factors, therefore, lead us to also expect none with humans. After a period of months, then, medical professionals noticed the cessation of minority pregnancies in both locations. Approximately eight weeks after that, pregnancies resumed, with the result that a devastating seventy percent of conceptions were defective in some way. There seems to be a tendency towards specific genetic disorders with different minorities."

David paused for breath. He sipped his soft drink. The room was deathly quiet.

"Doctor Livingston." It was one of the men David pegged as Mossad. "Did the pregnancies resume on a gradual basis, or all at once?"

"Good question. Allowing for natural leeway involving conception, of course, the answer is all at once." The man nodded. David resumed his narrative.

"Subsequent investigation revealed a domestic effort to initiate what might be called ethnic cleansing within our borders. This was a loose confederation involving political, scientific and intelligence personnel. Many were powerful figures. A shadow conspiracy, if you will. We have not finished this investigation, but its effectiveness has been destroyed. And, if we hadn't done it, G-11 would have. The assumption had been the target populations would cease to procreate, perhaps with the aid of subsequent inoculations. The reality, resumption of births with hideous rates of defects, was unforeseen by the group. This was unacceptable within the United States. Which leads me to Brooklyn."

If he had their attention before, they were transfixed now.

"Our information, partly supplied by you folks, was that the primary alternative to G-11 was an agent being bio-engineered somewhere in the Middle East, possibly Syria, maybe Iran, utilizing personnel from several Arab states. Certainly a finger points at Syria, since they still claim the Golan, where the bottling plant was inoculated, and the infiltrators you captured were Syrian nationals from over the border. But do they have the sophisticated facilities for this kind of engineering and production? That's a real question. We also are aware similar work has been ongoing in Japan and perhaps North Korea, in a rudimentary way. We gave this alternative agent the code name R U R."

One or two smiles appeared in the audience. The reference to the 1920 Karel Capek play involving genetic engineering was not lost.

"Because both G-11 and R U R had developed from the same basic research, the similarities are probably greater than the differences. Our intelligence indicated R U R affects the male, unlike G-11, and we would then have a quick way to differentiate between them in the field. What now seems apparent, based on the Brooklyn test, is that the R U R unleashed there, and likely in your bottled water, was a specific cocktail designed for a specific result.'

'I should tell you something here. When the G-11 was stolen from the California lab, a small portion of that substance was sold to agents who, we suspect, were working for Middle Eastern interests. We theorize the G-11 was used to advance their own development of R U R and may have in fact sped up that research to the degree that the Brooklyn test became operational much more quickly.'

'We don't know how the Brooklyn population was inoculated. We've eliminated the water supply. It may be tied to a specific cultural more. As you may know, my day job – my doctoral specialty – involves selective genetic defects."

David paused to drain his soda bottle. There wasn't a sound in the room. He continued:

"We have to allow that whatever the delivery system is, it has been proven effective. In the Hasidic neighborhoods of Brooklyn, pregnancies suddenly ceased. Blood tests revealed the males were affected, not the females. The conclusion, then, was an R U R inoculation that had no effect on either surrounding or embedded non-Jewish populations. Yet it was almost a hundred percent effective among the Jews."

David paused again and made a gesture. As someone handed him another soda, General Ben-Reuven spoke.

"You paint a dark picture, Doctor Livingston."

"I'm afraid I haven't gotten to the worst of it." David drank, then set the bottle down. "When the pregnancies resumed – and the hiatus with R U R was significantly shorter than G-11 – we tested the fetuses right away, of course. Among the Ashkenazi Jews, there was a seventy percent rate of Tay-Sachs disease."

Doctor Meir gasped. Heads turned towards him; he was clearly shocked. David could see that most of the people in the room did not understand.

"Doctor Meir, perhaps you would like to explain to these men just what we're dealing with."

There was a pause. Doctor Meir did not get up. He spoke in a flat voice. "Tay-Sachs is the most common genetic disorder in Ashkenazy Jews. It is caused by a mutation of the HEXA gene. That gene catalyzes hydrolysis of ganglioside GM2 to GM3."

He realized no one was following him. He sighed.

"Here is what this means. Within months of birth, usually, symptoms appear. Loss of motor skills, jerks, tics. Visual attentiveness goes next. Then loss of voluntary movements, seizures, unresponsiveness. A lucky child dies by age two. One not so fortunate will die by age four. There is no cure. There is no effective treatment. There is only heartache, all-consuming care, and great expense."

One of the uniforms David pegged as Mossad spoke up. "What is the percentage of Jews that are Ashkenazy? It's way over half, isn't it?"

Heads nodded. "Seventy percent."

"I think eighty percent."

"Eighty to ninety percent, in Israel, anyway."

Murmurs gave away to silence. David gave them time to absorb this catastrophic news. Then he spoke.

"None of the affected Brooklyn fetuses has reached term, of course. Press coverage has been limited to the brief cessation in conception. There has been some speculation regarding connection with Arizona and California. You have the exact date the springs at Salukiya were compromised. From that you can work out when the R U R effects will occur, from infertility to conception to detection of, presumably, Tay-Sachs."

There was a heavy silence as the men in the room struggled to accept the dreadful knowledge David had imparted.

"Do you have more to tell us, Doctor Livingston?" asked Major Ya'ari.

"Yes. Why would the perpetrators infect New York at all? We asked ourselves that. We knew the source was Middle Eastern, as I said, perhaps a coalition of some Arab states. What did they care about Brooklyn? Why not just infect the Golan? That's Israel. These were obviously tests. So what was the point of the Brooklyn test? Method of delivery, yes. But that was a secondary consideration, we believe."

"Who is the 'we'?" asked Major Ya'ari.

"Myself, Richard Haycock, key scientists at both U.S. sites and certain members of the intelligence community we knew were not involved in the original domestic contamination," David replied.

"And what is the primary reason, do you believe?" Ya'ari asked.

"So they could monitor the results. Eventually, everything would be in the American press. Cessation of pregnancies and, most important, resumption and any subsequent consequences. In other words, they would be sure to hear about the Tay-Sachs. This would not necessarily be true in Israel. It leads to a doomsday hypothesis."

"Which is--?" asked General Ben-Reuven.

"The replacement of nuclear warfare, nuclear deterrence, with genetic warfare against which there is little or no real defense for the targeted people. Far more deadly, producing total results and little environmental damage. The ability to selectively and effectively neutralize an ethnic population without harming others, no matter how geographically proximate. The ability to wage lethal warfare without harming infrastructure or damaging the environment. An enemy crippled with a new generation of severely mutated offspring, requiring twenty-four hour care with an overwhelming financial burden. Overwhelming grief, paralyzing despair. The breaking of the collective spirit. In other words, not just the slow fading away of the Jewish people. The genetic insult of Tay-Sachs upon Israel is a plague of biblical proportions, and some entity, some force, whomever, some diabolical coalition may be deliberately engineering it. They may believe this is what the Qu'uran and the Bible refer to, and thus a third reason for the Brooklyn test. R U R is an instrument of God, the very core of Revelation. The deliberate destruction of the subsequent generation, the debilitation of the current population from the consequences of seventy percent Tay-Sachs babies, and the descent into chaos that would rapidly follow. In other words, the end of Israel, the ultimate Holocaust for the Jews on earth. The final *jihad*."

74

David was sure none of the Israelis in the living room – the informality of which seemed grotesquely incongruous to him – had considered the potential consequences of the Golan Heights incident. For one thing, they hadn't possessed all the intelligence, particularly from Brooklyn, and they just hadn't had enough time to work it through. Perhaps as important, the implications for Israel were almost too devastating to accept.

Another silence. David thought he heard birds outside. Life goes on. Or does it? The men began to talk with each other, in low voices, breaking into groups. David sat patiently; he knew these men, so accustomed to authority and decisiveness, would need to find their bearings before formulating a course of action. Finally, General Ben-Reuven spoke.

"How much time do we have? If they have a significant quantity of this - what is it? - R U R, then we can presume they will introduce it on a widespread basis."

David said, "We believe there are many risks involved in the inoculation of R U R on a greater scale. The risk of detection becomes intolerable without an assured result. It is an all-out act of war equivalent to nuclear aggression. They can't go to war with weapons that might misfire. Their enemies have weapons that won't misfire. They need reliable test results."

"In a land of suicide bombers, you may be ascribing too much rationality to the perpetrators," Major Ya'ari said. It might be true,

David thought. "We need to find where this material is manufactured. What can you tell us?"

"Very little, I'm afraid. Our intelligence is sketchy. Saudi Arabia is a distinct possibility, despite the evidence pointing to Syria. The Saudis have sophisticated laboratory facilities and one or two leading lights in this area of research. It's also the home of *Wahhabi*, the most radical form of Islam, sworn to destroy Israel. You know all about that; the Saudi veneer of alignment with the West is paper thin. Under that veneer, they are aligned with and finance extremism and terrorist organizations everywhere. But the fact is that we just don't know. We have little human intelligence – no one we follow knows anything about it. We've got a couple of thin leads in the U.S., but we don't believe they'll pan out. This appears all too insulated and sophisticated. You've got a much better chance of ferreting out leads than we do.'

'As to the substance itself, R U R cannot be made in an ordinary commercial lab or the usual academic facility. There would be specialized equipment required. I have brought a list. Security would be ironclad, and a Level 4 containment facility required. That should narrow it down. In addition, certain specialized materials used in manufacture may be traced if one knows the formula for R U R."

"Do you have the formula for R U R?" General Ben-Reuven asked.

"We don't know the formula for R U R."

"How can we effect an antidote then?"

"We don't know. You have to destroy it."

75

"They call these hush puppies in America," Hashim said, inspecting his dish of *luqaymat*, the dumpling-like caramel coated affair that was a popular dessert in certain parts of the Middle East. Mamdouh and Abdul-Haq knew Prince Hashim was a closet fan of American junk food and Hollywood movies. Hashim had been educated at Davidson College in North Carolina and had a fondness for grits, although his fellow Royals thought it an affectation. Mamdouh had said they looked and tasted like wet cement.

The three princes of the Royal branch were poolside at the Moevenpick Resort al Nawras. The hotel, located on a private island just off Jeddah's Corniche, featured individual swimming pools for each of the 89 suites, all overlooking the sea. Mamdouh was staying for three days while tending to family business in the city. The others had arranged to stop by in the afternoon.

"Truly Hayyan has been sent to us by Allah," Mamdouh said, after Hashim had broached the subject.

"Are we certain of Hayyan? Can we verify his story?" Hashim asked.

"Haifa's brother comes to us from Allah, I repeat."

"Perhaps. We must be cautious."

"There are only two possibilities," Abdul-Haq said. "He is either telling the truth or he is in league with the Black Prince. I have reason to believe he is telling the truth. In either case, we have played our hand. We must move forward."

"Why do you believe he is telling the truth?"

"Not one but two people were slain in London. Sharif was in London."

The others contemplated Abdul-Haq's statement and realized it was true. There was no turning back. They had to proceed now. There were a few moments of silence.

"Hayyan is what we have been looking for. He will be the instrument."

"We are repeating ourselves like old women. We must act like men."

"I cannot think of a situation where he would lead Sharif back to us."

"I can."

A sudden wind came in from the Red Sea, rustling the palms, riffling the pool water.

"And what of Syed?"

"Yes, what of him?"

"He is of no consequence." Abdul-Haq replied to their questions.

"What do you mean?"

Abdul-Haq smiled. "I believe we need another dish of your hush puppies, Mamdouh. In either case, Syed's fate is sealed, is it not? He is useless to us now, no matter what."

"Is he not our friend?"

Abdul-Haq laughed, but not with his smoldering eyes. "Do you think you would be fit to rule with a woman's sentiment? Allah has seen that he has served his purpose, bringing Hayyan to us. Can there be any argument?"

*   *   *   *

It was only a few hours before Sharif learned the three royals had met off the coast of Jeddah. He still knew nothing of Hayyan, prince of the Cadet branch, simply because he hadn't been there.

76

David was lucky enough to hitch a ride on another G-150 back to Washington. The interior of this airplane was less accommodating, primarily because it didn't exist. David spent the flight in the cockpit, peppering the crew with questions. Although not certified to fly heavy jets, he had accumulated fourteen hours in the 747 Pan Am simulator in Miami, having overshot the runway at the old Hong Kong airport half a dozen times. He had electronically died each time before wobbling the make-believe airplane in successfully on his last attempt.

David waved so long to the flight crew after thanking them for the lift; they would be airborne as soon as they were cleared for takeoff, headed to Dallas for the plane's fitting out.

David's solution to avoiding jet lag was to drink plenty of water. As he sat in front of Richard Haycock, he realized it hadn't worked. He brought his boss up to date on events in Israel.

"What is your plan now?" Haycock asked.

"There was a message waiting for me at the CDC," David said. "A detective from Brooklyn homicide."

"What could that be about?"

"I'm not sure. The message was sketchy. I don't know what it could have to do with the R U R event, but I need to chase it down right away. We've missed each other a couple of times."

"Keep me in the loop, David."

"Certainly, sir."

As David left the townhouse, he considered his options. As he stood on the sidewalk, he called Detective Mulvaney from his cell phone. This time, the Brooklyn cop was in his office.

"Thanks for calling me back, Doctor. I don't know if I have anything here, really, but better safe than sorry."

"What's up, Detective?"

"Well, we had a homicide not long ago. A rabbi was slain and his body disposed of in a dumpster. Made all the New York papers."

"Okay." David didn't know what else to say. "I hadn't heard about it."

"Thing is, he was murdered in a factory during the night. The factory makes matzo. This is in a Hasidic section of the borough. Forensic evidence revealed two perpetrators. They made no attempt to sanitize their fingerprints, but hauled the body out of the factory and made a half-assed attempt to clean the place up."

A spider crawled lightly up the back of David's neck.

"All right, I follow."

"I'm figuring they didn't want the crime scene discovered, at least for a little while. So what were a couple of guys doing in a matzo plant in the middle of the night, you get my drift? Nothing to steal except matzo. What's worth killing a rabbi? These weren't drug users looking for a place to crash. They took the door jamb apart to get in, and screwed it back together to get out. Stealth, you know?"

David realized he was holding his breath. "I see."

"I didn't. I kept thinking about it. I went back to the crime scene and wandered around. I found something that didn't belong in a matzo factory. It way didn't belong."

"What did you find, Detective?"

"An empty container. The container had masking tape on the outside dividing the container into thirds. It had originally been sealed, and somebody tried to reseal it, even though it was empty."

"Keep going."

"Why reseal an empty container? So here's where my imagination gets way out there, maybe. The papers have been running this stuff about pregnant women suddenly becoming pretty scarce in the Hasidic community, you know? I figure you people knew about that."

"We know about that."

"So I'm thinking and thinking. There are three water tanks in the matzo plant. You probably don't know this, but the water is blessed by the rabbis and locked up overnight for making matzo in the morning. Which is just water and flour, okay? Especially when it's made for Passover, they leave out the garlic and other crap. Now this jug was marked into thirds, like I said. Almost as though whatever was in the container was for all three tanks. So I check the locks on the tanks. Your kid locks his bicycle with a heftier lock. There were scratch marks where they'd been picked. And here's the really odd thing."

"What's that, Detective Mulvaney?"

"There's writing on the bottom of the jug. Indented into the plastic, you know, no ink. From when it was made. We almost missed it. And it's not Hebrew. It's Arabic."

"What?"

"Yeah. We had it translated. It says 'two liters'. It's a two liter Arab container from someplace. What the hell's an empty raghead container doing in a matzo plant in the middle of Hasidic Brooklyn?"

Of course, David thought. Nothing but flour and water. How brilliant. How perfect.

"Did you open it? Where's the container now?"

"We may be in Brooklyn, Doctor, but we ain't that dumb. It's in a sealed heavy plastic pouch. The lab boys wanted to open up the container, but I nixed that. What the hell, I'm not through having kids. I've got it right here."

Within five minutes, David was back in the townhouse.

77

During the housecleaning at Jergens Labs following exposure of the eugenics program, work on the G-11 project had been temporarily suspended.   With the knowledge that R U R was apparently being field tested, an expanded team of researchers, bio-engineers, molecular physicists and geneticists had quickly been assembled to try and reverse engineer the R U R. A primary tool was the blood samples of the Brooklyn Jewish males provided by Doctor Mordecai Rubin as well as theoretical input based on the body of G-11 research. A similar program was underway at the classified military base that had assisted in the development of that agent.   Because amniocentesis carries a significant risk of miscarriage – one in 200 – and the fetuses were not quite sixteen weeks old, the teams were operating under a significant handicap. There was no opportunity to analyze the chorionic villi, the future placental tissue, a vitally important step.

Placed in a thick protective foam cooler, the plastic container from the matzo factory was rushed by police escort to Islip Field. When Detective Mulvaney stepped from the squad car onto the tarmac, he was immediately met by two men in civilian dress who escorted him aboard a waiting Gulfstream jet, a CIA asset that had been inbound from Glasgow, diverted to Islip and refueled. Richard Haycock had moved quickly indeed.

Aboard, Mulvaney eyed the oddly spartan interior and turned to his escorts.

"You boys the flight attendants? I've seen better heads on nickel beers. How about a double scotch?"

When David boarded N379P in Washington, he found Detective Mulvaney welcome company. What you saw was what you got.

"Call me Harris," Mulvaney said, sticking out his hand. "This damn airplane has no whiskey, no beer, no flight attendant, no nothing. Just those two mannequins." He jerked his thumb at the two men standing by the doorway. "Is this how you people treat a New York City Irish cop?" he said with a grin. The Brooklyn detective had no way of knowing he had ridden in the infamous "Guantanamo Bay Express" used to transport terrorist suspects to Cuba.

"Sorry for the dry run. Detective, you probably have no idea what you may have done here. The country already owes you a huge debt of gratitude."

"Save the Washington bullshit. Hell, the country owes me dinner," Mulvaney grumbled. "And a case of Guinness." He gestured to the front row seat where the cooler was strapped in. "Well, here's your baby. Let me know how it all turns out."

"Don't worry," David said. "I'll tell you what I can, that's a promise. Here's my card. Catch a first class flight back to New York, eat an expensive steak, buy the case of Guinness, and send the bill to me."

"Yeah?"

"Yeah. I want to frame it." His grin told the detective he was kidding.

Mulvaney nodded. "That's good," the detective said. "When I told my wife I wouldn't be home for supper, she said I'd find the meat loaf in the refrigerator."

Winging westward, David looked over at the Styrofoam cooler. As he thought about it, his admiration for the tough

Brooklyn cop grew. Mulvaney's stubborn streak and deductive reasoning might turn out to be a priceless break for the Jergens team.

*　　　　　*　　　　　*

David tried to sleep, but only managed an airplane stupor for perhaps an hour, drooling down his chin. He never missed the chance to view the Grand Canyon, anyway, which was off the right wing. Even the moon went someplace, but the canyon never went anywhere. David loved the idea that it didn't do anything, or need to do anything. It just was. It was absurd to think some dinky river made all that, even if it did. It was the same every time. Just as his mind seemed about to grasp the majesty and scope of the terrain, it always slipped past.

Gaining three hours, it was only four p.m. when David brought the cooler into the Jergens lobby. He had a brief flashback – his visit to the facility with Leslie seemed a million years ago. He felt a pang of regret about Ken Holliday, and a second one for not having thought of his murdered friend since that terrible day. There just hadn't been any time, really. A team was waiting on the fourth floor. He called Leslie as he suited up.

"You're going back into the Level 4 containment lab?" she asked, disbelieving.

"Yep. Have to. Don't exactly know when I'll be out. I'll see you as soon as I can."

The team analyzing the container was headed by Doctor Emily Werner. The alphabet soup after her name took up most of a line. David liked her right away. She had a kindly face, smile wrinkles around the eyes, and appeared perhaps fifty years old. Her make-up was just a suggestion, but a nice one. She reminded him of somebody's mom. Maybe everybody's mom.

"I'm Emily, Doctor Livingston." Emily, David thought. She's got more degrees than a thermometer and she calls herself Emily. "I've been briefed on the history of this container, but I'd like to hear it from you before we start."

David reviewed the background. Emily nodded. "Okay, we'll put the package under the hood and open the outer plastic." The laminar flow hood, with a high efficiency bacteria-retentive filter, would ensure the biological integrity of the package and its components. "We'll remove that pouch and analyze it separately. Then we'll remove the seal and probe the air inside the container. Finally, we'll attempt to remove residue from the inside walls and the inside grooves in the lid as well as the tape. I would think we will find traces of the R U R, but is it enough? Can we use the ETEC? Can we prep what we find? Those are going to be some of the questions."

They got started. After two hours, all the time zone changes and the tension finally caught up with David. He wasn't really performing any useful function anyway. Emily assured him she'd call as soon as they had anything to tell. Exhausted, he followed the decontamination procedures, barely able to doff his protective gear. Checking in a half hour later, he dissolved into the motel mattress without even a thought of dinner.

78

At eleven a.m. Doctor Emily Werner, David and two senior members of the analytical team, Doctors Fladeland and Rush, assembled in the second floor conference room at Jergens. David had gotten Emily's call at 7:15. The team had finished their analysis, having worked through the night, and she was going to crash for a couple of hours before discussing their findings.

David, fresh from a deep nine hour sleep followed by eggs, bacon, toast and coffee, felt alert and invigorated. Emily and her group also seemed to have benefited from a couple of hours in the rack. Outside, it was another gorgeous California day. The little red helicopter glowed like a jewel. Sunlight streamed in, laying a bright diagonal path across the pale blue plush carpet and gleaming mahogany table. One thing about Doctor Jergens, David thought. He had known how to spend Uncle Sam's bucks.

Emily began:

"There was sufficient material in the container for our purposes. Because an attempt was made to reseal the container, which was only partially successful, there was enough liquid remaining for definitive analysis. First, however, I will address the blood samples of the biological fathers of the infected fetuses.'

'The physician collecting the Brooklyn samples was quite thorough. Using venipuncture, he collected both clotted and heparinized blood. Thorough analysis reveals – I can get into the methodology later, involving isoelectric focusing and leukocyte pellets for hexosamindase - but the bottom line is that there is no abnormal evidence of carrier ancestry. There are other, subtle changes we will need to study. The conclusion is that the fetuses have developed Tay-Sachs strictly through the introduction of R U R."

Although this was expected, David felt a sense of shock. In other words, the stuff really worked. Emily continued:

"R U R appears capable, then, of creating an artificial deficiency of hexosamindase, more specifically β-D-N-acetylhexosaminase. Deficiencies in the fetuses encompass both α-locus and β-locus hexosamindase. The result, as expected, is Tay-Sachs. The ability to accomplish this is incredibly sophisticated. So that's the background. Now on to the container."

She paused to pour a cup of water and drain it. The phrase 'thirsty work' crossed David's mind, probably from a horror movie.

"Oh, there's one other important thing. Not all the subjects were Ashkenazy Jews. Tay-Sachs is an affliction primarily confined to that branch. We did some quick research. Ashkenazys comprise about eighty percent of the world's Jews. The blood work-up indicates two of the subjects were Sephardic Jews. This is statistically very significant. With a seventy percent infection rate, R U R would eventually eliminate fifty six percent of the world Jews if confined to the Ashkenazys. That would have been your best case scenario without intervention. Now, of course, it's fourteen percent higher. Of perhaps greater significance is the fact that they could have done it at all. It implies a modification not found in nature.'

'Okay. The liquid carrier for the R U R is common. Almost all the ingredients in the residual agent found in the container – and there are several – are common. We don't understand, as yet, why there so many, or what they do, if anything. But the bottom line here, Doctor Livingston, is that you can't trace the stuff by any the ingredients except one, and you can't trace it anyway. That ingredient is a dimeric enzyme, heat-labile hexosamindase in serum.

Specifically, Hex A. Mutations in either of its subunits α or β can produce either Tay-Sachs or Sandhoff diseases, as you probably recall. And we are speaking of very small quantities in the four liter container."

Emily paused. "You with me?" she asked with a warm smile. She might have been describing a recipe for apple pie.

David nodded. "Yes."

"Okay," Emily continued. "It would appear someone has made considerable progress, I would say astonishing progress, in refining the protein purification steps to prevent partial enzyme degradation. They purified enough material to investigate and modify, apparently, the polypeptide within. This appears responsible, then, for the causation of Tay-Sachs in the Sephardic subjects as well as the Ashkenazys, something without real precedent. How this works, we don't know. How an effect can be made a cause, we don't know. We may not know for quite awhile, but if you are trying to find it, you need to know what's in it, and that's what we've come up with. There's no field test, like on TV where the cops do for crack, where they swirl something on a car hood and it turns blue. You are going to have to track the source, and there is no source. Someone made it. They didn't get it, they made it."

Silence as the import of Emily's presentation sifted in. David realized the likelihood of finding the substance quickly dimmed with the gravity of what he had just heard. He gazed out the window, past the helicopter, the immaculate lawn, and into the forest beyond.

Twenty four hours later, he repeated the gist of Emily's findings as he sat facing Richard Haycock. The Special Assistant to the President was silent for a time, then frowned.

"So if I understand this correctly, the—let me rephrase that, because of course I can't understand it – we have to try and trace a compound that we have no idea where it comes from? It's not something that gets bought on some black market someplace?"

"Yes, but it's not quite that bleak. In order to synthesize this heat-labile hexosamindase, you need other ingredients, and those would be acquired in combination. We have a shot at finding it, but the problem is those ingredients are not rare."

"The 'we' will have to include Mossad."

"Yes."

"You know how they are. They'll have to sort it all out, who does what, between them and the Shin Bet and Aman."

"No doubt. They were all at the Lod meeting, as you know."

Haycock nodded. "Let us hope they've put aside their tiresome rivalries. A forlorn hope in this country, of course. Anyway, they will have to trace the key ingredients to wherever they lead. We can help, but it's their backyard."

"Yes."

"Here's the key question – by revealing the key substance to this R U R to the Israelis, will we compromise our own national security?"

David wasn't sure he followed. "How so, sir?"

"You know, David, they've been living on the goodwill of the Holocaust for a long time now. There really are no black hats, white hats. Just AK-47s and Galil assault rifles and RPGs. Illegal walls and cluster bombs on civilians. Human shields leading convoys. Toy rockets from Palestine. Well, not so kiddie anymore. And now, liquid death in containers."

"Yes sir." This was a small surprise. David wondered if Richard Haycock reflected the President's real views. Probably, he decided.

"I wouldn't want to find we regret giving the Israelis the key ingredient. That would be a major worry."

"I don't think so, sir. Doctor Werner was clear on that. She said just because you can buy paint doesn't mean you can turn out Whistler's Mother."

Haycock smiled. "I've never met Doctor Werner but I've heard about her. She's supposed to be really something. And not bad looking."

Somehow, coming from Richard Haycock, the remark seemed completely out of character. But then again, maybe not.

79

Royal Albert Hall, on Kensington Gore in southwest London, was not one of Sharif's favorite venues. Before the installation of giant damping mushrooms in the 1960s to null the disconcerting echo, the gag had been that a patron got two concerts for the price of one. To Sharif's exquisite ear, the mushrooms were an annoying imperfection. Nonetheless, a rare performance by the Royal Scottish National Orchestra of Shostakovich's Symphony No. 5 in D minor – a masterpiece despite its alleged apologetic intention – merited his attendance. As always, he would sit in Loggia Box 7, Seat 1. Yousif, whose tin ear would otherwise make his appearance without purpose, was usually booked into Seat 5, directly behind, where he would attend Sharif's needs and provide security.

Prince Abdul-Haq did not need to hack into the Hall's computer reservation system to know Sharif would be in attendance. He was aware The Black Prince had flown to London the week before, bringing not only Yousif but the ethereal Fatima, the green-eyed Libyan, who by now had become a constant companion. Sharif had instructed Yousif to procure another woman from the usual source, an elite service based just north of Hyde Park in a Connaught Square Georgian townhouse, a few doors down from Tony Blair. The woman, a Polish Jew named Wera, was also a mistress of Abdul-Haq, and at his direction had steered a sum to her employer so that she would be sent when Yousif called. Perhaps not coincidentally, the escort was musically knowledgeable and, in fact, an accomplished cellist who had performed with the London

Philharmonic before poisoning her husband while in a cocaine haze. She had not been convicted. Abdul-Haq had realized the value Wera might have, both as mistress and instrument of his will. He originally thought she might repeat her act with Sharif, if he could arrange for her to be called to the Piano Suite, but now the task would fall as agreed to Hayyan.

Wera spent an interesting two hours in Sharif's lair. She found the liaison rough, but a heightening experience. Afterward, while he was occupied in the bathroom, she engaged Fatima in discussion.

"It is a beautiful piano."

"Yes."

"Will you or the prince play something?"

"No. Perhaps another time," Fatima said. "I would play if you accompanied with your cello. Would you like to do that?"

"Yes. What would we play?"

"Fauré, I think. Perhaps Sicilienne. Do you know it?"

"Of course, Opus 78. I love how the melodies fade and intertwine." Wera probed. "Does the prince attend the Proms?"

"What is this – Proms?" Fatima asked.

"Concerts at Royal Albert Hall."

"Oh, yes. We are going this week. Shostakovitch."

As she left the Claridge, Wera placed a cell phone call from the taxicab to relay the news that Sharif would attend the concert at Royal Albert Hall four days hence, and that Fatima would accompany him. Sharif had evidently decided the tone deaf Yousif could sit this one out.

Abdul-Haq's scheme had worked better than he had hoped. Not only had he learned of Sharif's plans, but thanks to Fatima the Black Prince would be without his bodyguard that evening. He immediately relayed what he had learned to Prince Hayyan, and a plan was set in motion.

80

David realized that someday soon he was going to miss jetting around the globe, with all the aircraft of the United States government seemingly at his disposal. He hoped it would be soon if this crisis could somehow be solved. He had hitched a ride on an Air Force C-17 Globemaster III back to Atlanta, and was packing for an indeterminate stay in Tel Aviv, involving himself in the search. Finding the manufacturing location for the R U R was going to be a daunting task, even utilizing the resources of both the United States and Israel. Mentally, he was organizing the leads as he took a load from the washer and stuck it in the dryer. The mail pile was halfway up to the slot; it took him an hour just to pay pressing bills. To complicate matters, he had forgotten to record a check in the register – how could he do this every few months? – and he couldn't keep track of his balance. At least he was on his last batch of checks, he thought wryly, and had neglected to order a new supply. Life interfered with everything.

David understood Richard Haycock's reluctance to share critical R U R information with the Israelis. Their scientists, capable and well-equipped, would immediately initiate offensive as well as defensive research into this new weapon of stealth. The Special Assistant visualized a frightful vision of tomorrow, where nuclear capacity seemed almost benign.

He was probably right, David thought. Not given to introspection, David thrived on action and problem-solving. He would have liked to have seen Leslie in California, and wondered if little Derek had eaten any of the Erector set. The ring of his cell phone dissolved his reverie. It was Emily Werner. She and Haycock would really like each other, he thought.

"David? How are you?"

"I'm fine, Emily." He looked at his watch. "How's it going?"

"I'll let you decide. We know where the container came from."

A jolt of electricity. "What? How? Where?"

Emily laughed. "Well, put it this way. It wasn't through biological or chemical analysis. It was through dumb luck."

"I'm all ears."

"Well, okay. There's a woman on our team, Doctor Navi Zahedi. You didn't meet her. She was originally an exchange student, post-doctoral at MIT. She was working on the container and the seal. Who told you the writing on the bottom was Arabic?"

"What? What do you mean? What the heck is it?"

"It's Farsi."

"Farsi? They speak that in—"

"Yes. Iran and Afghanistan, Navi told me. She's Iranian."

"That's incredible news. Does it still say two liters?"

Emily laughed again. David really did like her. "It always said two liters. But wait, I'm not done. Did you notice the little symbol after the writing?"

David thought back to the container. He had assumed whatever was there was part of the text.

"No, I just thought it was all part of the text."

"It's not. It's a manufacturing mark. Doctor Zahedi worked in yellow cake production. She was involved in converting uranium to uranium hexafluoride."

Uranium enrichment. For reactors or bombs.

"Keep going, Emily."

"She worked in the yellow cake plant in Bandar Abbas. That's in Iran, you know? Most of their lab equipment came from a small local scientific materials production plant, not from Tehran. The mark belongs to that company. That means, in all likelihood, the R U R was synthesized in or around Bandar Abbas."

"Emily, if that's the case, it's an incredible break."

"Sure. And there's one more thing."

"What's that?"

"Navi's full name is Navideh. Know what that means in English?"

"Uuh – Merry Christmas?"

"Funny, David. I like your sense of humor. Navideh means 'good news'. You owe me dinner."

81

"What exactly did you tell General Ben-Reuven?" asked Richard Haycock, after David brought him up to date on the extraordinary stroke of luck with the container. The Special Assistant to the President was eating a cup of homemade chocolate pudding with a little milk on top of the skin. Slowly. David had finished his cup, which was light years better than the instant variety.

"I said I was delaying the trip because we had a lead on the R U R manufacturing location and I'd call back as soon as I had any further information. I got off the line before he could press me for details. Then I came right here."

Haycock nodded as he took a small spoonful of pudding. "Reasonable enough. You didn't take that little death trap of yours, did you? That tinny – *airplane*?" He made it sound like a profanity.

"No, sir. I took a direct flight from Atlanta."

"I hope you're saving all your receipts, David. This is all a whirling dervish, here, there, everywhere. Aah, well. Maybe when I was younger." He dabbed again at the pudding.

"Yes, sir. I still have the receipt from the fuselage repair. After the landing gear incident."

"Landing gear accident," Haycock corrected. He couldn't keep the trace of a smile from appearing, David noticed.

"As you say, sir."

"All right, then. What do you know about Bandar Abbas?"

"Not much. Sits right on the Strait of Hormuz. One of the Iranian cities involved with uranium conversion or enrichment, along with Esfehan and Natanz."

"Colorful history. Quite strategic. Something under a half million people. Flat. Didn't care for it much, myself." That surprised David, mildly. Where hadn't he been? "Of course, it wasn't the same world, then." He had finished his snack.

It wasn't the same world three months ago, David thought.

82

Hayyan had arrived at Royal Albert Hall at 5:30, an hour before the scheduled performance, and made his way to the Second Tier just as the boxes were opening. His ticket, catering order and prepaid parking had been paid for in cash two days prior. He left the spare key to the Honda Accord, registered to one Afzal Hadad, a naturalized British subject, on the left rear tire. He kept the remote in his pocket, just to ensure he could find the vehicle quickly. If Hayyan did not return for the car, it would be picked up two hours after the performance. The automobile was the preferred escape route, but Hayyan had familiarized himself with the location of the South Kensington and High Street Kensington stations, as well as the stops and destinations of the No. 9, 10 and 52 busses. His ticket was for Second Tier Box 83 Seat 5, deliberately chosen; in that corner location he was somewhat above and across from Sharif, with the curtain behind and no one to his right. He was also able to purchase Seat 4, directly in front of 5. He would have bought out the entire box, but four of the seats had already been taken.

Two days before the performance, a thirty three year old Building Services Technician at the Royal Albert Hall, a Yemeni immigrant named Muhammad Baakrime, entered the Hall as he normally did, carrying his large metal tool kit. Under the top tray, sealed plastic pouches contained a Beretta 92F semi-automatic pistol, specially equipped with GreenBeam 2000 laser sight and a fast-attach Advanced Armament M9 silencer, along with a full clip of hollow point 9mm Parabellum rounds. The weaponry was secreted in an electrical locker until just before the performance, when it found its way to the bottom of a champagne bucket containing a bottle of Marquis De La Tour Brut sparking wine along with the order of open smoked salmon finger sandwiches delivered to Box 83 at 5:45.

Hayyan, alone in the box, immediately fished out the parcels from under the ice. The M9 attached in seconds. He stuck the assembled weapon in his waistband; the icy cold metal chilled him uncomfortably for several minutes. His heart was thumping. Hayyan made an effort of will to calm himself; although he hadn't felt hungry he devoured the finger sandwiches. The more he ate, though, the more famished he became. He knew it was nerves. Although not a drinker, he sipped a half glass of the sparkling wine and felt a soothing warmth flow into his chest. It felt good after the cold of the handgun. He wanted more wine, but knew that would be unwise.

The hall began to fill as Hayyan contemplated the arrangement he had arrived at with Syed. The conspirators would assist him in his vendetta and Hayyan would share in the reward, should one of them ascend the throne. The sharing was unspecified but from Hayyan's point of view it did not need to be spelled out. He was committed to his action and the rest was a bonus, really.

The dress code at Royal Albert Hall was simple. There was none. Sharif and Fatima entered Loggia Box 7 at 6:15. Sharif, of course, was impeccable in Anderson & Sheppard black tie, Fatima breathless in Jean Paul Gaultier black dress, Dolce & Gabbana Black Floral Leopard Frame Chiffon Silk Square and Manolo Blahnik black suede pumps. Hayyan was able to observe their arrival from his position across the hall. Evidently Sharif had been able to switch seats with another of the box occupants, as Fatima sat directly next to him.

The other four attendees in Hayyan's box arrived at 6:20; two London couples whose gaiety was evident; the women prattled and chirped high-pitched laughter. Hayyan could not understand a word they were saying. The men appeared to be arguing good-naturedly about something called relegation:

"Middlesbrough's gone, mate. They can't beat Everton, for God's sake."

"And you think Derby has a prayer at Anfield? A fiver says you're daft."

It was all nonsense to Hayyan.

"Big spender. Make it a pony."

"You're on."

They had smiled and nodded to Hayyan, who nodded back before burying his nose in the program. He was keyed up, nervous; the words on the page did not seem to fit together in any meaningful way. At 6:35, the program began.

Hayyan appreciated good music, he believed, but everything he heard now was through the pounding of his pulse in his ears. It was all musical gibberish. It took a great effort of will to achieve a measure of calm; he was tempted to pour another glass of the Marquis De La Tour.

But he didn't. Hayyan got his breathing under control by 6:50. At 7:05 the brother of Princess Haifa got up from his chair as quietly as possible and stepped backward behind the crimson curtain at the rear of the box. None of the other occupants seemed to take notice of his action. Hayyan withdrew the weapon, readied it, then slowly opened the curtain slightly. He drew a steadying breath and took aim.

Across the hall, Sharif was enjoying the evening. Fatima looked incredibly beautiful next to him. He perhaps did not agree fully with the Royal Scottish National Orchestra's interpretation of Shostakovich's work, but then again—

From the corner of his eye, he was startled by something very small and vividly green that flashed over his black jacket. As he instantly realized the meaning of the deadly firefly, his left eye seemed to burst with a blinding green flash. Reacting with astonishing swiftness, he threw his upper body to his right while yanking Fatima to her left, in front of him.

Sharif heard the beginning of an exclamation from the normally silent Fatima, followed by the sound of a raw steak slapped down hard on a kitchen counter. He fell to the floor, Fatima atop. There were sounds of commotion within the box, and then screams. Sharif felt a slickness; his clothing was wet and warm. Was the shooter still on his deadly errand? He remained on the floor while the pandemonium increased. In seconds, the house lights came up. He became aware the performance had come to a ragged halt. Fatima was lifted off him and laid gently alongside. He glanced over. The middle of her chest was raw meat, open, glistening, like a thing no longer recognizable run over on the road, the top half of the beautiful haute couture dress with a ragged hole and slick with gore, the scarf vanished from her neck. Her eyes stared fixedly and she wore an expression of mild surprise. Sharif looked at his clothing. Ruined. The entire evening was ruined. He was really going to have to do something about his brother and his friends.

83

Across Prince Albert Hall, behind the curtain at the rear of Second Tier Box 83, Hayyan had been dismayed to realize the green beam was faintly visible in the air above the Hall floor. Dismay turned to horror when he realized the shaft connected him to the Black Prince for all to see. That realization caused him to lose concentration for a split-second, and the dot wavered across Sharif's chest and into his face. He lowered the dot and squeezed; there was no audible sound above the music. The Beretta's minimal recoil would have allowed a second shot, except that to his horror Hayyan realized Sharif was no longer there, but instead his beautiful consort had somehow taken his place and as he watched her chest exploded in a hail of red rain and red matter and what was left of the woman fell backward and disappeared.

And now, suddenly, it was all a nightmare. Even as Hayyan turned and fled the box, his mind froze in disbelief. He had failed, he still had the weapon, there was an escape plan but somehow he couldn't remember it. And now he was downstairs, and outside, and people were milling around. Strangely, there were no sirens, he realized, but then he heard them, faintly, one, and then another, klaxons and sirens and then a cacophony of noise and flashing lights as he entered the Imperial Car Park. Of course, he could not remember where he had left the car. What color was it? He rushed to and fro while he pressed the remote but heard no return honk. It seemed to take forever. Finally he stopped and remembered to hold the device to his chin, effectively doubling the range, and pressed the button. He was rewarded by a distant honk. He hurried to the car, which, he saw but did not remember, was a muddy brown. Hayyan retrieved the key from the tire and heaved himself inside the Honda that belonged to the unseen Afzal Hadad. He still had the pistol and could not remember what he was supposed to do with it. Why would anyone buy a car that wretched color? Maybe so the invisible Afzal Hadad would never have to wash it. He looked at the gun, now an alien thing in his hand. It smelled sharply of – death. And then he suddenly realized he had killed a woman. He began to shake without control. He had slain an innocent person, someone unconnected to the whole terrible web of malice that had been spun by the Black Prince and that held him fast. And then followed the further realization that now he was no better than Sharif and actually quite the same, and for a moment he contemplated the Beretta and what he might do with it, what he should do with it if honor really meant anything, as he sat shivering in the dark vehicle in the Imperial Car Park, some 9,000 kilometers from home with only memories of the sanity he had left there.

84

Within an hour of receiving Richard Haycock's phone call concerning the possible R U R manufacturing lead, General Ben-Reuven and the group present at David's initial visit were meeting in Tel Aviv at the most convenient location on immediate notice: the Collections Department at Mossad headquarters, 1,158 km northwest of Bandar Abbas. They began formulating a strategy for locating and neutralizing the laboratory involved in synthesizing R U R, armed with the knowledge that, in all likelihood, the facility was in the vicinity of the Iranian port. Simultaneously, an intensive intelligence effort was underway to unearth any suspicious travel to the city. Complicating the effort, Bandar Abbas was readily accessible by air, rail, ship and highway.

Within a second hour, Israel's Eros B satellite, launched in 2006 with the specific mission of monitoring Iran's nuclear program, trained its eye on Bandar Abbas and began sectoring the area, utilizing medium resolution, for possible targets. Those targets were then scrutinized with a resolution of 70 cm – about two feet – and the process of elimination begun.

Within a fourth hour, Ofeq 5 had been enlisted into the search. That satellite's ultraviolet and visible imaging sensors, resolving to 0.8 meters, were trained on Bandar Abbas on each of its six daily daylight orbits. The search area, split between the two birds, included the offshore islands of Hengam and Qeshm in the Strait of Hormuz as well as the nearby mineral mines.

By nightfall, larger industrial structures such as cotton textile manufacturing facilities, refining, aluminum smelting, steel milling and fish processing had been scrutinized, evaluated and eliminated. With its ultraviolet capability, Ofeq 5 kept looking through the night on each pass.

At daybreak, full optical investigation resumed. Unites States satellite coverage had not been offered, nor was it asked for. Richard Haycock had evaluated the American surveillance capability as considerably less, with higher orbits and fewer passes over the area, and thus redundant. By ten a.m. Bandar Abbas time, the electronic inquiry was focusing on three truck and trailer combinations, positioned triangularly approximately two miles apart, surrounding a large construction area.

One hour later, Major Ya'ari, standing next to a large mounted LCD HD display, used a laser pointer as he addressed General Ben-Reuven and three of the other intelligence officers present at the original meeting with David Livingston.

"The images you see were rendered by the Ofeq and Eros satellites. They are not live images; however, they are less one hour old. Please observe. These three vehicles have been identified as TLVs – Transporter Launcher Vehicles. They are for the Russian-built Tor M-1T surface-to-air missile system," he said, pointing to the truck and trailer combinations. "The Tor M-1, as you may recall, carries a 15 kilogram high-explosive fragmentation warhead and is activated by proximity fuse." Major Ya'ari knew at least one of the men in the room was unfamiliar with the details of the Tor system. "Its effectiveness against cruise missiles is very high – sixty to ninety percent – and it is lethal against aircraft, with a kill rate over ninety percent."

The men in the room were looking intently at the area depicted in the satellite image.

"The presence of these mobile launcher vehicles was previously undetected in the general region. Naturally, they evoke a high degree of interest. These three form a triangle surrounding a large construction site we have identified as the Hormozal Project. This is a Dubai Aluminium smelter potline facility not yet finished. We quickly obtained the plans for the project and evaluated them. Now notice an area to the left of the main construction site." Ya'ari indicated the area with his pointer. He pressed a control device in his other hand; the view enlarged, revealing more details. "It is an unknown compound, not present on the plans. This compound consists of a three story main building, a structure that appears to be a dormitory, and other outbuildings. Visible piping and support equipment are consistent with a Level 4 containment facility. Chain link fencing topped with barbed wire surrounds the compound."

Major Ya'ari had his audience's full attention. The officer from Shin Bet spoke first. "Major, what is the launch capability of the Tor?"

"All three operate independently and simultaneously. Reaction time from target detection to launch varies from 3.4 seconds to 8 seconds."

Other voices, more rapidly now.

"Can they be jammed?"

"They are designed to operate in an intensive jamming environment."

"Effective target altitudes?"

"Tor is designed to destroy targets ranging from medium to low and very low altitudes."

"Number of missiles per launch vehicle?"

"Eight. Just as importantly, each fire unit can engage and launch against two separate targets."

"Do we have confirmation this is the R U R laboratory from alternate sources?"

"How do we take out the installation?"

With no ready answers, the questions stopped. The room seemed charged with furious thinking.

"One further indication," Major Ya'ari said. "Bandar Abbas is the site of the Iranian Navy's largest base. There are an unusually large number of patrol boats in the Strait. At our last observation, two Houdong-class vessels, probably equipped with four C-802 missiles apiece, and one C-14 catamaran carrying an indeterminate number of anti-ship cruise missiles are within a hundred miles of port."

Everyone mulled over the implications of this further news. As if on cue, a phone rang. General Ben-Reuven picked up the secure line.

"Ben-Reuven."

"Sir, it is Major Feld."

"One moment, Major." He lowered the phone and addressed the group. "Let's reconvene in thirty minutes." As everyone filed out; Ben-Reuven motioned Major Ya'ari to stay. He resumed the call.

"I have Major Ya'ari here and I'm going to put you on speaker." He pushed a button. "All right, proceed."

"Major. We have the following preliminary results from scrutinizing twenty four month travel records to Bandar Abbas. Doctor Arash Yazdani, Professor of Bio-engineering at the University of Tehran College of Science, has been on sabbatical for eighteen months. He flew from Tehran to Bandar Abbas seventeen months ago and we have no record of his return. The same for Professor Shaheen Saber, Chair of the Department of Bioengineering at Azad University in Tehran. They were on the same flight. We believe these records reliable, but since it was a domestic flight we cannot be completely certain. We can be certain of the scientific personnel from Syria, who arrived in Bandar Abbas sixteen months ago, led by University of Damascus Pharmacological Chair Ashur Chammas. They were all on separate aircraft, which might not be unusual. We are beginning to obtain similar information regarding small delegations of scientists from Iraq, Yemen and Saudi Arabia." He paused. "Oh, and two guys from UAE came by ship."

"Any estimate on the overall number, Major?"

"Not yet, sir. Certainly more than twenty, probably less than forty."

"Thank you, Major. Please have a complete list with affiliations delivered here in fifteen minutes. Can we do that?"

"Certainly, sir."

Ben-Reuven rang off and turned to Ya'ari. "Can we get the names to David Livingston as soon as possible? We need to ask him to check with his American scientists if they've heard of any of these characters and just how capable they might be."

"Yes, sir."

"Think these people are housed in the dormitory there?"

"Is there any question?"

General Ben-Reuven leaned back in his chair. "You know, Major, I wonder why we didn't pick this up at the time."

"At the time, we didn't know to look," he said.

*   *   *   *

David had managed to get Leslie on the line as yet another limousine whisked him to Reagan National. "Hi, Leslie, how are you? I've got about one minute. Listen, anything further on the pregnancies?"

"I'm fine, David. Still the same. No change. The rate of conception is back to normal. The defects are still very high."

"How's the little guy?"

"He's great. You can't imagine what he's built with that Erector set."

"A cruise missile? No, wait. Hexosamindase?"

Leslie laughed. "It's taken over from the television. Can you believe that?"

They had arrived at Reagan. Ten minutes later, he was preparing to board another Israeli jet for Tel Aviv when his cell phone rang. Signaling the flight crew to wait, he hurried back inside the VIP lounge and wrote down the names of the researchers from Major Ya'ari.

"I recognize two of these names," David said. "These are heavyweight guys – Yazdani's published cutting edge stuff. Let me make another call."

He reached Emily as she was eating in the Jergens cafeteria. "I like the prices here, David," she said. "What've you got?"

"Emily, the Israelis have tracked a number of Middle Eastern scientists to Bandar Abbas. Can I read you some names? We need to evaluate just who these guys are."

"Of course, David. As long as you don't mind me talking with my mouth full of hamburger."

David read the list.

"Wow. Lemme think a minute." David could tell it didn't stop her from plowing through her lunch.

"You'll have to change the name to Bandar Badass," she said. David rolled his eyes, looking out at the waiting plane. It was drizzling; the tarmac reflected the flashing beacons on the waiting aircraft. And Emily was making puns.

"Those guys are the real deal," she continued. "Especially Yazdani. He's right at the top of the list, David. Are you going after that rogues gallery?"

"I'm jumping on a plane right now."

"Listen, y'all take care, y'hear? I want to collect on my dinner."

"That's a date. Good bye, Emily, and thanks. I will."

David phoned Major Ya'ari and gave him their evaluation. He was still smiling at Emily's phone call as he boarded, a smile that quickly faded as he contemplated Major Ya'ari's eclectic list. The scope of the operation, the number of Arab countries whose scientists were involved, was breathtaking. Several had high profile positions, and that implied governmental awareness, suggesting complicity, a unification of the Islamic Middle East at an international level in the horrific scheme against Israel.

Who was behind it? A person, an organization, a government? There was, David was beginning to realize, no ready list to compile, no obvious roster to contemplate, no usual suspects to investigate.

Whoever it was, whoever had organized and nurtured and was keeping the monstrous affair together under a cloak of total secrecy, had power in the Persian Gulf beyond anything dreamt of in the West.

85

Thirty six hours later, Captain Chaim Sayar reduced speed from one third to slow ahead as he guided the *Tekumah*, last of the original Israeli Dolphin class Type 800 diesel-electric submarines, eastward from the Persian Gulf and into the treacherous Strait of Hormuz towards Bandar Abbas. All three Dolphins had been built in Germany in 1998 and 1999, which then, in a burst of magnanimity triggered by Israel's having discovered the Fatherland had aided Iraq's chemical weapons program during the First Gulf War, donated 2 ½ of the vessels to Zion.

The *Tekumah* had been on patrol in the Persian Gulf when Captain Sayar received his encrypted orders. As the 1,900 ton submarine steamed toward the Strait, the four nuclear-armed turbojet Popeye Turbo cruise missiles, which, like Facility 1391, did not exist, were withdrawn from the 25.5 inch torpedo tubes in favor of four Popeyes with conventional warheads.

The Strait of Hormuz was dangerous business: a narrow constriction between the Persian Gulf and the Gulf of Oman, riddled with shipping lanes, islands, patrol boats bristling with cruise missiles, shallow water and complex currents. Over it all rushed the *shamal*, a prevailing cyclonic wind from the northwest. Giant tankers carried over twenty percent of the world's oil through the narrow lanes, approximately sixteen million barrels per day. At its narrowest point, the water separated Oman and Iran by only 34 miles. These second most heavily trafficked sea lanes in the world had seen collisions between American submarines – the *Newport*

News in 2007 and before that, the *Philadelphia* - and surface vessels. Sayar's orders made clear the need for stealth, stressing the likelihood of encountering Iranian patrol boats deployed in the region.

Although widely reported that the Popeye Turbo's effective range had been extended to 1,500 kilometers, the truth was any launch distance over 80 km made pinpoint targeting an iffy matter. The *Tekumah* was ordered to operate from the Iran side of the Strait, and to avoid Oman waters. Other potential problems facing Captain Sayar included the ever present naval vessels of all types, flying various flags, to the same common purpose: ensure the Strait remained open and oil continued to flow.

The veteran skipper conferred with his executive officer, Jaron Eban, as they studied the charts of the Strait of Hormuz.

"Tel Aviv says we can expect Iranian patrol boat activity," Sayar said. "The most obvious plan would be to shadow a tanker and fire from the shipping lane. The tanker would mask our position and provide a safety umbrella. They wouldn't risk a shot and maybe blow a ULCC sky-high."

"Who knows what those madmen would do? But yes, that seems our best plan."

Captain Sayar smiled at his executive officer. "Which is one reason not to do it. A direct route from the shipping lane towards Qeshm may be our best bet. They may not look for submarines in very shallow water. Agree?"

Eban thought for a few moments, then nodded. "They may not think the Israeli navy would hire a crazy captain. How close do we have to get?"

"As close as we can. There are ground-to-air installations around the target."

"Type?"

"Tor M-1. Fast reaction time. Very accurate. We can't have our birds in the air very long. That's the other reason we need to be close."

"Mmm. Firing sequence?"

"One, three, two four. All four tubes to remain loaded with conventional warhead Turbos. We dial one, two and four in for very low trajectory, three a hundred meters above. I'm thinking we fire one and see if the element of surprise allows it to get through. If not, we rapid-fire the remaining tubes and hope one of them reaches the target. The higher trajectory shot may mask its brother underneath. It'll be our only salvo; we can't chance a reload. We'll have to get the hell out of there. Those patrol boats will have C-701s and at least one gun."

"What about the missile battery on Qeshm?" Eban asked. "Aren't they equipped with the newer Silkworms?"

Captain Sayar hesitated for a fraction. "They've got the C-802A in their tubes."

This was a chilling statement. They looked at each other. Both men had studied the July, 2006 incident involving two C-802 missiles fired by Hezbollah at an Israeli warship as it shelled Beirut. One had heavily damaged the INS *Ahi-Hinit*, killing four Israeli naval personnel and nearly sinking her, despite the advanced Barak anti-missile system deployed on the corvette. The second had tagged an Egyptian merchant ship. The C-802 was impervious to jamming. Both men knew the A version, first seen in November 2006, had an improved range, but other specifications were not available. They doubtless included other upgrades to an already deadly weapon.

Captain Sayar spoke. "We're too close. There's no trajectory. If they rig them for surface skimming, they'll only have our sail for a target, and that'll be head-on. We won't give them a silhouette.

God knows what they might hit. They could tag a ULCC. We might be okay."

A hit on an Ultra Large Crude Carrier could probably be seen from Mars with the naked eye.

Might be okay, Jaron thought. The success rate for the advanced C-802, a joint product of Iran and North Korea, was said to be ninety eight percent.

"Tomorrow – today, really – it's my daughter's birthday."

"*Masel tov*, Jaron. How old is little Esther?"

"She is six. There's a party."

"We'll be okay."

Eban grinned wryly. "Well, Captain. It's as you say. They have gunboats and missiles, but at least we'll be in very shallow water."

*   *   *   *

Captain Sayar guided his vessel in the two mile wide buffer zone between the inward and outward bound channels. The riskiest parts of the mission had now commenced: Sayar had to cross the westbound shipping lane and finish his approach in waters less than twenty meters deep in places. The *Tekumah* carried a draft of 6.2 meters. Fortunately, there was no moon in the cloudless night sky, only starlight and the faint city glow.

The Popeyes would track directly over the city of Qeshm, on the island of the same name, before slamming into the biochemical compound in Bandar Abbas. Tel Aviv was forced to rely on two factors: one, that the radar clutter from Qeshm would conceal the low missile track until it streaked over the short space of open water before Bandar Abbas, and two, several extra seconds of reaction time from missile crews not on alert status. Launch was timed to coincide with a pass of Ofeq 5 at eventide, next occurring at 2:43 a.m. IRST. It would be 1:13 a.m. in Israel.

Tel Aviv, and David Livingston, would have a front row seat.

As the *Tekumah* approached the point where it would cross the shipping lane, Captain Sayar, at periscope depth, eyed the navigation lights of a VLCC – Very Large Crude Carrier - approaching from the east. Radar showed the *Vela*, under full power, steaming at 13 knots. The supertanker held enough crude to supply a small city for a year, or all of Japan for eight hours. At 333 meters in length and over three hundred thousand tons, with a draft of 32 meters, there was nothing for Sayar to do but run his vessel at dead slow for steerage and allow the behemoth to pass. He was not overly concerned, but he knew time could become a factor if there were more delays. If the *Tekumah* missed the designated firing time, he would have three hours until the next satellite pass to loiter in the Strait, an almost intolerable risk given the complications. These complications would include an unusual Hormuz phenomenon: a strengthening eastward current along both coasts.

The supertanker passed without incident and Sayar, at two thirds speed, crossed the westward lanes. He began the shallow approach towards Qeshm.

"All ahead slow."

The Tekumah crept forward. Sayar rotated the periscope a full 360 degrees.

"Prepare to surface."

The submarine breached; Captain Sayar and his executive officer took the conning tower even as the water streamed off the bridge. Sayar ordered a gun crew on deck. Perhaps their assessment that the patrol boats did not regard this path as a serious risk was correct, as no Iranian vessels were detected visually or electronically. As the 57 meter long *Tekumah* crept past the Patrick Stewart bank and approached the small island of Jazireh-ye Larak to starboard, the water shallowed to 23 meters. Captain Sayar further reduced speed to dead slow, keeping the city of Qeshm at a heading of 000°, knowing they could approach to 20 meters and no further before the bottom rapidly rose to 5 meters.

The submarine was nearly there when Jaron poked him.

"Captain!" He pointed to the northwest. A surface vessel had suddenly come into view from the north, around Qeshm. Simultaneously, word came up from the radar operator as the sub's Elta surface search I-band radar detected the speeding craft. Distance was four nm, speed 23 knots, course 210. The officers watched the boat pass the lighted buoy, moving fast to the southwest across their bow and leaving a phosphorescent wake. If the vessel turned to starboard, it would run right into the *Tekumah*. It could only be an Iranian patrol boat. They held their breath as the submarine's Timnex 2 electronic measures support system detected an active radar sweeping the area.

The boat kept straight, on a southwest heading, and passed no closer as it sped out to the main channel, around the other side of Jazireh-ye Larak. Captain Sayar turned to Jaron with a grin. The exec realized he had been holding his breath.

"That could have been interesting, eh, Jaron?"

Jaron looked at his skipper. "Yes, captain. Especially if the radar operator had been awake."

The *Tekumah* continued inching forward. By 2:31 a.m. IRST, they were one nm offshore. They were so close the sound of Persian music wafting across the water could be heard on the conning tower.

Few of the *Tekumah*'s thirty five crewmen had been aboard during the initial test firings of the Popeye Turbos off the coast of Sri Lanka in 2000. None had ever fired cruise missiles intent on harm. The crew was keyed up; adrenaline flowed in the electric atmosphere.

In Tel Aviv, the Israelis and David were in front of the High Definition LCD display, where the satellite image would show the results of the attack in visible light. As the satellite homed in, the sparse lights that vaguely defined the city of Bandar Abbas, and a smaller number in Qeshm, dotted the screen.

All we need is popcorn, David thought.

At 2:40:46 a.m. IRST, this is what they saw:

The display suddenly went gray, then onscreen appeared a continuous image transmission from the Electro-Optical target seeker on an Israeli Delilah-GL surface-to-surface missile, fired from a mobile rocket launcher inside the Golan Heights, as the missile acquired the Syrian Special Forces communications and relay building outside Qatana, twenty three kilometers west of Damascus. The black and white building grew larger as the missile closed until it filled the screen. The screen again went gray.

Major Ya'ari addressed the assemblage. "Gentlemen, the Syrian Special Forces advanced communications relay station outside Damascus has been destroyed."

The image switched back to the satellite picture above Bandar Abbas.

At 2:43:03 a.m. IRST, this is what they saw:

A flash, surprisingly dim, just offshore Qeshm, almost touching the island. The track clearly visible, streaking over Qeshm, lost in the lights, reappearing a moment later as the Popeye hurtled over open water towards Bandar Abbas. Approximately eight seconds after initiation, a flash from the vicinity of the compound, followed rapidly by another from the same location.

David gasped. The supersonic high tech game was on.

The Tor M-1 surface-to-air missile tracks were somewhat obscured by the lights of Bandar Abbas. The Popeye's track also became intermittent, difficult to follow as it reached the city. The Tor missiles, closing at 700 meters per second, then intersected the

Popeye track, mushrooming into a much larger, much brighter incandescent bloom directly over Bandar Abbas.

The explosion of light gradually faded. Everyone in the room stared at the display, transfixed. The only sound was electronic humming and clicking, as if the equipment was ruminating over the information it had displayed. David was reminded of the strange scene from *Fail Safe*, when the staff had cheered the wrong side. The first Popeye had been destroyed.

86

It seemed like an eternity to the men in the room in Tel Aviv, but it was actually eleven more seconds before three dim flashes appeared on the big screen. To the untrained eye, two were close enough together to appear as one. Captain Sayar had launched his remaining Popeyes. Six seconds later, two additional flashes came from the same Tor battery around the target followed by a third flare from a second mobile launcher. The remaining battery remained dark. Phase two had begun.

Only two incoming tracks could be seen racing in from offshore. All five converged over Bandar Abbas; there was another large flash, this time brighter than before. The men in the room in Tel Aviv held their breath. Moments later, a very large flash appeared at the target. Missile three, flying over the Popeye from tube four, had indeed masked the lower missile. The intercepting blast had wobbled Popeye four but not deterred it. The missile had continued to the target, delivering its 340 kg HE blast-fragmentation warhead to the three story laboratory building, demolishing it. The mission was successful. The *Tekumah* was already running towards deep water and relative safety—

Until two new missile tracks appeared on the screen, one from a land battery on Qeshm and the second from offshore, launched by an Iranian Houdong FAC/Missile Boat whose faint heat signature had been unnoticed by the men in the room, converging at Mach 0.9 on a point just offshore where Tekumah was running at flank speed.

*   *   *   *

Closing at almost supersonic speeds, fired from impossibly close range, INS *Tekumah* had 7.4 seconds to react to the incoming missiles, except that the lack of time seemed like an eternity to Captain Sayar before the Silkworm or the C-802 would reach his submarine and the 165 kg time-delayed semi-armor-piercing warhead would, with over ninety eight percent probability, blast his ship to –

A loud CLANK! reverberating throughout the submarine, followed by a deafening explosion as the *Tekumah* rocked violently. Yet, incredibly, the boat continued on. Unable to dive without a damage assessment, all Captain Sayar could do was race towards the shipping lane and hope for the sheltering safety of a tanker.

It seemed like an eternity to the men aboard the submarine before they reached Omani waters and the westbound shipping lane. Radar and sonar showed no targets speeding towards them, either patrol boats or missiles. If the Iranian patrol boats were still at work, they might have thought they had sunk their target. As planned, Captain Sayar tracked diagonally eastward across the lane, away from Iran and other island based missile installations, transited the buffer zone, shadowed an eastbound LNG tanker and headed due south through the Gulf of Oman and into the Arabian Sea. All this before little Esther Eban celebrated her sixth birthday.

87

"Cream or sugar?" asked General Ben-Reuven.

"No, thank you," replied David, sipping from his cup. The two were alone in General Ben-Reuven's office in Herzlia, a short drive north of Tel Aviv. Forty eight hours had elapsed since the missile strike from *Tekumah* had destroyed the laboratory building in Bandar Abbas.

"So what happened?"

"They were unable to dive until they could go topside and inspect the damage. The sail had been dented all to hell but not pierced." The general paused, made a gesture. "No one's certain, but Captain Sayar believes it was a combination of factors, what I believe is called pollyanna. Or is it serendipity? Or just incredible luck. We're studying the possibilities."

David smiled. "I'm sure you're looking forward to the debriefing of Commander Sayar when the submarine docks. It does seem he made some brilliant and inventive choices. It was very risky business."

The *Tekumah* had indeed been incredibly lucky. They would never be certain, but in fact the two cruise missiles had sideswiped each other just before reaching the submarine, whether confused at proximity to target and each other or because they were in the process of switching to terminal phase flight too soon after launch. The damage to the sail was six meters above the surface, indicating the Silkworm had transitioned down to impact height, despite never having reached its optimum flight altitude of 25 meters. They were all simply too close; the time delayed fuse was too short on the Silkworm that hit the Tekumah. The second fuse, on the C-802 fired by the patrol boat, had worked, exploding harmlessly upon impact with the sea, the missile having spiraled out of control after one of its fins was damaged by the collision. To the Iranians, it appeared they had scored a hit and neutralized the invader.

"The Strait is a very hairy place," David said.

"Hairy? Is that American slang? I'll have to remember that. Hairy."

"Well, don't go by me. It's probably a generation out of date."

"But then again, we are all a generation out of date, I suppose. At least I am. You can see why we place our most experienced men at the helm of the Dolphins?"

"He must be some leader. I'd like to meet him someday."

Ben-Reuven smiled. "Not likely, but perhaps you will, who knows? I believe you two have much in common."

"That's a real compliment."

The general smiled. "We have had no official or unofficial statement from Iran, nothing. Our people were surprised at the quickness of the response from the anti-missile batteries, as well as the fast missile response from Qeshm and the patrol boat."

"What about the dormitory building?"

"Aman advises that casualties were light. There were no scientists in the laboratory building in the middle of the night, just guards and maintenance personnel, apparently. The laboratory was destroyed, as you know. The dormitory suffered moderate damage, particularly the west-facing windows. Hospital admissions in the area included several of the people on Major Ya'ari's travel list. We'll be monitoring the situation, of course, to make sure they go home. If they recover, of course."

David thought he saw the trace of another smile, one without warmth. The general continued.

"We will monitor the pregnancies in the affected areas, where the mineral water was not recovered, and we will be most interested in the Brooklyn developments."

"Yes. I will keep you abreast."

"I'll give you a contact number for Major Ya'ari. Perhaps you can advise us on the results in California and Arizona as well."

"Certainly. We'd be most interested in following the scientists from Bandar Abbas as well as your final conclusions about the Iranian defenses."

Protocol was established. The general nodded slightly before switching gears. "Have you been to Herzlia before, Doctor Livingston?"

"Herzlia? No, sir. I know this is a resort area. Very beautiful, I've heard."

"Yes, quite so. Perhaps you can return when the dust settles. We would invite you to be our guest in Pituach."

David was appreciative. "Thank you, general. It would be my pleasure."

"Perhaps you might want to invite your Doctor Riordan." David thought he saw a twinkle in the general's eye. Why aren't I surprised, he thought. After all, he is the head of intelligence around here.

"I don't know what to say except thank you."

"That's exactly all you should say. Now please give my personal regards to Richard Haycock. More coffee?"

It was time to go.

88

Sheriff Winfield sat in the corner booth of the Moon Valley Diner, feeling the day's Lunar Special – hot dog with onions, chili, mustard and special pepper sauce - ooze its way down as he eyed the occupant of the booth by the door. The lawman prided himself on his cast iron stomach, but today it felt rusted through. He loosened his belt, still staring at the guy in the far booth as his young deputy, Daryl Phipps, worked a toothpick and poured real cream into his coffee, just refilled by Sally. It had been a slow morning.

"What if it goes through this time?" Daryl asked. The deputy was referring to an upcoming voters' referendum to cede law enforcement to the county. The estimated savings were claimed to be north of a hundred thousand dollars per year. Sheriff Winfield, an old hand at local politics, had countered at the last city council meeting by alleging the average response time for emergency calls would be extended by up to two and a half minutes, an eternity in a life-threatening situation, given the distance to the nearest county substation. It was a figure he had plucked from the air. He asked the assemblage to consider the consequences of having an armed burglar or a "crazed assailant" inside their homes for an extra two and a half minutes. Daryl had never heard of such an incident in Moon Valley, but he had been as impressed as anyone. The sheriff's laconic delivery had made the message that much more ominous.

The sheriff shrugged. "We go to work for the county. They got better uniforms."

"You kidding? They're hot as hell."

"The deal's not going to pass anyway."

Daryl didn't appear convinced. "What're you eyeballin'?" he asked.

"Check out this guy three booths down," the sheriff replied. "The one by the door."

Daryl turned, accompanied by the creaks of his various leather straps and belts. The deputy lifted weights and wore a tight uniform, unlike his boss. He squinted at the foreign-looking, nervous occupant with the scraggly beard whose eyes darted here and there, everywhere except the sheriff's booth.

"Looks hinky, doesn't he?" Winfield said.

"Don't recognize him. Must be an out-of-towner."

"Way out-of-towner."

Daryl respected his boss' judgment. The guy did look wrong, and foreign to boot, not like he belonged in a town like Moon Valley at all. Winfield signaled Sally for the check. The cops paid the bill and left the diner just as Sally served the strange patron the blue plate lamb's stew. Through the large window, they could see an exchange between the two as they walked to their patrol car.

"That's got to be his van," the sheriff said from behind the wheel as they sat in the parking lot several slots away from a dented, five year old Ford van with Maricopa County plates. "I'm going to run it." Winfield pressed keys on the computer mounted between them. The screen flashed moments later.

"Al-Asharq Trading," he said. "It's some A-rab company van on Buckeye Road in Phoenix."

"I knew he was a camel jockey. Look how scruffy he looked."

"Can't say that word."

"Scruffy?"

Winfield made a face.

"I didn't know they had ragheads in Phoenix," Daryl said. "Guess it's the desert."

"Yeah, you did. Remember that story in the paper about putting in the foot washing stations for the cab drivers at Sky Harbor? They got every damn thing in Phoenix now." The sheriff dialed his phone. Inside the diner, another waitress signaled Sally to pick up.

"Sally, this is Winfield. I'm still in the parking lot. What'd that guy say to you when you served him? The foreign-looking guy in the booth by the door."

"Hi, sheriff. That guy? It was hard to figure out. His English isn't so good. He wanted to know how to get to Desert Vixen Road."

"That all he said? Did he give a specific address or place?"

"He was looking for a number. Wait a sec, lemme think... 2499. I think. . . yeah, 2499."

"Thanks, Sally."

2499 was the professional building, Winfield was pretty sure. So here was this Arab from Phoenix, or at least a wrong-looking guy in a van registered to an Arab company near Sky Harbor airport, driving out to Moon Valley, all hinky and nervous in the local diner, looking for someone in the professional building.

"That guy look like he needs a lawyer?" he asked his deputy.

"He looks like he needs more than that. Maybe he needs to see a doctor."

Maybe he does, Winfield thought. Leslie Riordan was a doctor in the professional building. Someone had rammed her Jeep on the road to the migrant camp a few months ago, the sheriff knew. Someone from out of town, who probably had flown in to Sky Harbor right near where the van came from. Someone had waited outside her son's school on what appeared to be a poorly planned kidnapping attempt.

"Maybe we oughta find out."

The deputy looked over at his boss. Well, it had been a quiet morning. Ten minutes later the Arab – Sheriff Winfield had decided that's what he was – came down the steps and walked towards the van, looking around in every direction. He was slight, maybe a hundred and fifty pounds, about thirty years old, and he was dressed foreign, as Winfield judged. He would not have seen the sheriff's cruiser, now backed into the gas station down the street.

Winfield followed two cars back as the van proceeded down the street and turned onto Lowell Avenue, cutting across the white line.

"This guy's a shit ass driver," Daryl observed.

"Now he's ten miles over," the sheriff said.

"You going to light him up?"

"Not yet." The guy was wandering out of lane, tailgating the car in front of him.

"They all drive like that?" Daryl asked.

"I heard they do, yeah."

Five minutes later, the van slowed as it neared the professional building, then turned into the parking lot. Winfield turned on the wig-wags, lit up the roof bar and parked behind. He approached the driver's door as the deputy came up from around the other side.

The driver's eyes were wide as he looked up at the sheriff. He made no move to roll down the van window. Winfield signaled a circular motion and the driver cranked it down.

"Howdy," the sheriff said. "How're you this morning?"

The man made no reply. He was starting to sweat. Winfield, right hand resting on his holster, knew something was definitely wrong.

"I stopped you because you were driving twelve miles over the speed limit. Let me see your driver's license and registration, please?"

The man looked uncomprehending. Sweat rolled down his forehead. Sheriff Winfield unbuttoned his holster. The driver made no move, except to react when he saw Daryl in his right side view mirror, coming up just behind the passenger window.

Inside her office, Leslie was looking at Mrs. Pinder's chart before heading into exam room #3. Five months into her pregnancy—

Something was flashing through the blinds, she realized. Something red. Shouts and commotion from outside the window, followed immediately by three loud bangs. Heart pounding, she pulled on the blinds and saw the sheriff's cruiser, lit up, a van, and someone in uniform lying in a spreading pool of blood. Months earlier, she would have stood there, stupefied. Not now. Now she wheeled and darted for the closet and her purse containing the small 9mm 10 round Glock 26, just as she heard the crashing of glass and shouts, louder now, coming from the waiting area. Leslie came through the hallway door, low, weapon at ready, just as she heard a louder bang and saw Fred Jamison fall as Mary Jo screamed from behind her desk. She had time to see Sheriff Winfield stagger in through the shattered glass door as they both fired at the wild-eyed, bearded stranger in the center of the room who had turned and was pointing a weapon at her, and then she felt like a pick-up truck had slammed into her as the 9mm round from his Luger P08 found its mark and the floor rose up to slam her head.

89

Harry Deutsch sat in the Lobby Lounge of the Ritz-Carlton at 22nd and M Streets trying to decide if he should try to work out at the Sports Club/LA or just have a few more vodka tonics. He sat comfortably near the fireplace, admiring the fresh cut flowers and handcrafted paneling. He hated working out, actually, and he loved vodka tonics. As he polished off the one in front of him, the choice seemed easier. He gestured to the barmaid.

It had been an anxious day at the Permanent Senate Subcommittee on Investigations. The missile strike on Bandar Abbas had become an item of curiosity to two of the members. Was our intelligence community aware? Had they played a part? Were we militarily involved? Questions like those didn't make Harry Deutsch's day. He had managed to deflect interest, but probably only for awhile. And now a phone call from that guy who worked for Richard Haycock, David what's-his-name. He looked like a kid, for Chrissake, Harry thought. But he knew better.

He had wracked his brain trying to assess whether they could know about his connection overseas. There was just no way, he was certain. The only possible link might have been his father's wartime duties in Germany, but that was too distant. But then again, the kid had cut through the yacht deal like a knife through butter. All the pawns had been booted off the chessboard, all except Harry, who prided himself on being cool under fire and a survivor. Well, maybe not pawns. There was a bishop or two in there, maybe a rook. Harry

Deutsch himself was no pawn. If anything, a knight. White or black. What the hell did it matter?

Yes, he would meet with Haycock's flunky. No, he would disclose nothing, no matter what they thought they had. He knew, Senator or not, that to reveal his affiliation would be fatal. It would be all right.

Harry suddenly had a new thought. Mario, the slime ball trainer at the gym, had promised to introduce him to the blonde he had noticed while strolling on the treadmill last Wednesday. Like a moron, he had picked up the pace and his heart was just about redlining when she looked over at him. This was Wednesday; she'd probably be there. Besides, being fueled with vodka would probably help him through the stupid machines. He'd get his gym bag from his car; it contained the new burgundy and gold sweat suit with the words REDSKINS TRAINING CAMP on the front. He had bought the thing for occasions just like this. When he had tried it on and looked in the mirror, he suspected he looked more like the guy in a Burger King ad, but he quickly suppressed the thought.

Anyway, things were perking up. He paid his bill and slid off the stool. As he walked towards the gym, he was already mentally charming the blonde. Harry only revealed his Senatorial office as a last resort, but he disliked taking that risk if he didn't have to. Although what the hell did Mrs. Deutsch care, really? She'd probably be glad, as long as he didn't bring home some STD. Nobody else would give a crap in this day and age.

An hour and a half later, Harry regretted his impetuous choice. The blonde hadn't been there, and the vodka hadn't helped one bit. He thought those stupid sessions were supposed to get him in shape, not kill him. Harry had taken a long cold shower but was still red as a lobster. He resolved to start the diet he had put off months ago. Well, after the weekend, anyway.

Those were Harry's thoughts as he entered the garage behind the hotel and descended to his car. Which was – where? He pushed the key button. There it was, winking at him from behind the pillar. He climbed in and tossed his gym bag in the back, where—

"As-salaam aliekom, Senator."

What? Suddenly his heart pounded even harder than in the gym. Much harder.

"What? What are you—?"

90

Thirty minutes after hanging up the phone with Harry Deutsch, fifteen minutes after the tragic events at 2499 Desert Vixen Road, David Livingston learned of the shootings in Arizona and that Leslie, her partner, a deputy and the assailant had been gunned down. He was overwhelmed with a wave of sudden nausea. He had been home for two hours, his body still on Israeli time, when he called Leslie's office and a deputy sheriff answered. David used all his persuasive powers to pry information from the officer. Details were fragmentary. News crews were everywhere and still coming. The assailant and a deputy were dead; Sheriff Winfield had been hospitalized for observation, although against his will. He had stopped a 9mm round with his bulletproof vest but was being checked for internal injuries. Leslie and Doctor Jamison were in Critical Care; neither had been conscious when wheeled away. Jamison had been airlifted to Phoenix. Did that mean his wounds were more life-threatening? There was no way to tell before he could get out there.

And finally, no, the shooter was not a blond man, nor a dark-haired woman, but a slight, dark-complected bearded male, oddly dressed.

On the way to the airport, David called Richard Haycock and told him what had happened. Haycock said he would monitor the situation closely. There could be federal involvement in the investigation, especially if the perpetrator was not an American citizen, as they both suspected.

Flying west, David wrestled with the guilt that he had left Leslie unprotected, but from what? The domestic threat had ended. This attack was almost certainly from the Middle East, and completely unexpected: most likely the work of whomever had put together the Arab coalition. He should have seen it coming, insisted on her accepting some measure of protection. They had slain a rabbi and infected a matzo plant and maybe that wasn't all. And if they had done those things there would have been no compunction about taking out a rural obstetrician. For what purpose, he couldn't imagine. Leslie Riordan had played only a peripheral role, and it was over. What she had done impacted the domestic shadow conspiracy, not the Arab plot. It was unfathomable.

With the tragedy came a crystallization of thinking. Never one to prioritize feelings over action in a critical setting, he had kept the warmth of genuine feelings for the capable and beautiful obstetrician tucked in a small corner of his mind, confined, feelings he knew he had wanted to explore when the crises were over. But now she lay in Critical Care, perhaps mortally wounded, and those feelings had burst forth in a rush: first at the sickening, physical realization she had been shot, and now in a great anxiety of concern and closeness. He had never really spun the soft gossamer of lovers' thoughts; they had shared not so much romance as danger, not a mutual quiet acceptance but the heightened feelings of the battlefield. They had been comrades-in-arms more than anything else, and now she was a casualty.

He knew then with certainty that he loved Leslie Riordan. The concept of whether or not she loved him was not one that would occur to David Livingston. Below, the Grand Canyon slipped by unnoticed as he became desperate for the plane to land.

91

While Leslie hovered between life and death, undergoing two emergency surgeries, there was little David could do to help her. Catherine had driven over immediately with little Terry and taken charge of Derek. Waiting was not David Livingston's forte. He visited a toy store and bought a large Erector set.

"I had one of these as a kid," he told Catherine as she examined the box.

"It says ages eight and up. Make sure they don't eat the little parts."

David stayed in Leslie's guest bedroom and helped Derek construct a working ferris wheel and other Erector set staples when he wasn't at the hospital.

"Where's mommy?" Derek was screwing girders together. At first, he'd had trouble with the small screws and nuts, but the five year old quickly became dexterous.

David looked helplessly at Catherine, sitting on the couch watching the construction project while she read *Curious George* to Terry.

Catherine lowered the book. "She's at the hospital for a little while."

"When will she come home?"

"Soon."

"Can I go see her?"

Catherine uttered the life-saving words all parents used. "We'll see."

The straightforward approach seemed to work. Derek resumed his construction efforts.

Sheriff Winfield was discharged the following day and immediately sat down with David in the surgical waiting room. The man wanted answers, and David knew he deserved some watered-down version of the truth. The tough lawman had been proclaimed a hero as far away as Phoenix, with page one stories in both the Arizona Republic and Phoenix Gazette. With his deputy slain and two local obstetricians wounded, he was not easily mollified with talk of national security and need-to-know protocol. He (and David) was further incensed when a Phoenix radio show host speculated the medical practice might have been an abortion clinic, and the perpetrator a deranged right-to-lifer.

David wove a cheesecloth version of the story, full of holes, without stressing the foreign connection. The sheriff was not entirely mollified.

"CDC researcher, my ass," he had said. "I knew from the first time I saw you you weren't some test tube putz."

"Thanks for the compliment."

"Half-assed James Bond. Every time you showed up you brought some kind of mayhem."

"I'm sorry about your deputy, sheriff."

"Yeah. Me too. He had a family, you know. He was a good guy. At least she'll get a decent pension. I got the folks at First Baptist praying for Doc Riordan."

"I'm doing the same."

"And when she's all fixed up don't screw with her or I'll be all over you like white on rice, you know what I mean?"

"Yes, sheriff."

Winfield held a press conference, which seemed to go well, and said the FBI had taken charge of the case and was following strong leads back to Phoenix. Richard Haycock had seen no need to limit the Bureau's investigation, and they quickly discovered the Al-Asharq Trading Company on Buckeye Road was engaged in illegal activities and shut it down. Detailed drawings and blueprints of the nearby Palo Verde nuclear power plant, the nation's largest, were seized along with manuals on pressurized light water reactors and several bays of ammonium nitrate. The operators, Yemeni nationals, were taken into custody and subjected to extraordinary rendition. Four individuals were flown to the CIA "Black Site" at Mihail Kogălniceanu airport in southeast Romania, where they were rigorously interrogated. While several other promising lines of inquiry were opened by the FBI, none led where David wanted to go.

92

White everywhere, indistinct, and the impression of tubes and wires and bandages and machines glowing with green LED numbers, beeping out the drama of her struggle from moment to moment. As Leslie rose and fell from consciousness she came to realize she was in a hospital bed. She thought she saw Derek, but wasn't sure, and maybe Catherine, and at one point was certain she recognized David sitting next to her, but then he was gone. Had they been dreams? In fragments, she recalled the last things that had happened to her. She came to the scary realization that she had been shot, followed by relief in the knowledge she was still alive, followed by horror when she remembered Fred Jamison falling in a heap with red spattered on his exam coat, and someone who might have been Sheriff Winfield who had likely been shot also, lying in a pool of blood in the parking lot. Except that it couldn't have been the sheriff because he had come through the door seconds later and fired at the – who? – intruder who had pointed his weapon and shot her.

And she had fired too, she was pretty sure. Maybe. She had to find out about Fred. She turned her head – slowly, as it seemed disorienting - and there was David, looking at her from a chair next to the bed, smiling reassuringly. She was surprised and glad to see him.

"What—" she croaked. Her throat was like parchment. There was a tube in her nose. She swallowed painfully. David held up his hand.

"Don't talk. I'll tell you everything. They said you can have ice if you want." He poured ice from a pitcher and held it to her lips. Leslie sucked, relieving the dryness. The look in her eyes said tell me please now.

"You're getting fluids through an I.V. You're still in Critical Care but you're going to be okay. I'm not supposed to be in here, really. I'm not supposed to tell you anything, really, the doctors said, but what the hell. That's ridiculous. Listen, you were unbelievably lucky. Three days ago you were shot with a 9mm Luger, which you might not remember. It was a one in a million deal. The bullet hit your stethoscope bell, can you believe that? The bell took up a lot of the energy of the round. The doctors said if you had taken the hit directly you'd probably be dead. As it was, it was pretty much touch and go until yesterday. There were fragments of the bullet and the bell throughout your chest. You've had two surgeries. You might not be playing mountain goat for awhile. The doctor will explain what they did better than I can. He said he's a friend of yours, his name's Hartzell. Seems like an okay guy. Besides all that, when you fell you smacked your head on the tile floor and got a nasty concussion."

Leslie reached up and felt the bandage around her skull. No wonder turning her head had been disorienting. Looking down, her chest was completely bandaged and all manner of wires and tubes were sticking through.

"What about . . .?" she whispered. She gestured for more ice; David fed her more shavings as he spoke.

"Your partner was airlifted to Phoenix and rushed to surgery. A bullet shattered his rib and nicked his right IMA, among other things." Disrupting the internal mammary artery was a potentially deadly insult. "He's going to be okay, too, but he'll be in the hospital for awhile longer, like you. Sheriff Winfield took a round to the chest but his bulletproof vest stopped it. He's just bruised. Unfortunately, his deputy Daryl Phipps wasn't wearing his. "

Leslie gasped. She had known Daryl from Lamaze class, where he had been an enthusiastic husband to sweet Kathy Ann. Leslie had delivered little William. Now Kathy Ann was a widow and the little boy without a father. What a tragedy.

David read her face. "I'm sorry to tell you that. A whole bunch of people have come by to see you, but Hartzell is keeping everybody out. I told him I was your fiancée to get in here myself."

Fiancée. Another jolt. This one not so unpleasant, she realized. Maybe David could read her face, because he gave a short, quick smile. Apologetic?

"Where's Derek? How is he?" A whisper.

"He's fine. Your sister Catherine rushed right over and took charge. She's staying at your house for the duration. Actually, so am I. She brought little Terry."

"When can I see him?"

"I don't know, maybe she can bring him later today, though. I'll ask the doctor. We'll prep him first so you don't scare him looking like the mummy's curse."

"Thank you, David."

"Okay, there's a guy named Ted Winslow, the other O.B. guy in town here, who says he'll take your patients on an emergency basis until you can get back to the office, so he says don't worry about that. He's been here a couple times, too. I think he likes you."

"Who was—who was that person?"

"His name was Aden Haddad. He was from Yemen and in the country illegally. What happened was that Sheriff Winfield spotted the guy at the diner and got suspicious. He pulled him over as he drove into your parking lot. Saved your life. Twice, actually. It was his bullet that killed the perp."

"I shot too, I think."

"You hit the guy right in the stomach. It wasn't a killing shot, so you won't have that on your mind. I hope it hurt like hell before Winfield put his lights out."

Leslie started to lift her head from the pillow. "I need to—" But things started swimming and she never completed the thought as she closed her eyes.

93

General Ben-Reuven leaned back in his chair at Mossad Headquarters in Herzlia. He had poured two cups of Wissotzky Rooibos. David thought the better of telling the general he couldn't abide the stuff.

"It's a big industry here in Israel, you know," Ben-Reuven said with a smile as he raised his cup. "This tea's good for you. Lots of antioxidants."

David looked at it. "It's red."

"Of course it's red. It's red tea."

David looked dubious, but sipped anyway. He couldn't stop an involuntary shudder.

During the next half hour, David reported that the ongoing search for the shadowy figure who had unleashed the terrible genetic onslaught was not making quick progress. The same was true from the Israeli end, the general said. David moved to the shooting of Leslie Riordan and the investigation of the Al-Asharq Trading Company and her assailant.

"The Yemeni entered the U.S. illegally just two days before, through Mexico, and went directly to the trading company in Phoenix. How he got from Nogales to Phoenix – it's 300 kilometers - we still don't know. The other employees were interrogated and claimed to have known nothing about his mission. We don't believe that, because someone told them to supply Haddad with a company van. Al-Asharq did all sorts of illicit and illegal things."

The general poured himself another cup of red tea.

"It is a dead end here as well. Haddad was a non-entity from Socotra. That's a Yemeni island off the coast of Somalia. Seems an odd place, doesn't it?"

"Whoever is behind the whole thing uses people indiscriminately from all over the Arab world."

"We're still looking at ties between the rest of the infiltrators in your country and operatives in Yemen. So far no concrete information. How are the shooting victims?"

David said that both Leslie and her partner had been discharged three weeks ago.

"What was the purpose of the shooting, do you think?"

"No real idea. I wish we knew. Doesn't seem to make sense."

"I'm glad you are taking up my offer to enjoy Herzlia," Ben-Reuven said, when they had finished exchanging intelligence.

"I thought I'd take two or three days to unwind before getting back."

"Your Doctor Riordan arrives today, does she not?"

Another piece of intel from the General. The guy got around.

"Uh, yes, she'll be taking the train down from Tel Aviv. Her flight gets in later today."

"We've arranged more personal transport. The train is no way to travel for the walking wounded," Ben-Reuven said. "And taken the liberty of upgrading your hotel accommodations. You're at the Okeanos as a guest of the government of Israel. I hope that's all right with you. It's in Pituach and has a lovely beach."

"Uuh – that's –"

"I hoped so. There are a number of things you and Doctor Riordan will want to see and do. Diving - for you, anyway -, good restaurants, we even have a strange restaurant in a cave. I believe you'll enjoy your stay. I've arranged a driver who knows the area."

94

Seventeen and a half hours was just about her limit, even in first class, Leslie decided as the Continental flight began its descent into Tel Aviv. Normally a coach passenger, David had arranged the upgrade. She knew she could not have made the trip in steerage, even though she had been recuperating more rapidly than predicted. Despite the spacious, soft seat she had needed to shift her weight often and gingerly; she was still fragile. Leslie had boarded just before eight a.m. the previous day, having spent the night at her aunt Jane's in Phoenix. After changing planes in Newark, she had managed a fitful night's sleep. Now it was late afternoon. It had been clear over the Mediterranean, and Leslie had gazed at the blue green panorama below, fascinated with thoughts of great mythic and historic deeds on those waters. Armed with the map from the airline magazine, she had spent the time trying to identify islands along the way.

Of course, David had given her almost no advance notice, but she was now reconciled to his pace. He seemed to live in a pinball machine, careening through life, bouncing off the bumpers, and just when you thought he might disappear down the chute he flipped back up again while bells rang and lights flashed. She sighed. Leslie remembered her conversation with Fred those months ago - good old Fred, strong as an ox and back at work already, pretty much on a full schedule - when she wondered if there was more to life than the Moon Valley Country Club and weekend climbs. She smiled. Boy, had she found out, falling down a black hole to glimpse a shadowy world of people she only thought existed in novels, almost having been killed several times in any number of places: the containment facility, a luxury yacht, the Potomac, and finally her own office. It seemed like a strange dream, sped up and breathless, without a chance to slow down and assess things. It had changed her. She knew it had always been her inclination to weigh, to measure, to evaluate. Not so much anymore. Now she was close to her pilot's license (although a bit rusty now), jetting to Israel on virtually no notice, and found she was actually getting used to it.

David was not a person she could evaluate, measure, judge, determine her feelings for, she had realized. It was a waste of time to even try. He was simply David - or rather complex David, at least in terms of skill sets - and there was nothing else to think about or figure out. To care for the guy was to risk death, it seemed. An unusual way to base a relationship, but there it was.

After deplaning, Leslie looked for her luggage in the Arrival Hall. While she was trying to make up her mind whether she was supposed to take the Red or the Green Channel, she heard her name being paged, directing her to the nearest Israeli customs official. For a moment, Leslie felt a chill, remembering the last time she had heard her name at an airport in Washington, DC.

She identified herself to a young woman in customs uniform, who spoke into her radio. Within a few moments a young man in military uniform approached.

"May I see your passport?" After a moment, she handed him the document. He inspected it briefly. "Yes. We have your luggage. Will you come with me please?"

"Where are we going?" There was apprehension in her voice.

The soldier looked at her. "Really, it's all right. We are taking you to Doctor Livingston."

What choice was there?

*   *   *   *

The suite at the Okeanos was first class, David saw, with a large bedroom, living room, bath, kitchenette and views of the Mediterranean from everywhere. He stepped out on the balcony and looked out at the sea. The pool was directly below. He stood in the sunlight for several moments, letting the warmth bathe his body. David could feel his muscles relax for the first time in awhile. Now he could clear his head and look forward to two wonderful days.

When the object of his thoughts stepped out of the car at the hotel entrance, after the short drive from the airport, David broke into a big grin. They rushed into each other's arms, although David took care to do so gingerly, oblivious to the passersby who smiled as they glimpsed the pair. Finally, Leslie turned to the driver, a young, handsome man who was hefting her luggage. He was tall enough to look like he belonged in the NBA.

"David, this is David. He's our guide for the next two days."

"Hello, sir." He stuck out his free hand and grinned. "Another American. Another David. Rock and roll," he said. He brought the luggage upstairs and gave David his cell phone number before departing with a grin. He'd pick them up in the morning and the tour would start with the Art Museum, if that was all right with them.

Leslie was delighted with the Okeanos suite, and beamed at the spectacular views.

"What's across there?" She pointed directly east from the window.

"Well, straight east you go right out the Strait of Gibraltar into the Atlantic. We're on the opposite end. Up there," he pointed northeast, "is Turkey and Greece and down there is Egypt and Libya."

"I saw Cyprus on the way in. I could tell some of the islands from the airplane map." She yawned. "I'm not really tired, but maybe I'll just lie down for a sec. Will you lie down with me?"

Before he could adjust the pillow, she was fast asleep. It was about four thirty, and he wondered if she would crash for the whole night, but she awoke at seven. They decided to order room service. People laughed and splashed in the pool below as they dined on the balcony overlooking the Med. When they finished, daylight had faded.

They sat, contented for many minutes, drinking coffee. Then David took Leslie's hand and led her into the bedroom. The drapes were open to the night; the soft hiss of the Mediterranean floated up on foam droplets, blown skyward by the offshore breeze. The air was heavy with the sea. A few lights dotted the water far offshore; vessels on unknown paths edged across the horizon. Light from the pool eight stories below reflected somehow on the glass, dancing, mixing with the moonlight. The sky was purple-black and very clear. David recognized constellations in unfamiliar quadrants here and there.

For several moments, he held her close and then they lay down on the bed, in each other's arms, and David kissed her: first tenderly, then with passion, mindful of her damaged body and then surprised at the vigor of her response, and so they became lost in each other, unmindful of the sea and the vault of glittering sky or anything else. They matched each other's pace without thinking, truly as one, without effort, rising and falling as the sea below, and fell asleep together afterward.

They explored the Art Museum, and marveled at the craftsmanship of the Sidna-'Ali Mosque that, perched on a cliff, overlooked the shore. David went scuba diving while Leslie read on the beach. They sailed, ate in trendy restaurants, and enjoyed the funny and informative banter from their guide, whom they dubbed Little David, since he was a full head taller than David at 6'5". Nights were romantic, spent on the balcony overlooking the Mediterranean, talking of lovers' things, holding hands and sipping wine. They glowed of passion and contentment. They talked around the future.

Leslie surprised David with news that she had taken up flying, and had completed her first solo before being gunned down. David was delighted.

"I want to get back in the air soon, David," she said, "I've got the flying bug. I want to fly your Arrow and put the wheels up. Do you think I have to take another physical?"

"Legally, no, but you should ask Doctor Hartzell."

"I'm pretty much pain-free, you know. Except if I sneeze or cough hard."

"So I've noticed," he said with a grin. "You know, you don't need to rush things."

"I know I can't climb again for months."

It was the last night. The blue water, the blue sky changed to orange and green, then purple. They watched in silence, enjoying the slow, quiet majesty of it all. David, fortified with a half bottle of Chateau Golan Eliad 2001, broached the subject.

"Leslie, I'm not too good at this. You know what I do. Well, sort of."

That last statement spoke volumes, she thought.

"You know I love you and little Derek," he continued. "I told you a while ago I could live anywhere."

He paused. For breath? Leslie waited, not wanting to say anything and distract David from what he obviously felt a daunting task.

"Well, okay. I suppose we could – well, continue seeing each other like we have if you can bear with my erratic travel schedule. I mean, though, it's not right for a little tyke to have an unstable situation, not knowing what, wondering – I mean, other kids in his class and all—"

This boy needed help, she realized. She interrupted quietly. "David?"

"Aah—"

"Why don't you just say what you want to say? Without the parenthetical expressions and footnotes."

Did he look relieved or in pain?

"Leslie, will you marry me?"

"Of course, you nitwit. I thought you'd never ask."

95

"Congratulations," said Richard Haycock. "I had you two pegged when you came in here dressed like Coast Guard twins. A cute couple, in a Ken and Barbie sort of way, with those outfits."

David sighed. He should have been prepared for this. "No, you didn't," he replied. "You're just saying that."

"I knew your feelings for her before you did. Even William said something to me."

David smiled. Maybe it was true. He felt like his boss had mentally had come over and patted him on the head like a good boy.

Haycock shifted in his chair. "Anyway, there was a note," he said. "The note rambled on about Deutsch's drinking and depression. It said he knew he was going to be exposed along with his father, and that all he had done was for the good of his country."

"What does that mean? Who was going to expose him? He knew we weren't going to hang him out to dry."

"We don't know who he was referring to."

"And what's that stuff about his father?"

"The note explained Karl Deutsch was going to be exposed as an *oberlieutnant* in the Waffen SS, in command of a mobile killing unit operating in the Soviet Union in 1941. Shooting Jews and gypsies in the fields wherever they had overrun resistance. Fields and ravines."

"Sir?"

"They're always ravines. Somehow the Nazis found every ravine between Bordeaux and Leningrad. They filled them all with Jews and gypsies."

Thank God the fireplace was dark, David thought. One day the tottering steward was going to fall in when he coaxed the fire. There was probably something wrong with the damper, anyway. Maybe it was stuck half-closed.

"A good lie is mostly the truth, isn't it?" he observed.

"In this case, it is. And it appears Karl Deutsch was what the note claimed he was. He died of lung cancer in 1987 at the age of 72, a retired postal worker in Yonkers, New York. And, of course, by saying his father was going to be exposed, the note did exactly that. "

"It's a stretch. I mean, his old man was dead. Who would believe the Senator would kill himself over that? Every German immigrant after the war was suspect, for God's sake. They could have exposed his personal life and made it more believable."

"What, his philandering? Hardly headline material these days."

Only Richard Haycock would use a word like philandering, David thought. He stared into the frozen ashes.

"There is one thing, though," Haycock continued. "His wife. His wife was a Russian Jew. Her parents, aunts and uncles were all killed at Mogilov."

"Whoa."

"Yes. One would conclude she didn't know about his father. Interesting. There's a remote possibility that…" He shrugged.

"Senator Deutsch was killed to cut a link, protect someone else. Someone we haven't found. He was half the link between the G-11 and R U R programs, wasn't he?"

There was a pause. Haycock followed David's gaze into the dark fireplace. William would need to clear the ashes soon.

"Yes."

"We have to find the other half. The R U R contact. It will be in the Middle East."

Again, Richard Haycock seemed to be weighing something. He looked up at David.

"The other half died in the Bandar Abbas raid."

"It did? How would we know that, sir?"

Richard Haycock gave David a measured look. "Because we said so, David. That's as far as it will go."

There was a long silence. The Special Assistant to the President studied David's face as he worked it through.

"No," David said, finally.

"It has to be," Haycock said. "It would bring everything down."

David's mind turned the pages of history. Of course. One needn't turn very many. After all, the United States was the world's largest arms supplier, accounting for more weapons of death than all other countries combined, selling indiscriminately to an endless parade of eager buyers. While pursuing his doctorate, David had read studies like the World Policy Institute's Special Report on U.S. Weapons at War. He had glanced at a recent Congressional Research Service publication on Conventional Arms Transfers to Developing Nations, sitting in the pile on his desk at home. The report listed agreements to sell over ten billion dollars of American weaponry to the developing world alone. Adept at playing multiple sides, the United States exported new F-16C/D fighters to Pakistan while giving nuclear technology to rival India, all the while sanctioning North Korea and Iran for enriching uranium. In the early 1980s, supplying Saddam Hussein with billions in weaponry to fight Iran, a year later arms for Iran to kill Iraqis. In the twelve months following nine eleven, America sold weapons to eighteen of the twenty five countries actively at war: Israel, Angola, Chad, Ethiopia, Colombia, and on and on. Over half the countries receiving American arms were run by nondemocratic regimes.

Military aid to Uzbekistan and Georgia. In Afghanistan, al-Queda freely purchased American weapons on the open market, including large quantities of .50 caliber sniper rifles manufactured in Tennessee. The only Weapons of Mass Destruction in Iraq had been American, with over five hundred million dollars of "dual-use" weaponry exported to that country, and another billion finally halted when hostilities broke out. Rifles fired at American soldiers in Iraq – almost everywhere, for that matter - were often made in the good ole' U.S.A., American laser sights illuminating U.S. military camouflage.

And perhaps most disturbing of all: much of the chemical weaponry Saddam had used on the Kurds in the north of Iraq had been supplied by the United States.

And later, in Iraq, letting loose modern day privateers like Blackwater with no rules, no accountability, no restraint, mercenaries sanctioned by the State Department: the dogs of war unleashed.

An endless parade of misery and mischief, stretching far back into the past, supplying virtually anyone and everyone, from more F-16s to Singapore and South Korea to F/A 18s in Thailand, all the while claiming the high ground, holding news conferences showing Iranian serial numbers on weapons in Iraq, while peddling everything from guns to attack aircraft to missiles throughout the region. Running prisons at Abu Ghraib and Guantanamo that rivaled Lubyanka in its heyday. Iran-Contra. Shooting down 290 civilians in an Iranian Airbus A300 over the Strait. Assassinating heads of state: Trujillo, Lumumba, Allende, Diem. Laos, Cambodia. It went back forever. Dealing cards at every table, from every deck, from the top and from the bottom, all draped in the American flag. The U.S.S.R. invades Hungary and Afghanistan, America invades Grenada, Panama, Somalia and Iraq. And in Iran itself, ousting Prime Minister Mossadeq and installing the Shah. Coups everywhere; twisting the Monroe Doctrine to justify overthrowing elected heads of state from Chile to Guatemala. Destabilizing neighbors like the Dominican Republic. Funding clandestine CIA activities, including Noriega in Panama, with massive drug runs, then kidnapping and imprisoning the Panamanian leader with a raid leaving thousands dead.

And then there was Cuba, Bobby Kennedy's obsession and repeated object of the worst CIA mischief. Rolando Cubela, code named AM/LASH and possible double agent, one of the first of endless and failed assassins targeting Castro, drifting into farce with props like exploding cigars and beard poison, the involvement of Johnny Rosselli, Sam Giancana and the Chicago mob. JM/WAVE, AMWORLD, Task Force W, Project Rifle, Operation Mongoose, Bay of Pigs. On and on, unabated even after the Cuban missile crisis, which in itself was the predictable outcome of a campaign of aggressive harassment against the Russians, all the way back to the manufactured "missile gap" of the 1950s while drawing the nuclear noose ever tighter around the Soviet Union: airborne bombers on nuclear alert, minutes from Soviet borders, strategic nuclear missiles encircling the country and Polaris submarines stationed in the waters around Russia. Strangling the Soviets with fear, closing the ring of death with placement of Thor missiles in England and Jupiter C IRBMs in Turkey and Italy, prompting Khrushchev's failed and desperate gamble to place nuclear missiles in Cuba and the subsequent energizing of the Soviets' own nuclear sub program, all headed towards Armageddon. At sea, a soundless underwater campaign of aggression, capped with the ramming and sinking of the Soviet nuclear submarine *K-129* in 1968 by the USS *Swordfish*, just seconds before the rogue vessel would have launched a nuclear attack against the U.S. mainland: a self-fulfilling prophecy when a Soviet Echo-II class submarine torpedoed and sank the *USS Scorpion* months later in retaliation. And all in silence, in secrecy, with fabricated cover stories - a shadow war by madmen from both countries.

And David had no doubt how the Israelis got the young Syrians to cooperate. Facility 1391 existed, all right. It was as real as Abu Ghraib, as brutal as Bagram, where U.S. interrogators had beaten an innocent Afghan cab driver to death, as cruel as Andersonville, as deadly as Bergen-Belsen. David had seen the disturbing "Taxi to the Dark Side", Alex Whitney's meticulous video documentation of America's infernal Gulag, the torture prisons of the 21st century, detailing the beatings and killings by American soldiers of often indiscriminate victims with the tacit approval of their superiors. The Geneva Conventions and the Bill of Rights and the Constitution, all shredded in the blender of war, or the perception of war, trampled in the mud of national interest, washed away by the tears of the lost.

The high ground was indeed a graveyard; the violated crypt of the Founding Fathers.

And now, the game continued: pro Zion publicly, 89 octane privately. Just as the CIA had paid off Ali Hassan Salameh and Black September following the Munich Olympics massacre, and provided protection to the Red Prince, Zion was sold out again. Israel was expendable, but oil was not.

David's eyes were drawn once again into the dark fireplace. As he stared at the ruined ashes he came to a realization about the fires that burned fitfully there, the flames that carried no warmth and little light, an understanding he might have grasped much earlier.

Pogo had gotten it right after all.

*   *   *   *

Later, David stood in the doorway of the townhouse and turned up his collar. At the curb, the limousine door opened. He shuddered with a sudden chill. It had started to drizzle, a fine mist that showed the wind.

In Washington, it was not a cleansing rain. He hurried to the car.

He called Leslie from the airport, but she was at the hospital with a patient. He left the message that he'd be arriving before nightfall. He wanted badly to be with her. All the way westward, David thought about the implications of what he'd learned. The bandage had been pulled back and David had looked into the gangrenous wound that was United States foreign policy. The stench from up close was overpowering. He knew he was an action figure, not a philosopher, but he had to think things through. Even Richard Haycock had told him that as a boy growing up, he had been taught the Soviet Union was the godless state. Now they worshipped freely in Russia while the U.S. took In God We Trust off its coinage. David Livingston was not a particularly religious man. He knew that every religion thought heaven was their club: we're in, you're out. The Jews threw out nineteen minute matzo, the Catholics turned away non-Catholics at the Communion altar, the Islamics recruited nine year old suicide bombers and had their own innumerable versions of insanity. It was all too sad: the collective madness of organized religion, which David knew had nothing to do with God, who perhaps had whispered to Detective Mulvaney to look down and notice an empty jug, who might have nudged an alert Iranian scientist to recognize a manufacturing mark, who maybe deflected a bullet to hit a stethoscope bell, and who could have put Captain Sayar at the helm of the *Tekumah*.

There were clouds over the Grand Canyon. By the time the aircraft had started to descend, he had made his decision, his thinking clarified with single malt Dalwhinnie scotch. He was what he was. Those with the will to manufacture and use horrific weaponry against civilian populations could not be thwarted with the olive branch.   And, he had realized, that was everyone and everywhere: from Dresden to Auschwitz to Hiroshima to Palestine to Iraq to nine eleven, from Parkerville and Moon Valley to Brooklyn and northern Israel.

David Livingston did not know if he was a realist or an idealist, but he knew this:

If you want to dance, you've got to pay the band.

He would remain on the job, and loyal, but use his skills and his contacts to find the R U R link, track down and eliminate it. Friends were dead.   Babies were being born, deliberately made defective. It couldn't get worse than that. He would continue to try and protect a way of life, not an administration.   It would not be for his superiors, the policymakers, the politicians. He would soldier on for good and decent unsuspecting Americans watching television and drinking beer, building bridges, cutting lawns, making love and buying Girl Scout cookies, and for Leslie and little Derek, and maybe for Richard Haycock, who was, as all fathers are and all sons invariably learn, imperfect, but with no illusions as to motive or means.   Somehow, the words of Dalton Trumbo's Johnny Got His Gun, read so long ago, popped into his mind *You plan the wars you masters of men plan the wars and point the way and we will point the gun.*

96

As David Livingston's plane turned eastward onto final approach, the Gulfstream 5 carrying the prince who had become Sharif climbed and circled to the west, setting a course for London. As the aircraft banked, he looked down at the Strait of Hormuz. The Strait was the size of his little finger. He held up the digit and crooked it, mimicking the shape. The flashpoint of the world, he mused, and just as big as his little finger.

They had not been successful. Their enemies were cunning and perhaps had been underestimated.

Harry Deutsch had been— enlightened, eliminating any trace back to Sharif himself. Tapping into America's power had been ever so easy with a little money and information. Deutsch, with his Teutonic heritage, had been eager to help anyway, spoon-fed into enabling the theft of G-11. And those whom Sharif had not corrupted with money, he had done so with a twisted recycled vision: a revitalized America, purged of impurity, a Fourth Reich, cleansed of mongrel races, from sea to shining sea. The Swiss and the Yenish gypsies. Australia and the Aboriginals. Saudi Arabia and the West. Harry Deutsch thought he had inherited a legacy. The irony was, of course, that Hitler had copied it himself, studied and gotten inspiration from the U.S. government's treatment of the American Indian – propagandize against the target, restrict civil rights, decapitate the leadership, displace the population, exterminate. And for an instant in time, gliding through the troposphere, Sharif and David Livingston shared the same thought:

so it goes, East vs. West, Arab vs. Jew, Christian vs. Arab, white vs. black, country vs. country, and so on down to the most basic and intimate relationships. Region against region, town against town, Shi'a against Sunni, neighbor against neighbor, husband against wife.

And brother against brother. The Black Prince smiled as he thought of the plans he was formulating, plans to deal with Syed and his sibling's friends, plans that would remove at least two rivals for the throne. It was all coming together, and Sharif had the gift of patience.

He looked down at the sparkling water. New plays were opening in London. An important Bach concert was to be held in Bath. It would be an interesting season.

The supply of R U R and key scientists had been destroyed; they had suffered a serious setback. One key individual in the United States had been primarily responsible for ferreting out and destroying his network, one of the darker shadows in the penumbra of the American intelligence services. Sharif had sent the wrath of Allah to descend upon his woman accomplice, a nice but, unfortunately, non-fatal touch. This time.

Yousif had been responsible for the dispatch of the Yemeni and would require a measure of enlightenment.

Yes, they had failed.

This time.

But they were too far down the road to be stopped for long.

He would forge new links, and penetrate the revitalized research programs in the United States. Progress on G-11 would be used to regenerate R U R. After all, it was preordained, written those many centuries ago.

A deeply devout Muslim, he opened his Qu'uran to Chapter 17 and took comfort from the well-worn pages, the words of the Children of Israel.

"If thou shouldst respite me to the day of resurrection, I will most certainly cause his progeny to perish except a few." – verse 62

Epilogue

The new G-11 contract with Jergens Laboratories was invigorated with significantly more funding and a new set of strict security controls. Scope was expanded to include anti-agent research re R U R. Parallel programs at the classified base in the southwest were up and running. The number of scientists and support personnel on the projects increased threefold under the temporary Director of Operations, Dr. Emily Warner. A robust industry was born.

The government of Iran never admitted complicity in the R U R program. No reprisals were taken against Israel for its missile attack on the Level 4 facility at Bandar Abbas. There was no mention of the affair in the world press.

Three of the scientists wounded in the attack, including Doctor Arash Yazdani and Professor Shaheen Saber, inexplicably worsened and succumbed to their injuries while hospitalized on the Bandar Abbas Naval Base.

In Brooklyn, a total of two hundred and forty Jewish women gave birth over the ensuing eight months. Of those, tragically, one hundred sixty two babies were afflicted with Tay-Sachs disease. There was significant media coverage throughout the nation. The usual culprits were investigated, including cellular phones, diet pills, vitamins and high tension lines. Talking heads with endless theories and conspiracy accusations filled the television screens. There were no substantive conclusions. Pressure was brought to bear on the CDC, who never found the cause. In northern Israel, the number of defective newborns was two hundred and eleven. In both areas, pregnancies returned to normal after that time. Subject mothers, in subsequent pregnancies, would show no aberrant signs or defective births beyond statistical norms. Media coverage faded. The brief mini-holocaust was over.

Birth defects in the affected areas of Arizona and California involved most minorities in similar percentages. Total babies affected were eighty two.

Following Leslie's phone call to the Imperial County Coroner's Office in El Centro, an autopsy performed on Richard Garrison, M.D. noted bruising and a puncture mark in the neck area. Toxicological results revealed the presence of digioxin, digitoxin and ouabain; a deadly cocktail that had stopped his heart. The obstetrician's death was ruled a homicide by person or persons unknown.

Despite all efforts, the identity of the blond male and his female companion remained unknown.

David took Emily Werner to dinner at the nicest restaurant in Parkerville. She was charming, knowledgeable and radiant in a cocktail dress, David decided. Richard Haycock thought it might be a good idea to fly out for a meeting, ostensibly for an update on the R U R research. David only later learned the Special Assistant had taken Emily to dinner in the same restaurant.

Sheriff Buford Winfield was named Lawman of the Year by the Arizona Police Association and featured on America's Most Wanted. He won re-election in a landslide. The referendum to transfer law enforcement to the county was defeated 88%-12%. He declared himself a candidate for Arizona governor and won the Democratic nomination.

Senator Harry Deutsch's death was ruled a suicide.

Captain Chaim Sayar received the *Itur Ha'oz*, (Medal of Courage), and the entire crew of the *Tekumah* awarded citations.

Captain Sayar still commands a Dolphin class submarine patrolling the Arabian Gulf and other locations.

David and Leslie were married in Moon Valley. Derek looked splendid in his mini-tuxedo. He had gained a little weight, perhaps from drinking chocolate milkshakes.

"He was too skinny to begin with," David told Leslie who, being a licensed physician, didn't believe him. Fred Jamison, fully recovered but having perhaps lost a step on the racquetball court, handled the combined patient load during their honeymoon in Paris.

In a surprise telephone call, Richard Haycock asked David to be the best man at his wedding to Emily Warner. He interpreted David's strangling noise as a chuckle.

"Keep laughing, David. You're not so clever, you know," Haycock said.

Three weeks later, Leslie passed her flight test and became a licensed pilot.

The shooting of the Libyan beauty Fatima Heggi in the middle of a Royal Albert Hall performance was an instant headline news story in England and abroad. Due to the sensational and international nature of the case, the investigation involved several English law enforcement agencies, including MPS Specialist Operations and Detective Sergeant Peter Wilhite. A number of patrons claimed to have seen a faint green beam in the air seconds before the shooting. The trajectory of the bullet was successfully traced back to Second Tier, Box 83. A description of the occupant of seat 5, a tall, thin, handsome man, perhaps early thirties, of Middle Eastern appearance, was circulated. Hints of Fatima Heggi's lifestyle in Dubai engendered a rash of tabloid stories. Provocative photos of the Libyan came to light and received front page coverage. Bookings for U.K. visitors to the U.A.E. state increased considerably.

The papers speculated about an Arabic lover's vendetta played out on an English stage. Scant usable information was supplied by Sharif, who lamented the tragedy and claimed to have no idea who would shoot his companion. Little focus came on the Black Prince; he was just another rich Arab on the town with a beautiful escort. Prince Hayyan left England immediately and returned to the Middle East, shattered by his actions. As his numbness wore off, his resolve to avenge Princess Haifa hardened into obsession.

Over Wimpy Burgers and a couple of pints of Guinness, Detective Sergeant Peter Wilhite and his friend FME Colin Blake speculated on a possible connection to the Morris Fine homicide. Wilhite found Sharif's former attendance at the London Business School a curious coincidence, and he didn't much believe in coincidences. Colin Blake was full of theories.

David Livingston, with the help of his old roommate and NSA analyst Owen Hamilton, delved more deeply into Harry Deutsch's life. Still bothered by the corporate name of the *Tradewinds* holding company, Red Crescent, he followed the insurance claim for the destroyed yacht. Herbert Harris, the multimillionaire philanthropist and Harry Deutsch's largest campaign contributor, had deposited the funds in the Channel Islands and written checks from the Red Crescent account to the beneficial owners.

One of these beneficial but unlisted owners was the West London Mosque in Parsons Green, SW London, with a postal address and no active worshippers, and whose existence was unknown to the Islamic Cultural Centre on Park Road. The mosque's banking records were also in the Channel Islands. Signature authority was to one Yousif al-Hazmi, whose address was listed as 30 Charles Street, London W1J 5DZ. Analysis of the checking account revealed large monthly payments to Vodafone UK. Vodafone records, in turn, indicated twelve active mobile phones on the account. Examination of Harry Deutsch's international call records over the two months prior to his death yielded several calls to two of the mobile phones registered to the West London Mosque.

David made plans for a trip to England.

In three days, scattered and unconfirmed reports began to trickle out from Dandong, a city of six hundred fifty thousand inhabitants in the Liaoning province of China, directly across the Sino-Korea Friendship Bridge over the Yalu River from Sinuiju, North Korea. The reports described a statistical oddity: all the babies born in the prior forty eight hours were female.

Two days later, the phone rang. David picked up.

"Pyongyang," the voice said.